LEGACY

Legends of the Deft

Book I

Alastair Pack

First published in Great Britain in 2018

1

Cover by Christian Bentulan
www.coversbychristian.com
Cover copyright © 2018 Alastair Pack

ISBN: 9781718168176

For

James and Edward, I'll always be here for you.

Author's Note

To all who value the English language as it stands, I apologise for repurposing the word 'deft'. A truly Nachmairian thing to do.

CHAPTER ONE

Thick morning mist failed to dampen the noise of the bell. It rang urgently, sounding the alarm. It disturbed the tranquillity of dawn and Brande was sure the whole village would be awake by now. He would heed the summons and take his family to the village square to learn what was amiss. It was cold. The heavy mist had rolled in off the hills during the night. Despite the early hour, Brande was outside collecting logs from his stockpile. He had planned to start the fire early before his wife and child awoke. It would now remain unlit.

Brande ducked through the front door and into the peaceful interior of their hut. He rubbed his arms, agitating the blood, stirring some warmth into them.

His wife was already awake and sat on the edge of their bed, removing her nightcap. Auburn hair tumbled about her slender shoulders. She stretched out her arms and rolled her head around to ease the stiffness in her neck. She stopped suddenly and looked at him inquisitively. "Who's ringing the bell?"

"I don't know," he replied, "but we should hurry."

A rustling sound behind him.

He turned.

"Father?"

His daughter was already dressing.

"Morning, sweetheart." His gruff voice barely conveyed the fondness he felt for her, but he tried to make up for it with soft words. He cracked a smile, but the tolling bell drove it away. "Hurry."

His wife rose and splashed water from a bowl onto her face. A shudder travelled the length of her body. "There's ice in this," she complained.

"Leave it, Aithne," he urged, "we must go."

Brande pushed open the shutters on the window. The village was obscured. He could just make out the gable end of his closest neighbour's hut. He harrumphed and turned away.

Their stone fireplace seemed to radiate coldness as surely as it would have blazed heat if he'd had time to light it. The mist had crept into their home during the night, and there was little protection from it. It wasn't a morning for idle conversation.

His wife was hurrying their daughter. "Fia, we better get there soon or-" Her point was muffled as she dragged a smock over her head. The fabric sliced through the cloud of breath she'd left hanging in the air. When her face emerged again, she cursed, "Nachmair's tits, but it's cold!"

Brande grunted his agreement and went outside. He liked to see the morning arrive. It was a soldier's habit, forged long ago.

"Brande! Brande!" Someone called to him. He peered through the mist but couldn't see anyone. A figure emerged from nowhere, a stone's throw away. "Brande! You must get along!" He recognised the voice. A local man. A tanner.

"What business?" he shouted.

"They're almost here," the tanner yelled in reply. The figure waved and then was moving away again, fading.

"King's men!" If he said anything else, it was swallowed by the relentless clanging of the bell.

Brande shook his head. His thoughts were piling up with all the worst possibilities. As a father and husband, he felt the need to flee, but an old soldier's instinct drew him to the fight. He could make no decision without further information.

His wife appeared beside him, now in a long woollen gown with a cloak pulled about her. She nodded to indicate readiness.

"Village hall's that way." He gestured in its direction, as if she didn't know better than him. She'd lived in Bruton her whole life.

She handed him a chunk of bread, crudely torn from a day-old loaf and softened with the juices of last night's stew. "Here, eat something."

His daughter appeared a moment later, tying a cap over her short, dark hair to protect it from the damp morning air. Her mother helped her, briefly fussing with it. Hanging at Fia's chest was a wooden pendant hung from a leather necklace. It took the shape of a dragon. Brande had carved that himself and given it to Fia for her eighth birthday. She was twice that age now but still wore it when going anywhere. He had told her that it would protect her. She assumed it to be some supernatural enchantment. In truth, it reminded the local boys she was Brande's daughter, and those who knew Brande knew better than to get on the wrong side of him. "Come on, let's go," he ordered, through a mouthful of bread.

Together, they marched through the thick mist towards the village square. It wasn't long before they made out the sound of someone running. As more people joined the fray, they heard muffled shouting. The sound of horses' hooves and carts being mobilised was unmistakable. Everyone was heading to the centre of the village. Somewhere, someone screamed, but the sound was short-lived. A raven was perched on the chimney of the blacksmith's, meaning the furnace was cold, and it cawed relentlessly. A bad omen.

"What could it be?" asked Fia, her voice betraying her anxiety.

He tried to think of something placatory to say, but nothing came to mind. It wasn't in him to lie to her, either. "An enemy approaches."

"Who?"

"Soldiers."

"Why?"

"Perhaps they'll know at the hall."

They passed an elderly couple who were bickering about something petty.

"We'll take a shortcut." Brande pointed. He led them over a fence and through the grounds of a property belonging to the local reeve. They passed close to the large half-timbered stone house, rushing past the wide-open entrance. A dog careered out of the property, its paws barely touching the ground, charging right for them. Barking and slavering, it swerved by them and away into the mist. No one called for it from the open door. There was no one in sight.

Brande's foot kicked something unseen. He looked down. A half-eaten apple lay there, abandoned and forgotten. Someone must have dropped it in their rush to leave.

Close by, an empty stable stood with its doors flung wide open. They walked past.

"Wait!" Fia said, halting mid-step. "Someone's in there." She made to approach the stable doors.

"Come away," instructed Brande.

"I hear it too," insisted Aithne. "Someone's crying."

"Aithne, we must go. Now."

"But we need to see who it is," she argued. "They might be alone."

Aithne and Brande locked gazes. A battle of wills took

place without words. He shook his head, a small movement. She frowned disapprovingly. He couldn't argue with her beautiful, determined frown. He knew there was no point in trying. It would only hold them up. He nodded acquiescence. "Let's be quick, then."

Fia moved toward the stable. He put an arresting hand on her shoulder. "Let me go first."

A sweet, sweaty smell hit him as he passed through the stable door. The stable was modest, just four stalls, but there were no horses inside. A bucket of water had been toppled, making the straw strewn across the ground soggy. Ample hay still filled the mangers, blankets lay over the stalls, and tack hung from a wall against which expensive tools stood unprotected. A ladder led to a loft where stable boys might normally have slept, but no sound came from above. He heard crying. It was weak. A small child. He found her tucked behind a hayrick. She was young and should not have been left alone.

"What's your name?" asked Aithne, stepping forward.

The girl looked at them with large, watery blue eyes. No answer came. In the distance, the bell was ringing, beckoning them, and reminding them to hurry.

"How old are you?" asked Fia.

The girl held up a hand with four fingers splayed and her thumb tucked away.

Aithne crouched down to talk to the girl face to face. "Where are your parents?"

The girl's lower lip trembled, and she burst into tears.

"We need to go," said Brande. "Bring her."

Fia took the girl's hand and pulled on it. The girl remained sitting. Fia tugged.

Brande snorted. "If she won't come, leave her!" He turned to go. Although his family was his only concern, his intention was to provoke a reaction from the girl. It worked. The girl allowed herself to be drawn out of the stable. Fia led her by the hand. Seeing that her little legs wouldn't keep up with the pace Brande set, she picked her up and carried her. "What's your name?" she whispered. She got no response.

They tramped across damp grass and over a small wooden bridge where the mist was less thick but seemed to lie across the water in the strangest manner. They made swift progress, despite their new addition. Soon they were in the winding cobbled alleyways that led to the village hall. The stench of village life was strong. Gutters ran alongside walkways, dried sewage sticking to them, the smell potent on the moist air.

Other figures appeared in outline. Shapes became people they recognised. "Brackham!" shouted Brande. The builder waved, but he, his wife and two sons did not slow for them.

The mist was disorientating and played tricks with their hearing. One moment there was bustling and shouting from all directions, the next there was eerie silence pierced by the distant bell.

"We'll find your parents in the village hall," assured Fia. The girl said nothing.

"Do you have a family name?" asked Aithne.

The girl turned to look at her with wide eyes. She was still too frightened to speak.

A loud yell of fury erupted from a side road. Brande's whole body tensed. He could see nothing in that direction.

The same voice cried out again. "Help!"

He looked at Aithne, already knowing what she was about to say. "No," he argued before she could say a word. She started walking in the direction of the plea. "There's no time," he protested gruffly.

"We must," she said, firmly.

She was a headstrong woman, but that was one of the things he loved about her, even though it drove him mad sometimes. He strode ahead of her. If there were some danger up in front, he would meet it first.

They found an elderly gentleman stood by a small, open-fronted horse trap. His attire suggested to Brande he had once had wealth, but perhaps no longer. The nag in front of the carriage barely looked strong enough to pull it. He noticed the trap faced away from the village hall. Evidently, they were leaving.

A footman was fussing about the old man. He called to Brande and waved him over like he was a household servant.

Brande strode over. He didn't recognise the elderly gentleman, but he recognised the footman who he had seen drowning his sorrows in the local tavern on occasion. "What ails you?" he asked.

Aithne and Fia had held back, keeping a respectful distance.

The footman looked up, startled, clearly not expecting anyone to offer assistance. He saw Brande and smiled. He recognised him. "I'd say good day to you, woodsman, but there's nothing good about it. The road is in poor repair here, and there are missing cobbles. The wheel got stuck. I couldn't see it in all this damnable..." He waved his hand around in the mist as if he detested it so much he wouldn't name it.

Brande stole a glance into the trap. An old woman smiled toothlessly at him. He thought she looked senile. He turned back to them. "I cannot help you. I have to get my family to the village hall."

"We've just come from there," said the footman.

"What news?"

"Troops. King's men. Heading this way. They've been sacking towns."

"Madness. Any idea why?"

The footman shrugged and shook his head. "Don't know. Look, can you help us? Together we could turn this wheel..."

Brande looked back at his family. He loathed having to

7

separate from them, but neither could he let this old man and his senile wife remain in this predicament. Aithne wouldn't forgive him if he did. "One moment."

He returned to Aithne who was speaking softly to the young girl that Fia carried. He broke into their hushed conversation. "Take Fia to the village hall. Find out what news. Perhaps find this girl's parents. I'll meet you there soon."

She looked at him approvingly. "You're a good man." She smiled and kissed him quickly on the lips. "I love you."

"Quickly," he said. "I won't be long."

He ducked to give Fia a quick kiss on the cheek, then turned back to the problem with the horse and trap. The footman had his shoulder to the carriage. Brande grabbed the spokes of the great wooden wheel and started to push on them, hoping to turn the wheel. The carriage rocked once, edging forward an inch, then collapsed back to its original position. Brande looked down to where the wheel was caught. It was stuck in a jagged gap where cobblestones were missing and lodged deeply there. It would take a great deal of effort to get it out, but it didn't look impossible.

"Again," said Brande. "Harder. Heave!" This time, the old man urged the nag to move forward at the same time. The horse seemed petrified to the spot. The footman grunted as he threw his weight behind the vehicle. The trap was not large, but it was solid wood and heavy. It rocked forward. There was a crunching sound as some gravel disintegrated under the turning wheel, but despite their straining, it rocked back to where it had been. "She'll have to come out to reduce the weight," declared Brande. He saw the old man lift his head to protest, but the undeniable truth of it stopped him. Lightening the load would improve their chances.

As he waited for them to help the old lady out of the carriage, Brande glanced over his shoulder in the direction of the village hall and imagined Aithne and Fia reaching its large front doors, which would be thrown open at a time like this. He wanted to be with them now and hoped this would not take much longer.

There was sudden silence. The bell had stopped.

Time was running out. The meeting in the village hall had ended.

"We must hurry," he demanded.

"I know, I know," said the old man. "My wife has difficulties, she-"

The footman put a reassuring hand on the old man's shoulder, and he quietened. Together, they helped her out of the trap and on to the ground. She stood there helplessly, concentrating on her balance and seemingly oblivious to the problem they faced. She shivered violently.

"We'll have you on the move soon, my lady," Brande assured her, trying to sound more confident than he felt. She gave him a crooked, toothless smile which somehow cheered him.

The sun was rising and the cold light of day gave him a fresh perspective. He turned to the old man. "Sir, take the horse's reins. Your footman and I will push and lift the trap from behind." He showed the old man where to stand in front of the horse, so he didn't get knocked down. "As it rocks forward, you make the horse take the weight. It might be enough to carry it over the lip of the crack."

He took position behind the carriage, braced himself against it, body, heart and soul. The footman did the same.

"Now!" he bellowed.

It happened so fast that it seemed to take no effort at all, yet when he looked at his hands afterwards they had deep red imprints in them, and his shoulder was numb. The carriage bumped up and out of the crack and rolled forward on to level ground. The nag whinnied in confusion.

"I must go," said Brande. They could take care of themselves now.

"If our paths cross again..." began the footman. He

didn't finish, knowing it would sound foolish. Escaping the village before it was attacked was all that mattered.

Brande lost no time. His great strides quickly brought him to the village square, which was thick with people. They would have been stood listening to whatever pronouncement was being made, but now were dispersing. Several eldermen remained standing on the steps leading up to the hall and shouted instructions and warnings. Brande looked for Aithne, hoping her cascade of auburn hair would stand out in the crowd. All he could see were people evacuating. They had heard enough.

Somewhere, in the far distance, he thought he could hear a reveille being blasted out on a bugle. After a moment, he noticed others cocking their ears and looking in the direction of the sound. "That's it!" shouted a grey-haired elderman who was perched on the steps. "They're here!" He waved a hand in the air as if dismissing all his duties and ran up the steps and into the hall.

Brande felt his composure slip for a moment. Where were Aithne and Fia? He ran up the steps and used the elevation to scan the remaining faces in the crowd, hoping to hear one of them call out to him. He conceded they weren't there and his heart began to beat hard in his chest.

Suddenly, he remembered the little girl from the stables. Aithne would be trying to help the child find her parents. He remembered telling them to go into the hall. He barely spared a glance for the young man he almost knocked over as he dashed up the stairs and through the building's entrance.

He had never before been inside. Large brass plates depicting scenes of warfare and agriculture hung at regular intervals along stone walls. At the far end of the entranceway, a huge portrait depicting a statesman of old dominated the space above a doorway. The floor bore a red carpet trampled thick with mud.

He heard voices and followed them. He passed through

hefty oaken doors, made his way down a corridor lined with a cheap tapestry on one wall and coat hooks on the other. Just one robe remained hanging there. He saw Brother Nathan shuffling steadily along in his habit, heading towards him.

"You need to leave," ordered the religious man. He gave Brande a well-meaning scowl. He was carrying a large ring of clinking keys in one tight fist and a hefty leather-bound book in the other. "It is not safe to remain!"

"I'm trying to find my family."

"I mean the village," he scolded, "you need to leave the village. We're to be sacked by raiders."

"Where should we go?"

"Go anywhere, but go now!" Brother Nathan marched on, intent on getting away. "I'm travelling to Bruke to warn them they're likely next." He was through the door at the end of the corridor and away before Brande could shout a further question to him.

Irritated, he rushed onward. He rounded a corner to find himself with a choice of doors. His heart was racing. He pushed through a set of double doors and into a large meeting place. Chairs were stacked hastily against one wall. The end of the room hosted a dais featuring an upturned desk surrounded by loose parchments and mangled vellum scrolls. There had been some trouble here. A dozen people were in the room, broken into groups of two or three. Most were talking urgently. Some were outright arguing. Documents were being passed between them. Brande couldn't imagine what they thought was more important than getting away.

He couldn't see Aithne or Fia. His heart was pounding, and a cold feeling spread through his veins. He turned to go.

A door on the far side of the room opened, and Aithne barged in followed by their daughter. There was no sign of the young girl from the stables. He let out an exasperated sigh.

"Just in time," said Aithne, running over to him. "We must go. Now." She took Fia by the hand, leading her to the correct exit. Brande followed.

"We found the girl's school teacher," blurted Fia. "She'll take her to Bruke with her."

"Bruke!" he grunted.

"Is that where we're going?"

"Definitely not. That's where the King's men will go next. If they've the nerve to sack us, Bruke will surely be next. It's a straight road through for them back to the Burnt Plains."

Brande found himself on the steps of the village hall again.

"We've none of our belongings!" realised Fia.

"No time for that now. We must leave."

They could hear the din of soldiers approaching, a cacophony of hoof beats and neighing, chinking metal and rattling, shouting and laughing.

"They're close," grunted Brande. "We need to get out of sight. They're coming from the south. Let's head around the back of the hall and go from there.

"They'll come here first," agreed Aithne, "but we can head north."

"No, that path is too close to Bruke's. We'll go northwest, away into the hills. Perhaps to Hightown. Somewhere remote."

They skirted the village hall, keeping close together. The bugle sounded and could only have been a street away. "Run!" ordered Brande. They heard the commotion as approaching soldiers made themselves known to the locals. Screams followed.

They broke into a run. Brande glanced at his wife. Her face was grim but set. He checked Fia. She was white with fear but looked determined. He was proud of them. There was something of the warrior in them both.

They heard metal clashing and screaming. Horseshoes battered off cobbles as the soldiers spread out and caused havoc.

"Horses coming," gasped Aithne in warning. Brande glanced back. They were in deserted streets, but they could hear the soldiers close behind. He cursed the little girl from the stables and the footman with his stuck horse trap. They could have been long gone. As stragglers, they could be easily run down if they weren't careful.

"We need to hide." He wanted to say more, to make the problem clear to Aithne, to explain that capture was unthinkable, but he didn't want to scare Fia.

"There's nowhere. We need to get out of the village," urged Aithne. She didn't slow her pace.

"They'll catch us."

"They'll catch us if we hide."

Fia pointed. "The Inn. It'll have a cellar."

"No," they barked in unison. She looked startled.

"First place they'll go," explained Brande, more gently.

"I'm running out of breath," panted Fia.

Aithne and Brande shared a look of concern.

"Ideas?" she asked, slowing to a halt to let Fia catch her breath.

"Into that doorway," he said. There was an apothecary's shop set back from the road with a deeply recessed door well. They crowded into it, and following Brande's lead they ducked down on their haunches. They were all breathing heavily from the run.

"We can't hide here," complained Fia.

"Just staying out of sight while I think," he replied.

He felt something that he hadn't felt in years. He wanted a sword in his hand. He wanted to feel the firm hilt pressing into his palm for the reassurance it would bring. It had been a long time since he'd fought. Even so, if he just had his wood axe to hand he would feel happier. It was a stupid thought, and he tried to decide what to do next.

He caught Aithne staring at him, waiting expectantly for instructions. She looked fearful, clearly unsure what to do for the best. "We'll never get clear of the village," she said. "We're too late." It was despair talking, but he nodded, acknowledging it as truth. "A runner came from Lakeside," explained Aithne, revealing what she'd learned in the village hall. "They sacked the entire place, Brande. Torched it to the ground. They have horses pulling wagons with cages. They're kidnapping women and girls. The runner thought they were taking them as slaves. They've killed hundreds of men. They've been raping girls and-"

"Cover your ears, Fia," he warned. Fia looked startled and upset.

"She's heard it already! She was with me when the eldermen were-"

"What else did you learn?"

"Lakeside wasn't the first. They've been all over. We mustn't be found, Brande."

"Makes no bloody sense," he said. "We're not their enemies."

"I know."

He eyed the apothecary's door. "Perhaps I could kick through it," he suggested.

"We'll be cornered in there," she countered. "We need somewhere with an exit, and we need to keep moving."

Fia screamed. It was the worst thing she could have done. She had seen two soldiers on horseback come around the corner of a building and just reacted naturally. It was too late to do anything about it. They were spotted.

Brande lurched to his feet and strode out into the street, putting himself between the soldiers and his family. Instantly, Aithne was by his side, shoulder to shoulder with him, making a wall between the men and Fia. They glanced at each other, a look that spoke too much and lingered a moment too long. It said I love you. It said this is the end. It said we will die to protect our daughter.

The men spurred their horses into a canter. Brande and Aithne took several steps forward to meet them. It happened fast. The men drew their swords and charged, one aiming for Brande, the other for Aithne. Brande pushed Aithne. It was wrong of him, perhaps, but she fell backwards, out of range of the swinging sword. He didn't see her land on the hard ground behind him, because he had thrown himself forward under the reach of his attacker's sword.

It had been a reckless and uncontrolled move, hurtling forward and down. He rebounded off the side of the horse's underbelly, but not before landing one solid punch to its ribs with all his strength behind it. That single punch contained everything he had, his whole body weight, his woodman's strength, and all his chances. He heard something snap and the horse skittered away from him, bucking the swordsman in the process.

Unfortunately, he'd given himself no way out of the encounter. He was dazed as he stumbled backwards from the impact. He caught sight of the second rider's feet landing on the ground as he dropped from his horse. The soldier moved toward Aithne with his sword pointed low to the ground. He didn't appear to have seen Fia, still cowering in the depths of the door well.

Half-stunned, Brande turned to check what had happened to his own attacker. He expected him to have been thrown by the horse. Somehow, the man had held on but was off his saddle, hanging to the side of the animal. Brande roared and lunged forward. The frightened horse reared and threw its rider right at him. The man flailed and by sheer chance landed on Brande, the weight of his body and mail hauberk driving Brande skull-first to the floor. Brande heard rather than felt his head crash against the cobbles. Darkness consumed him.

CHAPTER TWO

Brande opened his eyes. There was blood all over the cobbles next to him. He drew himself up on one elbow. His head was pounding. He blinked a few times, trying to clear the white stars floating in his blurry vision. Memory returned and, like water breaking through a dam, adrenaline flooded his system. He was up on one knee, then on two feet. He staggered.

His large hands clutched at his head as if keeping his skull from fragmenting. He stumbled forward a step. Pain seared through his temples and raged behind his eyes. He tried to remember what was happening to him.

The realisation struck him like a knife to the heart. Aithne and Fia were gone. He swirled, looking for them, and the world rose and fell before him like a ship at sea. He waited for the feeling to subside.

He staggered to the apothecary's entrance. The door well was empty. Fear filled him up, and he started shouting, "Aithne! Fia!" His own voice seemed unbearably loud. Lightning shot through his head. He gasped.

He looked for any sign of them, any clue. There was

nothing. Panic drove him to madness. He ran up and down the street, yelling their names as loud as he could manage. He didn't care who heard.

It was too much for him. He collapsed against a wall, his eyes screwed closed and his breath coming in ragged gasps. What was he doing? There were enemies around. He was a bloody fool. He crippled over, fear and shock taking control of his mind. He vomited.

The expulsion helped clear his senses. He tried to think logically. If they had been killed, he'd see their blood on the cobbles. His family were missing. They had been taken.

Why was he alive? Again, the blood. The soldiers would have heard his skull crack and seen the blood and thought him dead. They would have been too preoccupied capturing the women to take a second glance at him lying bloody and unconscious on the ground.

He slowed his breathing. Aithne and Fia were probably alive. He focused on that for a moment. One thought rolled into another. He had to find them. He had to see them and make sure they were unharmed.

How long had he been unconscious?

It wasn't mere moments. Aithne and Fia would have put up a fight. They'd have been dragged kicking and screaming onto the backs of those horses. He'd still hear them. And it hadn't been days. He hadn't been found and moved. Most likely, it hadn't even been half an hour. They couldn't have gone far.

He straightened up and took a steady breath. His eyes tried to find focus. As the immediate rush of adrenaline subsided, shockwaves of pain rippled through his head. He forced himself to consider his next step.

An obvious place for the soldiers to muster would be the village square. He walked in that direction, probing his head with his fingertips. It hurt, but his skull wasn't caved in. He dabbed the wettest patch of his hair and decided the bleeding was abating. Head wounds always bled copiously, it didn't mean they were terminal. "Come on," he growled to himself. He increased his pace. Aithne and Fia weren't getting any safer while he felt sorry for himself.

Perhaps they had escaped? He tried to entertain the idea, imagining how it might work, but his rational mind knew it was folly. They were no match for two armed soldiers. It occurred to him that Fia couldn't put up much of a fight and Aithne might have chosen not to so she could go along with Fia. Fia was their only child. She meant everything to them.

By the time he made it to the end of the street, the world was levelling out and his sight steadying. Regaining his composure, his confidence began to return. He would find them. Whatever fate the king's men intended, that would not be their fate.

The village hall was only a half-dozen streets away.

He became aware of a dull roar in the distance. He glanced at the sky and saw a thick black plume of smoke drifting overhead. It had begun. They were torching the village. On the edge of hearing, he could just make out orders being shouted. A good sign. There would be much for a small army sacking a village to do. Fia and Aithne couldn't have been taken far yet. For the briefest of moments, his imagination concerned itself with what the soldiers might be doing to his womenfolk, but he pushed those thoughts aside focusing instead on what he would do to anyone who harmed them.

As he approached the village square, he pressed himself up against the wall of the nearest building. He would get up close and assess the situation.

His heart pounded against his rib cage. Fear. It surprised him, and he suddenly felt old. It had been years, many years, since his fighting days as a soldier. When had he last handled a sword? Perhaps four or five years now. He kept a broadsword at home, which occasionally he took down from the wall to clean, sharpen and perhaps swing about a few times, reminiscing about old battles. Always, he put it away while tutting to himself about an old soldier's folly.

He was a family man now. If he admitted it, he was also older and slower. He was pushing half a century, but still strong as an ox. His body was less trim, a little broader around the shoulders and the waist than it had once been. Yet, the years hadn't taken such a significant toll. Life as a woodsman was hard, persistent and physical. He would bring what force he had to bear on those bastards up ahead.

He picked his way alongside empty houses, pausing in doorways, glancing around corners. All the activity seemed to be moving away from him towards the northeast quarter of Bruton. What lay in that direction? Not much. It was largely residential, and the inhabitants would have fled. It might still be of interest to looters. Whatever the soldiers' plan, they wouldn't be expecting resistance. He could approach unchallenged.

A shadow moved, perhaps half a street away. He caught it in the corner of his eye. Someone had flickered into existence and then was gone again. He realised at that moment that the morning mist had cleared. He cursed. He looked up at the sun. It was higher than he expected. He must have been unconscious for an hour, maybe longer.

He watched the recess where the fleeting figure had been, but nothing indicated a lurking presence. He kept it in mind. To do otherwise would be dangerously incautious. Being seen was a risk, but he had to press on.

The square was deserted. From where he stood, Brande could see the steps leading up to the wooden doors of the village hall. He heard running. Three soldiers flew out of the hall's entrance, followed by billowing black smoke. One still held a blazing torch. He barked an order to the other two, and they ran northeast. Brande could hear a commotion building from that direction. What was happening there? He recalled Aithne, crouched in the apothecary's doorway, telling him something bad, something about cages.

A noise behind him startled him. He was too slow to react. A thin sword rested by his right cheek, balanced on his shoulder, the point visible before his eyes. He didn't dare flinch.

"I got the drop on you," said a mocking voice.

Brande remained silent.

"You're not one of them. What are you up to?" asked the man.

"Tracking," he whispered. He hoped a suitably ambiguous answer would draw more conversation and help him determine which side his assailant was on.

"Oh-ho! Tracking. And spying. Turn around so I can see you. Slowly, or I'll take your ear off before I plunge you through."

Brande relaxed. If this were one of the king's men, he'd be dead already. Friend or foe? Brande thought friend. He turned to find a young man before him. He placed him somewhere between the age of fifteen and twenty. His voice gave away a superior social standing, and his clothing confirmed it. The sword itself had a hilt with a jewel encrusted into its intricate metalwork, suggesting it was largely decorative. That didn't mean it wasn't deadly. Blue eyes twinkled in a slender face framed by long, straight hair which was as blond in some places as it was brown in others. Brande felt he had the measure of him.

"Who are you?" asked the youth.

"Brande, a woodsman. I live over by the edge of the forest. I guess you're from the north side, one of the Audly family?"

The youth frowned. "Perceptive." He withdrew his sword. "We're on the same side, you and me."

"Yes, and you're wasting my time," said Brande, turning back to the village hall. He set to a fast jog, despite his pounding head, leaving the young man behind. He crossed to the steps of the hall. He could hear the roar of the fire inside. It wasn't safe to remain there, so he moved to the corner of the building and peered around. No one was in sight.

As he hoped, the youth followed. This meant Brande was now calling the shots. It also confirmed the boy wasn't a threat. He was probably alone, probably scared and might also be willing to help him attack the enemy.

"Eadlyn." It was his name. Brande had actually heard of him. He was the son of one of the richer men living in the northeast quarter of Bruton.

"Brande," he replied, in case the boy had forgotten.

"What's your plan? You seem to have one."

Brande snorted. "Do you know why they're doing this?"

"Not really. They came on horseback. Spread out. Started lighting houses. Some men stood against them but were hacked down. I'll be honest, I ran. But I ran to get my sword."

Brande nodded, impressed at the lad's honesty and latent courage. "So, what's your plan?"

Eadlyn took a deep breath, reluctant to reveal the truth to a stranger. He seemed to arrive at a decision, then let the breath go. They had to trust one another if they were to succeed. "My brother. Younger than me. Much younger. Eleven. They took him. Two men took him away. He struggled, and they were rough with him, but I think he's still alive. I have to help him."

"The rest of your family?"

Eadlyn's lip quivered, and he deflated. "The men stood against the soldiers but were hacked down." He'd said enough, Brande knew he could trust him. Their purposes were aligned.

"They took my wife and child," revealed Brande. "I plan to free them."

"That's not a plan, that's an ambition," groaned Eadlyn. Brande didn't care for his fancy wordplay, but the boy was right. Nevertheless, Brande started off and beckoned for him to follow.

They made their way across a wide road and into an alley which he knew led in the right direction. "If they're unharmed, I'll wait until nightfall to make my move. If not, I'll stir up the kind of fuss that might give them a chance to escape."

"You'll be slaughtered. They're animals."

"No. They wear uniforms. They're just soldiers, like any other."

"They're savages, I saw how they-"

Brande turned on the boy. "Wake up, Eadlyn. That's what soldiers do. They rape, they pillage, they slaughter people like vermin, and, if they can, come out alive and sing songs about courage. But they're only human. They will bleed if we cut them, cry if we torture them, run if we frighten them." Seeing alarm on the young man's face, he decided to soften his tone. "We can turn the tables on them."

Eadlyn nodded. He was grinding his teeth with anxiety, but his eyes were determined.

It didn't take long to catch up with the soldiers. Brande flattened himself against the side of a blacksmith's shop. They heard voices just ahead. Brande risked a peek around the side of the building. He saw people, horses, and wagons bearing cages filled with people. "Fuck," he cursed.

Eadlyn's eyes widened. "What did you see?"

"They're treating people like livestock. Move back, we're too close."

He signalled for Eadlyn to follow. The blacksmith's had been ransacked, so they picked their way over the debris and into the building. They found a window looking out in the right direction to see the procession of wagons rolling away from them. They kept low, barely daring to look over the sill to where a hundred enemies stood. "Why are they doing this?" asked Eadlyn. "The king would never sanction this."

"None of this makes sense," agreed Brande in a whisper. "Why sack a loyal village? Why torch it when people have already fled?"

"Unless you're harvesting people," said Eadlyn solemnly.

Brande considered the idea. "Which means they may not harm the captives."

"We pray."

Brande thought Eadlyn was right. It corresponded with what Aithne had told him in the apothecary's shop entrance. Taking captives was their aim. Yet, it still made no sense for the King to turn on his own people. Something was amiss, but he couldn't nail down what it might be. The whole thing disturbed him.

"Someone's coming," whispered Eadlyn, ducking low.

Voices approached, they were fearless and laughing gruesomely.

"They're coming this way. Probably going to torch the blacksmith's," whispered Brande. He felt sure of it.

"Here, take this." Eadlyn handed over a knife he'd been wearing at his belt. It had a strong blade with a wide tang driven straight down the length of its wooden handle.

"Thank you," he said, taking the weapon. Keeping low, Brande picked his way into the next room to investigate. There was a fair chance the blacksmith made swords, but he couldn't see any. Eadlyn followed on his heels. They found their way through the tangle of metal objects and strewn furniture to a back door. It was unlocked. In the yard behind the building stood a pile of wood for chopping, presumably intended for the blacksmith's furnace.

"Well, they won't have trouble torching the place," mused Eadlyn.

Brande grinned. He had just found what he needed. He picked up the long-handled axe and tested its weight and balance. "Not as good as my own," he said, "but it'll do." He handed the knife back to Eadlyn. "Shan't be needing this."

"You said you were a woodsman, didn't you?"

"That's right, but I wasn't always one." He grinned and made off over the low wall into the neighbouring property. Eadlyn followed. They were gone long before the torchbearers arrived.

Brande took them along at a good pace, sticking to a northeasterly direction, choosing a parallel path to the soldiers' wagon trail.

They stopped for breath in a back lane. "There are others like me," said Eadlyn. "We were to meet at the Inn. The Red Toad. It's up ahead if it's still standing."

"Good," said Brande. "Take me to them."

By the time Brande had a band of men together the soldiers were out of Bruton but had not travelled far. They were taking a well-trodden path northeast through the countryside towards the town of Bruke, which was on the way to the Burnt Plains and Charstoke Castle. The soldiers moved slowly due to laden wagons and many of the men travelling on foot. Brande thought there was arrogance on display. Why rush if no harm can befall you? He knew little about them, but few would want to fight king's men. They were well equipped and properly trained, not to mention that it was treason.

In The Red Toad, he had met seven men. The discussion had been fast-paced and short-tempered. Brande had been eager to return to the pursuit. After all, Aithne and Fia were in one of those wagons. Eadlyn had become melancholy; he wanted the fighting to begin. Brande asked how he was coping.

"I hate this waiting. I won't be happy until I've cut out one of their tongues."

Brande could tell he wasn't joking. Most of the other men had lost family and were either in shock or spitting bile. A bond between them formed quickly, but it took time to agree on a plan. In the end, they decided to ambush the king's soldiers by night.

For the rest of the day, they quietly followed the procession. The countryside grew wilder and more overgrown the farther they got from Bruton. The enemy didn't pause, nor did it rush. The wails of women, children and young boys grew less frequent as the day drew on. They were becoming resigned to their circumstances. It seemed the captive's lives were not immediately at risk, so Brande and the men kept their distance, careful to stay out of sight.

As the sky finally darkened, the troops halted and began setting up camp. It wouldn't take them long. Their arrogance seemed astounding. They had camped not far from a village they had just sacked. The men of that village were not far away. Some of them were fighters. Nevertheless, the king's men appeared to expect no retaliation.

Eagle-eyed, red-haired Adler crawled back through long grass to their position. "I count nine wagons with captives." He shook his head. "They're treating them like cattle, but let's hope no worse befalls them before nightfall."

"Slaves, concubines, whores and-" began Nye tactlessly.

"That's my family you're talking about!" hissed Emmett.

"All our families," replied Nye.

"Men," said Brande, firmly. "Listen to him." They were good men, but they weren't soldiers. They weren't trained to listen to orders and obey them without question, but they were all he had to help get Aithne and Fia back.

"Continue," encouraged Eadlyn.

Adler went on, "I reckon there are about a hundred ordinary soldiers there, at least ten per wagon. Some obvious leaders up front, but I couldn't see them easily from where I was lying."

"Don't worry about that," said Brande.

"If we can kill them, we should," urged Eadlyn.

"The wagons are all to the rear," Adler continued. "There are others with them. Not all men. Not all soldiers. Maybe a score or two of hangers-on."

Brande spoke. "That's about right. A marching army often attracts followers, sometimes the men's wives, sometimes looters. It depends on the reputation of the army and the discipline of its leaders."

"Oh, and there were some people in cloaks," Adler added.

"What do you mean?" asked Eadlyn.

"Religious types, I think."

Kingsley was a short, barrel-chested man. He lived not far from Brande, and they knew each other by sight. Gavin, the brother of Adler, sat quietly, listening. They both claimed to be handy with a sword. Kingsley had competed in tournaments not many years ago and swore he had once beaten Eadlyn at a summer fete, but Eadlyn claimed to have no memory of it. Eadlyn still competed and was good with a sword, by all accounts, which gave Brande some hope, but he knew none of them had experience in the battlefield and had never been properly tested before.

"It'll be dark soon," said Brande, taking charge. "We will attack their flank. Four of us at first. We attack one wagon. Don't split up, don't spread ourselves thin. Two of us open it, two stand guard to take on the first wave of resistance, which will be soldiers close by. At that point, the other three join us, coming in behind our attackers. All of us will be fighting by then, but the two who opened the cage will help the captives flee into the forest."

"Dankwood?" interrupted Nye. "Is that a good idea? It's not safe in there."

"We've no choice," said Brande. "The rest will hold back the soldiers. Once the captives are moving, you return and join us. Then we move to the second wagon and same again. We repeat the process until all the wagons are empty."

"Will it work?" asked Eadlyn.

"No," said Brande, bluntly. "If we can get the first wagon emptied and leave with any of our lives, we'll have exceeded my expectations."

"That's grim," said Nye. A quiet hush fell on them, but there was no suggestion they should do anything else but try.

It was late. Although a few fires still crackled away in the camp, they had to rely on the light of the moon. Brande led the attack, approaching silently, picking his way through the heath. The rich boy, Eadlyn, and the red-haired Adler and his brother Gavin were right behind him.

Three soldiers guarded the rearmost wagon, the rest having settled down for the night. Due to the uneven landscape and the long grass, they were able to draw up close before making themselves known. Brande waited until he was certain the moment was right. The soldiers were idling, no longer on guard, feeling sleepy. Brande turned to the others and nodded. They nodded back.

It was to be a silent ambush. Brande sprang up and charged forward. There were no battle cries as the other men followed him, their weapons already drawn. The two closest soldiers turned in surprise, barely having time to react before the attackers were on them.

Eadlyn engaged a soldier, bringing his sword around in a sweeping arc. Silence and surprise were their allies, but the soldier countered, deflecting the blow despite his sword barely being out of its scabbard. The sound of metal on metal clanged through the night air. They were committed. The camp had been alerted that something was amiss. The defending soldier roared and launched a counter-attack. The older man used his height and superior strength to drive Eadlyn backwards.

Brande drew the first blood, decapitating the first soldier

he encountered with a wide unstoppable sweep of his axe. The third guard ran around the wagon and joined the fray, but his resistance was short-lived. Gavin halted him, and Adler stuck him in the leg with his sword. Brande smashed the soldier's sword aside with his axe and stamped a foot down on the side of his knee, cracking it. The leg buckled and the guard collapsed. Brande's axe was lodged in his skull before he could even release the scream in his lungs.

Eadlyn neatly parried the older man's fierce attack and plunged his sword through his opponent's neck with the finesse of a showman. The man looked surprised and then crumpled before him, staring at his open palm which was filling with blood from his own neck wound. He fell slowly to the ground, choking and spluttering. Eadlyn drew his knife from his belt then stooped toward the body. He hadn't been joking about removing a tongue. Brande stopped him with a firm grip on his shoulder and took the knife from him. "No time. Stay sharp." Brande noticed the lad was shaking. He had no experience of battle. Eadlyn nodded, seemingly happy to have received an order amidst the chaos.

The camp was disorderly. The King's soldiers weren't prepared for an ambush. It was sheer arrogance, and it worked against them. It bought Brande and the men time. Noise erupted in the camp as an alarm was raised, but it appeared they weren't yet sure where the problem was. The yelling of orders filled the night air.

Adler hacked at the cords that tied the wagon door shut. He helped the captives from the wagon and started leading them away before he was spotted and the cry went up proper. "Gavin, go with him," reminded Brande. Gavin looked unsure, reluctant to leave the others, but he did as he was told. He took up the rear of the escaping prisoners, taking them away into the shrubs and long grass, and out of sight, heading for the forest at the edge of the wasteland. The darkness provided them with cover.

Nye and Kingsley appeared an instant later, ready for the inevitable onslaught. Too soon, thought Brande. They were meant to wait for the attack and come up behind their opponents. It would be a square fight after all.

Only seconds had passed, but it seemed like an eternity before they were spotted. Two soldiers, probably roving watchmen as they seemed to appear from nowhere, drew their weapons and yelled out, "The wagons!" They could see they were outnumbered and hesitated. Brande's axe and the three who remained with him made short work of them.

"Come, we've a chance here. We'll take the next wagon," insisted Brande.

The camp was awake now. Brande and his companions wasted no time. Three soldiers stood ready for them. The darkness was filled with cursing and violence. They despatched the first of them quickly, but the other two put up a strong defence. Nye moved to open the wagon, but it was shackled with a chain and locked with a padlock.

A woman's voice. "Brande! Brande!"

Brande turned sharply. A white face peered at him from between the bars of the cage. He could barely see her, but he recognised his wife's voice. "Aithne!"

More soldiers burst onto the scene, surrounding the wagon. Brande counted five. Kingsley and Eadlyn were being pushed back by the first two, and suddenly the situation didn't look promising.

Brande saw Nye's problem and decided to assist. He cleaved the chain in two with his axe. Nye opened the cage's hatch. They dragged the captives out like they were sacks of grain, throwing them to the ground. Aithne fell into Brande's arms, and he helped her down only slightly more gently than the others. Fia was suddenly on him, crying. He was on a battlefield with the two people he loved most in the world and wanted least to see hurt. He didn't know what to do. This was not like any battle scenario he'd ever been in before. He felt vulnerable.

Kingsley was as good with a sword as he had bragged in the Inn earlier that day. He took out the two remaining guard soldiers by the wagon. Nye rejoined the melee, and between them, they got the better of a third man. Some of the soldiers wore no armour, probably having been roused from sleep and, picking up the nearest weapon, had simply run towards the sound of battle. Their vulnerability meant they weren't pressing the advantage of their numbers as they ought to have. Eadlyn was holding three of them at bay with some fancy sword work, but he was struggling and would only be able to keep it up for a few seconds longer. Brande charged into the action. At that moment, Gavin reappeared on the scene. The tide turned, and the soldiers began to fall back. Two fell at their feet, just shuddering corpses where moments before they had been dutiful soldiers. Brande was surprised the whole camp hadn't come down on their heads, but they had moved fast and time moved slower in battle. It wouldn't be long before all hell broke loose.

"We need to go," barked Eadlyn. "We can't save any more."

"To the forest!" yelled Gavin, trying to lead the way.

Nye was leading the captives from the second wagon away. Brande saw that more soldiers were incoming. He put himself between them and his family. There were over a dozen. Most had swords. Three had spears.

"Brande, help!" shouted Eadlyn. He was parrying two swords at the same time. His skill was impressive, but their brutality outmatched him.

Gavin was suddenly facing soldiers who had skirted the wagon and come at them from behind. He fell under a flurry of unexpected strikes. His neck gushed blood out into the open. He fell, grasping wildly at thin air. Suddenly Kingsley cried out. He fell backwards, a well-thrown spear protruding from his chest.

Brande threw himself forward. He swung his axe like he

was reaping a harvest. One down. Two down. Three down. Some of the soldiers backed off under his onslaught. He roared in anger, knowing that once he could have finished this, but something held him back, something deep inside. An old vow. Fear of what he might unleash.

His party pulled back before they were completely surrounded. They turned and ran, trying to flee an enemy that would swamp them any moment. They jumped through the bracken and heather, burst through the long grasses and found they had caught up with the captives already. The prisoners moved slowly, weak from being crushed in cages and jostled by travel all day.

The camp was upon them. It was hopeless. Brande realised he'd been separated from Fia and Aithne. He tried to find them amongst the throng of bodies in the pitch dark. He heard a scream and somehow recognised it as Fia's. He looked in the direction he had heard the sound and saw two soldiers grab a slender figure and start dragging her away. He was sure it was Fia. The men were laughing. They pulled at her and ripped her clothing. He saw Aithne appear and leap at the first man, digging her fingernails into his eyes. He cried out, flailed wildly and landed on her, striking her randomly with his fists.

Brande was proud of Aithne. Through a red mist, he could see her fighting, clawing, battling to save Fia, but she was drowning under a rain of punches. Fia was half-naked and being dragged away. Everywhere there was screaming. Brande was faced down by a soldier swirling a morning star and another with a short sword. He charged at the first and then changed direction suddenly, catching the swordsman off guard. He plunged his axe through the top of the swordsman's skull and then turned, using all his body weight to bring the axe around in an impossibly tight arc to catch the second man. Brande let the swing take him forward, which only just brought him inside the sweep of the morning star to avoid being caught by it. He shoved the man away from him and brought his axe down like he was splitting a log. Somehow the weapon had got twisted around in the fight, so it was the flat butt of the axe blade that rammed into the man's chest. It hit like a sledgehammer causing an explosion of blood and bone.

Two horses ridden by men in armour galloped into the fray. More soldiers caught up with the escaping prisoners and started dragging them back to the camp. The women tried to fight back, but they were outnumbered by men in light armour and wielding swords. They stood no chance against them. Brande took the legs out from under a soldier with a low curve of his axe. He plunged deeper into the action. He had to get to Aithne and Fia.

A soldier leapt on his back. The man had no weapon but saw that Brande needed to be brought down. Brande struggled to throw him off. He fell to the ground, landing on his knees. He was by the body of the soldier he had just felled and saw a dagger sheathed at the man's belt. He grabbed it, span, and plunged it up into the soft flesh under his attacker's chin. The man opened his mouth to scream. Brande could see the red tip of the dagger in his mouth. He got up and, with a one-handed swing of his axe, cut deep into the man's neck. Blood gushed over the axe, and he withdrew it quickly.

He looked around him. Eadlyn was holding his own. One of the horsemen bore down on Nye, who, with no experience in battle, seemed to just stand there while the sword cut through his face. His body dropped to the ground like a lifeless sack. Brande saw that the other horseman had gone on ahead and found Adler and the first lot of captives. Other soldiers had caught up. He saw Adler fall to the ground under the trampling hooves of the stallion. The horse moved away, letting several soldiers dart in to start kicking him. Brande didn't need to see more to know what the outcome would be.

Brande hefted his axe, ready for the next attack. None

came. The soldiers were preoccupied. It was dark, and the escaped women and children were screaming and running in all directions. The soldiers chased them and rounded them up like sheep. Prisoners were precious to them, too precious to lose to the dark night and the deep forest.

He turned at a sound and found Eadlyn by his side. He hadn't come alone, a semi-circle of soldiers approached. They were taking their time, no need to die on a dark night when the enemy were few, and most were dead already. There had to be twenty of them, wearing light mail armour and wielding a variety of sword types.

"Run," said Eadlyn, turning to go.

Brande had other ideas. It was one thing running from battle to be with, and to protect, his wife and child, but he wasn't about to run away and leave them behind. "Charge!" he yelled, and somewhere in him, some long lost part of him began to re-emerge. Memories of past conflicts swam through his mind, crowding out all other thoughts. He threw himself at the semi-circle of men, who closed in on him. He felt relief that Eadlyn had joined him, attacking from outside the circle. Two of the soldiers turned away to face him. Brande lashed out with his axe, catching one in the back. Eadlyn plunged him through with his sword. Suddenly all he could see were soldiers. They were all over him. Mail. Swords. Flails. For a moment he felt like blood had splashed in his eyes because the world went red and then dark. Something in him had emerged, then been sucked back in and sealed away.

"We need to go," shouted Eadlyn. "Come on!"

Brande looked about him. Eadlyn was parrying blows from one remaining soldier. The others all lay at their feet, dead and dismembered. Brande found himself at a loss for a moment. What had happened? He didn't have time to think about it. He charged over to help Eadlyn. With two hands on the handle of his axe, he raised it overhead and brought it down on the bastard's helmet. The man was split from crown to clavicle. The downward force of the weapon took him to the ground.

At the edge of the camp, Brande saw horses milling. They were overseeing the prisoners being returned to the wagons. It wouldn't be long before they came galloping down the hill to finish off any remaining opponents and round up the last of the escapees.

They had failed. They were outnumbered and outmatched. The situation was hopeless.

Eadlyn and Brande ran side by side through long grass toward the promise of safety offered by the trees at the edge of the barren wasteland. Two men emerged from the trees, evidently having looked for more of their prisoners and not found any. Some kind of bloodlust had taken hold of Brande as Eadlyn didn't even draw his sword before two bodies lay at their feet, large gashes from the axe in their torsos.

They merged with the trees, finally out of sight. Brande glanced back and saw some new figure roaming by the wagons. Not a soldier. A cloaked figure. A monk?

"Come on," insisted Eadlyn. He had no qualms about running.

"Did you see your brother?" asked Brande.

"No," said Eadlyn. He sounded half-relieved. "He must have been in a different wagon."

Swimming in front of Brande's vision was the sight of Aithne being pummelled by mail fists, and Fia being dragged away screaming, her clothes torn, the soldiers jeering at her.

He followed Eadlyn blindly. Everything in him was blind. His heart was blind. His eyes were blind. His emotions were blind. He couldn't allow himself to think for the damage it might do him. It could tear him apart on the spot.

Aithne and Fia.

So close.

Out of nowhere, a man with a sword attacked. He was on his own. He struck at Eadlyn, a straight, low, blow. Unexpected.

Eadlyn grunted. Brande wondered how badly he was hit. Brande stepped forward before the fight could begin and struck the side of the man's head with the butt of his axe handle. The man dropped. Eadlyn lifted his sword to finish him, but Brande put out a hand. "Don't."

Eadlyn blinked at him, confused. He clutched his belly like he had a stitch from running. "Bah!" he said and kicked the fallen soldier in the mouth.

"We take a hostage."

"Is that necessary?" wheezed Eadlyn.

Brande grimaced and nodded. He was a warrior forged in the crusades. He played to a different set of rules. He hoisted the man over his shoulder.

Eadlyn grabbed the man's sword and threw it, spinning, away into the forest. "Don't want to leave too easy a trail," he gasped.

Was he hurt? Brande didn't ask. They needed to get moving. "Quick, before we're pursued," he ordered. He pushed on into the forest.

Feeling nothing, not tiredness, not weight, not anything, Brande carried the man with him as they jogged into the pitch dark of the dense woodland. After some time, when they were certain no one would still be following, they found a ditch to lie in. Brande dumped the soldier on the floor, where he emitted a groan.

"Time to wake up, you bastard. So I can hurt you."

CHAPTER THREE

They dragged their hostage to a tree and propped him up against it. There was nothing to tie him with, but he was unlikely to try to sprint away with both of them standing over him wielding weapons. He didn't look fit in a state to run anyway after receiving that hard blow from the butt of Brande's axe. The whole side of his face was swelling.

Brande didn't really see the soldier before him. He didn't notice that he wasn't much older than Eadlyn. He didn't see the man's pointed nose, his short brown hair, his hazel eyes or thin lips. He didn't hear his panicked whimpering. All he saw was Fia being dragged away half-naked. All he heard were Aithne's screams as fists rained down on her. Pride and fear churned together inside him as he recalled Aithne propelling herself into the fray to defend their daughter. He wanted to act. He wanted to fight. His body shook from it. He could feel the blood running hot through his veins. Hot to boiling.

Choosing his words carefully, he began. "I cannot tell you how much pain you will suffer if you waste our time."

In the darkness of the forest, known as Dankwood,

Brande could make out the soldier's eyes widening. They rolled to look at him. "I cannot," he continued, "tell you what will happen if you lie to us." He paused. He definitely had the man's attention. "And I cannot even begin to tell you how upset I am that my wife and child have been taken by your comrades."

The soldier released a weak, dispirited groan, realising what he was dealing with. Brande pressed his face up against that of the young soldier and eyeballed him. The soldier's eyes rolled to avoid Brande's fierce gaze, but eventually, they settled and took in his anger. "However, I can tell you, if you do as we tell you and answer our questions, we will let you live."

The soldier gulped.

"Now, explain to me what the King's own men are doing raiding the King's own towns for children and women."

The soldier didn't respond, perhaps too full of fear, or realising nothing he could say could please his interrogator.

"Let's try something simple. Are you a soldier in the King's army?"

The soldier nodded quickly.

"Did the order to sack Bruton and kidnap innocent people come from the King?"

The soldier nodded again.

"That's strange," said Brande, "because as the King's loyal subjects, we don't expect our King to do that. Perhaps you can explain it to me since you were so keen to carry out his orders?" He waited a moment. "You're going to have to use words now."

The soldier opened his mouth. Crimson saliva dribbled out. A tooth was missing, perhaps from the kick Eadlyn had given him. "We were told... orders from the King himself." The young man's voice shook with fear but was full of resignation.

This was taking too long. Brande swung his axe,

embedding it deep in the tree just inches from their captive's head. "I need to know why," he growled.

The man's eyes flicked from the axe back to Brande. "Just orders. I don't know!"

Eadlyn had moved and now rested against the nearest tree, slumped in a half-seated position. His sword was no longer in his hand, but was on the floor beside him, almost within reach. "Did none of you question these orders?"

The soldier paused thoughtfully. "At first we did."

"Why women and children?"

Brande's mind could all too readily conjure answers to that question, but the usual reasons didn't fit with what he knew about the king. He was no tyrant, slavery had long been outlawed, and there had never been rumours of deviancy. Good King Ignatius. That was what the children called him.

The soldier looked around wildly as if he might somehow flee past his captors. Brande felt his anger rising. Every moment wasted was one where his family were in greater danger. "Maybe you wanted the women yourselves. Maybe I'll cut off your cock to teach you the error of your ways." He pulled the axe from the tree, making it clear this wasn't going to be a surgical procedure.

The young man's eyes widened with alarm. "I swear. We barely touched the prisoners. Unharmed, they said."

Brande shot a glance to Eadlyn. He was clutching his side, clearly injured, but still paying attention.

Their hostage shook his head. "I don't know any more than that."

Eadlyn managed to ask, "Who were the men in cloaks?"

The soldier shuddered. "I can't talk about them. Orders."

"You'll talk," growled Brande. He ran a finger along the cutting edge of the blade.

"I think they're Deft," he said, trembling. "Terrible! They'll know if I speak. They get into your mind. I can't say more."

"Try."

"They'll know. They'll come for me. They'll come for you. You're nothing to them. Nothing." The boy started rambling.

"Now, just listen here-" began Brande. He was cut off by a deep growl in the nearby darkness.

A rustle in the undergrowth meant something was prowling. Somewhere behind them, a wolf howled. It was so dark he could be surrounded by them and not know. He saw a shape move in the undergrowth. He yelled and ran at it to scare it off. He swung his axe through the waist-high scrub, and, sure enough, an animal shot out, fleeing before him. He chased it a few steps but a smattering of moonlight allowed him sight of it, and it was too small to be a wolf. He let up the chase.

He heard Eadlyn shout with alarm and turned. Brande had not gone far, but the darkness made every step a meaningful distance. A terrible blood-curdling sound erupted, then silence.

Eadlyn was slumped on the ground, and the hostage was gone.

"My sword!" Eadlyn moaned.

Brande quickly realised the soldier must have dived for Eadlyn's sword and run into the black. Brande chased after him but quickly shuffled to a halt, seeing what had happened. Brande inspected the body of the fallen soldier. He called back to Eadlyn.

"You couldn't have stopped him?"

"I can't move," confessed Eadlyn.

The soldier had grabbed Eadlyn's sword, run several yards and then thrown himself on it. The angle was such that the blade had driven straight up into his heart. Brande had heard his terrible death cry. He'd have been dead almost instantly.

Brande returned to check on Eadlyn. "I doubt he could

have told us much more. But he must have truly feared those cloaked figures." Brande mostly felt annoyed at the man's death. The right information might have aided them. He looked at Eadlyn slumped before him. "What's the matter with you?"

Eadlyn started to unbutton his shirt. "I took a blade," he said, simply. He started to undo his belt. As he pulled his shirt free, Brande saw it was dripping with blood. "I can't really feel it, but I can't stand now."

Brande got close to him and saw how drawn his face looked. He took a sharp breath but said nothing.

"I know what's going to happen," said Eadlyn. "I can remember reading books about knights and villains. A stomach wound is a slow death. When the shock wears off, I'll feel the pain. It'll take a day or two, perhaps. I'll bleed to death."

Brande said nothing. He knew it was true because he'd seen it first hand as a soldier. He got closer and inspected the wound. It was worse than he'd imagined. The stomach flesh was ripped open. Now that the pressure of the clothing had been removed, blood and other matter hung from the cut. Their charging through the forest hadn't done it any favours. "No lad," he said, softly, "it won't take days."

Eadlyn smiled, finding the news comforting. The poor sod, thought Brande. He was young and brave, but naive. Raised on heroic stories and competition fighting, he probably thought he could win the day singlehandedly. Now he was food for the wolves, and there was no doubt about it, they and every other forest animal had already smelled his blood.

Brande stood up, taking his axe with him.

"Don't leave me," said Eadlyn.

"I won't lad," said Brande, reassuringly. "You got anything you want your loved ones to know?"

"Oh, probably," said Eadlyn, cheerfully. "But I can't

think of anything right now." He was actually trying to smile.

In the bushes, Brande could hear animals prowling. Darkly, he felt relief that they wouldn't come for him with all this meat lying around. He snorted at that. Perhaps he never had left the soldier in him behind. Years ago, he had lost many men, many friends, to war. This was a war. His war. And time was ticking. Fia and Aithne needed him.

"Do you believe in the old gods?" asked Eadlyn.

Brande remained silent as he considered what to do for the best.

"Me neither," admitted Eadlyn. "I just hope… that…" His voice trailed away and turned into a soft moan. He was weakening. The pain was making itself felt. He put his hands up to his mouth and dribbled all over them. His eyes filled with tears. He whimpered like a kicked dog.

Brande had seen enough. He turned away for a brief second, steeled himself, and then spun, swinging. The axe took Eadlyn's head straight off and ended the pain right there and then. "Be at peace," said Brande. He leant down and unstrapped Eadlyn's knife from his belt. He began to attach it to his own belt as he walked away, not looking back.

A few moments later, he heard a wolf baying behind him, and the cry was met by another, and another.

He increased his pace. Those wolves might have food, but he was still alone with blood on his clothing and making plenty of noise stumbling over roots and scrabbling through the scrub. He determined to keep up a good pace, navigate by the moon to keep a northeasterly bearing and keep going until dawn. He would head for Bruke. Perhaps there he'd find new companions to help fight the king's men, who would surely attempt to sack the town as they had Bruton.

The skirmish replayed in his head, erasing all other thoughts. Fia. Little Fia. Those men dragged her by the hair. They had torn her clothes. They would pay for that. They had struck her to the ground and humiliated her. They would die for that. By Hungrar's wings, they would die for that.

As he stumbled through the darkness of Dankwood, he fought an internal battle. He was on his own, and he could not truthfully be sure of his own abilities. Those warriors in cloaks posed a problem he hadn't envisioned. The enemy was many, strong, had the power of the King behind them, and a sinister purpose he could not fathom. He tried to shrug the doubts from his mind, but in the persistent darkness of the forest, the brightest thing around him was his thoughts. He focused on Aithne and Fia. He wanted them back. He would steal them back and then, together, they would flee as far away as possible.

A huge cloud had swallowed the moon some time ago, leaving the darkness complete. He trudged until his feet ached from stepping on roots and stones he couldn't see. As time went by, he started to imagine more noises about him in the forest. He was a large man and not light on his feet. No doubt he was attracting every predator in the whole expanse of the forest.

Just for the briefest of moments, he thought he heard a voice. Could the soldiers still be after him? He stopped moving and tried to be quiet but his breathing was laboured, and it took him a short while to get it steady and quiet. His aching body didn't want to stay still, so he moved until he was leaning against a tree and then tried to remain as quiet as possible. He listened. His right foot ached, so he moved it an inch, but at that moment he thought he heard another voice. Could it be his imagination? Did the sound of his foot moving sound like a voice? He quieted again but could hear nothing except the sounds of the forest. In the distance, a wolf howled. Nearer, an owl hooted. Small things scuttled and pitter-pattered across the forest floor.

Leaves rustled. The wind. A yawning sound, like the forest itself stretching and breathing. But no voices.

A twig broke. It was followed by a silence that was too silent. The animals were quiet. The forest stopped yawning. He felt like he had just gone deaf. The silence in his ears was so loud, so noticeable, that he could hear the blood pumping through them. Something was near. A predator. He kept his back against the tree. It provided protection from the rear. His best defence was to stay quiet and listen. He held the axe out in front of him, ready.

Time passed. It was excruciating, waiting in the blackness like this, listening. He would wait all night if he had to. He wouldn't risk being attacked while distracted by his own stumbling. Yet the need to press on nagged at him, urging him to catch up with the king's men. But there was something out there. Of that, he was sure. First the voices, then the twig breaking. It was enough for an old warrior to know that something was stalking him. In these deep, accursed woods, in the pitch black, it was all too easy for his imagination to run away with itself. If he was lucky, it was just a wolf. Yet, what of the things people feared in the dead of night, or the depths of an uninhabited forest? Satyrs. Centaurs. Demons. He had heard all kinds of tales about Dankwood although he didn't believe half of them. He was less certain about the other half, though, because he had already seen some unbelievable things in his lifetime.

He recalled a young lad, a trusted soldier, who travelled with him once. The lad, his name was Taylor, swore he had fallen in love with a woodland nymph, a beauty beyond comparison. She had lured him deep into a forest and there turned into a witch, in the midst of their passion as they rolled in the leaves. Taylor spoke with such detail at the horror of finding himself lying with this old hag, enjoined with her, facing the warts on her face, her wrinkled skin and her saggy two-hundred-year-old breasts, that it seemed completely plausible. Brande almost chuckled, recalling

Taylor's vivid retellings. He hadn't believed it then, nor did he believe it now, but it was so much harder to dismiss such tales when the darkness was closed in all around. The grin fell from his face as he remembered another story, a more recent one. A man had crawled out of Dankwood one day claiming the men in the forest who snatch people had done terrible things to him. He had heard voices in the dark too.

Brande remained still. The passage of time was hard to gauge. He decided to run through an old rhyme in his head. This was a soldier's trick. He knew how long it took to sing it and he counted each recitation on his fingers. If he ran through all ten fingers three times and there was no further sound, he would assume it was his imagination and move on.

Good King Ig,
He danced a merry jig
As he ate and drank his wine.

The feast was late
But it still tasted great:
Fish, poultry and roast swine.

He was on his seventeenth iteration, thinking the simple children's rhyme through in his head when he began to grow tired of it. He knew his survival might depend on him out-waiting his attacker, though, so he kept at it.

A beggar came along
And sang a merry song
And they got along just fine.

They ate like a pig,
Did the beggar and King Ig,
Said the king, "What's yours is mine."

Then he heard the word "axe". It was a distinct whisper from barely twenty paces away. It had broken through the sound of his sing-song thoughts like a stone through the surface of a still pond, sending ripples of fright through his system. It could be a soldier, but what soldier pursued a man this far into the forest, for this long, away from his comrades. No, this was a forest dweller of some description. He tried to cast thoughts of cloven-hoofed satyrs aside. He glanced down at his axe. Sure enough, it was gleaming in the light of the moon which had just reappeared. With his eyesight adjusted to the darkness, he could see his way for a short distance, but that meant so too might someone see him and the gleaming weapon. He had become so sure it was just his imagination that he hadn't taken the obvious precaution of lying low and staying hidden. He had thought the worst that could happen was that his fears got the better of him and he had to sit it out until daybreak. He was wrong. This was worse.

He tried to consider his options, but it was late, and he was exhausted. He had been awake before the village bell sounded that morning, and he felt like he had been running or fighting ever since.

There was no point in running. He would tire, and they would find him.

He could fight, although they probably knew the surroundings better than him and were more refreshed. The fact there was a voice suggested at least two people. "Axe." The word still echoed in his head. Someone had identified that he was carrying a weapon and had relayed that information to another as a warning. They didn't know he also possessed the knife he had taken from Eadlyn. His pulse quickened as he prepared to fight. He could take two of them, he was sure. More might be a problem.

Dry leaves crackled underfoot, and bushes pushed aside as something ran at him, something fast. The moon was still out, and he saw the low shape of the wolf just in time. He swung the axe and caught the creature on the side of its head as it leapt for him, knocking it to one side where it fell to the ground, rallied for just a moment on unsteady legs, then collapsed. He turned to see two more stalking out of the darkness toward him. Who had spoken though? He had heard of men that could become wolves, but it was yet another tale he only half-believed.

The first wolf approached tentatively, giving Brande an opportunity. He threw the axe and, without looking to see if it hit its target, he drew the knife with his right hand and lunged. He dropped on the second wolf as it attacked, bringing the knife down where spine met skull, even as its jaws clamped on to his side. It slumped and dropped away.

He heard the voices again. They were everywhere suddenly. There was shouting from all around him. The wolf struck by his thrown axe was back. It leapt on him and growled into his face, its paws clawing for purchase against his chest. He stared into those dark eyes, watching the life drain from them. Tension left the wolf's body, and he threw it from him, retrieving the knife dug deeply into its throat. As it fell to the ground, he saw it also had a gaping wound in the side of its head, where his axe had struck then fallen away.

He stood now, his bitten side aching, his arms tired, his heart pounding and his breathing ragged. He held the knife up, almost like a shield, as he staggered about looking for his fallen axe. The moonlight revealed it, and he grabbed for its handle. It was by a pair of feet. He looked up to find the barbed head of a nocked arrow pointed right at his face. He heard footsteps draw in all around him. He was encircled by men dressed in dark outfits designed for lightness of movement. Their faces were partially covered by masks or paints. Forest dwellers, he realised, slumping to the ground and dropping the knife. Several men held short horse bows with arrows drawn back. Another couple held knives. They were young men and the dark look in their eyes was unmistakable, even behind the masks. If they planned to finish him, it would take but a moment.

His mind flashed an image. A baby in a cot, giggling. Her dark hair just a wisp. Fia.

A figure, strong and beautiful, motherly, stood over the babe. Aithne.

"Tie him up," barked one. Brande turned to look. The instruction had been issued by a short, sturdy man wearing a boar's tusk on a string around his neck. His sword was by his side, not drawn as the others' were. Their leader, perhaps. Something in Brande wanted to snatch up his knife and plant it in the man's heart, regardless of how many arrows would pierce him during the attack, but he held back. Somehow, here in the darkness, surrounded, the fight had gone from him.

He smiled to himself, remembering the little girl who he led around as she sat on the back of a pony during a midsummer's festival. He recalled whittling a small family of wooden dolls for her seventh birthday. His life was flashing before his eyes. The bits that mattered, at least.

He was abruptly brought back to the present as hands grabbed him and hoisted him to his feet. His wrists were tied behind his back. The man on his right wore a fox's tail on a string around his neck, his face obscured by a cloth mask with eyeholes cut into it. To his left, one man wore a chunk of wood around his neck on a chain. Distracted by this, wondering what it meant, he didn't notice a tall, lean figure approach until the man landed a fist full of bony knuckles into his gut. Brande doubled over, being completely unprepared for it. He wheezed in pain, but he still noticed the wolf paw on the string around this one's neck. The man's face was painted grey. His eyes were black, even the whites were black. Had he dyed his eyeballs? "That was for Pain, Death and Taxes," spat the man. "They were my wolf brothers." Brande realised he'd just killed the man's pet wolves.

"Shouldn't have relied on them," spat back Brande.

The wolfman leapt forward in a rage and drove his knee into Brande's gut, knocking the wind from him again.

"That's enough," growled the leader with the boar's tusk.

From behind, a blow struck Brande on the side of the head. He didn't see it coming, just a hard object swung in the pitch of the night. For the second time since he'd woken that morning, he collapsed unconscious. This time it only lasted moments. He found himself semi-comatose and dizzy, his head spinning so fast he was sure he would throw up, his face pressed against the forest floor. He retched, but it had been so many hours since he'd eaten that he didn't produce anything. He glanced up to see, swirling before him, a boar's tusk, a wolf's paw, a fox's tail and a piece of wood on a chain. Other cloaked figures were also gathering, each with a different talisman hung about their necks.

Brande vowed that, before the night was out, he would make them pay for slowing him down.

CHAPTER FOUR

The forest dwellers gagged his mouth and blindfolded him. They dragged him to his feet and tied a rope around his neck. They shoved him forward, forcing him to walk. They lead him on like an animal, kicking him from behind when he slowed. They took him this way and that, back and forth. He was sure they had walked him in a circle more than once to confound him. If he stumbled over tree roots and fell to his knees, they would strike him in annoyance and drag him to his feet again by the rope. Disorientated and injured in the depths of Dankwood, he was hopelessly lost.

There was a time, not so very long ago, when he had been a different man. In those days, this could not have happened. He sighed, remembering a promise he had made. Memories of violence rose in his mind, but he forced them down again, suppressing them. He had been a warrior once, but now he was someone else. He had thought he could save Aithne and Fia and fight an army, but he had been a fool.

"Hang him over there," said the recognisable voice of the one wearing the boar's tusk, who Brande presumed to be their leader.

They yanked off Brande's blindfold. He took in his surroundings. The moon hid stubbornly behind dark clouds leaving the night sky black, but a raging campfire burned at the centre of the clearing. It illuminated a well-established encampment with timber huts and a stone-walled well where someone was drawing water. Makeshift tents and hammocks surrounded the permanent structures.

There had been talk of forest-dwelling people in Dankwood for some years. Brande had assumed there to be some truth to the idea that a few bandits had set up residence. He could now see that a proper, small community had been established. There were more of them than he had anticipated. He saw children, a mother carrying a baby, and many adults who wore masks or paint disguising them as forest animals or sprites. Every one of them wore a talisman around their neck. Brande wondered what they could want with him and whether he would live to see the dawn, which could only be a few hours away. He ground his teeth against the coarse fabric of his gag. Every hour lost put distance between him and his family.

A short distance from the fire, on the edge of the camp, a cross had been erected in the ground. It was made of two sturdy tree trunks, each as thick as a man's leg, overlapping in the centre to form an X. They dragged Brande over to it and tied his hands and feet to it. He dared not struggle because, although he could probably break free of the bindings, they had a noose around his neck and still pointed their crude arrows at him. They left him there, hanging from the cross, staring out at the camp.

The one wearing the fox's tail reached up to him, holding a serrated hunting knife. He slid it into Brande's clothing and ripped at his coarse wool tunic, exposing his chest and his arms. He chuckled. He ran the blade along Brande's cheek, not cutting his skin but sliding it under the fabric there. The gag was tied tightly around Brande's head, pulling on the sides of his mouth, suppressing his tongue, making it difficult to breathe or talk. The knife sawed and tugged until the coarse rag split. Brande spat the fabric from his mouth, and the gag fell away.

Brande's anger smouldered deep within him. "Who do you think you are?" he growled. He wanted to say more but decided it would be unwise to aggravate his captor while he held a knife near his throat. He little knew his capabilities these days, but he knew when the odds were against him. His initial outrage and despair when Aithne and Fia were taken had driven him on a mad pursuit, but almost a full day had cycled, and here he was in Dankwood. Lost. Captured.

They had set wolves on him. He had thought they intended to kill him, but now he was their prisoner. His head swirled with the meaning of it all, but all his heart cared about was that he was failing his wife and child. They were being carted away, and he was incapacitated. It wouldn't do.

Fox's Tail walked away from him without saying a word. The others had all lost interest and moved off, except for a woman who still stood to watch him. She wore a rabbit's foot around her neck on a delicate chain. The rabbit's claws were splayed outwards unnaturally to emphasise a jewel embedded in its paw. He tried to sound reasonable as he asked, "What do you people want with me?"

She stared at him, inspecting him like a piece of meat. He closed his eyes. He could still see the campfire's glow on the inside of his eyelids. Could they be cannibals? Would she use him as a mate? Whatever their intentions, they were wasting his time. His anger began to build. He opened his eyes, ready to swear some dark oath, but the woman was gone.

He shouted some questions in the general direction of the camp but got no response. Only the children looked at him, their little faces hidden behind grey and brown paints, soft feathers stuck to their jaws and temples. They soon lost interest, as if they had seen this performance already from the last person to hang from the cross. They flitted about like little birds, quietly playing with each other, oblivious to his torment or the late hour. He watched the other forest dwellers as they went about their business. Mostly, they performed chores. Drawing water. Feeding the fire. Preparing food. They were doing it without speaking to one another. For a moment, he wondered if he was awake.

Brande noticed Boar's Tusk and Wolf's Paw emerge from a hut. They were whispering quietly to each other, involved in some conspiratorial conversation apart from the others. It looked like their discussion might dissolve into an argument. He suspected they were deciding his fate.

Having completed their mundane tasks, the figures moved together and gathered around the campfire, forming a circle. One of them turned a metal poker balanced on a forked stick, its tip lodged in the heart of the fire. That sent a jolt of worry through Brande. Hanging on the cross being ignored was one thing, but now he had a suspicion about what was to come next.

He would have liked to know more. What possessed people to dress like this and hide out in a forest? He didn't like it. He watched them. None of them spoke. The sound of the fire filled the night air as logs crackled and spat.

The man tending the poker was tall and thin. Perched on a long scraggy neck, his bald head reflected the firelight, but his face was covered with a leathery mask that didn't look like any animal. He wore a human ear hanging from a string around his neck. Brande thought he knew what that meant.

He tried to see what other talismans were worn. A crow's foot. A rat's skull. A pair of bat's wings. Brande was a simple man. He liked his work. He liked cutting down trees. He liked spending his free time whittling figures out of wood. He liked the company of his family and those fellow craftsmen and tradesmen as he came into contact with on a regular basis. But he'd seen other things during his time as a soldier. He'd seen things that made his blood run cold. Vicious things. Truth be told, he'd done some of those vicious things himself. This, however, smacked of lunacy. It was a cult of some kind. He knew from experience that devotees of any cult could not be trusted to play by the rules of ordinary folk.

Were they worshipping demons out here? Animal spirits? He sneered in disgust. He had no time for these people. He wanted no part of it. He didn't even want to be seeing it. A knot formed in his stomach. Was all this hokum designed to scare him? It just served to anger him. They were playing this idiotic game while his family needed him.

Were any of these men soldiers? He thought about the knives they had held. They were hunting knives, not military ones. Their bows were poorly maintained, the strings fraying. The wooden shafts of their arrows showed signs of warping and were black with dirt having been retrieved and used time and again. He thought back to his capture. The knifemen had held their weapons clumsily. Only the wolves seemed well trained. No, these weren't soldiers. These were men who had fled their normal lives to be part of something new. They were loners, castoffs, outlaws and some were probably simpletons. Someone had forged a bond between likeminded strays and formed this forest-dwelling cult.

He reassessed his odds. He counted the figures around the fire. There were twenty-five, not including the children. Maybe a few of them were fighters, but not many. Maybe there were a dozen he would have to contend with should he break free. The camp was not large. If he could make it out of the clearing, then he stood a fair chance of escape. Suddenly the odds didn't seem so stacked against him. He just needed to get loose. He yanked at his bonds, but they were secure. He could feel his arms going numb, the blood running out of them as they remained aloft. They felt heavy. Even if he got free, it would be a struggle to fight until the circulation returned.

Eventually the inevitable happened. The tall man with the human ear hanging at his chest stood up and brandished the poker. The tip glowed bright orange. The man's face was unreadable beneath his tan leather mask. He and Boar Tusk walked towards Brande. Still, nothing was said. The others watched from their circle around the fire.

Brande growled at the approaching figures, determined that they would speak to him. "Show me your faces, cowards."

Boar Tusk spoke up. "Answer my questions, and you might live. First, give me your name."

Brande laughed, thinking how earlier that day he had tried the same tactic on the soldier he and Eadlyn had questioned. He spat on the ground at Boar Tusk's feet, narrowly missing them. He wouldn't submit to their demands willingly. Stubbornness had soaked into his bones long ago and settled there.

Boar Tusk stepped back and motioned for Human Ear to step forward. The poker was placed gently on the inside crease of Brande's elbow and drawn down his arm to his shoulder, leaving a long, red mark and the sickening aroma of burning flesh. Despite his arm feeling numb from being held aloft, he felt the pain just the same. A sound escaped him that began as a wail of pain but transformed into a growl of anger. His teeth gnashed at them. Unconsciously, Boar Tusk took a step backwards, staggered by the ferocity of Brande's reaction.

There was no doubt in his mind now. These fearful cowards were not warriors. He could take them, given half a chance. They would pay for this.

Boar Tusk smiled at Brande's reaction and, gaining confidence, stepped closer again, perhaps hoping to intimidate him. It had no effect on Brande. His anger burned within him, redder and hotter than any poker. The man was so close now he could smell his stink.

"I'll ask you again, prisoner. What is your name?"

Wolf Paw joined them. He wore a smirk, enjoying the display. He doubtless wanted revenge for the death of his pet wolves.

Another man came over and joined them. He wore little make-up and a small, well-crafted wooden spoon hung from his neck on a leather strap. A few of the others were rising now too, beginning to form a semicircle around the spectacle.

"Who are you people?" growled Brande. "Let me go. I must go."

"You killed my wolves. You're going nowhere," sneered Wolf Paw.

Boar Tusk raised a hand for silence. "Tell me your name, captive. I won't ask again."

"Nachmair take you, whore-son," cursed Brande.

Boar Tusk spluttered, aghast. His neck turned red. His hand dropped to the knife in his belt but stopped there. "Teach him a lesson."

Human Ear ran the poker along the same line on Brande's arm, only in the other direction, running from the shoulder up to the elbow. From there, he continued along in the direction of Brande's wrist. Brande's cry was less restrained this time, with the edge of a scream in it. Human Ear left a long red welt along his arm, but he was careless. The pressure on Brande's skin increased and decreased as Human Ear giggled. A simpleton who takes pleasure in pain, realised Brande.

It went on too long. Brande's eyes rolled up into his skull. He gritted his teeth and panted, trying to focus on anything but the pain. He had endured worse than this in the past. He forced himself to look at what was happening. He immediately saw the man's mistake.

Boar Tusk's expression changed when he saw it too.

"Unlucky," grunted Brande. The fibres binding his wrist to the cross were strained as he writhed in pain, and Human Ear had caught the taut rope with an accidental glance from the poker. The binding snapped. Brande ripped his hurting arm from the bonds, pumping his hand to bring blood back into it.

"Get more rope," ordered Boar Tusk, not realising it was already too late.

Brande stretched out and grabbed Human Ear by his scrawny neck. The man gasped. He began to lift the poker to retaliate, but he'd hesitated a second too long. His scrawny neck was no match for Brande's brute strength. One violent shake, a sickening crack, and the man collapsed to the floor. Brande snatched the poker from him as he crumpled to the ground.

Boar Tusk began drawing his dagger. One of the others, Fox Tail, turned and ran, probably to collect a weapon. Several others followed him. Wolf Paw clenched his fists and narrowed his dyed black eyes. The remaining few backed off.

Brande knew they were inexperienced and hoped those who stayed would be overconfident. He pressed the hot poker into the other bindings holding his right hand, and they snapped away. He reached around the back of the post to stop himself falling forward. He'd planned to cut his feet bindings, but Boar Tusk leapt forward with his knife shouting something incomprehensible. Brande propelled himself forward, ankles still tied to the cross and legs wide apart on the lower half of the X. He knocked Boar Tusk's dagger away with his free hand, receiving a gash on his wrist for his trouble. Simultaneously, he plunged the poker straight through Boar Tusk's chest and into his heart. He clung to the poker, letting it drag Boar Tusk down slowly. It was all he could do before he fell forward and the bindings broke his ankles.

He heard Wolf Paw issuing orders, probably too

cowardly to attack by himself. Suddenly they were on him, holding him, kicking him. The poker was knocked from his hand. He kicked out and found his feet were loose of their bindings. He didn't know how it happened, but they were free.

He kicked the nearest cultist. The rest of them piled on him. He couldn't defend against a fist to the eye or a foot in the gut. A knee pressed down on his neck. He tried to wriggle free, but there were too many on him.

He looked up at the man whose knee was crushing his throat. A bat's wing hung from the man's neck, which was suddenly no longer attached to his head. A fountain of blood erupted from the man's decapitated body. A sword swung past, attacking another of the forest dwellers. No stranger to the thick melee of battle, Brande knew instantly that he had an ally. The pressure on his neck relaxed, and he struggled to his knees. The other dwellers had recoiled, shocked at the sight of so much blood. Brande wiped the man's blood from his eyes. He didn't stop to find out what was happening. He forced his attackers off him and punched one square on the chin. The man stood like a statue. He had a crow's foot on a lace around his neck. Brande's arm ached from the burning, but it had only sustained a flesh wound, and his punch was solid. The man's eyes unfocused and he dropped backwards, falling like a stone.

An arrow hissed past Brande's head. It struck the cross and embedded itself there, splintering the wood.

Rising to his feet, he saw that the only person nearby holding a sword was a man with a shapeless piece of wood hung around his neck. He wore a wooden mask, and it was impossible to read his intentions, but a man wearing a rat's skull lay at his feet covered in blood. That was good enough for Brande.

An arrow zipped past Brande's face, a goose feather brushing his cheek. He turned and ran. He knew they were on his heels, but he didn't look back. His legs were still awkward from being strung up, but he shambled to the edge of the clearing as arrows flew past him. It took skill to hit a moving target at thirty yards, or blind luck. Fortunately, his captors had neither.

As soon as he could, he put a tree between them and him. It also meant he was out of the light of the campfire now and it was still night. He plunged into the darkness, trying to skip over roots and avoid thorny scrub. He could hear them close behind. He scrambled this way, then that, helter-skelter, with only the vaguest direction in mind. He didn't care which way he was headed. The important thing was to put the camp, the fire, the cross, and those crazy cultists behind him. His legs were slow, but he still hoped he could lose them.

Something landed on his back. It was heavy. He felt a searing pain in his shoulder. He fell, turning, driving his fist into the thing's side, expecting to find a wolf. Something furry was in his face. A fox's tail. He punched again and again and then rolled the man off him. A dagger fell to the ground. He'd been stabbed in the shoulder, but it was poorly done and left only a small wound. His energy was ebbing despite the adrenaline churning through his veins. He staggered to his feet, waiting for the next forest dweller to appear.

"Here," said a voice. Brande hadn't even noticed the man with the shapeless wood talisman standing by him. His ally. He had severed his ankle bonds and killed at least one of his attackers. The stranger jammed the sword he was holding blade first into the ground and stepped back. Brande chose to trust him. He grabbed the sword and drew it from the earth.

"Would've preferred an axe," he grunted, by way of a thank you.

"We must hurry. They've got more wolves. We need to put distance between them and us." He headed off. Brande wasn't in a position to argue. He jogged after the man, doing his best to match his pace. The injuries he had sustained meant he struggled to keep up. They ran into the thickening darkness of Dankwood. Whatever light the campfire had produced was of no benefit at this distance, and the moon was only barely visible behind a thin cloud.

"Where are we headed?"

"East, I think," replied the stranger.

It was good enough. A howl in the distance told them the wolves had been unleashed. They hadn't put much distance between them and the camp.

"The wolves will come, then the men," said the stranger. "For now, we just run."

They ran, but Brande was sluggish. It wasn't long before he called out, "Enough! I will make my stand here." He leaned against a tree as he caught his breath. He examined the sword that had been given to him. It was a crude longsword, the hilt worn and rough, the blade pitted.

"The edge has been sharpened recently," said the stranger, seeing Brande's look of disapproval.

"It's still not an axe." Brande tried to smile, but the situation made it impossible.

"We can swap if you want." The man showed his own sword to Brande, but it was almost identical. Brande shook his head, not knowing if it was meant as a serious offer or just proof that neither was at a particular disadvantage compared to the other.

Brande could feel his tired face pulling his head down to the ground, begging for sleep. He blew out a long breath and straightened himself up. He rotated his wrists and his ankles, then rubbed the wound in his shoulder. It wasn't as sore as the burns down his arm.

They heard the wolves before they saw them. They came hurtling out of the darkness like things possessed. The first to emerge leapt at the stranger and the next came for Brande. The two wolves were snarling, passionate in their attack, eager for violence. Brande swung the sword and missed. The wolf leapt up on him. Its teeth gnashed at his face. His ally lopped half its nose off with a wild swing that only just missed Brande himself. The wolf tore itself away, screaming in a high pitched whine.

Brande liked wolves. As a woodsman, he liked all the forest animals. He knew a wild beast when he saw one. He also recognised a half-starved, maddened beast that had been trained to track and kill. As the wolf struggled on the ground, trying to get away, he picked up his sword from where it lay and plunged it into the creature. He curled forward and drove it home with all his weight behind it. The wolf clawed the ground, blood gushing from its face. A moment later, it was still.

His ally had beaten off the other wolf, but it returned with renewed anger and leapt on him. It bit at him and clamped its jaw shut on the chunk of wood now rammed into its mouth. He struggled desperately with it, barely holding it at bay. He'd wrapped his legs around the beast's ribcage and was straining, crushing it, forcing the air from its lungs. Brande heard a rib snap. The wolf whined, and its hind claws scratched frantically at the flesh on the man's thighs.

Brande drew his sword out of the wolf he had killed, one foot on its flank as he slid it free. He barrelled towards his ally and drove the sword down into the beast's spine. It slumped forward, dead in an instant.

Brande took the stranger's hand. He pulled him out from under the wolf and up onto his feet.

"Thanks." The man's voice was full of gratitude. He was shaking from the attack.

"They'll know where we are now," warned Brande.

The man looked at him. His mask had fallen away at some point. He was younger than Brande expected. He had red hair and fair skin covered with freckles. His bright blue eyes shone with urgency within his narrow face. "My name is Silas," he said, quickly.

"Brande."

They shook hands.

The man began to limp away. Brande saw that he had been bitten on one calf. It didn't look severe and didn't seem to stop him bearing weight on it, but it would slow them down.

"We must go," Silas urged. "They have no more wolves. But there are many men."

They staggered on together, Brande desperately hoping each weary footfall took him closer to his wife and daughter.

CHAPTER FIVE

They had taken a deliberately winding course, not hesitating to choose a difficult path where an easier one might look more tempting to pursuers. It must have worked because they encountered no one else that night. At one point, perhaps an hour after the wolves were dispatched, Brande thought he heard footsteps and bid Silas be quiet and still. They waited. Brande was sure he had noticed something, but Silas shook his head to say he heard nothing. After that, there was nothing. They carried on their journey east through Dankwood.

"You've not taken that thing off your neck," said Brande in a challenging tone. They had exchanged few words as they tramped through the seemingly endless night, not daring to stop for fear of men at their heels. Brande decided it was time to break the silence and find something out about his travelling companion. He wanted to know why he had been rescued.

Silas raised a hand and touched the wooden block hanging from the chain around his neck. "I lost the mask when the wolves attacked. I forgot about this thing. I guess

I've got used to it." He looked at Brande apologetically. "Anyway, I couldn't just drop it in case they were tracking us."

Brande nodded agreement. "What does it mean?"

Silas took a deep breath and let it out slowly. He didn't seem to appreciate being interrogated after saving Brande's life, but he answered all the same. "I was a novice, an initiate. Wood is for an initiate." He paused, but as Brande didn't reply, he continued. "Once you are accepted into the community, you get something representing your skills, like a spoon for a cook, or a twig for a gatherer, and if you are highly trusted you get to sit in on the meetings and take part in the rites, and you get a forest animal. It's lunacy."

"Why did you join them?"

"Soldiers came to our village. King's men. Took my little girl. I came north, heading for Charstoke Castle. Got lost in the forest. The cult found me. Tortured me." He lifted his right sleeve and showed streaks of burn marks along it. Brande recognised the technique. "They gave me the option to join. I took it. I've wanted out ever since."

Brande pondered what he had been told. "How long?"

"Five weeks, three days," he replied. "That's how long since they took her from our home in Lakeside."

"What do they want? What do they do?"

"Who?"

"Your friends."

"Oh. Rebels. Cultists. There's no sense to it."

"I bet there's a story."

"I don't know everything," Silas replied and snatched off his wooden neck piece. "Novice, see?" He threw the offending article away into a bush. If they'd been tracked this far, the discarded item wouldn't make much difference anyway.

"Why did you free me?"

Silas paused as if asking himself the same question. "You killed their torturer and leader in less time than it takes for those imbeciles to nock an arrow. I took a chance on you."

"You recognised a fellow soldier," said Brande, approvingly. He'd always found it hard to pay compliments, so didn't look up as he spoke. "You swing a sword well." He continued onward, picking his way over roots and brambles. He was in pain, but he dare not show it. He needed rest. So too did Silas. He could see the man limping and trying to hide it. The wolf's bite to his calf was not severe, but no doubt hurt all the same.

Silas followed after him, not noticing Brande had changed their direction slightly. He had seen the first rays of dawn and turned them to face northeast. He had not lost sight of his need to get to the town of Bruke where the king's men would surely be taking Aithne and Fia.

"I was a soldier for seven years. Mostly fought the Skulluns."

"Nasty people."

"We won some battles." He shrugged. "Not all. But we won the war."

They walked in silence for a short while. Silas broke it. "I imagine that you fought in the Crusades."

Brande nodded, pleased the man could tell the difference between a regular soldier and those who had been through madness and back. "Yes, I fought in the Crusades."

"I could tell when I saw you fight. There's something about you old warriors."

"It was a different kind of war."

"Yes." Silas nodded respectfully but didn't say anything else on the matter.

Brande was warming to him. "That leg of yours all right?"

"I'll live."

"We have something in common."

"You lost family?"

"Yes."

"Those two men took them? The ones the cultists found in the forest? A soldier and another man with no head."

"The soldier was one of the king's men, yes. They took my wife and daughter. The other was a friend. I ended his life, he was in terrible pain."

Silas didn't comment on this. "You go after your family now?"

"Yes."

"I'll join you. I don't expect to find my girl alive, but I have nothing else to do but kill those bastards one at a time."

Brande laughed bitterly. "Join me, and there'll be plenty of that."

"Good," said Silas, earnestly.

"But don't lose heart. That soldier had orders to take them unharmed."

"Really? Did you learn anything else?"

"No."

"You killed him?"

"He killed himself. He was afraid of the cloaked men who rode with them."

Silas pulled a face. "Strange."

The cold light of dawn chased away the night, the stars, but none of the exhaustion. It became easier to find a path to walk between the trees, which Brande was grateful for. They trudged on in silence. Brande's thoughts grew morbid, thinking about what might be happening to Aithne or Fia. Images of Aithne being struck and Fia being dragged away filled his mind.

Silas's limp became more pronounced. Brande was just about to suggest they stop and rest when something caught his attention. His nostrils filled with a new sensation, unlike the other smells of the forest.

"Something's burning," said Silas. "I thought I smelled it earlier but dismissed it."

"I smell it."

"Wood."

"Scented wood. Did your cult burn scented wood?"

"Not that I know of."

"Could there be a house around here?"

"In the heart of Dankwood? Not likely."

"But not impossible."

"Could be a campfire."

"Who burns scented wood on a campfire? I've a feeling we're closer to the fringes now. Let's find out who is burning what. I'm hungry." He led Silas up a rise and, sure enough, through the woods they could see smoke rising into the sky on the slightest puff of wind.

"I'd wager that people who build houses deep in forests don't want company," proclaimed Silas

"Agreed."

"Then let's not-"

"But we need food and rest. Come on. The king's whole army can't be in there."

Silas grunted amusement. "And if they are, we can take them."

"Let's go."

They marched through the thinning trees and found they were now heading downhill.

"They've built their house low down, so it can't be seen," realised Brande.

"Someone who definitely doesn't want company," repeated Silas.

"What's that?" asked Brande, pointing to a low-hanging branch on a tree right in front of them.

Silas looked up at it and frowned. Hanging from a low branch was a strip of something like leather, like part of a belt or a strap. It was looped around then sewn below to leave two dangling tails.

"There's another one," said Silas, pointing. They moved forward to inspect the tree and found several of the branches were hung with these strange strips, each one like a short piece of a leather belt flung over and sewn to keep it in place. Some of the thinner ones rocked in the light breeze, but most hung still.

"Here," called Silas. He had moved on to another tree. "This yew has them too. I wonder if they signify something?"

"Probably decoration. Just signs of habitation," grunted Brande. "Come on, let's see what's up ahead."

"A lot of effort for nothing," mumbled Silas, eyeing the straps. As they walked on, they found straps on most of the trees. Usually, only one or two, but some of the more expansive trees held more.

The trees continued to thin, and they looked for an opening. All at once, the forest opened up to reveal a modestly sized cottage. Brande thought it impressive, considering its location and distance from civilisation. It had wattle walls and a mouldy thatched roof. From what he could see, it was in reasonable repair, and the scented smoke suggested someone lived there. There was a furrowed clearing by the cottage which functioned as a garden, judging by the herbs planted there. There was even a well at the edge of the property. Brande wondered who could live out here.

Brande and Silas had come upon the back of the property and began to round it, looking for a front door.

"Can you hear that sound?" asked Silas, quietly. "Like scratching."

Brande shrugged. "Come on. We need food. I could use a new tunic, too. We'll sleep away the morning and make progress in the afternoon."

"What if we aren't welcome?"

Brande furrowed his brow. "I may not give them a choice." He was in no mood for etiquette that might stand between him and his family. It seemed an impossibly long time since he'd seen them. He tried to imagine where they were and how long it would take to reach them. The biggest obstacle he faced right now was exhaustion.

At the front of the house, they found an old woman standing by an apple tree staring at them in absolute horror. Her expression did not go unnoticed by either man, but it finally relaxed into a half-hearted smile. She used a walking stick to move towards them, one awkward step at a time. Brande doubted such a frail old thing could survive out here on her own. Perhaps she wasn't alone.

The ground was littered with rotten apples. She obviously produced more than she required. She held one plump one in her free hand. "I grow all my own food," she announced, as she approached. "You gentlemen must be hungry." She dumped the apple in Brande's hand.

Brande couldn't quite place her age. Her circumstances suggested she shouldn't be too old because survival out here, isolated, must be hard, but she looked not a day under ninety. He briefly recalled a story he'd heard in the tavern late one night, a bard had been passing through Bruton and told a tall tale about the wicked witch of Dankwood. He quickly put it from his mind as nonsense.

"We mean you no harm," he assured her. "We seek shelter and food." He tried not to make it sound like a demand. "Unfortunately, we have nothing to offer in return."

The old woman paused, searching them with her eyes. They waited for her to respond, but the wait continued and made the pair of them feel uncomfortable. Brande was about to demand her hospitality, but Silas spoke up before he could. "Actually, I do have some coin sewn into my belt. It's yours if you can help us. It's not much, though."

The woman smiled. She eyed them up and down and sniffed. "You look like you've been fighting."

"We were attacked by wolves," explained Brande.

"We've been travelling all night. We escaped raiders, south of the forest," added Silas.

She nodded slowly, maybe hearing the truth in their words, perhaps picking up on the omissions. "You must be tired, gentlemen. Follow me. Come inside." She started moving toward her front door, one painful step at a time, making good use of her stick. Brande felt frustrated following behind her but was grateful for her hospitality.

Inside, the modest front room boasted a fire which made the place comfortable on this cold morning. A thick brown rug lay before the fireplace. The room was full of that sweet but sickly aroma they had smelled from afar. A rocking chair sat by the hearth. There was a table surrounded by chairs. For decoration, a vase of dried flowers sat atop it. The only other ornament was a small wooden carving of a man. He was perched on the rickety wooden mantelpiece over her fireplace and stood erect, leaning against the wall. It was a crudely fashioned item. Brande liked to whittle small objects in quiet moments. He wasn't exceptional at it, but he was skilled enough that he could sell his items at market and make a few pennies. This thing before him now was of far poorer quality than anything he would deign to sell. Strange that it should have pride of place on her mantelpiece. He wondered if she had made it herself. Perhaps it was something to talk to during the lonely nights. He stared at it, and his mind travelled back to Fia and the carving of a dragon he had made years ago. She had mistaken it for Hungrar the World Dragon, and he didn't want to disillusion her, so that's what it was from that moment on. She treasured it because he had made it, and that warmed his heart. But now she was in a cage on a wagon, and he was stood in some old woman's cottage in the middle of this accursed forest.

"Something ails you, sir?" asked the old woman, staring at him.

Brande broke from his reverie.

Silas jumped in. "I am Silas, this is Brande. We thank you for your hospitality. We cannot stay long but-" He paused, something distracting him. A scratching sound. He looked around for it but saw nothing causing it, and good manners demanded he continue. "We cannot stay long, but we do need some food and somewhere to sleep the morning away. We'll be gone by the afternoon."

She smiled. Toothless, noted Brande. Maybe that was why so many rotten apples lay on the ground outside.

"Well, one of you can sleep on the rug by the hearth. It's a cold morning, but you'll be warm there. The other can sleep in my bed, provided you're clean. I'll put a rug over it anyway. I'll be outside most of the day, or in the kitchen, which you are to stay away from at all times! I don't want you dirtying or interrupting me. I have my preparations to complete."

"Preparations?" inquired Silas.

"I brew medicines from herbs that I grow here, and sometimes I sell them. So keep out of my kitchen."

"As you say," said Brande. "What is your name, good lady?"

She stared at them through old, squinting eyes. "It's important to me that people don't find me living out here. I live alone, and I don't want company. I certainly don't want people sniffing around here stealing my herbs. There are strange types in these woods nowadays." She eyed the clothes that Silas wore, presumably recognising the garb of the cultish forest dwellers. "So you don't need to know my name."

Silas nodded. "So be it. But we will need food." He smiled devilishly. "Can you offer us anything other than apples?"

She clucked at his impertinence. "I have bread and cheese, which I bought recently. If you are honest and you give me coin, as you said, I shall be happy to supply you food and ale. I have some salted meat too."

That sparked a recent memory in Brande. "What are those things hanging from the trees outside?"

She paused. "They keep away bad spirits. Wait here." She turned from him and headed to the doorway leading to her kitchen.

Silas unbuckled his belt and started picking at it, trying to loosen the coins sewn there. Brande said nothing, wondering at the wisdom of giving money where hospitality might have prevailed without it. He quite liked Silas. They had some similarities, and possibly a combined purpose, but Brande already felt the man was slowing him down. He didn't need friends. He just needed to get to Bruke as fast as possible to meet the soldiers when they inevitably arrived there. He moved to another doorway and found a small bedroom. "Fire or bed?" he asked.

Silas looked back, shrugged, unwilling to choose.

Brande thought for a moment. He looked at the coins Silas had retrieved. "Heads you get the bed, tails I do." The bed was small but probably comfortable. The rug was soft and next to the fire. It was hard to say which would provide the best rest.

Silas pulled the last coin from his belt, broken stitching falling to the floor. "Do you hear that scratching?" he said, agitation in his voice. "It's getting on my nerves. Rats under the floorboards."

The scratching was quite distinct, but Brande chose to ignore it. He walked into the bedroom. He walked out again. "I'll tell you what, Silas. You take the bedroom. You can't hear the scratching so much in there. I'll sleep by the fire. It'll warm my bones after a night out in the air." Silas nodded appreciatively.

The old woman came back into the room and placed a wooden platter on the table. A moment later, she returned with two flagons half-full of ale. "There's not much," she said. "But if you're heading to Bruke, which is the nearest place worth visiting, then this will get you there."

"Thank you," said Silas. "I'm sure it will."

Brande's eyes narrowed, because to his mind, his

untrusting mind, the one that seemed to have awoken after years of comfortable family life, he had just heard the woman ask their destination and his companion foolishly confirm where they were headed.

He had learnt much during the Crusades and not giving away his name and destination was his most basic rule. Silas had broken those rules already. Brande began to wonder if he could trust this man. After all, he'd been a member of a cult intent on torturing him not a full day ago. Could he have known this house was here? Could he have somehow led him here and together they were stalling him until the forest dwellers arrived?

Brande blinked away the thoughts, deciding he was paranoid. Exhaustion did that to a person. He plonked himself down at the table and took a grateful draft of ale. He licked his lips and looked into the bottom of the flagon to find he'd emptied it. He took up the bread and tore off a chunk for himself, as Silas had already done. He could smell the cheese, and it made his mouth water. He crumbled some pieces on to the bread. He ate and was pleased. The fire was warm, the sun was rising, and after a few bites, he began to feel better. He relaxed, and immediately tiredness swept over him and dragged on his eyelids. His hands felt heavy and clumsy.

He looked up from the table. The woman was watching him. Silas had stopped eating and was watching him too. He felt alarmed, and a wave of panic rushed through him. As he dropped his hand to his sword, he realised it was too heavy to lift. He looked to the flagon, his foggy mind coming to a realisation all too late.

He stood up, using all his strength. He tried to speak, but all that came out was a slur. Even his thoughts were incoherent in his mind.

Silas stood up and the old woman - the witch, he now realised - moved closer. "Put him by the fire," she said. Brande slumped to his side and landed on the floor, his upper half already on the brown rug. Before he passed out, he heard the frantic sound of scratching from beneath the floorboards.

Brande was running through a forest and rats were chasing him, swarming over the tree roots, under and around leaves, up tree trunks, along branches, squeezing through bushes and shrubs, and they devoured everything that moved in their path. A nearby fox was minding its own business when Brande shot past it. He glanced back and saw it stripped to the bone in moments by the plague of rats mowing over it. Their little front teeth were red with its blood now, their fur sticky and matted. Brande was out of breath, but he ran, and ran, and ran. Rats dropped from the trees onto him, and he frantically brushed them off him, sometimes punching them as they fell towards him. On either side of him, they were starting to overtake him. Their swarming mass created a pincer movement which he could do nothing to stop. To his left and right, he saw them move past him and close around him. He was in the centre of an ever-shrinking circle of carnivorous vermin.

There was a campfire out in the woods. It was surrounded by men in cloaks. He rushed toward it, not fearing that they were enemies, just desperate to get to the fire. The rats merged and clambered on to him, their claws scratching at him, scraping him. He dived for the fire, stumbling as their rodent bodies squirmed and crunched underfoot. He threw himself in the flames, hands first.

Silas was pulling him away from the hearth. He awoke. His hand was red, sore. Had he plunged it into the fireplace?

He was in the cottage. Silas was there.

Silas! Traitor!

No, wait. He was helping Brande to his feet. A friend.

The witch! Poison!

No, wait. He was alive.

"You passed out," said Silas. "You seem to have slept very heavily. You stuck your hand in the fire."

Brande was panting and soaked in sweat. He got to his feet. He could still hear the scratching of the rats in his dream. The sound faded as he moved about, making noise himself. Silas was saying something. "It's alright, it's alright."

Brande settled on a seat and looked at his burnt hand. It wasn't particularly damaged, just sore. There'd be a blister or two.

"Sorry," he said, finally, feeling foolish. "A nightmare."

"No," insisted Silas, kindly. "A soldier doesn't have nightmares, he just scrubs his mind clean of the horrors he's experienced, sometimes reliving things, sometimes imagining others. I know this. I remember it from my first battles. You've been through a lot."

There was a dull thrumming in Brande's skull and he recalled being knocked unconscious near the apothecary's store by the soldiers in Bruton. He'd been surviving on nothing but anger and anxiety, it was no wonder he passed out the moment he reached sanctuary. He looked around for the old woman, feeling a little guilty about suspecting her of witchcraft. He sighed. "Where is she?"

"She went out to fetch something."

How could an old woman be a threat? He shook his head, trying to clear it. It was that silly story the bard had told about the witch in the woods. And sleeping too close to the fire had overheated him. And the traumatic events of the last few days had disturbed him. Rational thought regained control of his mind.

"Any food left?"

"I don't know. I've only been awake a short while myself. I woke to your shouting."

"Did you hear scratching?"

"No, but I don't think you can hear it in my room. I

suspect she's got rats under these floorboards."

Brande nodded. "Seems probable."

Silas shrugged. "Are you hungry again? Try the kitchen. We're not meant to, but-"

Brande got up and wandered through to the kitchen. It was a small, narrow room with a counter along one side. He was struck by the myriad jars and tied herbs that filled every inch of space. Various concoctions sat brewing in pots and jars along the window ledge, on the counter and atop every other flat surface. He could see that it was all neatly organised and why she might not want someone interfering. On one shelf, there was a jar packed with fish eyes. He looked around and saw a cat bowl. That made sense. She kept a cat and fed it fish eyes as a treat. He couldn't help inspecting the room, still feeling wary and uneasy after his dream. "I'm surprised she's got rats if she has a cat," he mentioned.

"Not seen a cat," replied Silas, poking his head into the kitchen too. He was rubbing his leg, the one that had been bitten by the wolf, and kept his weight on the other. He looked around the kitchen with interest. "I wonder if there's a pantry behind that door," he said, grinning.

Brande tried the handle, but the door didn't budge. It was locked. He snorted to indicate his lack of surprise.

After a short search, he found where she kept her bread and cheese. "This'll do." He stuffed his mouth with it as he spoke. It was something Aithne always chided him about, but he doubted Silas cared. "We need to get a move on soon. Judging by the light outside, I've overslept." He chewed. "When did she leave?"

"Just before I fell asleep. She didn't suggest she'd be gone this long."

The kitchen had a door to the outside with a round hole in it. A face was at that window. Brande jumped.

"There she is," said Silas, laughing at Brande's reaction.

The door opened, and she came in, picked up the bread

and cheese and knife in front of Brande and walked straight into her main room and slammed them down on the table. A piece of bread bounced onto the floor. "In my house, we eat in this room. I asked you not to enter my kitchen." As they joined her in the other room, she was standing staring at them, arms folded across her chest. She looked furious.

Brande spoke first. "Sorry, I just woke, I was hungry. We'll be gone soon. Don't worry."

"I am not worried," she said. "You will respect my wishes under my roof." Her voice was strained. She was angry, maybe a little upset.

"We understand. We've overstayed our welcome," said Silas. "We'll be gone soon." He reiterated the point, hoping she'd believe him. No doubt she would be afraid they were there to steal from her.

"I went to collect some Naril's Root from the garden," she explained. Her manner had calmed. Brande sat down and continued eating. Silas took a seat too and asked her what the herb was used for. She replied, "It's good for calming the nerves. You brew it in boiled water. But it has another purpose, too. They say it has Deft properties." She paused, then continued when the men didn't react. Brande knew well that she was a witch now. It wasn't that she seemed to think she had Deft abilities, because any madwoman might think that, but to so calmly introduce the subject meant she was quite sure of herself. He understood now why she lived out here, away from folk, and why she wasn't afraid of two soldiers turning up out of the woods and entering her home. During the Crusades, Brande had seen the relentless pursuit and bloody destruction of those who possessed Deft abilities. To reveal you possessed the Deft touch to two soldiers was usually an act of suicide. Her calm manner indicated a lack of concern about her being in any danger.

To Brande, that meant she was a witch. He shuffled in his seat, seeking the reassurance of the feel of a sword at his side, but trying not to make the motion visible. Nothing. A surreptitious glance around the room revealed his weapon lay by the wall near the front door. Presumably, it had been removed by Silas after he fell unconscious. Brande shuddered, the memory of the swarming rats in his dream briefly resurfacing in his mind.

"I wondered if you two might let me read your futures," she said. Her tone became wistful. "I often read my own, but it never changes and is so predictable. You look like interesting gentlemen with interesting futures. I could use the practice in reading the leaves. It's an old tradition amongst my family, and I am the only one remaining." Brande almost laughed. Perhaps he really was becoming paranoid. Reading leaves wasn't Deft, just folk tradition.

Brande shook his head. "I don't much go in for that type of thing."

"Oh, it's harmless," she pleaded. "The plant does all the work, I just read the signs." Brande had no time for superstition, but he didn't want to displease the old woman after all the generosity she had shown. He felt foolish for thinking her a witch and bad about entering her kitchen.

Plenty of folks would have looked around this place, killed her, made it home for a day, and moved on. Maybe once, he acknowledged to himself, shamefully, remembering the Crusades, he might have done so himself. Aithne had instilled a gentleness in him that he would never have suspected existed in those days. He could almost hear Aithne's voice in his head. She was always his guide in these matters. She had such a good heart, and a firm voice to ensure it was heard. He had to get to her. He was wasting time. But her voice insisted.

He acquiesced. "If it pleases you, you may read my fortune." Brande shoved aside the platter he had been eating off. It was empty. "But be quick, we need to be away from here soon." He did not explain why, as he felt Silas had already blabbed enough.

The old woman made them both grasp a handful of the herbs tightly in their fists, assuring them all the while that it would not take long. "So, now you have warmed it in your hands, I need you to chew it into little bits and then spit it on to the table in front of you." Both men looked at each other. This seemed like the madness typical of a summer day fayre. Silas grinned.

"You said it calms the nerves," said Silas. "I don't want to feel sleepy."

"Only if you boil and drink it," she explained. "A quick chew and spit will not affect you. I promise. Even the brew only lasts an hour or so…"

They did as they were bid. The leaves tasted like sewage. Readily, they spit them to the table. In front of each man, a small gooey mess lay, promising to tell them of their fortunes or misfortunes for years to come. The old woman inspected the globs of leafy spittle. Eventually, she prodded them with her finger. "Interesting," she muttered.

Brande was feeling better now he had recovered from his sleep. Thoughts of Aithne and Fia swirled in his head as he waited for the woman to come to some decision about what to say, and he was losing patience. This was an old woman's folly, and he didn't have time for it.

Brande started to become convinced she was merely keeping them around for company. Or was it something else? Another idea entered his head. She had left the house for longer than Silas had expected but returned with herbs from her garden. Could she have told someone they were here? Was she delaying them so men could arrive? Cloaked cultists? Or the king's men? But who was within reach? He could not answer that. She was out here in the middle of nowhere, surrounded by dense forest.

He could hear the rats scratching under the floorboards again. "We need to go," he growled.

"You first, Silas," she said. Her voice had taken on a reedy quality, just like the fortune tellers at a fête. "You have given me a small sample, but enough. Your time on this world will not be long." Silas went pale. "I see a pool of clear water, but a droplet of oil lands in it, covering the surface, then making the whole pool black. This will be your undoing, but not before you hang."

"I get hanged?"

"I did not say that. Your death is not because of hanging, but because of the oil. I do not understand what that represents. Perhaps you will be poisoned."

Silas baulked. "I don't like this prophecy. Do you have any good news for me?"

"Only that you will not die alone."

Silas didn't know what to say. But Brande did. He spat on the table again, getting rid of the disgusting taste, but also expressing his distaste for what she was prophesying. "I have heard enough. We'll be leaving." He got up and swept his weapon off the floor by the door. As he leant down, he could hear the scratching from under the floorboards more clearly. "Nachmair's tits, woman, have you heard these rats!?"

She smiled. "I have a pet that eats them."

"Not fast enough, it seems."

"You will burn, Brande."

"What?" He was startled.

"Your leaves. They say you will burn up, like a falling star, or a lit arrow, or a-"

"I get the message. Silas hangs, I burn." He had a little trouble standing upright. He felt woozy. "Ugh, I think that stuff is doing more than calming my nerves." This time he was sure she was poisoning them.

Silas fell from his seat to the floor. He scrambled along, getting closer to Brande, who held his weapon in front of him. It wavered. "Witch!" he cried, groggily.

She smiled and went into her kitchen. Silas and Brande were losing strength. Brande crumpled to his knees. He had fallen on Silas, who shuffled to get out from under him.

They heard her open the locked door in the kitchen and shout some unintelligible words.

"Basement," realised Brande. It seemed unfeasible that there should be one in a cottage this small. Perhaps it was just a little wine cellar, crouching room only. The scratching sound was loud now, and he realised it was because he could hear it from the open kitchen door.

"Rats," he said. "She's calling the rats. They'll eat us alive." He felt fear. He crumpled by Silas, his muscles steadily failing. They were both in a heap on the floor, embarrassingly tangled, like drunken fools who had been leaning on each other but had finally collapsed on one another. "Can't even grip my sword," he slurred. His eyes were getting heavy too. Inside him, anger was churning away. They were so close to leaving. Why had they not gone? They should have. They could have.

The witch came back out of the kitchen and strode right up to them. She smiled. "You should never chew Naril's Root, ingesting it at full potency. Now, I have a little surprise in store for you."

She stepped aside. "I am so, so pleased you decided to visit me." It was arrogance that brought her so close to them, and it was her undoing. Brande's anger fuelled one last surge of energy. He grabbed the sword and swung. He aimed for her chest, meaning to drive it through her frail old frame, but he missed. The sword skewered her face, then dragged her down with his falling arm. She had been too sure of her poisons. His blade was lodged in her face as she sank to the floor, screaming. Brande fell to the ground still clutching the sword hilt with every desperate ounce of strength remaining in him. She shrieked and shrieked but could not move away as the sword was twisted into her face.

Brande lay on the ground. He was paralysed throughout his whole body. He could feel a warm patch growing around his loin where he had pissed himself. His eyes still functioned, but his sight was blurring. He had no idea if Silas was still conscious. He watched the old woman finally stumble backwards, the sword sliding out of her face. She fell like a bag of rattling old bones to the ground. Hardly any blood escaped her wound as if her skin were dried parchment.

There was a scratching, shuffling noise from the kitchen. If they were rats, they were taking a long time.

"Silas," he grunted. The word was slurred but intelligible. "Silas?"

An unintelligible response came back, little more than a strained groan.

"Rats," repeated Brande, the fear of his dream still vivid. He froze. What came out of the kitchen was worse than rats, worse than anything he'd seen since the Crusades.

A man staggered from the kitchen, but he was only recognisable as a man from the shape of his body. He had two legs. Two arms. He had a head with eyes. He staggered because he was in pain, some terrible, terrible pain. His muscles gleamed red and fresh, and raw and bloody. His intestines were partially held in place by one of his hands. His bones showed through in several places. Most of his skin was missing. He had one hairy forearm that was partially intact, but a rectangular strip was missing right along the length of it.

The shambling horror moved towards them, slowly, purposefully.

"Silas!" yelled Brande, a new fear filling him so that his mind felt crazed. He couldn't move. His vision was deteriorating fast. He cursed the witch and her potent poison, and he cursed the thing dragging itself towards him. He cursed the day he was born. Fury burned and twisted inside him. He had to save Fia. He had to save Aithne. He did not have time for this! He felt his fingers twitching. He could feel the sword again, it was just at his fingertips. With a little exertion, he might be able to grab it.

The skinless horror was nearing. There had been no response from Silas which made Brande think he must have passed out on seeing the fleshless creature, or perhaps the poison had run its course on him and he was now comatose, or dead. Brande couldn't move his head to see. He was alone and paralysed. The monstrosity staggered awkwardly, relentlessly, towards him. It whimpered as it moved, revealing its pain. Its raw, exposed muscles contracted and expanded as it shifted its innards and its skeleton towards the fallen men.

His eyelids dropped over his eyes and refused to reopen. Brande realised what the missing strip from the man's arm meant. He recalled the trees outside with the leather strips sewn around the branches. She had said they warded off evil spirits. They were strips of leather cut from the man. No human could survive what he had endured. Truly, she must be a witch. His mind connected the staggering thing before him to the crude effigy of a man over the fireplace. Only the darkest arts would keep a man in this condition alive. Brande wanted to kill the thing, to destroy it, burn it, but he was in darkness now, his eyelids shut, and he could not even feel the sword against his fingertips.

CHAPTER SIX

It was a warm summer morning. Aithne was cradling Fia in her arms, rocking her back and forth. She was kissing her and talking to her little naked body, which lay in the crook of her arm. She was such a small thing. Last night she had wailed and wailed, and this morning she was floppy, and her eyes were rolling. But she was still breathing. Her little chest heaved with each hard-fought-for breath. Her body was hot.

Aithne spoke gently to her. "You'll be alright, little one. You'll be fine. Keep breathing, my love. Keep breathing." She picked up the cloth next to her, letting water drain from it back into the bowl. She compressed it, then dabbed Fia's cheeks. Gently, she squeezed cold water over her baby's brow and then wiped most of it away again.

She looked up at him. He stood by the door, full of agitation and anxiety. Her eyes were wide. "She's so hot." Her face relayed untold misery. They had tried for so long for a child, and their delight had been absolute when she had been born just three months before.

Brande felt uncomfortable and useless. There was

nothing he could do to help either his wife or his child in this situation. "The doctor is on the way," he promised.

"He won't try to bleed her, will he?"

"No. Not a baby." Brande tried to sound confident.

Aithne held Fia close to her. She walked up and down the front room of their little cottage, trying to keep the child awake and stimulated. She didn't want to put her down for fear that something bad might happen, that she might give up and her little breaths might stop. Brande walked over, held Aithne by her shoulders and kissed her on the forehead. He looked down at Fia. He had no words to explain how he felt. This was not a part of the world he knew or understood. It was not war or woodcutting. He didn't know how to face this, how to fight it. He just wished the damn doctor would arrive.

"Come on, Fia," whispered Aithne, stroking the thin wisps of dark hair on her child's head. "Fight this thing that makes you unwell. Be a fighter like your father." A lump caught in Brande's throat.

A friendly face popped her head through the door. It was their neighbour. "The doctor's almost here." She disappeared again.

"He'll know what to do," said Brande, with little conviction in his voice.

"Lots of little ones have fevers and pull through," agreed Aithne, for the tenth time that morning.

"That's what babies do. They get sick. They mend." He smiled at her.

The door opened. Aithne looked up at the figure silhouetted in the doorway. She gasped and dropped the child to the stone floor.

Brande, being a soldier, looked to the enemy before the fallen.

In the doorway stood a man, or the remains of one. His flesh had been removed, seemingly one strip at a time. His bones, his muscles, his tendons, his sinews, were all held together by some unseen force. His intestines, all ravelled up inside him, slopped about behind his stomach muscles. His hideous lipless grin and staring, lidless eyes were directed straight at them as he shambled into the room. Aithne screamed and reached down for their child. Brande went for his sword, but it was by the door and beyond reach. The creature leapt.

Brande yelled out. He awoke with sweat pouring down his face. He tried to move, but his muscles were frozen. He forced an eye open.

The creature lumbered out of the front room and away into the kitchen.

Silas was lying next to him on the floor in the witch's cottage. The old woman was missing, although he could see a small spattering of blood on the floor from the injury he'd done her. The fire must have died down because he couldn't feel or hear it. How long had he been comatose?

Brande felt movement in his fingers. As he blinked, he saw an afterimage of Fia lying helpless on the floor at Aithne's feet. He mentally shook the image from his mind. That never happened. Aithne nurtured the babe. The doctor arrived. He told her to put her baby down, her body heat would be making it too warm. He had some liquid, and he poured it into Fia's mouth. It contained willow bark, he'd said. He put a cold cloth over the girl's head. Soon she was sleeping peacefully and her little hand gripped Brande's finger again. He recalled the real outcome, not the one his fevered imagination had conjured after the poison the witch had made him chew.

The woman's body was gone. Brande decided the creature must have taken it. He estimated how much time must have passed for the fire to have had time to dwindle. Why were they still alive? He tried to twitch his fingers, and to his surprise, his whole arm moved. He rolled away from Silas.

"Brande! You're awake!" hissed Silas.

"Can you move?"

"A little. But I don't dare. That thing has been watching us. I think it wants to eat us."

Brande had been worried that they would find themselves in the basement, their flesh slowly becoming baubles for the trees outside.

There was no sound from the kitchen, so he assumed the creature must have gone outside, using the back door.

"We need to escape," said Silas.

Brande remembered his dream, the creature leaping towards him and Aithne. "That thing must die. We're not leaving here until it's dead."

"Why waste time?" asked Silas, fear in his voice.

"Because it has seen us and I don't want it showing up again." Brande was resolute. He wanted to get on, much time had been wasted, but he couldn't leave knowing that thing was about. It was a creature borne of the dark arts, and if the Crusades had been about anything, they had been about putting an end to such evil. If that monster was being held alive by the witch's skill even after she was dead, and Brande was sure he had killed her, then the thing might live indefinitely. There was little that could not be destroyed by fire, though. This he knew from experience.

"I think I can crawl," he said. He used his arms to pull himself along the floor a little way. "I can feel something in my legs. I can feel my toes."

"I had that," said Silas. "I'm fairly certain I could stand now."

Brande grunted, although not loudly, as he tried to sit up. He managed to get himself up on his elbows, but that was all he could handle. "That poison packed a punch. We're lucky to be alive."

Brande hefted himself into a sitting position. "Do we have weapons?"

"Yes. The creature has not removed them."

"What's this?" He was looking at peculiar red stains on

the floor. One was next to where he had lain and the other in the space Silas had occupied.

"I don't know, but you have red around your lips. Do I?"

"Yes, a little."

Brande rubbed the back of his hand across his lips. A smear of red showed there.

"It's not blood," said Brande. "I know the taste of my own blood in my mouth."

Silas shrugged, not offering any suggestions. He got to his feet, slowly. He turned his ankles and stretched up to the ceiling. "That feels good," he said, quietly. He retrieved his sword and brandished it. "Are you bent on killing this thing?"

"Yes, and we'll need fire."

"I can smell smoke, now you mention it."

Brande sniffed. "You're right. Look at the window." Black smoke drifted past the small open window. "It's trying to torch the cottage. We need to get out."

"Can you walk?"

Brande shook his legs. "Not yet." He flopped on to his front and started to crawl. "To the kitchen."

Silas gasped suddenly and stepped back. The creature stood at the kitchen door. Its face was a tormented, muscle-covered skull, locked in a rictus grin. It raised its hands toward them, revealing bone, sinew, tendons and raw muscles. Silas stepped forward, putting himself between it and Brande who frantically started crawling away from it. One of his legs was kicking out, meaning life was returning to it.

The creature made a noise. Its tongue moved in its mouth like a bloody serpent thrashing in a pool. It didn't move forward, instead just stood watching them. Its bulbous eyes had no lids, and those white spheres studied them intently.

Silas clutched his sword in his hands. He was shaking.

Brande pitied him. For all that he might have fought the ferocious Skulluns who raided their shores and pillaged villages, it was another thing entirely to fight a monster like this. Silas was no Crusader.

Brande was close to the front door now, where his sword lay. Tentatively, he shifted his weight to one arm and reached out and grabbed his weapon with the other.

The creature was looking intently at Silas's face. Suddenly it started yelling and gurning, its hands frantic and its motions getting wilder. It stepped forward.

"Stay back," growled Silas.

"Attack it!" yelled Brande, trying to get to his knees. His legs still felt useless beneath him.

"Noh!" yelled the monster, frantically waving its hands.

Silas hesitated. The monster took a step backwards. It lowered its arms. There seemed to be no threat from it. It stood there, awkward, an unfortunate thing, a thing stripped of essential parts that could never be whole again. It stood looking at them both, its eyes moving from one to the other. Its lungs expanded and shrank inside its ribcage. "Noh," it repeated, more quietly.

It turned away, then, and went back into the kitchen. Silas frowned, watching its back as it walked away from them. Brande was wary, waiting for some trick. "Follow it," he ordered. He strained and got himself up on one leg as if he was kneeling for a knighthood. "I'll be close behind."

Silas edged forward after the creature. Brande stumbled in a half-crouch to the table and pulled himself up to standing. He had one functioning leg and one that was still lame. For a moment, his mind went back to little Fia: floppy, ill, and the monster that came in place of the doctor. They had to kill that thing.

He staggered to the kitchen door and leaned through. No sign of the creature. Using the counter to support his weight, his sword clattering all the way along it, he edged his way towards the exit. Eventually, he leaned on the doorframe and looked out. Silas held open the door for him.

Outside, the sun had passed the apex of its arc and was working its way down. The length of time they had been at this cottage was disheartening to Brande.

He looked on with wonder at what was happening in the woman's garden. The creature had built a pyre from branches and twigs. It was a low, unspectacular thing, but it sufficed. The witch's corpse lay atop it, burning. Her clothes had all burnt away, and her skin was peeling and smoking. The creature had not tried to torch the house. He was destroying the remains of the witch. Good, thought Brande. Fire works best on things like her.

It was clear to them now. This was a man stripped of his flesh and held captive in the witch's basement. To what end she had kept him they could only imagine and tried not to.

Perhaps the creature had hoped to die when the witch died. Perhaps he had hoped his end would come when her mortal remains felt the lick of the flames. It looked like this would not be the case.

The creature twisted its head and gave them a doleful look with its lidless eyeballs. It pressed its hands flat to its chest then linked its thumbs, forming a gesture that resembled the shape of a bird, just as a child might to cast a shadow puppet on a wall. Silas gasped. "Bresal," he said, quietly, realising the truth of it.

The thing that had once been a man nodded. "Dorr-ee," it said. The word was warped by the loose tongue and lack of lips.

"Molly," said Silas. "I'll tell her."

Brande said nothing. He had long ago learnt not to make promises to dying men. It was impossible to even remember them all after weeks on a battlefield.

The creature shook its head. "Noh."

"I'll tell her something better than this," promised Silas.

The creature nodded.

Brande watched on, fascinated. After a moment, he realised he was standing unaided on his own two legs. He took a couple of tentative steps forward, using his sword as a poor substitute for a walking stick.

The creature bowed. It turned to the pyre.

"Wait!" Silas stepped forward. "Is there nothing we can do?"

The creature paused and shook its head, but didn't look back. It stepped up and onto the pyre, its strange, impossible form shuffling inelegantly and then clambering through the flames, disturbing the logs and branches, sending sparks into the air. It fell to its knees.

Through the flames, they saw the creature turn its head. It looked at Silas. Its mouth moved, and although all they could hear was the hissing and crackling of the pyre, Silas knew the word. "Molly!" he repeated loudly. The creature's face contorted into something that might have been a smile. It fell on its back. They watched as the fire consumed it. Smoke poured from its body.

Brande moved by his companion's side. "Someone you knew?"

"Someone I knew," confirmed Silas. He looked away. Brande couldn't.

The witch was blackened and her flesh all but burnt away. Her belly ignited brightly for a moment. Burning fats and muscle hissed and spluttered. Brande watched, feeling reassured that this was the last they would see of either of these abominations.

"His name was Bresal. In the cult, he wore skyte's wings around his neck," said Silas, using the common name of a local bird. He made as if to say more, but stopped. Nothing more seemed necessary. Except, after a moment, he added, "Molly was his little sister."

Brande knew he shouldn't, but he asked, "How long since your friend went missing?"

Silas thought for a moment and winced like he'd been

struck. "After I joined the cult. Four weeks or so."

They considered the possibility he'd been trapped in the witch's basement for a month, having strips of flesh peeled from him for all that time. It made Brande angry. He didn't show it, but deep, deep down in his core he felt burning anger. It was always present. It may have lain dormant for a long time, but it was still there. "The straps of flesh hung on the trees couldn't have all been his."

Silas accepted the assessment. "It is just as well we came here, then."

The flames consumed the witch and her unwilling familiar.

Silas took a sharp intake of breath. He'd realised something. "He saved us. The red substance on our lips. Antidote."

Brande's eyes widened with surprise. Silas was right. The creature had poured a concoction down their throats as they slept. It must have been difficult for it, with its shambling lack of coordination and the horrors it had endured. Somehow it had put aside the need it felt to destroy its captor and itself long enough to save them.

"He was a good man. Good to me, anyway. He shouldn't have had to burn on the same pyre."

Brande said nothing. He walked back into the house on ever-sturdier legs and left his companion to his thoughts.

"We don't want to be seen," said Silas, warily.

Brande scanned the rolling hills and the low-lying stone walls marking boundaries. A few trees, the occasional copse, were scattered across his view, but this was managed land. They were out of Dankwood and facing the trek to Bruke. They had emerged from the forest far from the beaten track, which meant they weren't directly following the convoy any more, but it did mean they could make a beeline for Bruke and not worry too much about entanglement with soldiers.

"We'll be fine," assured Brande. "We've emerged west of Bruke. Had I not been driven into the forest I would have been pursuing the king's men north, but we won't encounter them out here."

"I just…" muttered Silas, shaking his head, looking worried. A sheen of sweat glistened on his brow.

They were both well-built men and although they had been rattled, hurt and weakened by their recent encounters, both would doggedly pursue the villains who had taken their families from them. They had conversed freely as they made their way out of Dankwood and Brande was impressed by Silas's honesty and determination, but he had also noticed his pace slackening.

"Are you alright, friend?" he asked, concerned.

"Sure. Yes. I am," reassured Silas. "Let's keep going."

"You look like you might have a fever."

"No, just exhausted. I'm not used to it anymore."

Brande accepted his answer but decided to keep an eye on him. He didn't want Silas slowing him down, but neither did he want to lose a reliable companion. He thought the best thing would be to continue on their course as quickly as possible. Once they got to Bruke, they might be able to find him some medicine. Brande's priority, though, was still to pick a fight with some soldiers.

Silas seemed to sense Brande's concern. "It will pass, I'm fine," he insisted. "I still have some pain in my leg from the wolf bite, but it's not bad." He wiped some spittle from his lip and hiccupped, then laughed. "Bloody hiccups."

Brande offered a lopsided grin, then turned to the horizon. "Let's press on."

The next part of the journey was uneventful. As they tramped through fields and over hills, they exchanged stories about their pasts. Brande was careful not to say too much about his time in the Crusades, or to give too much away about his family, but he was happy to talk about his time as a regular soldier under King Leofric, predecessor and brother to King Ignatius.

"There was a time," he recalled, letting the memories wash over him, "when we were sent to investigate a gang that had taken root on the Drashford hills, somewhere southwest of Hightown, near the little village there. I forget the name of it." He hadn't, but sometimes omitting the finer details was prudent. "They had this leader who liked to wear a black bandanna. In that bandanna, he wore a white feather. It was a striking image, unforgettable, and the locals came to fear it. When one of his men killed someone, they left a white feather stuck in their victim's eyeball." He paused. "Sometimes, when they didn't have a feather to hand, they just rammed a stick in there. It did the same job. Anyway, I took four men with me to find them. I was sure that five of us would easily best seven of them. But the man's popularity had been growing. A full score of them had sworn fealty to the bastard. They were bad men. They raped, pillaged, looted, ran protection rackets, you know the sort. When we turned up, they were armed to the teeth and ready to fight, so we-"

Silas halted abruptly. "Smoke!"

Bruke was a speck on the horizon ahead of them. A wispy haze drifted skyward from it, but for that to be visible at this distance meant great plumes of smoke had to be rising.

"Perhaps we're not so far behind the king's men as we thought," Silas commented.

"So," continued Brand, truncating his story significantly, "we slaughtered every one of them and peace was restored."

"Nice story," Silas quipped.

"I always thought so. Let's move!"

They picked up their pace across the intervening fields.

The ground sloped off then rose again. It seemed like hours before they crested the final rise and saw Bruke spread out before them on the open plain. A narrow river ran between them and the town, but a couple of felled trees provided a makeshift bridge for foot travellers.

As they approached, Silas looked troubled. "It's quiet. I don't like this."

"We're too late," realised Brande.

Bruke was not a small town, but it had woefully inadequate protection. Lying southwest of Charstoke, it was unlikely to be targeted by foreign invaders. If invaders got this far, it meant they had taken the capital, and all hope was already lost. As such, Bruke had next to no defences. It was a sleepy place and a stop-over for tradesmen travelling from other parts. An attack from the king's men, who would typically be expected to protect it, would not have been something for which they were prepared.

The outskirts of the town were deserted but detritus lay strewn across the roads, and there were signs of battle everywhere. Brande shook his head disbelievingly. This was Bruke, always such a peaceful place, where travellers came to tell tall tales of their journeys. It was home to Bryan of Bruke, a famous bard, who had once kissed King Ignatius' niece during a performance and, for his trouble, been imprisoned for three days listening to a fat, tone-deaf, jail warden strum a lute he couldn't play and warble nonsense lyrics he invented on the spot. In the end, the bard screamed for mercy, and the punishment was said to have fit the crime. Brande smiled at the recollection. That was the Bruke he knew. This was now.

They picked their way amongst the buildings and found a town left in disarray. "A real skirmish here," shouted Brande, rounding a corner. Blood painted the walls. A dented helmet sat abandoned on the ground, and a dead horse lay half buried in a wooden building into which it must have careered before arrows finally took it down. The townsfolk had tried to fight back. A man lay against a smashed barrel, his chest gaping open with a weapon still embedded in it. Brande pulled at the wooden handle protruding from the dead man's torso, which heaved upward, rising with it, then slumped heavily as the artefact departed it with a squelch. He wiped the gore off it on the man's leg. "Just the thing," he said, examining it with pleasure. It was a small but impressive battle axe. It was single-headed with a crescent blade, engraved with a swirling pattern that culminated in the shape of a bear, and was socketed and mounted on a sturdy wooden haft.

He turned to show it to Silas, but Silas' eyes were wide open and alert. "I can hear shouting," he said. "Let's help them."

Their feet pounded the road. They reached the town centre quickly. "The church!" hissed Silas, pointing. Flames flickered from the eaves and climbed up over the rooftop. Tongues of yellow and red licked up the sides of the towers, spires and pointed arches. As they watched, one large stained-glass window exploded outward, shattered glass cascading to the cobbles below. Brande and Silas approached carefully, sidling along the side wall of a deserted barber-surgeon's shop, staying out of sight, and looking for men.

"Just two soldiers there," said Brande. "Let's take them out."

They sprinted into the clearing, remaining unseen, and crouched behind an overturned cart that only just provided adequate cover. It was just one item left in the aftermath of the battle, one piece of detritus scattered throughout the deserted town.

The two soldiers seemed to be guarding the doors of the burning building. No one would want in, so they had to be there to stop people from escaping.

Silas shifted as if he was about to charge them, then stopped. "Wait. Do you hear that?"

"What?"

"Screaming."

Brande listened intently, aware his hearing was not as good as the younger man's. Over the noise of the flames, the crackling wood, the chatter of the two men, and the cracking glass, there it was: the sound of voices, screaming, wailing in terror. It was constant, persistent, almost indistinguishable from the white noise of the raging fire. Brande's experience told him the king's men must have locked in some troublesome townsfolk before setting the church ablaze.

Silas drew his sword. Brande readied his newly-acquired axe.

"Get down!" spat Brande. "They're coming this way."

They readied themselves to spring an ambush. They waited. The men were taking too long. Silas stuck his head over the cart quickly. "They've turned," he said, "they're leaving. North. Rejoining the ranks, I'd wager." He was blinking madly, but when Brande frowned at him, he licked his lips and seemed to get the twitch under control. Brande realised Silas was fighting pain, probably in his leg. He wondered if the bite had become infected. "We have to get those doors open," Silas urged.

Brande took in the church. He almost declared it too dangerous, that they should go after the men, but even though it suited his need to keep moving and to find the military company holding his family, it was the wrong thing to do. He shouldn't have to rescue strangers when he could be searching for Aithne and Fia, but it was Aithne's voice in his head that told him he had to do the right thing. He wouldn't be able to look her in the eye if he left those people to die. This delay would just become one more reason why he was going to make those soldiers pay for their crimes.

The soldiers were out of sight. "Come on," he growled.

They raced over to the church doors. Wooden slats had

been nailed to the door as reinforcement. He hacked them off with his axe. He tried the handle and found the doors were locked. He brought his axe down again, trying to smash through to the locking mechanism. He hacked and hacked, swinging fast and repeatedly, but it made little impact on the solid oak doors. "I need a heavier axe," he grunted and started putting more of his weight behind each swing.

"Stop!"

The voice behind them was unexpected but distant. Brande swung round in surprise. The two soldiers were on the edge of the town square. Silas moved forward to put himself between them and Brande, his sword at the ready.

It was clear why the soldiers had returned. Each dragged a corpse, which they now unceremoniously dumped. They had intended to add the bodies to the funeral pyre. One of the bodies, a woman, started crawling away. They hadn't even killed her. They planned to burn her alive. One of the soldiers landed a heavy boot to the back of her neck, and she collapsed with unequivocal finality. They ran to stop Brande opening the doors.

"Keep trying the door," insisted Silas. Brande hammered into the wood again, sending splinters flying.

Silas raced forward to meet their attackers. Brande gave up his attempt on the doors and followed close behind. As Silas blocked the initial attack from the first soldier, Brande, who had been running to meet the second one, changed direction and leapt. He brought his axe down on Silas's opponent's head with his entire body weight behind it, splitting the man's head diagonally from crown to jaw. He tumbled into him, ending up in a heap on the ground. Silas wasted no time stepping over them and engaging the remaining soldier. He kept him occupied long enough for Brande to get to his feet. The soldier saw that he was in trouble and drove forward his attack hoping to finish with Silas before facing Brande. Silas was easily a match for him.

He parried the blows, ferocious though they were, and with a well-placed kick to the crotch, he dropped him to the ground. Brande didn't even have to move. With a calculated swing of his weapon, Silas knocked the man's sword away and plunged his own blade through the man's chest. The soldier's dark eyes screwed themselves up in pain and hatred, then relaxed in despondency and went dim. Silas and Brande didn't shy from it. They had both seen their fair share of opponents die. Silas looked up and round, as a soldier will. No other threats approached. "The church!"

Brande's axe did much of the work, but together they got the door open and jumped back as flames billowed out towards them. Inside the church, fire raged all around the walls. Flames tore at the wooden vaults, one already hanging loose and threatening to come crashing down. "We can't go in there," said Brande. Smoke filled the space making it impossible to see if anyone was alive.

They listened. There were no more screams. "Too late," said Silas. He was sweating, and spittle was hanging from his bottom lip. He had a crazed look in his eyes and seemed jittery. Brande didn't like the look of him. He watched him jostle from one leg to the other, like a child needing to pee.

"Come away," said Brande. "There's nothing we can do here now."

But he had spoken too soon.

In the depths of the church, there was sound and movement. Two figures emerged. They must have been enclosed in some back room that prevented exposure to the heat and smoke. They were yelling, although the words were indistinguishable from fearful screaming. They burst through the flames, fleeing the burning building. The old man's robes were alight. The young woman's hair caught fire. She screamed. Silas batted at it, putting it out. The old man cast off his ceremonial robe. He had adequate clothing underneath. The four of them stepped away from the collapsing church.

"We were the last," gasped the woman.

The old man, grey of beard, and bald, looked at Silas and Brande for a moment, then at the bodies of the two soldiers and the corpse that lay not far from them. His bushy grey eyebrows pushed down into the centre of his face. He seemed to read the events that had unfolded. Finally, he turned. "Thank you," he said. "Thank you." He coughed hard and crouched down.

The woman was coughing, too. Her eyes were streaming, agitated by the smoke.

"It's a miracle you're alive," said Silas. Behind him, the church continued to burn and crumble.

The old man nodded, but the girl spoke. "There were about forty of us in there."

Silas vomited. He turned, bent double, and released the contents of his stomach. Brande could not fathom why. A soldier would be used to witnessing events such as this one. It could only mean that he was ill.

"I am glad we could help," said Brande. "Who did this?"

The old man responded, his voice cracked with age, broken by rage, "They sacked the town! The King's own men!"

"Are they heading to the capital?"

The old man looked at him strangely, as if he wondered why that should be the next question. "Yes, I'd say they are."

Brande grabbed Silas and brought him to his feet. "I have to go. I have to catch that company of men before they reach Charstoke Castle. If you're unwell, you can stay and help these people."

Silas shook his head, but it looked like it cost him dearly. His eyes closed as if he was experiencing dizziness.

"Did you inhale smoke?" asked Brande.

Silas shook his head again and winced. "It'll pass."

"I must go."

"I am coming with you."

Brande turned to the couple they had helped escape. "I am sorry, I must go. They have my family."

"Go," they urged.

CHAPTER SEVEN

Brande marched off and Silas limped after him, still suffering from his leg wound. Brande was pleased to have his company but did not see him as essential to his mission. Silas was an ally, not a friend. A friend would slow him down. A friend might be a liability if this proved to be a suicide mission. A fire was burning in his belly, deep down, and it drove him onward to the fight. His wife and child were in danger, constant danger, yet there was a chance he could do something about it. There was still hope, and it made every wasted second feel like torture.

He knew Bruke reasonably well from his days as a soldier. He took a shortcut along the back of a row of tightly-packed houses believing it would keep him on a northerly path out of the town. Bruke had grown since he had last been here. It was more built up and stretched farther into the countryside than he remembered. Following the battle that had taken place, Bruke's back streets were strewn with dead bodies, nearly all men. He didn't examine them, just stepped over the obstacles and continued on his way.

"This way," Brande urged, gesturing to Silas. He ducked into a small cobbled alley, which wound around several blind corners, believing it to be a shortcut to a road which led out of town. They found themselves face to face with two men brandishing weapons.

The narrow alley meant the only way was forward for each party. The presence of weapons made it seem like a bad idea to turn their backs and retrace their steps, and it would waste too much time. The four men froze, none really sure what to do.

"Hail," said one of the strangers. He was a short man, with curly brown hair that fell almost to his shoulders. He had an impish face with a mischievous look, but was smiling through his neatly trimmed goatee. He was muscular, but not like the man who stood next to him. His companion was as tall as Brande and his shoulders almost as wide, his tunic revealing arms bulging with muscle. He was handsome, too, with a chiselled jawline and a swathe of blond hair pushed back into a ponytail. They were younger than Brande, probably younger than Silas, but looked handy with their weapons all the same. The short, dark-haired man bore a curved dirk, its blade already exposed, and he had a bow slung over his shoulder with a quiver full of arrows on his back. The tall, blond man held a bastard longsword in one hand. He made it look like it weighed nothing at all.

Brande and Silas looked at them with a kind of awe. They hadn't expected many confrontations and certainly not from opponents who appeared so capable. The two strangers seemed to be regarding them in the same way. "Well met," replied Brande, cautiously.

"Well, you're clearly not soldiers," said the short, dark-haired one.

"That's right," said Silas. "We're not."

"We need to pass," continued the stranger. "I trust we may?"

Silas began to nod accommodatingly, but Brande wasn't

prepared to take them at face value. "What business have you in Bruke?"

The short man looked surprised and glanced questioningly up at his tall companion. "What business do we have?" He repeated this a second time as if genuinely perplexed by it.

The tall one looked back down and said, "Well, it depends, I suppose. I expect there will be some killing."

"I expect so," continued the shorter one. He turned to Brande. "We expect there will be some killing."

Brande wasn't sure what to make of that. Silas asked, "Whom do you plan to kill?"

The men nodded as if this was the right question. "King's men," they both replied.

Brande assessed them. They seemed self-assured, and the smaller of the two had a natural arrogance about him. Brande didn't feel hostile to them, but he did want them out of his way. "There's no king's men back there."

"No?"

"We killed them," admitted Silas.

"The church?" asked the short one.

"We opened it. Two survived. Many didn't. Are you from around here?"

The short one looked at the big one again. "Are we from around here?"

"All over, really," replied his tall, blond companion.

"We're from all over," relayed the short one. He was apparently amused by the questions.

Brande decided he couldn't trust a word they were saying, so there was no point asking questions. Of course, it was this very fact that was amusing the shorter of the two. It didn't amuse Brande. "We're wasting time."

They were at a stalemate. Neither party trusted the other. Neither wanted to pass the other in close confines. Neither wanted to shed blood unnecessarily.

"I suppose," said the taller man, "that if they killed

king's men, then we could turn back."

"That would look like cowardice," snorted the shorter one.

"Do we know what they want?" asked the tall one.

"Well, they want to get past us."

"Yes, I know that, but they killed king's men, they say, so maybe our purposes are... aligned."

"So, you're saying we could all leave together. It wouldn't be us turning back, so much as us joining them in travelling in a relevant direction."

Brande wasn't amused by their repartee, but he was pleased they were willing to reach an amicable solution. "We kill king's men, you kill king's men. It sounds like we want the same thing, for whatever reasons. We'll follow you back along here." He indicated the passage in front of him.

The short one nodded. "I think I would like to know their names first. After all, if we're stabbed in the back, I would rather I knew my ambushers personally."

"You're too sociable," said the tall one, flatly. Brande couldn't tell if it was a jest or not. He wasn't about to answer, but he had the decision taken out of his hands.

"My name is Silas. This is Brande. The king's men have our families. We're pursuing them." Brande just managed not to roll his eyes. He disliked Silas' eagerness to blurt out their purpose to every passing person.

"You're slowing us down," added Brande. He was a blunt instrument. His strong point had never been diplomacy.

Rather than being offended at his lack of tact, the men seemed convinced by it. A small nod passed between them, some decision reached.

"I am Aldway," said the shorter, dark-haired man. "And this," he said, looking up at his blond friend, "is Eberhard."

"You look like you were soldiers once," remarked Brande.

"I'm glad you approve," replied Aldway, taking the

compliment but also swerving the implied question. "Now, let's make our way back along this alley. Eberhard, you lead the way. I'll keep an eye on our good friends here as they follow."

Brande and Silas grunted their agreement. All four moved off.

"Perhaps you could join us," said Silas, after a moment. "We plan to go after the company."

"I've been contemplating just that," admitted Aldway. "But I think we have something we need to do first."

Eberhard paused as he came to the end of the alley. He put his head out and checked to see if anyone was about. The place was deserted. They emerged into the open. Brande noted the eerie silence around them. It reminded him of Bruton when he woke from that blow to his head outside the apothecary's store. He could imagine the townsfolk fleeing for their lives, the bell tolling, the soldiers on horseback rampaging through the town, their trumpet blowing, and men being hacked to death in the streets.

"We'll be on our way," said Aldway, smiling cheerfully. "Pleasure meeting you." If he'd been wearing a hat, Brande imagined he'd have doffed it cockily at this point. Brande had met a few happy-go-lucky types in his time, and never thought much of them. However, he had watched how Aldway held his weapon at the ready the whole time they'd been walking. He didn't let himself become distracted once. He'd also noted how comfortably Eberhard held his sword, like it was an extension of his arm. He'd find their manner quite pleasant if he weren't so utterly sure that if they turned on them they would be very serious opponents. He was glad to see them go.

"If you change your mind..." offered Silas.

They bowed and left.

Brande and Silas walked on. When they were out of earshot, Silas asked, "What do you think they had to go and do?"

Brande snorted. "Well, they hadn't done much fighting. Their blades were clean. I suspect they are looters."

Silas rolled his eyes. "Of course!"

Brande and Silas knelt on a patch of firm ground, hidden amongst reeds and bulrushes. The soldiers and their captives, and the mysterious cloaked figures with them, had taken a direct route out of Bruke towards the capital of Charstoke in the Burnt Plains.

Not long after leaving Bruke, Brande and Silas came to marshland which extended on for miles. It was not difficult to cross, but an unwary traveller could fall foul of deep pools or end up wrong-footed in a boggy patch that would suck them under like quicksand.

Bullfrogs croaked all around them, invisibly, and insects zipped past just an inch from their faces. Soaring on the thermals above them, a skyte's dark silhouette contrasted against the glorious oranges and reds of the setting sun.

"I've never liked these marshes," confessed Silas. "And I hate insects."

Brande gave the barest acknowledgement. He had his eye on the enemy. The convoy was ahead of them by a mile, but across the green and black vista of the fens that was an easy distance to track their quarry. They kept low and out of sight behind feathery reeds, tall rushes and dwarf spruces, and camouflaged by the dirt that covered them from head to foot. Despite the abundant flora, they would be exposed if they attempted to cross the open ground too quickly.

"Oh my," groaned Silas. He let out a small laugh.

"What?" Brande glanced over his shoulder to where Silas was looking. He saw the two men they had met earlier wandering along the beaten path in full view. He rolled his eyes. "We'll call them as they approach. No point giving away our position before we have to."

"Agreed."

They waited until the men had just passed them, then Silas called out to them. "Aldway!" he hissed, remembering the smaller, talkative one's name.

Aldway and Eberhard turned. In a flash, Aldway had his bow in his hands with an arrow nocked. The arrowhead was pointed directly at Silas, even though they still couldn't see each other. "Show yourself," called Aldway.

He's swift, thought Brande.

Silas stood up, high enough that they could see him. "Over here."

Aldway relaxed the tension on his bowstring, and the two men came over to talk to them.

"We were looking for you," said Aldway, convivially. "Look, we brought you some bread."

Eberhard was carrying a satchel. He opened it and handed Brande a large chunk of fresh bread which he tore from a loaf. Brande assumed it had been looted from a bakery.

"Thank you," said Brande, accepting the offering. He was famished. He looked at Silas who was as pale as a ghost and doubtless exhausted. He gave the bread to Silas.

Silas wobbled as he took it from him.

"You don't look steady on your feet," observed Aldway.

Eberhard handed Silas some more of the bread and gave some to Brande too. Silas stuffed his face without speaking.

"Silas, you need rest," instructed Brande. "Go back to Bruke."

"Just hungry," replied Silas. "I'm not unwell."

Aldway frowned. "He didn't say you were unwell." His brow furrowed further. "Have you caught a plague? Should I be worried?"

Silas shook his head. "Exhaustion and hunger. I'm fine. Honestly."

"Come on, we need to move from here," urged Brande. He led them away, not unaware that Silas' limp was quite exaggerated now.

They kept pace with the troops for an hour. They were tracking a large body of people, horses, carts and who knew what else, so there was little to do but try to keep out of sight themselves. All the while, Brande thought about Aithne and Fia being trapped like animals in those cages. He also kept a wary eye on the two newcomers, not entirely sure what to make of them.

"It's a long way to the capital," said Aldway, after a time. He had slung his short horse bow from one shoulder to the next, clearly wishing he could put it down somewhere. Eberhard looked fine, always searching ahead, or behind, or about, making sure they were not going to be ambushed. As well as limping, Silas was now making gulping sounds, as if he was having trouble with his throat.

Brande shook his head. He would benefit from the help of these companions, but they were slowing him down. Ultimately, he doubted they could turn the tide against a confrontation should it arise. The odds were stacked against him. He had to hope that a surprise attack might confuse the enemy just long enough for him to free Aithne and Fia and get away.

"It will be dark soon," mentioned Eberhard.

"They'll make camp," said Brande. "When it's dark, we'll attack."

Silas looked pale, but Eberhard and Aldway nodded their assent. They looked at each other. Aldway grinned.

"Idiot," said Eberhard.

"You know I love long odds," he replied.

"You're suicidal."

"Come now, you love a challenge."

"The only challenge is staying alive around you."

Brande snorted with amusement.

Silas grinned then asked, "Do you also have family up ahead?"

They looked at each other as if deciding telepathically

what their answer should be. Eventually, Aldway answered. "No, we just hate the bastards."

Eberhard looked ahead. "They are the enemy. And we like a fight."

"They'll set up camp very soon," predicted Brande. "They won't want to do it in the dark, there's too many of them, even after their losses at Bruke. They'd be falling over each other. Plus, they have nothing to fear so they have no need to rush."

"King's men killing and kidnapping the king's subjects," spat Aldway. "I'm surprised there isn't an uprising."

"There hasn't been time," muttered Brande.

Night was falling. Crickets, hummingbirds and bograts filled the dying evening with their sounds. Bats already swooped and turned in the twilight. "So many bugs," complained Silas. He was the only one of them getting eaten alive, and the others found it funny, even though he clearly didn't. "There's one," he said, slapping his hip. "Drink someone else's blood, you little-"

"Shhh," hissed Aldway. "It's night-time. Sound travels at night. The lookouts will hear you. I don't want to die because your pale arse was a tasty treat for some bloated marsh gnat."

They had contemplated going back and gathering more troops to their cause. After all, there must be plenty of able men who had managed to hide and survive the attack on Bruke. Brande wanted none of it. He'd tried that type of assault last time and it hadn't worked. There just wasn't time to marshal enough troops. He wanted to get in by stealth and retrieve his loved ones. That was his only aim. If he could manage it without a fight, so be it. He'd almost rather try it alone, perhaps creep in and slip them away in the night.

Brande inspected his companions. Silas had no idea if

his daughter was with these particular troops or not. Right now, he seemed more concerned about the bugs. Eberhard looked like a capable fighter. He was tall, broad and strong. There was something about him that suggested he had been a soldier, but he spoke little and gave little away. Brande estimated that the man was at least twenty years his junior, and he was pleased to have him on his side. There was something no-nonsense about him, even if he was a looter. The shorter, dark haired one, though, was an entirely different sort. He appeared friendly, but Brande was sure he was every bit as deadly as his friend. His every movement bristled with energy. He had a smart mouth on him, but, in truth, he had entertained them with his banter. Brande suspected Aldway had more guile than his taller companion. Silas seemed quite taken with them. They were far more entertaining company than Brande who was not particularly communicative at the best of times.

The two newcomers hadn't explicitly stated their purpose in coming along. Were they soldiers? Rabble rousers? Spies? Troublemakers? He wasn't sure how they fitted into the picture, turning up late to the attack on Bruke and then, without much ado, agreeing to risk their lives by joining him. Aldway had the look of a person from Bruke, but Eberhard clearly had foreign blood in him. The blond hair and tall, strong physique more befitted a Skullun raider than someone from around here. Skullun bloodlines were not entirely uncommon.

The sun sank quickly, and soon it was dark. They ventured closer to the encampment. Brande noticed Eberhard keeping a constant lookout, never letting his attention wander. Brande wondered where he had picked up that habit. Aldway and Silas were sharing stories of past battles. Brande would have preferred it if they were discussing tactics.

Brande was focusing on something inside himself. He tried to summon the anger he had felt earlier, but it was dormant. Perhaps he was too tired. He gave up and listened to Aldway's latest story. Brande thought it a tall tale if ever he'd heard one, but Silas seemed to believe every word, and it kept Silas occupied, providing a distraction from his pain.

It was too early to attack, and the conversation ran dry. After a while, Silas whispered, "How did you two come to know each other?"

A slight pause. Aldway replied, "A forester needed extra hands to hunt down a prolific band of poachers. We volunteered. Worked together. It panned out well."

"You're mercenaries?"

"No, no, not mercenaries. We just had certain skills. We saw money could be made by someone who didn't mind getting their hands and morals a little dirty, so we went for it."

"I think that's how you describe a mercenary," laughed Silas.

"The definition's blurry," countered Aldway. "Anyway, we got offered more work."

"As mercenaries?"

Aldway shook his head. "I wouldn't exactly call it mercenary work." He didn't venture another title, though, nor did he sound particularly convincing.

Brande suspected they weren't getting the full story. "So you caught the poachers?"

"I caught them," interjected Eberhard.

"And I was nearby at the time, so technically I caught them too." Aldway grinned. "Team effort."

"And you became friends?"

"That's the idea," said Aldway.

"It's hard to trust others in times like these," commented Brande.

"We pick our battles as we like," said Aldway. "We're free men."

Brande was sure there was more to these two than they were letting on, but he didn't probe further.

The bugs continued to torment Silas, who was suffering enough without the constant irritation. "When do we attack?" he asked, impatiently.

"We need a clear idea of the layout of their camp," suggested Eberhard. "I don't want to run in blind."

Aldway seemed to be pondering something. "I have an idea."

Eberhard sighed and almost rolled his eyes, but didn't. "The last time you had an idea…"

"It's a good idea," insisted Aldway. A smile played on his lips. "I got the idea from you."

"Well, all the best ideas come from me," admitted Eberhard.

"And I also got it from the marsh bugs."

Eberhard rolled his eyes and didn't try to hide it.

It seemed like a sound plan. It was as good as anything Brande had in mind. The company had positioned itself out in the open. It was an easy position to attack, but they weren't afraid of attackers. It was also an easy position to see attackers coming, and that posed a problem for Brande and his allies.

Brande kept down among the rushes. He shivered. His clothes were almost soaked through, and it was cold in the night air. He gripped his axe tightly. His best hope was to get in close to the encampment and use its own structures, the tents and the wagons, for cover. The size of the convoy had grown since it left Bruton. Although they may have lost a few soldiers, they had taken more prisoners and stolen horses and wagons to accommodate them.

Off to one side, he saw Eberhard crawling along the ground on his belly. Aldway's plan was to pick off a few of their men silently, irritating the body of the men like biting bugs, until they became aware there was a bigger problem. Slowly, a ruckus would start as they found people missing or bodies left in tents. It was a vicious tactic just to provide a distraction, but the hope was that by causing trouble near the far end of the camp, Brande would have access to the prisoners. He would free as many as he could then escape with Aithne and Fia. He knew the name of Silas's daughter. It was Alani. He would hope Aithne might have heard the name or know of her, or her fate.

Silas was farther out, he would come in last since he felt unwell. He had been behaving strangely, complaining of headaches and nausea. Brande was convinced he was a liability, but for Aldway's plan to work they needed as much distraction as possible. He was convinced that the wolf bite Silas had sustained had become infected, causing the limp and perhaps the other symptoms as well, but Silas refused to admit to anything being wrong. An infected wound, Brande knew, could affect a man's mind if it became severe enough.

There was only the slightest sliver of a moon, and some clouds had blown in. As it had been a clear day, it was a cold night. Brande shivered and had to clench his teeth to stop them chattering. He thought murderous thoughts about soldiers warming their hands by a campfire while his wife and child froze in a prison wagon. He tightened his grip on his axe. He would split those soldiers from shoulder to crotch. He dwelt on this thought, feeling his anger grow, feeling its familiar glow inside him.

His shivering stopped. All the emotions he felt mixed within him, hatred, anger, loathing, all fuelling a fire that burned intensely. His eyes narrowed, and he started crawling toward the camp. He saw a sentry stood by the back of a tent. Moving when the man was distracted by others bringing him cooked food from the campfire, he was almost on him when the man staggered and fell with a grunt. In the darkness, he was little more than a silhouette to Brande, but the arrows protruding from his throat and chest were visible enough. Brande cursed silently. He was too close to Aldway.

That also meant he was too close to Eberhard. He crawled away. Looking back, he saw Aldway grabbing the body and dragging it away. He was as fast as a bograt. He dropped the body among some rushes about forty paces away. Hopefully, someone would notice the soldier was missing and go to search for him. They would spend time searching and, when they found him, lying there in the darkness, it would take them a moment to work out what wounds he'd sustained. They might think some animal had attacked him. A few more like that and panic would spread.

Brande went straight for the wagons. His mission was clear. He just wanted to free his family.

The soldiers were cooking, drinking and joking. They were on the home stretch, and it seemed that discipline was slack. They had but a few days journey ahead of them, their next destination probably being Charstoke Castle.

Brande found the first prison wagon. Its inhabitants were still locked up. A soldier walked past and threw something into the cage. There was a scuffle from within. He laughed. "Eat up, ladies!" The captives fought over the insufficient morsel. The soldier wandered deeper into the camp, still chuckling to himself. Brande felt his rage ignite and he nursed it.

He couldn't see a lookout, but he knew there must be one. He waited. He kept flat to the ground and remained vigilant while soldiers strolled past. They were arrogant and expected no retaliation, helping him remain invisible.

A cry went up from the other side of the camp. Brande smiled. Someone's work had been discovered.

He jumped up and flew to the first wagon. He was not seen, but he heard someone shout, "Check the wagons!" He cursed his luck. He peered between the crisscrossed bars of the cage. He couldn't see Fia or Aithne. Inside were seven or eight young girls, a couple of very young children and a woman who looked on the brink of death. He whispered to them: "I'll help you escape." The faces looked back at him, confused. He hated himself for it because he knew that they stood little chance of survival even if they did get loose. "Are any of you Alani?" he asked. The heads shook. He knew freeing them would make a noise and probably draw attention to him, but so would their wails if he walked away without helping. His axe collided with the lock and shattered it. The noise rang out into the night. He pulled open the door, hating himself as he did. They would flood out and cause a diversion, like lambs to the slaughter. It would buy him time to find Aithne and Fia.

He ran to the next wagon and saw Aithne's form inside. She was huddled over, eating something. His heart pounded in his chest. He was just about to call her name when a thin face, framed with short dark hair, appeared at the bars, shouting, "Dad!" He almost dropped dead with relief. It was Fia. They were both alive.

"Halt right there!"

He turned. There was the guard from before, the one laughing at the prisoners squabbling over his scraps. "Don't move!" he yelled. Brande wasn't afraid of this man, but his yelling posed a problem. He would bring everyone running. Brande sighed with relief when a horn sounded on the other side of the camp. Eberhard and Aldway had done their work well.

The guard was a big man and charged straight for him. He swung a flail overhead, the heavy spiked ball aimed straight for Brande's face. Brande threw his axe. It spun through the air and thudded squarely into the soldier's chest. The man's feet kept running. One leg lost strength before the other, and he careered sideways, collapsing on his side in the mud, his legs still twitching. Brande bent over and drew the man's dagger, which he wore at his belt. He positioned his body between the wagon and the man, so Fia wouldn't see the act of killing, and slit his throat.

He heard footsteps and heavy breathing behind him. He

grabbed the haft of his axe and pulled it clean from the guard's ribcage in one motion. The axe arched through the air and hit steel. The new attacker's sword was knocked away, but remained in his clutch. Another stroke and the axe sliced through the soldier's thighs. He cried out and fell. So violent and quick had been the manoeuvre that Brande lost his grip on his weapon and it flew into the mud by his side. Rather than go after it, Brande threw himself at the soldier. They grappled with each other, both gripping the soldier's sword and trying to gain ownership of it. The injury done to the soldier's legs made him weak and ineffectual. "Just die," grunted Brande, as he wrestled the sword into his own hands and then pressed the blade against the man's throat. They collapsed to the ground, Brande pushing the cutting edge of the sword into his opponent's throat until he was done.

He stood up gasping, looking for Fia's face and finding it, holding her gaze for just a second, seeing both shock and relief there.

He could hear that the camp was in chaos now. He retrieved his axe from the mud and took steps towards the cage. Hope filled him. Here was his chance.

In a blinding flash, the darkness lit up. A band of yellow fire, hovering at waist height, sprang to life around the camp. It was a cold, pale fire, flickering erratically, supported in midair by nothing visible. It was unnatural.

The flaming barrier of light encircled everything. It was as if the whole camp had been lassoed with an ethereal boundary. He felt helpless. This land was supposed to be cleansed of the Deft. Now, it would be hard to escape with the light exposing them. What he feared more was that this flaming boundary might have properties preventing anyone passing through it. He had encountered such a thing before during the Crusades.

His axe smashed down on the lock holding the cage door closed. Fia came first, scrambling out into his arms.

He hugged her quickly but was already helping someone else out of the cage. He needed Aithne to get out, but she was helping others go first. "Hurry," he insisted. She climbed out, her body awkward due to the cramped conditions it had endured. Others followed, and she wanted to help them, but he took her hand. "We must go. Now. Before they-"

The words died on his lips. A handful of soldiers burst onto the scene. Nearby, a man in a cowl, his face hidden, strode into sight. Brande froze. Typically, he would have already attacked to gain the advantage of surprise, but he had his wife and child here. They needed his protection. He stepped forward, putting himself between them and the men. He hefted his axe.

"Is that your family?" jeered one of the soldiers. "Gosh, you came close. So, so, close." He laughed.

The man in the cowl pointed. Brande saw more soldiers approaching. They were holding Silas, who was struggling, hissing and spitting ferociously. Brande hesitated, considering his options, then decided the game was up. He started to back away from the men, stretching out his arms to force Fia and Aithne backwards too.

Fia turned and ran. She hit the yellow flame marking the camp's perimeter. Where she touched it, it shimmered and became red. As she ran away, a strand of cold, red, wisp-like fire clung to her and trailed from her. She was tied to the camp by this snaking red rope of light. One of the men ran after her. Brande leapt and brought his axe down into the man's skull. It was a bad move. Immediately, the other soldiers were on him. He struck one with the handle of his axe, but a rain of blows came down on him and a blade pressed against his throat. He stopped moving. He was no good to Fia or Aithne dead.

He heard a scream. The men were forcing Aithne back into the wagon. Others had gone after Fia, who was traceable by the red strand trailing behind her. There could be no escape.

The figure in black came closer. His face was hidden in the shadows of his hooded cloak. He stood above Brande. A voice rasped from under the cowl, "Interesting."

Brande squinted and could just see the pale, thin face of an emaciated older man. Thin lips smiled as the man leant over him, studying him. Brande tried to pull away, but three soldiers held him down, grunting obscenities and threatening to cut his throat. The cloaked figure placed a cold, bony hand on Brande's forehead. He rasped a few arcane words, and suddenly Brande found he could no longer see. Darkness engulfed him.

He heard one of the soldiers say, "So, that's his daughter, is it?"

CHAPTER EIGHT

"Squawk, squawk, squawk!" Someone was jeering at him, and the words tore through his dreams and brought him back to reality with a start.

Brande could barely see through his puffy, bruised eyes. His head swam. His first notion was that he'd been in a scrap. Did he have a hangover? His brain was aching in his skull. It was dark, but what little light there was stung his eyes. His vision was returning. What had that cloaked man done to him? The panic beating in his chest started to subside as he realised he would regain his sight.

It was cold. Uncomfortable. Dark. Where was he?

Cold metal pressed against the back of his head and dug into his skin. He wondered if he was being tortured, which was a fair guess. When he opened his eyes, he was staring through bars at the ground ten feet below him. The same soldiers who had beaten him after the blindness took him were now striding away, laughing cruelly. He tried to make out their faces, but it was too dark, and he could barely see out from between his eyelids. Pain reverberated around his skull. He tried to listen, to make out what they were saying, but none of it made sense to him.

He felt the cold night air whistle around his legs and shoulders. He was suspended in a cage. He turned his head and saw the scaffold his cage hung from. He closed his pain-filled eyes and pictured the scene. A crossroads. A wooden gibbet rising into the air, one arm stretched out, with chains dangling from it holding a skyte's cage. In that cast iron cage, a crumpled man sat within the confines of the metal bars. Another wave of panic flushed through him, but an inner voice told him there was nothing he could do but sit still and recover from his injuries. He tried to go back to sleep, but the pain and cold prevented it.

Near him, he heard a groan. He began to say something but stopped himself, wondering if the person nearby might mean him harm. The groan continued. It was long and suffering. Eventually, it whispered, "Eb."

"Here, Ald," came the slurred response.

They were defeated. He and at least two of his three comrades had been imprisoned. They would starve to death if thirst or exposure didn't end them first. Of course, that was provided a passing traveller didn't take unkindly to them and stone them for his own amusement. They had been arrogant and foolish to think they could strike a blow at the King's soldiers.

His mind returned to the cloaked figure he had encountered. He had used some kind of profane artifice on him. Brande knew enough to suspect those cloaked figures must draw their power from the Rift. King Leofric would never have condoned such people travelling alongside his soldiers. He would have executed them before even considering employing their services. He would have done it himself! It would seem King Ignatius was of a different mind. He was utilising them for his own purpose. This was unsettling to Brande, but it was too late now for him to do anything about it.

He moved his legs and shuffled, trying to shift his back,

so the rungs of the cage didn't press into his spine. He was sore. Everything about him was sore.

He knew Eberhard and Aldway were alive, but what about the other. "Silas?" he hissed, through thick, senseless lips.

There was no response.

The cold of the night penetrated his clothing and nipped at his extremities. The wind was picking up. He knew it would prove a terrible torment as time passed.

His mind wandered. He recalled an incident during his crusading years. He'd travelled with two other warriors, good friends of his, to find a small village where supposedly a necromancer was in hiding. Wind and rain had beaten at them until they were forced to turn back. That night, both his men had died from exposure. The next day, wracked with guilt and sadness, he made makeshift graves for them and buried them under stones. The weather had calmed, and he prepared to head back to the small village to complete his mission on his own. Before he could set off, his two friends rose from their graves and attempted to kill him. He butchered them and burned them, ensuring they would never rise again. He never did catch the necromancer.

Memories of the past had led him into a dream. He awoke and tried to go back there, but the discomfort in his bones prevented him, and he stayed awake. "Silas," he hissed, louder than the last time. No response.

At least he thought he knew where he was. They were at the crossroads beyond the marshlands. It made sense that the company had passed here on their way to Charstoke.

King Leofric had had the most terrific moustache. The pain and exhaustion was causing Brande's mind to wander again. He had spoken to Leofric many times and fought alongside him on three separate occasions. He had always been impressed by the man's facial hair. Of course, it matched his commanding bearing, his huge physique, the sense of power that emanated from him. On their first meeting, Brande had been but a messenger, tasked with the unfortunate duty of telling the King that a platoon of soldiers had been ambushed by just two unknown bandits who had decimated their number and sent the rest running. They had sprung a surprise attack using their Deft touch to bring down an avalanche on the unsuspecting men. It was just one of many such tragedies that had occurred in the early days of the campaign before they became wise to the tricks of the enemy.

A noise drew his attention back to the present.

"Nnnnhhh."

It was a strange, inarticulate sound, but it was unmistakably Silas. So, we're all here, thought Brande. He felt oddly comforted by the knowledge. They could so easily have been killed. Apparently, they were being used as an example to others that might dare to challenge the King's own soldiers. They had been left to rot.

He awoke to the sound of someone screaming. His eyelids shot open, and then he screwed them shut again as the bright sunlight seared into them. He shifted uncomfortably. He remembered he was trapped in a skyte's cage, hanging about twelve foot above the ground. At least he was still in one piece. One leg dangled from the cage. He pulled it back in slowly, careful not to scrape his shin. The cage was too small for him to fully sit up, and his neck ached from being at an angle all night. His back was numb from leaning against the bars. The cage creaked and swayed from his movement. He could see another four gibbets behind him, on which similar cages hung from chains. Eberhard seemed to be in a very troubled sleep. Aldway was awake and briefly smiled at him, but his eyes lacked their usual liveliness. He pointed to the next cage.

Silas was a sorry sight. As Brande looked at him, Silas

began retching and then screaming again. It was almost unbearable to watch or hear. Brande let his emotions run cold, as he had learned to do during the Crusades. He watched dispassionately, waiting to see what would happen. He fully expected to witness Silas die in that cage.

Silas began to throw himself around the inside of his cage. His head clanged off the bars without him seeming to notice. The howl that emanated from him was barely human, more like that of a wolf. When he saw Brande was awake, he threw himself at the bars and breathed heavily, drool dripping from his bottom lip. His eyes were bloodshot and rolling. Brande kept eye contact with him and slowly, surely, Silas began to calm. Eventually, he sat back, then lay there, slumped, dribbling and muttering incoherently.

"They cut me seven times," said Aldway.

"Muh-huh?" mumbled Eberhard in his sleep, almost waking but not doing so.

"Seven," repeated Brande. He had no feelings. He had left Aithne and Fia behind. He had lost.

"I shot one with an arrow. Right in the neck. Dragged him down the hill a bit and dumped him in the rushes. That was a clean one. The next one, I got him in the eye with a dagger which I threw from at least twenty foot. I kid you not." He rattled them off like a list of groceries. "The next one, I shot but he moved, and the arrow took his ear off. He yelped, but so quietly no one was drawn to him before my next arrow got him in the heart, piercing right through his back. I dragged him into a tent. I almost didn't even notice the one in the tent because she was asleep. I slit her throat. I thought it would be silent, but she gurgled like a storm drain. Someone heard. A man came barging into the tent. We fought. It made noise. I choked him with the garrotte I keep in my pocket, but then another soldier came in before I'd finished him off. We tussled. I killed them both but left the tent to find it surrounded. There was," he paused for a second, his face turning grim, "a man in a cloak. As the soldiers grabbed me, he touched me on the head. That's the last thing I remember."

Brande said nothing. Aldway continued. "Eberhard was less lucky. He put his sword through someone's chest. A clean kill. I think, if I remember, he beheaded the next one. But the third kill went wrong. I don't know exactly what happened, but he got caught out somehow. He was dragged to the ground by three of them. They beat him up pretty bad."

Brande had no feelings about this. He said nothing. He thought about Aithne and Fia. He'd let them down. He began to grind his teeth.

"Silas managed to take out one or two. He made his way to meet up with you, but somehow he drew attention to himself. I'm not sure that's not what did you in. He wasn't acting like himself."

Silas did not respond to the suggestion he was responsible for Brande's failure. Brande was unmoved by the revelation. He remembered the soldiers had realised Fia was his daughter. His blood chilled as his mind worked against him, conjuring images. What terrible humiliation had she suffered? Guilt began to churn around and around in his stomach like a squid in a barrel.

He closed his eyes. Aldway continued talking, but he no longer listened. He moved each finger. He moved his toes. He moved his arms, his legs, his back, his chest, his neck. He was alive. Everything hurt, but he was not broken. It had been downright foolish to attack a camp of soldiers, but how arrogant of them to leave him hanging here in this skyte's cage when he held such a grudge against them.

A new feeling stirred in him. A feeling he welcomed.

He opened his eyes more fully. Aldway was watching him, but saying nothing now. Brande grabbed the bars of his cage and shook them. He roared defiantly as they refused to give to his strength. His cage swung from side to side as he shook the bars, willing them to yield. Eventually, he admitted defeat. He slumped back and waited for the cage to stop rocking.

"No use," said Aldway.

"No use, no use, no use, nyus, nyas, nyat, natnat," repeated Silas, his words descending into nonsense. He fell silent.

"What's wrong with him?" asked Brande.

Aldway shrugged. "Not himself anymore. Truth be told, I'm glad he's in the cage."

Brande eyed his travelling companion. Silas' clothes were in tatters, but something told Brande that Silas had done this to himself. He was streaked with blood. His hands were worn to the bone in places, probably done while attempting to free himself from the cage. In his madness, he must have scraped the flesh from his fingers. It reminded Brande of the creature at the witch's house, but that creature had, in the end, shown humanity. He saw none of that in what Silas had become.

He closed his eyes and breathed.

The night Brande met Aithne, his world had turned upside down. He had not long lived in Bruton. He had little to show for his years in the Crusades except for some gold and silver he had brought back, a handful of secrets, a skin-load of scars and a mind that ran with terrible thoughts. He had continued working as a soldier in the king's army for as long as he could bear it but found it very different from his life of fighting in the east. He had been given a division to command, but he preferred not being responsible for so many lives.

He kept himself to himself. He buried his gold and silver, keeping back enough to buy himself a large hut, ideal for the simple life of a woodcutter, and a couple of quality axes. He thought he might be happy in Bruton. He planned to live and die there. He wanted nothing more of the outside world. He wanted to be alone.

It was not that he disliked others, or distrusted them, just that he had spent his life in the company of soldiers, and now he wanted peace. Before, he had torn towns apart. Now, he wanted to walk among simple village folk and be one of them. He wanted to spend his days doing honest work and sleeping restfully without the threat of attack.

His nights were always troubled. He never slept through from dusk to dawn. Not once. While he did sleep, it was fitfully. In his dreams, he was always fighting. He saw horrors that he could barely have described if he'd been asked to retell them during the day. His dreams always ended in blood and fire, before he awoke.

He could confess to himself now that he had not been properly looking after himself. He would rise early, splash water on his face, pick up his woodsman's axe and head into the forest to meet with the other men. He cut down trees like they were enemy soldiers. He worked with a fury that kept the thoughts from his mind. Sometimes, he would undertake other tasks. He would strip a tree. Saw it into segments. Transport it. He would do the work of five men by himself.

At night, in his home, he sharpened his axe and oiled it. Mostly he ate berries he'd collected in the forest and bread he'd bought. Sometimes he would make a meal, a simple potage made from onions and vegetables grown in a strip of soil by his hut. If he couldn't get to sleep, he would make a fire and sit with a block of wood and, using a sharp knife, whittle it into small animals or figurines. Anything to keep the thoughts out.

There had been a terrible winter storm. It had raged for weeks. One awful night, even Brande went to the tavern for warmth, comradeship and ale. He spoke to a few of the men he worked with, but their merriment grew, and they descended into drunkenness. Eventually, he knew this was no longer his place. He decided to return home. No one would try to stop him, they were used to the way he kept himself to himself. He was an imposing figure, sullen, and rarely seen without an axe. He had heard children rush past whispering that he was mad, or demonic, and he smiled at these things knowing it meant their parents were also wary of him.

He stood up, draining the last of his flagon and banged it back on the table, wiping the back of his hand across his mouth. He could have left at that moment, but, for some reason, he stopped to survey the busy scene before him. He could not have said what he was looking for. Perhaps he was fixing a pleasant moment in his mind, one to replace the years of horror and battle. Perhaps he was convincing himself that the happy scene was something he wanted no part in. Instead, he caught her eyes.

Aithne was the blacksmith's daughter. It was well known that she worked in the smithy. Her arms were as strong as a man's, yet her figure was all a woman's. There were rumours about why she had not married, but what they were exactly, or if they were true, Brande neither knew nor cared. He turned to go, but couldn't stop himself glancing back at her one last time to see her smoky eyes and the long auburn hair that fell upon her shoulders. For a moment, he forgot his desire to be alone but instantly regretted doing so when he saw she was watching him. He felt embarrassed.

She was with a group of men and women, one of whom was her father. They were all drinking, talking and laughing. Some of them were playing dice and money was passing across the table. They were all distracted and had not noticed she had stopped to watch him. The world paused for a long moment. In his mind's eye, Brande remembered her smiling at him, but perhaps that was just his imagination filling in details. One of the men at her table stood and shouted to the barkeep to bring them more drinks. He had blocked their view of each other and broken the spell.

Brande turned and made for the door. As he pushed it open, he glanced back once more. It was uncharacteristic of him, but something about her had captured his attention. She was no longer there. He didn't look for her, because he was betraying his promise to himself, to live a quiet, solitary existence. He deserved no other. He struggled out into the wind and the snow, relieved to be away from the noise and bustle of the tavern. Yet, as he travelled home through the winter storm, Aithne's dark eyes stayed with him.

"Brande?"

He awoke. His mind had been somewhere more pleasant than this, he was sure. He twisted and moved his limbs. Pain surged through them. The hours in this skyte's cage were taking their toll. He realised he must have fallen asleep again because by his reckoning it was past early morning. He felt lightheaded.

"Thought you were dead, you deaf bastard," said Aldway.

Brande noticed a man standing beneath the cages. He was on his own and carried a large backpack on his back.

"Hail," said the man, looking up at him.

Brande looked down. From his vantage point, he could see the man's hair was thinning on top. He was older than Brande and his stature somewhat portly. He had something of the look of Bruke about him. His hair was shorn, his clothes simple.

"How long have you been up there?" His tone sounded casual and interested, not at all mocking.

Brande turned to look at Aldway, who shrugged. Eberhard was sitting still, with eyes closed. Silas was pawing at the cage, muttering to himself.

"I think this is the second day. Maybe the third." He smiled. "Hard to say."

"What did you do?" asked the fellow, forthrightly. His

look suggested he was taking the measure of them. Brande saw potential in the situation.

"We attacked the king's men, the ones that just sacked Bruke."

The man laughed. "Sure you did."

"It's true," growled Brande.

"But you weren't there during the sacking?"

"No, we arrived on its heels."

The man turned his lips down in a sour but contemplative expression. "Why did you attack them?"

"We each have our reasons, but mine is simple. They took my child from me. I hoped to get her back."

Brande had to tell the truth, or most of it, because the man was studying him, head tilted to one side as he examined the cage and its occupant. Anything he said had to ring with truth if he had any hope of making the man trust him enough to release him.

"Maybe that's the case," said the man. He stood, thoughtfully.

"I know I'm in no position to ask," began Brande, "but would you tell me where it is you travel? You look like one from Bruke, but I know Bruke to be more or less deserted. You can't be a trader as you carry no wares."

The man studied the ground for a moment. "It's true. What you say is true. I have no wares. What I intend to do is go to the capital and see for myself what has happened to the king who once ruled us so fairly."

"You think something has happened to him?"

The man sighed. "There have been rumours." A thought occurred to him, it lit up his face. "If you did attack them, you'd have seen they had those that fought but did not wear armour. Can you describe them?"

Brande cracked a half-smile. "That sounds like a riddle, but I know whom you mean. The cloaked ones, with the cowls pulled about their faces. One of them put a hand on my head, like this, and made me blind for a time. They've the Deft touch, but also experienced in darker arts, by my reckoning."

The man looked interested. "Is that all you know of them?"

Brande shrugged. "They maintained some kind of invisible perimeter around their camp to stop people getting out. Didn't stop us from getting in."

"You speak true. I saw such a thing myself. A yellow band running around the camp, just for a moment."

"Do you know anything about them?"

The man paused. "If I released you, where would you go? What would you do?"

"We'd continue," promised Brande, firmly. "We'd go together in the direction those men are heading and hunt them down again and somehow attack again, with a new strategy."

"It is said those cloaked men are acolytes of a warlock who worships Nachmair. They are fearsome warriors in their own right." He was revealing what he knew. "I heard they come from the east, beyond where the Crusades were fought. Their leader, some say, has the ear of the King."

"How could that be?" asked Aldway. "King Ignatius might not possess the hate-filled fervour of Leofric, but he has no love for the Deft."

"I have heard that he has many of these acolytes in his employment now. They have terrible powers, but there is a rumour that more powerful beings await in the wings, ready to attack when the moment is right."

"You seem to know a lot," exclaimed Brande. "How did you learn all this?"

The man shook his head, indicating that line of questioning would get Brande nowhere.

"Tell me, what is your name," said Brande, eager to change tack, not wanting to put the man off helping them.

"Carantok."

"Well met, Carantok. Mine is Brande. Please, let us

down. We can work together. We can protect you on your way to the capital. We'll break off if we come across the company again. You would not be obliged to help us attack them." He felt like he was bartering at market, but it was their very lives at stake.

The man paused for a moment, in contemplation. Brande could see he was weighing them up. Finally, he spoke. "I have a sword. I might be able to break one of you out if the lock is rusted or weak. Who is most likely?" He looked up at the cages sceptically.

Silas shook his cage.

Aldway said, "Let me out, I can free the others."

Eberhard opened his eyes. "You would help us?"

The man nodded. "Are you all together?"

"Yes," confirmed Brande.

"This one is much lower," said Carantok, pointing to Silas. It was true. The beam was lower. "Is he all right? Would he be able to help me get the rest of you down?"

Brande shrugged. "We are all worse for wear at the moment. Take your pick. We would all help each other."

Silas rested his head against the side of the cage. "I can… out," he whispered.

Brande hoped Silas was well enough to help. He didn't want to suggest he wasn't, in case Carantok decided one of them was plague-ridden or bewitched, in which case he might fear they all were and would just walk on.

"Can you throw a sword up to me?" asked Brande. "If I had a sword, I could probably lever the lock and break it myself."

Carantok tried. He took out his sword and threw it up into the air, then bolted out of the way before it came down again. With each try, the sword either didn't get high enough or was at the wrong angle so Brande couldn't catch the hilt. After four or five attempts, it was apparent that it was a futile endeavour.

"I think," said Carantok, "that I can climb up the gibbet

and then get to the lock from above. Failing that, pass the sword down into the cage."

The man stood at the base of the gibbet that held Silas. "I think this will be the easiest. It's lower than the others. See how there's a peg there? It will serve as a foothold. In fact, it's different from the rest, older. The lock looks smaller too." Brande could tell that Carantok was nervous about climbing and was talking himself into it.

Brande cast a sideways glance at Aldway and Eberhard. They both looked uneasy about the man's choice to free Silas, but neither voiced an objection. No doubt, they were also concerned about scaring Carantok away. And they probably considered Silas and Brande to be friends and did not want to upset Brande, as Silas would surely free him first and then it was up to Brande to determine whether or not to release them. Their eyes spoke volumes about their concerns.

Brande decided to let fate run its course. Something was wrong with Silas, that was certain, but none of them wanted to disrupt the enthusiasm of the man that could save their lives.

"Hurry," growled Silas to the newcomer.

CHAPTER NINE

Brande watched as Carantok climbed the scaffold and edged his way along the beam. His inability to help left him feeling useless and all he could do was grunt the odd word of encouragement. The man was not young and not slim, and it took him a great deal of effort to get to where he was now. Perhaps it would have been comical if so much had not been at stake. Carantok winced as he caught his shin on the sharp edge of the timber and paused a while until the pain subsided. He edged further along the horizontal beam that held the cage imprisoning Silas. Finally, he got to the end of it. He pulled free his sword from its scabbard and reached out with it and took a swing at the lock. He missed. He swung again and this time hit the lock. There was a loud clang, but nothing else.

"This won't work," he said. "If I drop the sword down to you, will that do it?"

Silas grinned, and his bloody hand emerged from the cage.

Carantok looked up. "Your friend isn't the most talkative soul."

Aldway spoke quickly. "No, but we are all extremely grateful for what you are doing. Pass him your sword. He will free us. Together, we will head to the capital."

The man nodded. He sheathed his sword and, with some effort, managed to pass the sheathed sword down to Silas's outstretched hand. Silas grabbed the sword eagerly, and it disappeared into the cage. Soon, the sound of scratching, scraping and banging proceeded. As Carantok climbed down the gibbet, Brande strained to see what Silas was doing.

"He's doing it," cheered Aldway, his cage swinging as he enthusiastically leaned toward Silas to watch his efforts.

Carantok reached the ground and walked around to where he could see Silas. "Be careful, take your time. Otherwise, you'll hurt yourself, and that will slow you down." Silas grunted and cursed, savagely attacking the rusty lock on his cage. His exertions were violent and frantic.

There was a metallic snap, and all sound stopped.

"Done?" asked Eberhard.

"My sword," groaned Carantok.

Silas launched straight into his savage attack on the lock again, this time using a sword with a broken blade. It was less than half the length it had been. He did not halt again.

"Your friend is eager," said Carantok, sounding merry but looking disconcerted.

Brande nodded. "Like I am," he said, calmly. "We all are." He didn't feel calm, though. Something was very wrong with Silas.

Despite his captivity, Brande was starting to feel more like himself. He was growing accustomed to the aches and pains. His eyes were opening more easily. All his thoughts were bent on freedom. He wasn't sure releasing Silas first was a good idea at all.

"If someone comes this way, I'll have to go," blurted the man, perhaps deciding Silas would have no luck. "I can't be seen trying to release you. That doesn't mean I won't come back, but there's no point me being caught here because I'll just end up like you."

"I agree," said Brande, sensibly, "and if you return, we'll hold you in even higher esteem for it. We know you risk your neck. Tell me, do you have much family?"

"Yes. A wife. Two daughters. A sister. I sent them away a week ago before Bruke was attacked."

Brande thought about that for a moment. He wasn't entirely sure what to make of the man who stood before him. He was travelling alone but didn't look like the type that would. He was older than Brande. He had a paunch around his midriff and was balding. Like any lone traveller, he wore a sword, but he didn't look like he would be up to much in a fight. He had known about the magical perimeter and seemed to know a lot about the acolytes. Now he seemed to be suggesting he had a week's forewarning of the attack on Bruke. "You knew the attack was coming?"

Carantok paused, then shook his head. "Merely expected it based on the attack on Bruton and the towns south of there. Word travels fast among traders."

Brande mumbled his understanding, seeming to accept the answer, but he was looking at Carantok in a new light. There was a strange confidence about the man. Something tickled the back of Brande's mind. The man reminded him of someone. A man he had met a long time ago in the east, but that man had the Deft touch. Carantok might have the same gifts, although would never have been trained in these parts. With the King's traditional stance against Deft folk, Carantok would never admit to his latent abilities. Brande considered that if the man had the gift of foresight, and they journeyed together, he could be useful.

There was another loud, clanging snap. Brande saw the result. The lock from Silas's cage fell, hit the road and bounced. The broken sword followed after. Silas kicked the metal door open and slid out, hanging from the cage by his hands. Drool was slathered all over his chin. He dropped and landed feet first, falling forward and then curling to a ball on the ground.

"Yes!" yelled Aldway, pumping his fist in the air.

Brande felt a rush of relief, followed by concern when Silas did not move.

Carantok rushed over to help him. He grabbed Silas under the armpit and attempted to help him to his feet.

Silas rounded on him and dragged him to the ground. He started pummelling the man with his fists.

"Stop! Stop it!" screamed Aldway, who was closest.

The two men fought. Carantok grabbed up his broken sword from the ground. For a moment, it evened the odds. Silas was like a wild thing. Brande looked on, helpless to stop it.

Silas jumped on Carantok and bit his face, clawed at his eyes, punched him and kneed him in the ribs. He ripped a fistful of Carantok's thinning hair from his head. The attack was ruthless and relentless. Carantok screamed and managed to retaliate with a few stabs of the broken blade, but Brande knew from the outset who would win. Silas was a soldier. He had a fighter's build. Some disease of the mind had maddened him and made him aggressive.

Carantok, despite whatever Deft ability he might or might not possess, had no cause for confidence now. He was submerged beneath the brutal attack. Aldway and Eberhard were screaming at Silas to stop, trying to reason with him, even threatening him about what they would do if they got free. Finally, they too gave up. Eberhard shouted an apology to Carantok, who was now a bloody mess on the floor, trying to scrabble away but failing. He turned his face to the sky, just as Silas leapt on him once more. They knew it was almost over, but somehow, with a wild, hopeless swing of a broken blade, Carantok caught Silas across the throat. Silas fell on him, furiously plunging his thumbs into the man's eyes.

Brande considered it his fault. He alone had known Silas had been bitten by a wolf. He alone suspected the wound was infected. He had watched Silas's deterioration but raised no alarm. In his defence, he hadn't known Silas was this far gone, but now he owed it to Carantok to witness his death.

Carantok stopped moving. Silas scrabbled about in the blood and flesh for a few moments. He was trying to stand, but failing to rise. Whatever madness drove him, it couldn't keep him alive forever. Eventually, his body came to rest. He lay prostrate across his victim's corpse. Blood was scattered from them. It was a like a slaughterhouse, chunks of meat and streams of blood surrounding them in every direction.

"In Nachmair's name," cursed Eberhard, eventually. "Was he possessed?"

Aldway was stunned into silence and said nothing.

"Rabid," said Brande. "I think he was rabid."

Eberhard looked at him in bemusement. "You said nothing?"

Brande shrugged and looked away. "Carantok chose to release one of us. I wasn't about to argue with that." He didn't look back to see if the two men accepted the answer, because it did not matter. They would die in these cages now. No one else would rescue them, not with evidence of the last disastrous rescue attempt rotting below.

"And now, we're going to die," announced Aldway, who had evidently reached the same conclusion.

If the night brought rain and four-legged scavengers, the dawn brought a belly aching with hunger and coldness like he had not experienced in a long time. Brande awoke, shivering. He looked down at the mess below. Some of the blood had washed away, but much of the corpses remained, now torn to pieces. He shivered.

The wind died down as the sun rose. The morning was crisp and his clothes still soaked through from the night's rain. He saw that Eberhard had removed his shirt and tied it around a bar, presumably hoping it might dry. Brande couldn't fail to notice the muscles that layered every aspect of Eberhard's physique. Aldway was still asleep.

Aldway and Eberhard had spent some time talking that night, lamenting Silas' actions and their misfortune. Brande had been half-asleep and hadn't listened to much of it. Eventually, Eberhard had tried to sleep, but Aldway spent much of the night shooing away animals. Brande could see no reason for it but said nothing despite resenting his rest being broken up. The only comfort now was in sleep.

"Are you awake, Brande?" called Eberhard.

Brande turned and nodded.

"We have a visitor."

Brande frowned, puzzled.

"Look to the distance."

Wearily, Brande looked in the direction Eberhard indicated. Sure enough, in the distance, he could see a figure approaching. A lone figure, a man, scrawny, meandering along the road towards them.

"Don't get your hopes up," said Aldway, suddenly awake.

"He's coming from the direction the soldiers went. He might have news about the company," said Brande, thinking of Aithne and Fia and what they might be enduring while he was swinging in a cage.

Eberhard said nothing. Aldway spat between the bars of his cage. "Lightning doesn't strike twice. He won't help us."

"I just need information, that's all," said Brande. "Don't scare him off."

Eventually, the man reached them. He stopped and looked at them, each in turn, as if assessing each of their chances of survival. He then studied what remained of the corpses below them. He wandered around looking at the grisly remnants, occasionally humming or talking to himself. He paused before Eberhard's cage and looked up, a grin on his face.

He was scrawny, with a face that was as pokey as a weasel's. His clothes were those of a beggar; multilayered for warmth, but torn and dirty. Occasionally he ran his hand through his black hair, tugging on it at the end before letting go, then wiping his hand on his trouser leg as if cleaning away the grease he had pulled from his hair. He walked over to Brande's cage and looked up. "Alive then?"

Brande nodded. "Barely."

"What did you do?"

"Fought some soldiers. The ones you passed on your way here."

The man inclined his head to one side but revealed nothing. Travellers were wary of those in skytes' cages.

"What's your name, friend?" asked Eberhard.

The man said nothing. After a moment, he giggled. "So, you fought King Ignatius' men?"

"That's right," affirmed Brande. "We killed a few. But they hung us up instead of killing us. Why would that be?"

The man tilted his head to the other side. He rubbed his right eye, which was twitching. "I don't know."

"Did you not ask them?"

The man looked at him strangely. "Your time in that cage has addled your brain, fool. I only just met you. Why would I have asked them before I even knew you existed?"

Brande shrugged and laughed. "Good point." He knew now that the man had seen the soldiers, which meant he knew the direction they travelled. They had not gone directly to Charstoke Castle.

"The soldiers took my child," revealed Brande. "When you saw them in Thornaway, were there children with them?"

"Thornaway? No, no, no," he chided. He tilted his head the other way and laughed. "You killed King Ignatius' men!

So, so, so!" He hopped on the spot for a moment, doing a little jig. "Tra la la," the man sang, and danced in a circle and giggled to himself.

Brande realised they were dealing with a madman.

"Stonenife," said Eberhard. "You saw them in Stonenife?"

Well done, thought Brande.

The man stopped and looked up at Eberhard. He pointed to the corpses of Silas and Carantok. "Are these your friends?" As he spoke, a crow flew down and landed on Silas' face and pecked at his eye, drinking the liquid within.

Eberhard shrugged. "Yes, in a way."

"Looks to me like one escaped his cage then killed a traveller. Wouldn't want that happening to me! You all locked up in there?"

Eberhard sank back against his bars and ignored the fool.

The man seemed annoyed that he had lost the attention of his audience. "Are you hungry?" he asked.

Eberhard leant forward. "Do you have food?"

"Don't be taken in," said Aldway. "He has no food. He is tormenting us." The more guileful of the two, thought Brande.

The man picked a fresh apple out of the bag he carried and waved it in the air. "I'll throw it to you!"

Eberhard eyed him suspiciously.

"If you catch it, it's yours!"

"You're on," grinned the big man. He thrust a hand out between the bars and nodded for the man to throw the apple up to him. "I'm very grateful to you, sir."

"Wylie," said the man. "You may call me Wylie. Most people do. Well, most who know me." He seemed to twist on the spot as if he was about to buckle and fall to the floor. He sprang and chucked the apple. Eberhard was in the process of saying thank you to the man, using his name this time, and suddenly had to lunge for the item as it sailed through the air. He banged his face against the bars trying to reach it, but its apex was just short of where it needed to be, and it fell down beneath the cage.

"Wasn't ready," said Eberhard. "I'll get it next time."

"Oh, oh, oh, but we agreed," said the man. "If you catch it, it's yours. But you didn't. So now it is… not yours." He smiled almost innocently and picked up the apple and bit into it.

Eberhard looked to Aldway, who gave him a look that said I told you so. Eberhard slumped back in his cage, closed his eyes. He was finished with the man. A moment later, Aldway leaned forward and said, "So, Wylie, from Stonenife, who met the passing army, anything else you'd like to tell us about yourself?"

The man stopped mid-bite and frowned as if realising he might not be as entirely in control of the situation as he thought. He picked something up off the ground and examined it. "A broken sword. Interesting," he muttered. He kicked the corpses over and about a little, to see the damage done to them. Silas was a ragged thing, ripped apart by night animals. The kindly man who had tried to help them was still mostly intact, but he looked even worse because of the damage Silas had inflicted. His entrails were spread out across the ground to one side where a fox had tugged at them and drawn them from the body.

Wylie searched the bodies and found a small bag of coins on Carantok. He danced a little jig, pleased with himself. Brande's eyes narrowed. He felt, at that moment, he had the measure of the man. A cutpurse, a thief, maybe a cutthroat. Not someone to be trusted.

"You killed King Ignatius' men," laughed Wylie, suddenly remembering they were there and looking up at them hanging in their cages. "That's probably treason!" And then he sang.

Fool King Ig
He didn't give a fig
He liked to drink and dine

Sloshed on a swig
He danced a merry jig
And spewed up half his wine

It blew off his wig
When he farted like a pig
And he swallowed like a -

Eberhard's shoe hit him hard on the back of the head, stopping him abruptly. He turned and looked up at the warrior, anger in his eyes. "Your singing voice is weaker than your throwing arm," bellowed Eberhard. He threw back his head and laughed.

"Are you laughing at me? Laughing at me?" He threw the apple in anger.

It sailed through the bars of Eberhard's cage and straight into his lap. This made the blond giant laugh even harder. "Thank you, fool. I was wrong about your throwing arm." He took a bite from the apple. "But not about your singing."

Wylie collapsed to the ground as if he'd been punched in the gut. He sat there looking stupefied.

Brande, however, had seen an opening. "You obviously have no love for King Ig. Maybe we can be of some use to each other?"

Wylie looked at him a while, assessing him. He eventually stood up and started walking along the road, back the way he came. Brande watched him. He had not expected much, and this behaviour did not surprise him.

"You're going the wrong way," yelled Aldway.

"No, no, no," replied Wylie, simply, as he left them behind.

They watched him go. "I don't understand," said Eberhard. "Why is he going back towards Stonenife?"

Brande snorted. "Because he knows we want to go that way, but can't."

Silence fell. They hung there, in their cages, all hope leaving them.

It was about an hour later when Eberhard grunted, "At least I got half an apple."

Wylie was not the last person to come to the crossroads that day. Several travellers passed them by, but in general, they refused to speak or, in some cases, didn't even bother to look up. Brande could feel himself weakening. He had been through much and although he was all too tempted to dwell on his predicament, all the time he tortured himself thinking about where Fia and Aithne might be. Most likely, they were at Stonenife. From there, the army would inevitably head back to Charstoke.

Brande could feel the hopelessness of the situation weighing on him. He tried to stir himself, to feel something, to feel anger, but he couldn't. It wasn't in him. He had been a young man and filled with rage once, but now he was of a different temperament, and he found, caged, hungry and frozen as he was, that he could barely summon the energy to complain about his situation.

He spotted two figures heading their way, from the same direction they had come, from Bruke. Brande held on to no hope that they might help them. He suspected the lack of food and drink, the exposure and the cold would just about finish him in the night.

He was apologising to Fia and Aithne for not being there for them. For a short time, he thought they were in front of him, and he started apologising out loud to them. He found himself shouting, "I'm sorry!" He shut his mouth. He should never have let them get captured. He should have had a better plan. He was a strong man, hard, forged in the wars and tempered in the Crusades. If he could just get free, hope would be restored. It seemed, though, that his time had run out.

"Over there," said Eberhard, noticing what Brande had seen.

Two horses with riders. One was sat up straight, the other bent over, hunched. They were barely more than silhouettes in the setting sun.

"Is it any use?" asked Aldway, sounding weak. Brande didn't blame him for his pessimism. Their luck had run out.

"This could be our last chance," said Eberhard. "Few travel at night. These could be our last travellers."

The riders halted their horses in the distance. Aldway groaned. "I knew it. They aren't even coming close."

"There's nowhere else for them to go," said Brande. "They will come."

Over the next hour, darkness descended. The riders had made themselves a camp in the distance. Brande could see their campfire.

The metal rungs of the cage were biting into his flesh now. His skull felt like it had ridges worn into the bone. He cursed everything. His foolishness. King Ignatius. Aldway. Eberhard. Silas. All of it. He cursed the moon.

"Eberhard," said Aldway. "I want you to know something."

"Don't," said Eberhard. "I already know."

Aldway stretched a hand out of his cage toward Eberhard's. They were on opposite sides of the road, there was no hope they could reach one another. Eberhard put his hand out of his cage too, stretched it towards Aldway's. It was just a small act, and it was over as soon as it started, but it represented something. The end of hope. "I am dying," said Aldway.

Eberhard spoke, his voice steady. "It has been a pleasure, my friend."

Aldway whispered, but Brande could hear because the night air was clear and carried sound. "My love."

Brande understood now. He understood why their story of how they met, the one they had told in the marshlands, had somehow been lacking. Their friendship was more than a friendship.

Eberhard looked over at Brande. "I am sorry we did not tell you, Brande. Maybe you are glad we did not?"

Brande smiled. "At least you'll die together. Aithne is…" He couldn't find the words.

Aldway spoke, "Eberhard, I was ever yours."

"I know," said the bigger man, gently. "And I yours."

Eberhard turned back to Brande. "Your discretion…"

"Is assured," replied Brande. He didn't care if they were lovers. He had only one care in the world, and that was his own family.

Eberhard nodded thankfully.

"We won't last the night," whispered Aldway. He had reached the point of despair.

"I know," replied Eberhard, quietly.

A cold chill went through Brande. King Ignatius, if he ever got near him, would need to explain why he had broken so many families and ruined so many lives. He was not a weak king. He controlled his forces. He was responsible for them. Why, then, had he allowed these atrocities under his own banner? Brande looked through the darkness at the spot of orange fire in the distance, then leant back and stared at the stars wondering if it might be his last night.

Eberhard and Aldway continued to whisper to each other as the cold and the dark destroyed the last vestiges of their hope. Brande sunk in his cage and put one arm over his ear trying to make himself comfortable while blocking out what they were saying, which was private and did not need to be heard. He could feel himself on the edge of sleep. The real world and the imaginary conflated, confusing him. His mind was awash with images of witches and fire. The witch had said Silas would hang. He'd been trapped in a skyte's cage. She had been right. She had also told them that Brande would burn. It seemed that had been wrong.

The sound of hoof-beats woke him with a start. "Hey!" he shouted. The two riders were approaching. "Hey! Hey!"

They stopped amongst the cages, in the dead centre of the crossroads. The hunched figure was still hunched. He was a man with a substantial growth rising out of his back and deforming his shoulder. His face was also misshapen. Next to him, holding the reins of her horse, was a young woman whose visage contrasted starkly with that of her riding companion. She was beautiful. She seemed tall, maybe because she sat with her back so straight. Long, blonde hair was evident beneath the hood of the brown cloak she wore to keep away the chill of the night air.

"You travel through the night?" asked Brande.

"It is almost morning," said the woman. "We press on because we seek someone."

"Who?" asked Brande.

She paused. "His name is Silas. He is a pale man, with red hair. Have you seen him pass this way?"

Brande let out a sorry sigh. He didn't know which way to take the conversation. Explaining they had just ridden through his meagre remains did not seem to be the best place to start.

"He died."

"You knew him?"

"I travelled with him."

The woman looked suspicious. "Prove it."

"He wore a piece of wood on a chain around his neck."

"That just means you saw him."

"He told me that his daughter was kidnapped by the king's men."

She nodded. "So you spoke to him."

"He and I went to Bruke together, chasing the soldiers. He to retrieve a daughter. Me, a daughter and a wife."

The hunchback leaned forward and straightened up somewhat. He was not as old or crippled as he first seemed and was probably of an age with the woman. "How did Silas die?"

Brande paused. "Infection took him, in the end. He was bitten by a wolf back in Dankwood."

They looked at each other, then seemed to shrug as if the story seemed plausible to them.

"Please," said Brande. "I will answer all your questions. But get me down, because I won't survive the night."

"What is your name?" asked the woman.

"Brande."

The woman and her hunchback friend exchanged a meaningful glance. "We will get you down," said the woman. "You look in no fit state to cause us harm, and I am interested in what you have to say. These two are friends?"

Brande was momentarily lost for words. She had told him he would have his freedom as if it was such a little thing she did. He was reeling from her answer. He could never have expected it.

"They are, and they were friends to Silas too."

The hunchback stood, crookedly. "If I move the horse under-"

"No need. I can break the locks," said the woman.

Brande sat quietly, shivering, while the woman dismounted and threw her cloak over the saddle. He could see she was strong and capable.

"Who first?"

"Aldway," said Eberhard. "He is unwell."

"No," said Brande. "He is weak. You go first and then free Aldway. Perhaps this lady will release me while you do so."

"Yes," confirmed the young woman. "That's what I'll

do."

Despite Eberhard's gibbet being the highest, moments later she was above him, having scaled it, and was crawling along the beam from which the cage dangled. She drew her sword and, just as Carantok had tried to do, she leant down and swung the blade. Only, she was hanging from the beam by one hand and one foot, and her swing was true and fierce, and the padlock exploded. The rusted ring holding it to the lock, its weakest part, shattered. Eberhard kicked the door open. He untied his shirt and put it back on, despite it still being damp. He watched as the woman slipped down to the ground and ran over to Brande, who was free before Eberhard had even straightened out his painful joints and dropped, like a sack, to the floor.

"How about I just free your friend myself," she said.

Brande laughed, despite himself.

Eberhard nodded, "Please, I am still weak."

Brande sat on the cold ground, rubbing feeling back into his legs and arms. "We do not yet know your names," he said, posing the question to both her and the hunchback.

"I am Githa," she said. "Silas' cousin. And this is Alland."

"Also his cousin," explained Alland, the hunchback. "Come, we should get away from here in case other travellers pass in the morning. We'll go somewhere quiet and start a fire, since you'll be cold and hungry."

Brande's gaze fell momentarily along the road to Bruke. He had no memory of Silas saying he had cousins who might look for him, but then perhaps the conversation had never tended that way. He put it from his mind. He looked along another road, towards Stonenife, thinking of the woman and child he loved. Finally, he smiled. There was still hope.

CHAPTER TEN

They moved slowly, but eventually got themselves out of sight of the cages and any travellers that would pass.

Brande said, "I'll fetch some wood. Do you, by any chance, have an axe?" Alland seemed unsure about whether he should trust one of the released prisoners with a weapon, but Githa scowled at him, and he handed it over.

Brande brought back some wood. Alland used flint and steel to start a fire. They gathered around the small campfire and Alland cooked bacon over the flames. Githa produced some bread, dried apples, honey cakes and a small bag of nuts from her saddlebag. Brande and Eberhard tucked in.

Aldway drank some water and was eventually persuaded to eat something. He was the worst of them. The exposure had got to him during the night. He had taken a turn for the worse. They put a blanket around his shoulders. It was a chilly night, and the sun was slow to rise.

They sat around the flickering fire, drawing warmth from it and staring at it like it was an imprisoned creature that might break free. It spluttered fiercely as if trying to frighten away the darkness. Few words were exchanged at first, but as the warmth and the food began to ease their discomfort, Brande had questions he needed to ask. The feeling of urgency in him felt like strangulation. Fia and Aithne could not wait.

"You are a cousin to Silas?"

The hunchback, Alland, nodded. "Yes, several years his younger."

Brande had first assumed the hunchback to be older, but his disfigured face aged him. Alland held his head at a slight angle, stooped and crooked, because of the hump on his back. Alland spoke before Brande could ask his next question. "I know I look older, but I did not always. I was a good-looking young man. I was blond then. Now I have this matt black hair. I was tall and muscular, not unlike your friend." He nodded towards Eberhard. "I was as beautiful as my sister and women loved me." His squinting features twisted, which Brande took to be a forlorn smile.

"So he says," broke in Githa. "He was not as beautiful as me." She laughed as if this was an old joke between them. Brande could not deny she was beautiful. She reminded him of someone, but he couldn't think who.

"And now I am this," sighed Alland, splaying his hands wide open and taking in his whole form with a gesture.

Githa became solemn. "It's true. He and I are twins."

Brande's eyebrows raised in unhidden surprise.

"You say little, Brande. But I understand. It makes no sense. You see, I was born beautiful, like Githa, but a Deft attack left me looking like this."

Brande sighed. "I fought in the Crusades." By this, he meant he had seen things like this before.

"Good, then, like us, you must hate the Deft."

Brande shrugged. "I have fought for that cause, yes. Yet, did not your brother Silas dabble in such affairs?"

"Nachmair's tits, he hated everything to do with it!" stormed Alland.

"When I met him, he was with cultists in Dankwood."

The cultists had captured Silas, but Brande wanted to test how much these two knew about him.

"Those thieves and fools?" spat Alland. "Did he fall in with them? They raid villages and attack travellers. Scum."

Brande thought back to those thieves and fools and the torture they had inflicted on him and the revenge he had meted out as he escaped. "There are less of them since they met me," he said, in a voice that revealed his contempt for them. "Silas came with me. It was during our escape that he was bitten by a wolf."

"I cannot believe he would have joined them," said Githa, although she sounded unsure.

"He was forced to. Tortured."

Githa put her hand to her mouth. "When you met him, was he hurt?"

"No, he was in rude health. As I said before, he wore a chain around his neck holding a piece of wood. He was soon to be accepted properly into their ranks. But he told me he always intended to escape when he could. It wouldn't have been easy. Tell me, did he have any other family?"

"A daughter," said Alland. "Alani. Soldiers killed her mother and took her. We went after them with Silas. We became separated. We didn't know what had befallen him in the forest, although we started to piece the story together as we tracked him here." Brande felt there was something rehearsed about Alland's answer, but he couldn't put his finger on why it lacked authenticity.

Githa seemed about to say something, hesitated, then spoke anyway. "Where is he now?"

Brande pursed his lips, debating what to tell them. He opted for the truth. "He was caged," he said, pointing back the way they had come. "A friendly traveller released him, but the bite he had sustained was infected. He'd become rabid. He turned on the traveller. They killed each other."

"Were the bodies removed?" asked Githa.

"Only by night animals," said Brande, avoiding details.

She lowered her eyes. Alland was looking at him intently. "Are you saying he's nearby?"

Brande shook his head. "I'm saying there is nothing left of him."

Githa moaned quietly, imagining the result. She hung her head, her fair hair falling to cover her face.

Alland nodded grimly. "Dark talk is best kept for daylight."

"I agree," said Brande. "Where are you headed now?"

"Silas may be gone, but little Alani may still be alive. We will go with you in your pursuit of Lance Company."

"Lance Company?" Brande had not known the king's men were from Lance Company. He had heard of them. They were selected from the finest of the King's soldiers and famous for their bravery and chivalry. How strange that they were now raiding the King's own villages.

Brande grunted his appreciation of Alland's offer to join them.

"People are starting to realise this isn't just some party of Skulluns raiding them," explained Githa. "It's their own king. Worse, some of the men in the Company are Deft. People are angry, they're ready to rise up!"

"Careful, Githa. That sounded a little like treason," warned Alland. He rested a gentle hand on her shoulder.

"If we can't trust him, brother, who can we trust?" She paused. "He was a friend to Silas. He has family at stake. He fought in the Crusades." She looked at Brande. "You want to rescue your wife and daughter, but there's a bigger picture! A rebellion is underway, and we plan to be part of it. We have connections in Charstoke."

"That's how you came by these packhorses?"

"Yes, an Elderman leant them to us, and we are returning with news from-" She looked at Alland, obviously questioning if she was telling too much after all.

Alland sneered, "The Deft have already ruined my life. Look at me. I'm deformed. I intend to get my revenge."

Brande saw something new in them, then. As he had suspected, there was more to them than met the eye. They were right that he only wanted to rescue Fia and Aithne, but his aims did correspond with theirs, and they would be useful allies.

"What's the old saying?" he asked.

"The enemy of my enemy is my friend," suggested Githa.

"My priority is my family, but our purposes are aligned. Let's travel together. Assist one another. You say you have a contact in Charstoke?"

Githa gave a firm nod. "We do."

"That could prove useful. First, though, I am going to Stonenife. Aithne and Fia may still be there."

Githa nodded her consent. "We'll come with you. Now, Brande, you should get some sleep until the sun is up and we can make our way."

He agreed. He got to his feet a little unsteadily. Exhaustion wore upon him. He shook out the blanket Githa gave him and knelt down on it.

Eberhard was tending to Aldway. "How is he?" asked Brande.

"Same."

Brande lay down. He thought he heard Eberhard ask him a question, but the moment his head touched the blanket he was asleep.

Brande felt weak but knew he could go on. His wounds were healing. Eberhard, equally, seemed to have been restored by the food and the ability to stretch out and sleep. This morning, he had spent his time monitoring Aldway who still looked unwell. Eberhard looked after his partner tenderly, but also stoically. Aldway groaned almost continuously and kept his eyes closed as if the dawn of the new day displeased him.

They all agreed it was best to get moving again. They helped Aldway up into a saddle. He wore the blanket about him, occasionally complaining he was still cold. His head hung low, and his skin looked grey. Githa led the horse. The others walked alongside, apart from Alland who found walking long distances painful due to the misalignment of his bones, so he took the other horse.

Brande felt buoyed by his new travelling companions. Just a few hours out of the cage and he was starting to feel better. Food, drink and the ability to stretch were enough to start his body mending. Somehow having a weapon tucked into his belt brought life back to him, even if it was just a small hand axe.

They travelled slowly and spoke of mundane things, but all had grim thoughts on their minds. Light conversation did not come easily. After a while, Brande brought the discussion back to the matters at hand and asked, "When they took Alani from Silas, were you there?"

Alland looked to Githa as if making sure she was paying attention. "No. We pursued them after they left his hometown of Lakeside. There was a skirmish. A few of us escaped with our lives. They're like a pestilence, sweeping the land, taking all that is good, destroying all that remains."

"Yes," agreed Brande. They walked on in silence for a while, then he asked, "When did they do this to you?"

"My disfigurement? Many years ago. A group of Deft cultists attacked our village. There was much fighting. Much destruction. They wielded power like it was nothing to them. I got caught in it. This happened."

"What did it look like?"

Alland shrugged. "The man held up his hands. A grey light poured out. I felt pain and blacked out. When I woke up, I was told my body had writhed on the floor until it was misshapen." He finished by spitting toward the side of the road.

"Does it hurt now?"

"No, but it is not comfortable. Why so curious?"

"I fought against such power during the Crusades. It is not the darkest magic, but it is along that path."

"You've seen worse?"

Brande nodded. He thought about how to describe some of the things he'd seen. "I have seen power drawn from the Rift amidst unspeakable acts of cruelty performed in the name of Nachmair. I have a suspicion these acolytes are drawing their power this way."

Alland shuddered. "Then they all must die."

Brande's rumbling stomach told him it was well past lunchtime. They had just arrived at the outskirts of Stonenife, the last walled town before the capital of Charstoke. They looked up at a watchtower and saw a soldier standing guard. Next to him, there stood a figure in a dark cloak.

"We'll not find allies here," said Brande.

They had stopped by a watermill. It was a crisp, clear day. Birds sang in the trees, and the soothing sound of water rushing past would have been relaxing to any other travelling party. Warm sunlight from clear skies made for a picturesque day, although the wind had a chill in it.

Eberhard was tending to Aldway. He had been asleep but was now sat up on his horse. He finally seemed to be recovering.

"I can hear something," warned Alland. They were out of sight of the main road in their present position, so they waited. Soon they saw a procession of horses and soldiers making their way along the road from the west and into the welcoming gates of Stonenife. "Well," said Alland, ruefully, "looks like the King has several companies out ransacking the villages of his own countryfolk. I'd hoped it was just Lance Company, but no."

Brande grunted. "That means there will be a lot of

prisoners in there. Aithne and Fia are probably in there too. Alani might be in there. Are we going in? What are we waiting for?"

"You're right, Brande," said Githa, "We've no time to waste. Let's go. It looks like this place hasn't put up much of a fight. The soldiers are using it as a rendezvous point before heading to the capital. Stonenife is a big place. I think we'll be able to get in easily."

"For all we know, those men on the gate are the ones who put us in cages. We need to be careful," cautioned Eberhard.

"We'll split up," she said. "We'll be less suspicious if we travel independently."

Brande had expected as much.

"We'll meet up at nightfall, by the hermitage," she instructed.

Brande patted the axe in his belt. "I'll go first."

Brande had been to Stonenife before. It didn't take him long to find the garrison, where he expected the prisoners were being kept. As he approached its tall wooden walls, he could hear the telltale sound of the prisoners moaning and weeping. He heard harsh voices and thought he heard the crack of a whip.

There were soldiers everywhere and no obvious way in. He slunk into the shadows and watched the entrance. At one point, he saw Githa go past, maybe looking for him, but he kept out of sight. He hadn't made his way to their rendezvous point by the hermitage, and they would wonder where he was, but he didn't have that sort of time to waste. He would keep watch and seize the first opportunity that came along. He would free Fia and Aithne. At this point, after all he'd endured, everyone else could go hang. Alland and Githa's little rebellion meant nothing to him. Their friendship was valuable, to some extent, but their motives were suspect. He was better on his own. He would draw less attention and be more effective.

He slumped himself down in a corner, near a drain, like some down-on-his-luck beggar. It wasn't a good begging spot, almost no one saw him and those that did ignored him. Some tossed him a scowl, but none tossed any coins. He looked the part, though, in his tattered clothing and with days of pain and exposure on his face. Night began to fall, and he knew, if he waited, sooner or later, an opportunity would arise.

He was not surprised to hear rowdy voices approaching the garrison entrance from inside. Soldiers who had just arrived that day would want to go and find a brothel and the local taverns. He heard them approach and noted the mixture of accents. One booming voice seemed to be in charge. What emerged disturbed him. There were twenty soldiers, most wearing swords. Three young women with sacks over their heads and with their hands tied were dragged behind them on ropes. The men were rowdy, their voices high and merry. Brande was half-convinced several of them were already drunk. He pulled back into his hiding place, and they didn't notice him as they went past. One stopped to take a piss, and Brande smiled. An opportunity had presented itself.

"Don't dally," called one of his comrades.

"Whose dallying?" boomed a voice from the front of the procession.

"Sergeant Major, it's Private Natt, sir. He's taking a piss."

The garrison's sergeant major was taking a few of them for a night out on the town. No doubt more would follow later. He believed several companies had descended on Stonenife on their way to Charstoke. It was a favourite place to stop over, full of gambling dens, brothels and several notorious places to drink.

He caught a glimpse of the sergeant major. He was a

large fellow, not unusually tall but broad and rotund, with a ruddy complexion and clumsy features. He had a big nose, large ears, fat lips and greasy brown hair. He swaggered as he walked, clearly the big cheese around here.

The soldiers carried on out of sight. The garrison gates had been shut behind them. There was no visible guard stationed outside the garrison now that night had fallen. Brande found himself looking at the back of a soldier pissing on the garrison wall, letting his urine flow down a shallow drain in front of it. They were alone.

The soldier was just shaking the last drops away when a large, strong arm closed around his neck. He tried to shout, but the world was going black, and he had no breath. The ground disappeared beneath his feet, and he was lifted up. He could see what was happening more than feel it. He grabbed on to the arm and tried to turn his head to free his windpipe. Suddenly, he was on his back, and something cold was pressing against his exposed penis.

"Feel that?" asked Brande. "Cold metal against your Johnson? That's my axe. Now, you are going to answer some of my questions, or you'll go from having a John-son to having a John-daughter. Understand?"

The soldier nodded, but the look on his face suggested he was angry and waiting for an opportunity to strike.

"Simmer down," growled Brande, and pressed the axe down more firmly. The man squirmed but didn't move or speak.

"The first thing I want to know is: where did your company travel from?"

"Bruke," replied the soldier through gritted teeth. "What's it to you?"

"Second question. Where are the women and children you kidnapped?"

"In the garrison," said the man, guessing Brande already knew the answer.

"This is going well, isn't it?" Brande smiled. "Now, the

third thing I want to know is where you are taking them."

"It's common knowledge," smirked the soldier, thinking he'd got one over on him. "Charstoke."

Brande continued, without a pause. "What happens when they get there?"

"I don't know."

"I see," said Brande, grimly. "Well, that's your first wrong answer."

"Really, I don't know."

Brande growled, turning the axe handle to let the cold metal press into the soldier's crotch, so he didn't forget it was there.

"It's true," protested the soldier. "We have orders. We've done it before. We drop 'em off. Don't know what happens to 'em."

"That's why it was the wrong answer," said Brande, levelly. "No man should be kidnapping women and children without knowing what happens to them. Tell me, what do you think happens to them?"

"Well, you know…" The soldier smirked.

"Bearing in mind you have my wife and child," added Brande.

The soldier's face went blank. He stared at him, suddenly lost for words.

"Do tell me," said Brande, "what you think happens to those little children, those young girls and those women?"

"I… I think…" said the soldier.

"Is it something good?"

"Well, no, I…"

"Wait. You're handing them over for a purpose you suspect isn't good? Careful now."

The soldier knew he was beaten. "Just following orders."

"Yes, following orders," growled Brande. "Now, you're going to trot along and be sure not tell anyone you saw me, right?"

The soldier hesitated, looking confused and not believing his luck. He'd just begun to nod eagerly when Brande spoke again. "One last question." He grimaced. "Did you come across a girl called Fia? She has short dark hair, and she's from Bruton. She escaped but got captured again."

"Oh, escaped near Bruke?"

"That's right."

"Yeah, know the name. Heard it. Sergeant Major took an interest in her. She your daughter?" He grinned menacingly, realising he suddenly had something to use against his assailant.

"That's right."

"She's one of them ones with the sack on their heads. Better hurry if you want to catch her." He laughed. "Can I go now?"

"I guess so."

"Get your axe off my cock then," he spat.

"Don't worry. I'm not going to chop it off. That would be nasty. And tell who you want about me, I don't expect you to keep a secret."

"Then get the fuck off me," shouted the soldier, trying to sit up and edge away from Brande's axe.

"But I do expect you to die slowly."

The soldier flinched. Brande struck hard at the man's throat with the edge of his hand, taking his breath away. He watched the soldier's bulging eyes trace the hand axe as he lifted it and brought it down into the man's stomach. The man spluttered. Brande made sure the axe head was well sunk into the soldier's gut and lodged against his ribs, then used it to drag him down a nearby alley. The soldier grabbed the axe handle, trying to prevent the blade ripping through him. When Brande dumped him in a dark corner, the soldier barely moved. Blood ran from his mouth, and his intestines trailed down by his feet.

Brande patted him down. He found a small bag

containing just two coins. He took it. He was no thief, but he had nothing against equipping himself for what lay ahead. If he was going to a tavern, he might just need to buy a drink. He considered whether he should put the man out of his misery, but after a few nights in a skyte's cage, his compassion was nonexistent.

He upped and left. If Fia was with those men, he had a chance of rescuing her tonight. He could still hear the garrison sergeant major and his rowdy men in the distance, and he could guess where they were headed. He jogged after them. Time was not on his side. They could not have good intentions towards those girls.

CHAPTER ELEVEN

Brande sat himself down at the bar. The tavern was busy. He disliked being amongst so many people. He had drawn a few stares on the way in. It was to be expected. He had a bruised face, his clothes were torn and soiled, and he looked like he had just come in from an abattoir. The reason he didn't draw more attention was that he wasn't the only one that looked like that. Plenty of the off-duty soldiers were no better off. They had evidently met resistance in some of the towns and villages they'd sacked and still bore the signs of it.

The tavern was called The Black Bull. Soldiers came here. Men of the town came here. Many travellers came here too. They were used to strangers in Stonenife. Everyone seemed to be drunk already, which suited him fine. Let them sing, shout, swear, drink and fight. He had his wits about him.

As he'd entered, he'd just caught sight of the sergeant major leading the girls upstairs. They didn't struggle, just stumbled along, blindfolded by the sacks over their heads. He couldn't tell if one of them was Fia.

He didn't have to wait long before he saw the men come back downstairs. From what he could tell, they must have tied up the girls, presumably each in a different room. The sergeant major sauntered over to the bar and loudly ordered a drink. He exchanged pleasantries with the barkeep for a while, noisily quaffing his ale while the man took his turn speaking, and they laughed raucously at their own jokes. The landlord had a massive smile on his fat face. The tavern was crammed, full of soldiers and locals. Business had never been better.

A band on a raised platform in one corner of the room struck up a jaunty number on their instruments. Two men played lutes, a lady played a pipe, and a young man banged a drum. Brande hated all of it. He thought he had left all this behind him. He had forged a good life, an honest living, working hard and finding a use for his hands that didn't involve killing. How had it come to this?

The music must have had some effect on him because he suddenly remembered dancing with Aithne one Nachmair's Night in the local inn in Bruton. Nachmair's Night was the one night of the year when tradition demanded that vice was celebrated and people went wild. He had walked over to her and offered his hand, requesting a dance. She had seemed a little reluctant at first but later admitted that she had been playing hard to get. He had felt confident, though, as she had been flirting with him with her smoky eyes from across the room.

There had always been something about her, some foreign element that made her stand out from the other women of the village. All at once, she seemed unobtainable and mysterious, like some will-o-the-wisp, yet she glowed with an inner strength that made her feel more real than anyone around her. Even though she'd lived in Bruton her whole life, there was something worldly about her that Brande recognised in himself.

He enjoyed the settled life he had created for himself,

but she provided something missing, something he wanted to cling to in himself, a passion, something like wildfire. It was like wildfire that they danced. The music got faster and faster, they danced and span and laughed, and the night went on and on.

The morning broke with her in his arms and a ray of sunlight piercing through the window and lighting up the small wooden figurines on his mantelpiece. He gave one to her as she left. She smiled at the gift but rejected it, momentarily upsetting him until she added, "I'll be back for it tonight." She swirled away into the day and, true to her word, that night, she returned and became his Aithne. His strong, dark, intelligent, fearsome Aithne. He missed every single thing about her.

Suddenly the music stopped, and people began shouting for more of their favourites. He was back in The Black Bull, refocused on his deadly purpose. One of those girls had been Fia, their child. He had to find a way to get upstairs without bringing every soldier in the place down on his head.

He moved over to the stairs, knowing he wouldn't be allowed up if he hadn't paid. The door to the tavern opened and shut, letting in a blast of cold air. He didn't look over. It had been doing that a lot.

The sergeant major was by the bar, talking and laughing with the landlord. He was drinking ale like he had to slake a thirst he'd had for days. The fat landlord chuckled at something the soldier said, and he gestured to the stairs. Brande watched them, knowing time was running out.

He could imagine how it worked. The King wanted women and children, but he had no idea how many were taken so a few would slip through the net and get sold as slaves or whored out by the hour. He didn't let his imagination run away with itself, because it could be Fia up there and he wasn't going to allow it to get to that stage. He knew all he needed to. There were three girls upstairs and the soldier he hurt, Private Natt, said one of them was his daughter. He was going to rescue her. He felt bad for the other two, but he wasn't here to change the world, just to save his family.

It seemed strange that no one was going near the stairs. If he did climb them, he would be conspicuous. Similarly, while no one else was upstairs, he hoped no harm was coming to the girls. It seemed unlikely that situation would last long.

He looked around the room full of people. They were mostly men, because of the proportion of soldiers, but there were plenty of women and a number of serving girls too. Some were innocent, most not, he decided. Deep inside him, he seethed. These people were just going to let it happen. He kept that anger there and fanned the flames of it. Still, he carried on observing.

Pretending to look out of a window, he edged to the foot of the stairs. There was a strange oasis of stillness and emptiness around the foot of the stairs. No one wanted to look like they might be about to head up without permission. That told him a lot. There was danger here for anyone who broke the rules. He needed a plan. He looked up. Once up there, there was a door directly at the top of the stairs. The corridor disappeared left and right. He could open the door on either of those rooms without being seen, but not the one at the top of the stairs.

He needed something to distract the inn's occupants so he could get up there.

"Looking for someone?" asked a female voice.

He expected a prostitute but found Githa.

"You have blood on your hands," she said.

"I needed some answers."

She turned to face him, her face both beautiful and terrifying. "Why did you not meet us at the hermitage at nightfall?"

He repeated himself, "I needed some answers." His

voice was gruff, hiding how glad he was to see her.

She looked into his eyes, searching for something, perhaps the truth of it, or an indication of just what he had been up to. After a moment, she shrugged. "No matter. What are you doing?"

"Three girls upstairs," he said. He lowered his voice, but there was no need to whisper because of the general hubbub and the band playing. "One is Fia. I need to get up there."

"Difficult," she acknowledged.

"Where are the others?"

"Alland is outside, in case of trouble approaching. Your two went to steal some weapons."

She meant Eberhard and Aldway. He acknowledged this with an affirmative grunt. "How do I get up there?"

She looked around the tavern. "If something bad happened to the band, that would give you a moment or two."

"It would at that," he said, appreciating her suggestion. "Any ideas?"

She winked at him. "Just get ready to run."

"The garrison sergeant major and the landlord mustn't see me," he warned.

She looked at him solemnly. "Trust me, I've got this."

Brande watched her slink across the busy room. She was young, with everything going for her. She was tall, slim, blonde, but there something about her that screamed warrior. He liked her, and, moreover, he trusted her. His eyes weren't the only ones watching her. She walked deliberately past the sergeant major, rolling her hips, and drew his gaze. She turned, flicking her hair, and winked at him. She then stumbled, seemingly by accident. There was a cry as she grabbed someone's arm and their flagon went tumbling across the floor. The sergeant major and the landlord both moved to help her, but as she stood up, she punched the man closest to her and grabbed his drink, throwing it at the landlord. There was uproar. Everyone's eyes were on her. Brande froze for the briefest of moments, wondering what in Nachmair's name she planned to do next. She drew her dagger and threw it. It hit one of musicians square in the chest and stuck there. He looked down at it with dismay and staggered backwards, stumbling over his chair.

Brande didn't stay to watch the pandemonium unfold. He had no idea how Githa hoped to rescue herself from the situation. She was likely to get herself killed, but she had certainly done her job. He was halfway up the stairs in one bound. No one would be looking his way.

He darted left down the corridor and threw the door open. A girl was tied to a bed, the sack still on her head. He could see her long brown hair jutting out from under it. She heard him enter and squirmed, but he closed the door before she could scream. He darted along to the other side. He threw open the door, and the girl in there was naked, tied to the bed, and crying. She took one look at him and screamed. She had long red hair. Not his daughter. He slammed the door shut, cursing his bad luck. The noise downstairs continued. He heard a window smash and a woman screaming. He hoped it wasn't Githa, although suspected it was.

The third room was at the top of the stairs and visible from the ground floor. If anyone looked up, they would see him enter. It was time to take the risk. He dashed for it.

Inside, he found a slender girl tied to the bed. He rushed over and pulled the sack from her head. She screamed and buried her head in her arms and chest, trying to keep away from him. Her short dark hair was all he could see. He grabbed her face and turned it to him, saying, "Fia, it's me! It's your father!"

She looked at him in bemusement and fear. It wasn't Fia.

All too suddenly, he realised his mistake. So eager was

he to hear news of his daughter that he hadn't picked up on the fact that Private Natt had been making fun of him. Of course his daughter wasn't one of these three. It was a fiction designed to make him hurry away after her. It was so obviously a lie designed to rile him.

She screamed with mighty lungs for one so small. It was a wonder every person in the tavern didn't freeze on the spot. The door behind him was ajar. He just had to get out now. He just had to run. If he got caught, he would be mincemeat.

He threw open the door and hurtled towards the stairs. He hadn't been as quick or as inconspicuous as he'd hoped. The sergeant major was already climbing the stairs with two of his cronies, no, three, four, right behind him. They were falling into place as quickly as he could count them. "Who are you?" yelled the fat man, his face beetroot red and spittle forming on his thick lips.

Brande looked up. He couldn't see Githa. Most people were pushing and shoving to get out of the tavern, although not the soldiers who had arrived with their sergeant major. They had seen their commanding officer head for the stairs and were ready to back him up and protect their assets.

Brande was trapped at the top of the stairs. He couldn't go down, and the sergeant major couldn't come up. Fia wasn't here, and to Brande, this was now a waste of time. This wasn't his fight. He was in trouble, and it wasn't going to help Fia or Aithne one bit if he won here. He pulled the axe from his belt.

A soldier charged up the stairs, past the sergeant major. The stairs were narrow and fell off sharply at one side. The soldier jabbed his sword point-first at Brande, but Brande knocked it away with the head of his axe. Another soldier was close behind and tried to stab at Brande's ankles. He attempted to climb further up, thinking the other soldier had Brande's full attention. Brande brushed another attack away with his axe. The clanging metal had everyone's attention. It wasn't going to be easy to fight his way out of this one.

He considered other exits. Could he jump from a room to the ground outside? He saw people were still trying to leave the inn, but they didn't seem to be able to get out. He wondered what was blocking them, but he didn't have time to dwell on it. He was pushed back up the stairs by the soldiers' swords.

He knocked aside the sword being thrust at him and then kicked out, catching the lower soldier in the head. He tumbled off the stairs. The momentary distraction gave Brande the opening he needed to hack at the first soldier's shoulder. The man screamed and fell backwards, his arm hanging severed and useless.

The sergeant major growled. It was guttural and feral. "You'll pay for that, scum. I am Sergeant Major Pith. You may have heard of me. I am not known for my mercy."

"Fought in the Crusades?" asked Brande, judging the man old enough.

"That's right." His eyes narrowed.

"Then you may have heard of me. I was Major General Brande, and I was not known for showing mercy either." He made sure only the sergeant major heard him. Brande watched the man's mouth slowly start to gape as understanding dawned.

Brande had the advantage of being elevated. Another soldier pushed past to defend his sergeant major, but Brande was ready. He knocked the man's sword to the wall then swung his axe round at the man's head. As the axe struck, he snatched the falling sword from the man's hand and kicked him off the stairs.

He swapped the weapons in his hands, the sword in his dominant right hand while the axe remained a useful off-hand weapon. He looked up to see the sergeant major edging away. He wasn't sure if it was his name or that he had just despatched three soldiers that made the man wary, but Brande was determined to press his advantage. A handful of soldiers now waited for him at the bottom of the narrow stairs.

"You are him," growled Sergeant Major Pith. "I saw you once. I recognise you. You're a wanted man." He had managed to back down to the bottom of the stairs, and his men went ahead of him, eager to show their mettle.

"Wait. I remember him!" shouted a tall soldier from the back. "You were the father of that girl that ran away near Bruke."

Brande's heart sank. Now they knew his purpose, it increased the danger that Fia was in. He didn't wait to hear more. Anger that should have already been bubbling began to rise up in him from hidden depths. His gut churned with it. He roared and threw himself down the stairs, one shoulder scraping along the wall, pushing his opponents precariously close to the edge of the stairs. His sword deflected blows while his axe cleaved two throats with one wild swing. He fought. He saw the sergeant major getting closer, but his men were all around Brande already. The crowd in the inn, their lust for blood already strong, turned on him. He fought with his axe, using the sword to defend himself. His back was to the wall, and he stepped left, then right, dodging attacks and hacking at those who got too close. Men started to pile up at his feet, some dead, most screaming in agony as he took them apart.

He was outnumbered, but hadn't he always been? He would happily fight to the end but for the fact that he needed to escape and find his family. He swung out wildly with his axe, catching an oil lamp on the wall. Flaming oil splashed through the air and splattered on a chair and a wall hanging. The wood was old and the fabric dry. They quickly caught alight and flames leapt into being. People jumped to attend to them. The barkeep called out in alarm. Fire in a wooden building was a dangerous business, and it took some of the attention away from him.

A surge of people came back in through the tavern's front door. At first, he thought they were coming for him, but they seemed to be pushed back by some force. A moment later, Eberhard stood in the doorway, his tall, muscular frame filling the space, a longsword held by both hands. He swung it easily, and the arc of his blade took the head off the soldier who was right in front of him. Aldway was right behind him, a crossbow in one hand. He loosed a bolt and people scattered. He dived into the space they left. The dagger at his waist appeared to spend an equal amount of time in his belt and in his hand as he tried to fit a bolt to the crossbow while striking out to carve a hole in the crowd. Brande appreciated their assistance. He almost smiled.

Sergeant Major Pith barked orders, ushering his men forward. Brande found himself faced with the dual danger of five armed men and flames flickering up the wall behind him. He heard a scream and saw a red-haired girl at the top of the stairs. She had freed herself. She saw the lie of things and ran off into one of the other rooms.

Flames flickered through the air again. Githa was back in the tavern and smashing lamps all around the room while the barkeep screamed obscenities at her. Eberhard was still in the doorway, now facing the other way to stop people entering. Brande hacked at the soldiers before him, and blood flew. Aldway joined him.

"Head out," yelled Githa. "The fire is spreading." They moved toward the door as one.

Sergeant Major Pith was standing near the bar, barking orders. He hadn't yet got involved in the fighting. "Coward," growled Brande. The axe swapped hands again, and he threw it. It arced through the air and landed with a thud in the sergeant major's leg. He yelled and collapsed backwards, falling on his arse. He attempted to pull the weapon free, but it was embedded deeply, and he screamed.

Black smoke began to fill the air. The barkeep was

making his way out of a back door behind the bar. Brande signalled to Aldway to follow him and finish him.

Pith had managed to remove the axe and was standing, holding on to the bar for support. He held the weapon in one hand. He turned and shouted at Brande, "You're here for your daughter, aren't you? She's here in Stonenife, all right."

Brande marched over. Pith swung the axe at him, but he grabbed the soldier's arm in mid-strike and held it firmly. He placed his sword against the man's throat.

"Hurry Brande!" yelled Githa. "The fire is spreading fast!"

Brande slid the sword slowly along the side of Pith's throat, drawing blood. Pith snarled and leapt forward, trying to bite him. It took Brande by surprise. They fell together, under Pith's weight, and the axe clattered against the bar and got hooked there, leaving their grasp as they dropped to the ground. Pith landed on top of Brande. They punched and kicked at each other, and somehow Pith got a foot on Brande's arm and forced him to drop the sword. Brande landed a punch, and the soldier fell away.

Brande stood and grabbed a bottle from the bar. He smashed the end of it, creating a jagged weapon. He lunged forward and dug it into Pith's neck before he had a chance to reorient himself. Brande saw red. "You have my daughter?"

Pith could barely speak. The bottle had struck an inch into the side of his throat but missed his windpipe. "She's here," he sneered, alcohol and anger preventing him from appreciating the injury he'd just sustained.

"That's all I needed to know."

The fat man laughed, despite the blood squirting from his neck. "She's been sharing my bed. A right little-" Brande twisted the bottle, opening the man's throat. Arterial blood spurted all over Brande. The man seemed to laugh as he choked on his own lifeblood. He knew he'd upset Brande.

The smile faded as he dropped to the ground, his head colliding with a stool on the way down.

Brande grabbed the axe from the bar and turned to realise the tavern had emptied. He ran for the exit, black smoke stinging his eyes. His companions were outside, fighting for their lives. The hunchbacked Alland had a mace, and he swung it left to right, scattering anyone attempting to get near. Githa was standing back, her face covered in blood. She was blinking and wiping it from her eyes, trying to ready herself to fight again.

"What now?" called Alland.

"Trouble!" replied Aldway, seeing soldiers approaching from various directions. Presumably, the garrison was emptying as soldiers came to sort out the troublemakers. Brande turned to see fire engulf the tavern. He hoped the girls had managed to escape through a window on the first floor. The noise and flames would be seen and heard across the whole town. He didn't much care.

Aithne's face flashed before him. He did care. He had to. Not caring took him back to who he was during the Crusades, and he was no longer that person. Aithne had stopped him being that person.

Githa rushed forward, swung her sword and executed a soldier with one strike. She jumped back and let Alland take over again. Her face was bleeding. Brande realised she must have cut it jumping through the glass window as she escaped the building after creating a diversion for him. She was brave. "Your face?" he called to her, wondering just how injured she was.

She glanced over at him. "I guess Alland is the good looking one now," she laughed, ruefully.

The heat of the fire consuming the inn drove them away from it.

Three soldiers rounded a nearby building and pointed at them. "There they are! Get them!" It was hardly an inspired battle cry. Brande rushed in with just his hand axe. They had swords and leather armour. He brought his axe around through the first soldier's helmet and skull, where it stuck fast. Brande swung the man around by the handle in his head, using him as a shield against the slashing sword of the second man. In an instant, he had the man's sword out of his grasp. He turned it on his attacker and struck.

One man now knelt before him with an axe in his head. A second fell to the ground with a sword wound in his gut. "You'll die, bastard!" screamed the third, charging at him. Brande's sword swung up in a perfect arc, catching the third man right under his chin. He stepped backwards, tipping over his heels. His flailing sword narrowly missed Brande's crotch. Brande stepped forward and finished him off by plunging his sword through the man's chest. It was child's play, but something at the back of his mind screamed at him to remember that this wasn't who he was anymore. He shouldn't be doing this. He would regress to who he had once been.

"We need to split," shouted Aldway. They were outnumbered. The townsfolk had chosen a side, and it wasn't theirs. There was no way his merry little band could defeat an entire town. Brande accepted the decision.

From nowhere, Githa was next to him. "Did you free your daughter?"

"It was a lie," he explained quickly. "She wasn't there." A peasant who had just emerged from a nearby house charged Brande with a homemade sickle, the curved blade passing inches in front of his face as he pulled back from it. Brande ran his sword through the man's guts, regretting having to do so.

Half the street was joining in.

"This is getting out of hand," shouted Eberhard. "Let's go."

Brande was armed with axe and sword again. He threw the axe at a man's face. A bad throw, it hit handle-first, but it gave the man pause for thought. He staggered backwards, clutching his bruised face. A short, angry man wielding a dagger lunged for Brande, thinking him distracted. "Die, outsider!" He didn't make it far. He dropped to the floor with a crossbow bolt in his gut. Brande raised a hand of thanks without looking round to see where Aldway was positioned. He approached the man whose face he bruised with the thrown axe and ran the sword through his shoulder. He had no desire to kill townsfolk, but he would happily put people who attacked him out of action.

It was turning into a bloodbath. This wasn't the approach he had hoped to take. It didn't help him rescue Fia or Aithne.

He looked about him and found that Aldway and Eberhard were long gone. Alland was fighting his way out with Githa at his side. She despatched the man she was fighting with swift, unerring moves, then turned and ran. Alland crushed a man's skull with his flail. Soldiers were approaching him. He turned and ran too, making good speed despite his limp.

Brande now faced a street full of angry onlookers and about fifteen soldiers. This wasn't a fight he wanted to pick. These townsfolk were trying to quell a disturbance they didn't understand, and the soldiers were just grunts.

His way was blocked, so he ran for the tavern. It was crazy because the building was ablaze, but he knew they wouldn't follow. Inside was a furnace. He could feel the heat singeing the hairs on his face and head as he ran into it. Sight was almost impossible because of the temperature and the smoke. He ran, trying not to breathe. Moments later and the place would have been an inferno, utterly impregnable. He leapt up to where the band members had been. The dead one still lay there, a dagger in his chest.

He jumped through the glassless window through which Githa had previously exited, snagging his sleeve on the jagged glass but not injuring himself. He landed outside. No one wanted to be trapped in a narrow alleyway next to a burning building, so the way was clear. He hoped they would assume he was dead. The townsfolk would soon realise their more pressing priority was the burning building and would start to fetch buckets of water to help prevent the fire spreading. He could hear the town bell clanging away, warning people of the danger and calling them to assist.

Brande heard a hue and cry and realised he'd been spotted. Looking over his shoulder, he saw it was so. He'd merely bought himself a head start. He was tired, his muscles ached, his heart was pounding, his spirit was heavy with the thought of all this time wasted, but he ran off at full speed. Each turn, he darted down the quietest route.

He was pursued relentlessly. People saw him, pointed and shouted to assist their fellow townsfolk. Men came out of their houses and saw him, ran after him, called to their friends. He felt that he may have taken on too much this time. He could not defeat a town united against him.

He dashed between two buildings, treading through sewage that had been tossed out. He slipped and slid, but stayed upright. The smell was atrocious. He pressed on and found himself in the back garden of some landowner's estate. There was a hole in the ground. A square hole. He looked into it, hopeful. Was it a sewer? It seemed unlikely. Just a cesspit.

He looked around, realising he was temporarily alone and this was his only chance. "Shit," he grumbled. He had a split second to make the decision, and he took it. He jumped in, feet first. It was deep. Too deep. He felt himself submerge under the effluence and his eyes, ears and nose all filled with it. He coughed, and that was a mistake. His mouth filled with it. He couldn't breathe. The sides of the pit were straight and flat. He scrabbled against them, trying to find any kind of purchase to pull himself up. His eyes were screwed shut, he started to see lights dancing in front of them. He saw Aithne's face, Fia's face. He saw their little home in Bruton. He saw their fireplace. He saw the delicate wooden figurines above it. He saw himself picking one up and giving it to Fia. It was her birthday.

He frantically clawed at the walls all around. Finally, his hand caught onto something. He clung to a single stone that was an inch out of place. He hauled himself up, lifting his body using just the strength in his fingertips. His lungs were burning. He coughed out the mess in his mouth and spat freely. He inhaled a great, stinking lungful of waste gas and air. At least his head was above the surface. He gasped and spluttered. He brought up a hand and wiped what he could from his eyes, which blinked open for a moment, giving him the chance to spot a missing stone higher up that would provide a better handhold.

He was gasping noisily, and he tried to quiet himself because he knew they would still be looking for him, but his lungs hurt and he couldn't stop himself from spluttering in disgust and heaving loudly. His stomach tightened, and he wondered when he would throw up.

It happened. His innards gushed up and out, making it even harder to breathe. At least it removed the foul material in his nose and mouth. He could barely hold on while this was happening, but it took only moments. He puked out green bile, and it burned his throat, and he knew his stomach was empty. The noise would surely have alerted someone to his predicament. He had hoped to hide down here.

He clung on with one hand, his feet sliding against the wall, waist deep in it. He used a hand to wipe the muck from his hair. He wiped his hand on the stone wall of the pit. He blew hard through his nose and gunk ran out and down over his mouth. He could breathe through his nose once more. He wiped at his face again, desperate to free up his senses from complete bombardment.

Finally, he paused to take stock.

He looked around. It was disgusting, but he was safe.

He could hold on here, and breathe, and provided he wasn't found, he could make his getaway at night. He looked up, finally, at the opening above him. Three faces, surrounded by blue and white sky, looked down at him. One of them spat on him. "That one's got a price on his head," the man said. The other two were chuckling.

The first lowered the sharp end of a spear down to him. "Catch on, and we'll lift you up. Unless you'd rather I just spike you through the head like a fish in a barrel?"

Brande had no choice.

CHAPTER TWELVE

This was the second day. It was dark and cold. Brande could see very little. He'd woken in the night again. He cursed out loud.

A droplet of icy water hit him on the back and rolled down his spine. Another drop repeated the journey. Outside, it had begun to rain. He thought the sound of rain must have woken him. It beat against flagstones somewhere above.

He sat with his back against a stone wall. Manacles clamped his wrists and ankles. They had chained his wrists to the wall and his feet to solid brass rings affixed to the ground. He couldn't feel his arms. He tried to move one, and his chains clanked. He groaned. Pain wracked every muscle and joint in his body.

He was naked. They had poured several buckets of water over him, but still he stank. When he'd awoken, he thought he'd crapped himself, but then remembered the cesspit. He still bore the bruises of the beating they'd given him. He'd been barely conscious when they dragged him to this place.

He didn't know what building they had taken him to, but he could tell that the dungeon was below street level. There was a small hole near the ceiling, directly above him. It had a half-circle shape with the flat edge along the base. No daylight came from the hole, so he assumed it was night outside. This is where the sound of the rain came from. And the trickle of water that ran down onto his back. He would soon be sitting in a cold puddle. The temperature in the room dropped. He shuddered.

A slice of silver light, starlight or moonlight, came through the hole affording him just enough light to make out the shape of the dungeon cell, or at least different shades of black. Blackness of varying intensities swam before him making it difficult to judge depth. To his right there was blackness. To his left, there was hazy greyness. He surmised he was closer to the wall on his left than his right. His cold, naked back felt the wall he was lying against. A steady trickle of ice-cold water continued down his back. He shuddered uncontrollably for a moment.

Lightning flashed outside, and he drew a sharp intake of breath. In that instance of half-blindness, he saw the room. It was bigger than he imagined. A bare wall to his left. Ten strides forward and there was no wall, just bars making up the front of the cell. Beyond that, the blank far wall of a corridor. To his right, another wall, maybe ten strides away, and he gasped at what he saw there. A black shape was bundled in the far corner. He had thought he was alone. He blinked, but all was darkness again.

A dullness sat upon his mind. Not despair, because a warrior would fight to the last breath. Not hopelessness, there was always something to be done. But he felt weak. He felt impotent. He had no hope of escape, and it had hardly been any time since he had been trapped in the skyte's cage. Deep inside, somewhere in his gut, somewhere right in the very centre of his being, anger simmered, but it was out of reach and sealed away.

They had thwarted his efforts to rescue Aithne and Fia yet again. All he wanted was to be with his family, and he was sure that was not something anyone in the land had a right to prevent.

"Speak," he demanded, addressing the bundle of black clothes he'd seen in the corner of the room. "Speak!" He thought he heard a light shuffling, but it might have been his imagination.

Brande was quiet. He suspected someone was in there with him. Movement, not accompanied by any clinking sound, suggested the other person was not chained down. That concerned him. When nothing happened after a moment or two, or even after an hour, he decided he must have been mistaken. He needed to think about something else before his imagination ran away with itself.

He allowed himself to remember Aithne, the woman who had captured his heart. She had changed him. Normalised him. He could see her sweet smile and hear her strong voice. She told him of all the goodness in him, and all the good in the world, and all the positive changes he could make. But in this wet hole, chained to the wall, her image was a little bit dimmer than it used to be, her voice a little quieter. It upset him. She failed to prevent the other images that resurfaced, the dark memories of the Crusades.

Brande the Butcher. That's what they had called him. He had once been captured like this before. He had been tied and tortured by a Black Monk, a twisted individual with one eye. The man had done unspeakable things. Brande flinched as he recollected some of them. He always wondered how much of his younger self he had lost during that episode. He had escaped. Two days later, he returned. He returned to murder every last one of those bastard monks. He killed his captors, and he slaughtered their entire community. He singlehandedly annihilated every last man, woman, child, slave and animal. Nothing escaped his wrath. He'd rejoined the Crusade and been celebrated as a hero. After that, what else could he do but keep fighting?

Down here, Aithne seemed distant, and there was no protection from those memories. But she had saved him. She had saved him on more than one occasion, and one of those memories came to him now.

How long had they been together at that point? He was unsure. They had travelled together for months, to the far north and into the western mountains. It had been a hot summer when they set off, and the journey had been wearing on both of them. He endured it for her sake and she for his. They had been very much in love, back before Fia was born. He and Aithne had lived together as husband and wife for a year. He had told her, the night before their wedding, precisely who and what he was. She had been startled, but not surprised. She married him the next day, under a blossoming arch where they held hands and kissed, exchanging vows before her relatives and many of the village folk. For a moment, he was lost in the warm swirl of that memory, smiling to himself in the darkness.

A year later, during a hot summer, she had taken him away. She had heard of a woman who lived remotely in the Strangled Mountains and had once been a Sister of the Stone. The Sisters were individuals with great power and esoteric knowledge. This one had turned renegade and escaped the strict religious regime in which she had grown up. Brande had believed the Sisters a myth, but Aithne insisted they find out for sure. He had been wrong.

Deep in the mountain range, on a hilltop, they found a small hut with a fenced garden where chickens roamed. Brande had expected to meet some kind of haggard old witch, but the woman was far from old and, in a certain way, handsome. She was probably only ten years their elder. She did not welcome them at first, but when Aithne revealed who they were, it became apparent she knew Brande by reputation and her interest was piqued. Aithne explained what they wanted, and the Sister took pity on them and invited them to stay with her. It might have been summer when they set off, but it was autumn when they arrived, and it had been cold on those mountains. She gave them shelter and talked to them, day and night, for a week. Eventually, she acquiesced to Aithne's pleas and agreed to help them.

It had been a starless night. Brande, Aithne, and the woman who would not give up her name went out into the fields and slaughtered a lamb. They dragged it to the top of a peak, so they were in full view of the sky and could see the world all around them. None of them had experience of Rift power, but that is what they summoned that night. It went against everything each of them believed in or had fought for, but they each saw the necessity of it.

"You have a rage in you, Brande," she had said. In the moonlight, her scarred, stern face was as frightening as it was beautiful. Her scars did not hide her kindness. "This incantation will seal that rage in you. It will still be there, but it will be dormant. You will still have the Deft touch, but no longer will you be able to call on it. It will be stowed away. You will be at peace."

"I am no longer a warrior," he said. "I am a family man. I have no need of rage."

She smiled at him. "There is no knowing what the future may hold."

He shook his head. "Take it away. Make it irreversible."

She smiled, but she did not promise. What followed he did not like to think of but, smeared in blood and excrement and on top of that moonlit mountain, the woman who had been a Sister used her Deft powers and arcane knowledge to draw power from the Rift to quash the fire that burned in Brande's belly.

Aithne had brought him there. She had cured him. She had saved him from himself. And he loved her all the more for it.

The warmth of the memory faded, and he found himself

in the cell again, pressed against the hard, stone wall.

Hours passed. The pain kept him from sleep. "Speak," he would say, occasionally, but the man he imagined bundled in the corner never replied. He would have to concede that it was just a pile of dumped rags. The rain was persistent and a comfort to him. It reminded him of where he was and stopped him losing his mind in the darkness. The moon had gone behind a cloud, and the room was pitch black, yet he felt oddly safe for the time being. Apart from that bundle of rags in the corner.

The most significant difference between this prison, and the skyte's cage, he realised, was that he was alone here. Where were his travelling companions? Had they escaped? If they hadn't, there wasn't much hope for them. He could do nothing for them, and they could do nothing for him. There was no chance of passersby offering him release, either, as he'd burnt down the townsfolk's tavern and killed a sergeant major from the garrison. They would not underestimate him again.

He wondered what lay in store for him, and why it hadn't happened already. He dared hope the others had escaped, and his delayed execution was due to resources being redirected towards their capture.

He tugged his chains, seething at his inability to move. He couldn't even stand up. They were taking no chances.

He realised there could really only be one end to all this. There would be no trial. There would be no bail. It was the hangman's noose or burning at the stake for him. He smiled and nodded to himself. Perhaps that would be his fate. Hadn't the witch said Silas would hang and he would burn? She was right so far. Silas had hung in a skyte's cage. Perhaps he would burn. He wondered at that.

He remembered the girls in the tavern and was grateful Fia hadn't been one of them. Although, as a father, he could readily imagine the horror their parents would be feeling, if they were still alive. Anger stirred in him again, biding its time. He could not let harm befall his family. Yet, here he was, chained up.

He was full of guilt. He hoped he had killed so many soldiers and caused so much chaos that they wouldn't think to take revenge on the prisoners nor realise his connection to two of them.

Eventually, the sun rose, and he spent the whole day looking at the immobile pile of rags in the corner of the room. It was a substantial bundle, but as the light came in from outside and a wet, miserable, grey day came and went, it didn't move once. Dusk arrived, and he realised he had been watching the bundle all day. A rivulet of water ran down the wall and under his calves and away across the floor. There was no other movement in the room. The bundle could not be a person, he decided. He had only imagined the shuffling. All the upset and discomfort had tricked his imagination. It was a pile of rags.

He was amazed that no one had come for him yet. Probably they would come for him tomorrow. Of course, perhaps they planned to leave him until he was so emaciated and helpless he could cause them no trouble when they started on him. It was a depressing thought. He couldn't allow that to happen, yet what could he do but wait?

He was awake much of the night. The rain had stopped. It was hard to sleep after being still all day. Pain wracked the joints and muscles of his elevated arms, and he shivered in the cold. His buttocks hurt from sitting on the hard stone floor. His wrists were red where the metal chains chafed against them every time he moved.

He was submerged in pitch blackness. He was aware that no guard had walked past the bars of the room. At one point, he had heard distant voices outside the small window above him, but nothing from inside the dungeons. He thought he must be in some remote place. He called out occasionally, but there was no response. He was completely isolated. He saw neither prisoners nor guards and had not even been brought food or water.

Brande had long since stopped thinking of himself in terms of how dangerous he was to others, but sometimes old thoughts resurfaced as if they'd never gone away. He was beginning to think like his younger self again. His concern was that if they left him here, unfed, for long enough, he wouldn't have the will to escape or fight. It was strange to him that he hadn't been dragged out to a hangman's scaffold already. It would have given him a chance. No, they had stumbled on his weakness. Put him in a room of people, helplessly outnumbered, and he'd fight his way out, but chained up like this there was little he could do. They would defeat him through attrition, through inactivity.

Hours later, it dawned on him that maybe something worse was in store for him. Perhaps some hideous display was to be made of him. He knew of a tribe that would boil a captured enemy's legs while keeping him attentive to watch the flesh slough off his bones. Perhaps they'd make him fight a bear for the locals' amusement. His memory conjured no end of possibilities and his imagination filled in the gaps.

Of course, maybe they had made the connection between him and Aithne and Fia. In which case, perhaps something unthinkable was happening to them. He couldn't let himself think that! In that direction, madness lay. He closed his eyes, then jerked wide awake and sat upright, fully alert, panicked. His heart pounded inside his chest. He was certain this time. Completely certain. The pile of rags had moved.

He held his breath for an age. The vague, grey-black shape in the gloom that he sometimes thought he could see in the black of the cell made no further sound. He refused to doubt his senses this time, though. He was sure it had moved. He would not be fooled. He had seen a slight shift in the darkness, but there had been a noise. A shuffling sound. It had been accompanied by a sound like a tiny sigh, like the last breath escaping from the mouth of a dying child.

After a time, he spoke. "I am defenceless." He willed the bundle to attack if that was its plan. He would not live in fear of it. His hands were shackled, but he could move a little and might be able to grab fabric. He could lift his knees and maybe strike someone from below if they leapt on him. He had the movement of his neck, which meant he could headbutt and bite. He waited. Nothing. No response.

After some time, he started smacking the manacle on his left wrist against the wall to which it was chained. Metal clanged against stone. It made an unbearably loud noise in the darkness. He banged it hard, and he banged it again and again, each strike coming quickly after the last. He couldn't keep it up for long. His arm was numb, and the angle of it meant he was striking backwards, shifting the heavy manacle. He could feel the muscles of his left shoulder straining.

He had no hope that the manacle would break. The relentless clanging had another purpose. It made sitting in the darkness uncomfortable. The deafening sound reverberated around the stone chamber. He wanted to infuriate whoever was in this cell with him into action. He didn't take his eyes off the bundle, although all he could see in the darkness was the dimmest of grey shapes.

He wondered if banging might bring a guard. It would be a pleasure to see another human being, even if they were only going to smack him in the mouth to teach him a lesson for disturbing their sleep.

Nothing.

He kept banging away, smashing the metal off the stone.

Slowly, the moon came out from behind a cloud, bringing just a little more light into the room.

The face, inches from his own, was hideous. Moonlight reflected off its wrinkled skin. Beady black eyes had feathers where eyebrows should be. A fleshy beak protruded from its face. It had no discernible chin but a long neck disappeared into the cloak of rags. Dark holes listened where ears should have been. It was humanoid, but not human. Brande froze, his heart stopped.

His reactions kicked in. He struck forward with his forehead, and his knees came up. His hands strained to reach its tattered robe.

It was out of reach. The thing continued to lean over him. This deformed creature, with a head like a vulture's, hung over him, staring at him, balancing on back legs. Brande couldn't see much in the dark, but it wasn't attacking him. For now, that was all he needed to be able to face it. He had smoked out the threat with his banging, and that reassured him. He still had some element of control.

It hung over him, tilting its head back and forth, staring at his face from just inches away. This thing, he realised, was why he had been left alone. The danger was in here with him. Now it came down to one thing: who was the most dangerous.

"Potential." It choked out the word in a rasp, some awful noise generated in a voice box unsuitable for the spoken word. "Huge potential."

It raised a hand from the folds of its cloak. Not a hand. A talon as sharp as a razor. It pointed one long nail at him, almost reaching his face. He didn't flinch. He looked the creature directly in its soulless black eyes.

"What do you want with me?"

The corners of its eyes wrinkled. Was it smiling? "Your future," it croaked.

Brande thought he knew now what it was talking about, and he didn't like it.

"Why do you fight it?" asked the thing. "Why struggle?"

This hideous creature represented all that Brande hated: power used for evil, power used to deform a living thing.

"You were human once," said Brande.

It moved away, retreating into the darkness. "Now I have real power." He could still see it in the moonlight, a shape shifting through the black. It shuffled, but he knew it could move quickly when it wanted to, just as it could wait motionlessly when it desired.

"I am not like you," he said.

"You will be." It cackled.

The hairs on Brande's arms stood on end. He had fought the Crusades to destroy the destructive powers that were not of this world. Now, he was trapped with this creature, a thing twisted by the same dark forces. It would twist him too. He understood now why he had been left alone with it. He was pleased that the reason had nothing to do with Fia or Aithne. Now, it was just him and this enemy, and he would chance a fight any day.

"You think I am helpless, but I will kill you," he swore.

The creature cackled loudly. "You have no idea!" it screamed. It swung around, its face up against his own. Its beak was wide open, and a small, worm-like tongue vibrated rigidly with anger. The scream was somewhere between a bird's cry and human anguish. It sucked the certainty from him, leaving him hollow and without confidence. It screeched again, and he felt like a smaller person, a person lost in a vast sea of darkness. He thought it would stop, but it screeched again and again. His will to fight was ebbing away. He turned his face away from it.

"You see, now," rasped the creature. "Neither of us will

die. You will weaken, and I will rebuild you in my likeness." The thought of ending up like that hideous thing brought Brande back to his senses. His face was a grimace of disgust. He was not like this thing and would not be made like it.

He felt something kindling in him, a new anger, born of fear.

The thing regained his attention by scratching him with one of its talons. It was like a dagger being drawn across his rib cage. He felt the skin snagging and tearing. Pain seared through him. He wriggled, trying to move, but there was little he could do to get out of its reach.

It screeched again, and he felt hope drain from him.

"I will never be like you," he growled. "I would rather die."

"You don't get to choose," it cackled. It leant down and stuck a pointed talon into the sole of his bare foot, causing him to howl in pain and retract into himself. Lying frozen, starving and naked on the stone floor, his back against the wall, he could do little to protect himself.

It screeched again, a long, fierce call. He could feel it driving the will to live out of him. He had to stop it making that noise. The sound was some kind of weapon, some kind of Rift power that deadened his will to fight back. He had to halt it. He couldn't take much more. The screeching was pushing his resiliency to its limits far faster than he would have thought possible.

He couldn't reach the thing. He could only combat it with words, and words were hopeless, and hope was leaving him. But anger wasn't. He had plenty of that.

He concentrated on his anger inside, and it lifted him, strengthened him, made him want to keep fighting.

"Yes, that's it," squawked the creature. It moved closer to him, screeching louder and louder. It seemed to be growing physically in size, or he felt he was shrinking before it, just as it diminished his desire to fight for his sanity. He focused on his anger, stoking it. He could feel the core of it, like a ball of molten lava held together by some internal force, morphing into a sphere of red-hot fury. He bolted forward, straining against his manacles. His muscles tensed, the veins on his neck stood out. He rocked up on to his feet, straining at his chains. Stone dust fell from the bolted plates holding the brass hoops to the wall.

"That's it," it croaked, sounding pleased.

Brande faltered. It was encouraging him. It could see his determination growing. It was feeding off it. He had been around long enough to know how these things could work. Some of the Black Monks used to try the same technique, using his Deft touch against him.

He slumped back against the wall. The thing snarled at him, scraped him with its talons, sneered and jeered at him. He fell back, beaten. His anger subsided. He closed his eyes. He thought of Aithne. She would run her fingers through his hair to calm him after some injustice had been done to him, reminding him that violence was not always the answer. There were other ways.

The thing shrieked in annoyance, still sucking away the fight in him.

The world went silent. Its wretched voice croaked, "Nevertheless, you are the one."

He opened his eyes. A tiny amount of light had entered the room. It was dawn.

The thing was gone. Brande's eyes shot to the corner of the room, but it was bare. He was alone.

He had survived.

Under his breath, he thanked Aithne for her help. He could imagine her smiling at him.

He heard a noise from outside the bars of his cell. Someone had been alerted by his banging and the creature's shrieking. He could not tell how long it had gone on for, but for him, it felt like an eternity. He had no strength left to deal with whatever was coming.

Approaching torchlight brightened the corridor beyond the bars of his cell.

CHAPTER THIRTEEN

In the flickering torchlight, Brande counted four of them. His heart sank. He knew what that meant.

The first was an ugly young man holding a bunch of keys dangling from a large, rusty ring. He selected one and slid it into the keyhole of the iron gate. Before opening it, he glanced around the cell with a wary eye as if suspecting something untoward had taken place. He swung open the gate and stepped inside, holding it for the others. Brande pegged him as being of low importance. He was the jailer. He looked nervous, so probably new to the job.

Brande inspected the other three. A fat, sweaty man with a glistening face and patchy hair held a bundle of wrapped cloth that clanked in his hands as he moved. He was not in a guard's uniform, just the grotty rags of a man who had no real purpose in life. This morning, however, he looked confident and eager. He unravelled the cloth to reveal a selection of metal implements, each of which was clean, shiny and sharp. Brande took an instant liking to him. This was a man who took pride in his work, even if not in any other aspect of his life. Without a doubt, he was their torturer.

The other two were also easy to identify. One was tall and imperious. He stood in the centre of the room, assuming a commanding presence. He was in charge of the others and would let the underlings do the work unless they were not getting results, then he would step in. He had dark eyes and a droopy moustache. He looked too keen, his face twitching with eager anticipation. Brande figured him for a sadist itching to see another's pain. A real villain, he thought, sent here to get the job done. He would need to keep an eye on him. There was no knowing how far a person would stray once they deviated from the norms of regular behaviour.

The last one, a short, wiry, red-haired fellow, wore the local uniform but had a swarthy look which made Brande think he had travelled. He was the muscle. Brande couldn't dislike him. He'd done that job before now.

"Right at the break of dawn," said Brande.

"Peaceful night?" the officer sneered.

Brande smiled back. "That's right. But you're up early. Did some noise wake you?" They didn't want a docile prisoner, and he wouldn't let them down. Equally, he didn't want complacent enemies, he wanted agitated ones that might slip up.

The wiry, redhead approached and leaned in to sneer at him, right up close, nose to nose. "We'll ask the questions around here." There was a sickening crunch, and he dropped, landing prostrate across Brande's legs. A patch of sticky red stuff lingered on Brande's forehead from the impact.

Brande turned to the officer. "Looks like you'll have to ask the questions now."

The officer signalled to the jailer, then pointed to the fallen man who lay stationary. There was every chance the blow had killed him. "Remove that waste of space."

"Yessir!" The nervous jailer hurried forward, slipped his

forearms under the fallen man's armpits and dragged the unconscious body out of the cell, dumping him face down in the corridor by the far wall.

The officer turned to the torturer. "You. What is your name?""

The fat man ran a hand through the remaining hair on his sweaty, balding pate. He had removed a long, thin scalpel and was examining it. "Peri."

"Peri?"

"Short for ex-peri-menter."

The officer snorted his amusement. "Well, if you would oblige." He swung his gaze to Brande, indicating the work should begin.

The ugly young jailer stepped back into the room, assuming his position by the door again. He fidgeted nervously with the keys he held.

Peri, the torturer, edged closer to Brande. "Got to be careful with this one, I see."

"Yes," the officer agreed. "Keep your distance. Perhaps I should run him through first, to loosen him up."

"Won't be necessary."

"No, it won't," chirped a cocky voice behind them all.

A soft twanging noise was accompanied by a wet thud. Brown and grey feathers protruded from one side of the young jailer's head, while a barbed arrowhead tipping a thin wooden shaft protruded from the other. He staggered forward, then slumped to the ground, knees buckling beneath him. His keys clattered to the floor.

"What the-!" The officer drew his sword.

Aldway appeared. Brande sighed with a tremendous release of anxious energy. "About time," he muttered.

Eberhard strode past Aldway into the cell, while Aldway notched another arrow with the speed and grace of a fox.

Eberhard smiled at the officer. "You know the saying 'what friends are for'? Well, this is what friends are for." His long bastard sword clashed with the officer's one-handed sabre, knocking it to the side. Brande paid no attention to the fight because the torturer was leaning down to retrieve something from his cloth bundle. He pulled out a thin throwing knife. Fortunately, he was fat and slow. This was not the sort of confrontation to which he was accustomed. Aldway loosed an arrow, it struck the man in the backside.

Brande smiled to see Githa arrive, her already-bloody sword held before her. "We'll have company in a moment," she warned, as she strode into the room and assessed the situation. The torturer turned to her, ready to strike with the knife, but she kicked it from his hand, and it chimed as it hit first the ceiling then the floor. She held her sword to his throat, inviting him to make a move and pay the price. He was too busy clutching his arrow-pierced buttock to care.

She glanced at Brande. "It took us a while to locate you," she said, half-apologetically.

He shrugged and grimaced.

Peri's throwing knife lay on the ground. Githa kicked it, sending it soaring into the air towards the officer, who was fighting Eberhard. It was a skilled move, uncannily accurate. The officer batted away the airborne object with his sword, foolishly leaving himself open to attack. Eberhard ran him through so fiercely that the man staggered back towards the wall and off the end of the blade. He slid to the ground, his eyes wide, his expression aghast.

The torturer started screaming, "My arse!" Githa grabbed him and slammed him against the wall. He howled with pain as the arrow knocked against the stone.

"I may let you live," she said, "if you tell me what I want to know."

The irony of the situation was not lost on them. The torturer was being interrogated. Unfortunately, he was the least likely to know anything.

"Anyone?" asked Brande, casually shaking his chains.

Eberhard laughed, lined up his sword with the chains and struck. The sword bounced off them without doing any damage.

"There," said Githa. She pointed to the key ring the young jailer had dropped on the floor. Shaking his head at the simplicity of the solution, Eberhard retrieved them and went to work finding the right one to release Brande from his shackles.

"I know nothing," winced the torturer, clutching his buttock. "The first I learnt of this was when I was woken this morning."

Eberhard released one of the manacles. Brande shook his arm and felt the blood starting to return to it. Excruciating pins and needles coursed along his arm and through his shoulder. He placed it against the wall, leaning on it, trying to slow the flow of blood. "Looks sore," said Eberhard.

"I'm grateful, all the same," grunted Brande. Eberhard released his other arm.

"All I need to know," said Githa, "is who gave the order to torture this prisoner?"

"Him!" He pointed to the dead officer slumped against the wall.

"Quickly," said Brande, indicating his ankles. Eberhard fumbled with the keys, trying one then another in the rusty locks. He managed to free one leg, then the other. Brande shuffled away from the wall and into the centre of the room. He stretched out on his back on the floor, exceedingly grateful not to be slumped in a sitting position any longer. He rolled over and lay on his front. All the agony in his body demanded his attention at that moment, so he waited for it to pass, gritting his teeth.

"But who gave him the order?" insisted Githa. Brande knew what she wanted. She wanted the torturer to say something to implicate the King. He recalled she was part of some rebel faction that was planning an uprising, but her questions wouldn't help him acquire the knowledge he wanted.

The torturer shrugged. "I don't know. Honestly." He grimaced, still pressing a hand on his punctured rear and trying not to put weight on that leg.

Alland burst into the cell, limping because of his hunchback and slightly twisted right leg. He'd been keeping watch. "We need to go. Ten soldiers heading this way."

Brande sat up. "Only ten?"

Alland shook his head. He looked white. "There's an acolyte with them."

Brande got to his feet awkwardly. His joints were stiff. He knew why Alland looked so fearful, having been on the receiving end of Rift power once before, transforming him from a handsome young man into the deformed cripple of today. They were powerful beings. They had surrounded the camp near Bruke with a yellow barrier that had prevented Fia escaping. One had stolen Brande's sight with a simple touch to his forehead. They were to be feared.

The torturer grinned, revealing misshapen teeth, full of gaps. He forced a chuckle, but it did not hide his fear.

Brande looked at each of his companions. He was grateful for being rescued, he was glad of them, but he wasn't sure they were any match for an acolyte. He walked over and moved Githa aside. He looked the torturer in the eye. "One question. One chance. What information were you told to extract from me?"

"Any moment now, there will be a man here who will strike you all dead with a wave of his-"

Brande grabbed him by his flabby throat. He tightened his grip. "That was your one chance, fool." He started to squeeze the life out of the man, who suddenly changed his mind about how cooperative he would be.

Gasping and spluttering, the man began, "They wanted… to know... if you still... had…"

Suddenly Brande knew what he was going to say. He tightened his grip and shook. The man died gasping, his eyes bulging.

"Um… didn't you want to hear the end of that sentence?" asked Aldway.

"No," replied Brande. "How do we get out of here?"

"You don't. Not ever." The voice was cool. Distant. Standing at the point where the corridor turned and met the stairs was a man in a black cloak, his face old and pale, his nose thin, his lips cruel. Brande thought he recognised him as the one from the encampment, the one who blinded him. Almost as if he'd been reading Brande's mind, the acolyte responded. "I recognise you, too, Brande." The acolyte sounded like he was pleased, but he did not smile. There was no trace of emotion on his face.

Githa looked surprised. "You know this one?"

Brande shrugged.

"Tell me when we get out of here," she shot, trying to sound confident.

Brande appreciated her optimism. "Later," he agreed.

The acolyte snorted. "Oh, you won't be leaving here."

Guards rattled into place behind him, beside him, at the door and on the stairs. These were not town guards, Brande noticed. They wore a uniform he had not seen before. They had a black kerchief around their necks, perhaps denoting their allegiance to the acolyte. They looked sharp, alert, professional. They were not like the guards they had just fought.

The place was crowded. The bodies of the jailer and officer took up space on the floor. Brande stood by the left wall, the bulbous corpse of the torturer lying at his feet. Eberhard stood near Aldway, who was behind him notching an arrow. Githa and her brother Alland stood next to each other, defending the way in through the open prison gate.

The black-scarf guards edged into the room. They held short swords, ideal for this environment. By contrast, Aldway's archery would be less useful at such a short distance. Eberhard's bastard longsword was an encumbrance. Githa and Alland held sabres liberated from the guards, so were the best equipped. Brande stooped and swept up the scalpel the torturer had intended to use. He didn't have time to explore the cloth for other utensils.

"Attack," hissed the acolyte. He took a step backwards towards the stairwell. He had a good vantage point, and the bars of the cell prevented anyone from reaching him.

An arrow zipped between the bars and struck the wall beside the acolyte.

"Almost," laughed Aldway.

The acolyte leaned forward calmly. "Now you have one less arrow."

The guards rushed them as one. It was a surprising and powerful opening gambit.

Alland and Githa were forced back by the onrush. Brande stood behind them with the scalpel, waiting to take on the first one to make it past their defensive barrier. One guard went down with an arrow in his chest, which left another at the mercy of both Alland and Githa's blades which finished him off quickly. Eight more pressed forward, bottlenecking at the door, which gave the prisoners the slightest advantage.

Brande stayed at the back. He edged toward the guard who had fallen, hoping to get his sword, but stopped in his tracks as he saw the acolyte raise his hands and fill them with a layered weave of grey mists. He massaged the vapours with swirling hands and then pushed. The guards didn't react to this and pressed their advantage. Better weapons, greater numbers, and the prisoners' shock at seeing Rift energy summoned, all worked in their favour. Alland froze in fear. A guard came at him, and Brande prepared to dive forward and help him but was relieved when Alland automatically blocked the attack and found his focus again. He struck the soldier.

The woven energy was like a ghostly apparition which twisted and tumbled no faster than an old man's walking pace as it worked its way through the air towards Brande. He moved backwards, then sideways. The hex took a straight path toward him but stopped above the fallen black-scarf guard who had died with Aldway's arrow embedded in his chest. The grey weave hung in the air for a moment, then dropped and sunk itself into the dead man's mouth, as if he was sucking it in. Quickly, it was gone. The corpse sighed, then blinked and looked around. Even the guards took stock of this. The fallen man groaned as he rose to his feet. He pulled the arrow from his chest, evidently feeling no pain, snapped it then dropped the broken pieces to the floor.

It was a long time since Brande had witnessed necromancy. It chilled him to see it again after all these years. He lunged at the deceased guard, who raised a feeble defence but the small sharp knife proved enough. Brande slashed at the man's throat, the scalpel cutting through cleanly. He grabbed the top of the guard's head and then snapped it backwards and off. The decapitated body slumped to the ground.

Brande's four companions had driven the guards back to the iron gate of the prison cell, preventing them controlling the space around them. Brande saw three more ghost-like energies floating through the air. One dropped low and entered the severed neck of the corpse Brande had just decapitated. The body came to life and reached towards its own head. It grabbed it, then replaced the head on its neck and began to stand up.

"We have a problem," said Aldway. He released his last arrow at the throng of guards, and one of them screamed and staggered sideways. Aldway dipped and grabbed a sabre from the ground. "They're not staying dead."

Eberhard roared and rushed forward with his sword pointed out like a lance, skewering two black-scarf guards at once. It turned the fight, and they pushed them back through the door and out into the corridor. Four remained, beyond the bars.

Githa tumbled into the corridor, followed by Alland. Aldway was close behind.

It was a mess. The floor was awash with blood. The acrid stink of sweat filled their nostrils, turning their instincts animal. The fighters were like pigs crammed in a cart being taken to market. They grunted and squeaked and shoved and tussled. All the while, Brande stayed at the rear, now with a sword in his hand, decapitating the guards that had already fallen but were crawling across the floor. "We're surrounded," he realised.

Alland took a soldier's arm off at the wrist. The soldier screamed out but another guard, just behind, poked his sword over the injured man's shoulder and pierced Alland just above the collarbone. It was a quick stab, and the sword was withdrawn again. Alland cried out, then headbutted the first soldier with his deformed, but weighty, forehead.

Aldway was now dual-wielding sabres, one in each hand. He and a guard had been pushed to one side by the flow of the battle and were battering each other with blow after blow, evenly matched in their swordplay.

Githa took one on, her back to the bars. Brande thought she was at risk from the resurrected men stabbing her from the cell, and when one tried it, he leapt forward and pulled its head off for the third time. He almost laughed to see it roll away along the floor again.

Githa drove her sword through her opponent's bony breast-plate with such force that when blood spurted out and hit her in the face, it caught her by surprise. The man almost exploded.

The fury of the events had reinvigorated Brande. Some part of him had left all this behind, but another part of him, a part he was ashamed of, revelled in it. He exited the cell and pushed past Githa, making his way to the acolyte just as two more guards appeared at the stairs.

"Let me past," he grunted, as a guard ran forward to block him. He pushed the man, who slipped on some gore underfoot and fell against the wall. Eberhard's bastard sword passed through him and struck the wall with a loud clang. Brande barged past and came face to face with the acolyte. He could see more soldiers lining the stairwell, just regular troops, no black kerchief, waiting to get in on the action when some space cleared. This was bad news.

Brand propelled himself forward, intending to headbutt the acolyte and put him at a disadvantage, but the acolyte brushed him aside with one hand, smashing him into the wall. He smiled down at the stunned Brande. "You disappoint me," he rasped, "but I've learnt what I needed to know." He turned to go.

"Wait! I'm not finished with you!" barked Brande gutturally. He launched himself from the floor. The fire in his gut began to enliven but was kept in check by that dark incantation cast atop the Strangled Mountains long ago.

All around him were limbs and steel, thrashing and flashing, and the ferrous smell of blood. Screaming, shouting, sweat, hatred and fear surrounded him. Every primal instinct in his body was electrified. He swam through the air and grabbed the acolyte. With incredible force, the acolyte shrugged him off, but not before Brande had drawn the cowl over his face causing him to hiss in annoyance. Brande still had hold of the hood as he landed. He ripped it from the man, taking the cloak with it, exposing his fleshy frame beneath.

He was repulsed by what he saw. The acolyte's head may have seemed normal, if grey and wrinkled, but his upper torso was saggy and striped with unnatural crevices, and his legs were thin as a spectre's, no thicker than the bone and bandaged up, so no part was visible. The guards on the stairwell paused, equally horrified, but remembered their training and joined the attack.

Aldway's two swords penetrated the man he was

fighting, who had grown tired and slow. He let the man fall away from him. He eyed a spent arrow lying on the ground. Grabbing his bow, he nocked it and shot it into the next guard to descend the stairs.

A guard grabbed Brande and shunted him toward the bars of the cell. Brande tussled with him and landed a solid elbow to his jaw. The corridor was crowded as fists struck and blades hacked in every direction. Two soldiers now stood in front of the acolyte, offering protection. They needn't have worried. He was weaving some black art in his hand, a swirling vortex of strands and fibres. He threw it in Brande's direction, but Brande was gone. The black mass coursed through the bars where he had been, melting them, and driving into a section of the stone wall leaving a blackened hole. Brande escaped the wrestling soldier and launched himself at the acolyte. He thrust out a foot and smashed the acolyte's stick-thin leg. He heard the bone snap as the rag-bound bone folded in on itself. The acolyte stumbled forward, but held himself upright against a wall, showing no sign of pain.

Meanwhile, three guards had pushed past Brande and were attacking the others. It was a bloodbath. Githa and Alland managed to work their way toward Brande, who was smashing two soldiers' heads together. It was not the act of an annoyed parent. As he smashed their heads together a second time, then a third, their skulls cracked, and one cried out. The other was already unconscious. A fourth time ensured neither would ever trouble him again. Sopping in blood and brain matter, Brande stood up and took in the scene.

Aldway and Eberhard fought as a team, watching each other's backs. Alland was aggressive, he fought vigorously, if clumsily. He had just turned his attention on the acolyte. Githa was a force to be reckoned with. Her swordplay was precise, not a movement wasted. He could barely keep up with her swift, accurate strokes. He would have to find out where she learned to fight like that because it wasn't military and it wasn't self-taught.

Two approaching soldiers took one look at Brande's expression as he swung to face them, then turned and ran back up the stairs. Eberhard was battering the pommel of his sword into the head of a soldier who had made the mistake of turning away from him.

A barked instruction from above and the same soldiers came racing down the stairs again, this time with more soldiers on their heels. Brande picked up the nearest sword and took them on as they poured from the stairwell. He slashed and struck, his growl like thunder, his sword like lightning. He began to see red, and his blade tore through them like an oar slapping water, blood splashing in every direction.

He returned his focus to the acolyte, who was hopping towards the stairs, one arm on the wall, the other constructing something eldritch and convulsing in his palm. He reached the stairs and threw the creation at Brande, who jerked to the side, just managing to dodge it. Suddenly, the acolyte took on incredible speed and started crawling up the stairs, one hand over the other, one leg kicking and the other boney, broken limb just flailing, like a spider with several legs pulled off. It scrambled up the stairs, hissing and spitting its annoyance.

Brande was already two strides up the stairs after him. The acolyte kicked out with his intact leg and caught Brande in the stomach. Brande felt like he'd been kicked by a horse. He landed on his arse three foot away from the bottom step. He gasped, desperately trying to draw breath as he got up off the floor.

"Finish them." The acolyte was ordering someone at the top of the stairs. Gasping in ragged breaths, Brande looked up and saw more soldiers gathering. Reinforcements were arriving. They blocked the light from above as they crowded at the entrance. Alland stood by Brande, watching the acolyte finish crawling up the stairs.

The enemy was above them and had the advantage in both numbers and positioning. They watched as soldiers hauled the acolyte to his feet and to safety.

Brande looked back along the corridor. Alland was by his side, his grim face set in grimmer determination. Githa stood, poised, ready for anything. Aldway and Eberhard stood by each other, both were covered from head to foot in gore. Brande almost smiled. They were a good team. Nearly as good as any he'd had in the Crusades. "Up!" he growled.

Followed by the others, he led the charge. Anger drove him forward. There was no waiting this out, and no other means of escape. He had a sword in his hand, and he used it. He barrelled up the stairs and into the awaiting soldiers, knocking them back. A blade glanced off his shoulder, leaving a bright red line. Upon seeing him, the acolyte howled in rage and started muttering another incantation under his breath. Even as he was helped away by a black-scarf soldier, he was chanting. Brande and his four companions were immediately locked in battle with the fresh influx of soldiers.

"Don't let the bastard escape!" yelled Alland. He was almost dribbling with fury at seeing a servant of Nachmair escape. His fear was gone. Acolytes had once deformed him, and he wasn't going to let this one get away. Brande recognised bloodlust when he saw it.

Brande narrowly avoided an axe blade that swung past him, reaching for his shoulder. He almost missed the relevance of it as he engaged with another soldier, just dismissing it as another threat. Then it sank in. A proper battle axe. He grinned from ear to ear. Eberhard arrived by his side at that moment and seeing Brande's expression knew precisely what he wanted. He swung his longsword and took the axe wielder's head clean off. Brande plucked the fallen weapon from the floor, pausing to admire it for just a moment, before turning back to his opponent and, with a mad glint in his eye, clinging to the haft with both hands, made good use of it. It had a smooth black blade with a recently sharpened edge which cut through his opponent with ease. The axe's beard curled into a nasty hook at the bottom of the blade. A long metal spike, the sort that a poleaxe might feature, jutted from atop this exquisite instrument of death. Leather strapping wound the handle in two places, higher up near the shoulder and lower close to the pommel. It was a thing of beauty. He knew good fortune when it struck.

Having the space to fight, and the prospect of freedom before them, gave them all the impetus they needed to turn the fight, drive their enemies to the wall, and leave their lifeless forms in a tangled pile there. For now, they had won.

They made their way through the rest of the prison complex. It was deserted, but for occasional stray guards, each of whom met a swift demise. Brande took the clothes from a larger-than-average soldier and found they just about fitted.

"That's better," said Aldway.

"Why are there no other prisoners?" asked Eberhard.

"They saw you coming," said Aldway.

Eberhard lifted his sword. "Wise move."

"It's not your sword, it's your smell." Despite everything they'd been through, Aldway's sense of humour seemed to be returning.

Eberhard pulled a face at him.

They found chairs knocked over, and food and drink abandoned. Soldiers had deserted their posts. "It wasn't like this when we came in," said Githa. "But we did take a shortcut. Over the wall. And through a window."

The acolyte had fled, and his remaining black-scarf soldiers were gone with him. "The place is probably riddled with passageways, we'll never find him," said Alland, furious that the twisted figure had got away.

When they finally emerged outside and sunlight hit their faces, they found they were in the garrison on the edge of town. The lack of other prisoners confirmed Brande's suspicion that, when trouble arose, the companies had moved on. Most likely the same day they threw him in the dungeon. Their main instruction would be to get their prisoners to Charstoke. Stonenife wasn't safe with him and his allies around. He wondered exactly how much of a head start they had on him.

They emerged from the garrison and onto the street. Townsfolk gawped at them like they were gods descended from the sky to wreak vengeance. No one came within forty foot of them. They walked together, side by side, brandishing their weapons, covered from head to foot in blood, and none wore an expression that invited conversation.

"This won't last," spat Alland, sourly. "That acolyte will be back. Two or three of those bastards and we won't stand a chance."

Brande grinned. "We fought him, and we survived. Don't overestimate them. If he'd been more powerful, he'd have let us know about it."

"He made the dead rise," said Alland, "and drove a hole through a stone wall."

"And he threw you across the room with a gesture," added Eberhard.

Brande laughed, releasing some small amount of his battle rage, but it made him seem like a madman. "We survived." As he said it, his sense of victory suddenly soured in his mouth. They'd won just one small battle, but the war raged on. He was alive. He could say nothing about the health of his wife or daughter. They were in more danger now than ever.

He took stock. He had good companions. They fought well and were loyal to one another. He was just about to say something along those lines when Aldway patted him on the shoulder.

"A thank you wouldn't go amiss, old man," he said, a wry smirk on his face.

Brande looked puzzled.

"For busting you out of prison."

Brande grinned. "I had it under control."

Githa snorted in amusement. "You were naked and about to be tortured."

"Look," said Brande, changing the topic, "the sun's shining, the sky is blue, and I have somewhere to be."

"You're not going to get far covered in blood," said Eberhard.

Brande glanced at him askance. "It's never stopped me before."

Accepting this for truth, Eberhard asked, "Well, where are we going?"

They waited a moment for the answer, during which time Brande's expression soured. He set his jaw. "Charstoke."

CHAPTER FOURTEEN

Brande entered the city of Charstoke alone. Its huge walls dominated his vision as he approached the barbican, a towering gateway draped with fluttering banners. There was much traffic today. Peasants, traders, performers and knights with their squires all made their way into the city. The wind carried the sound of merriment and music from within the walls. He was surprised to pass unchallenged as he entered. It was the Fayre of the Fallen. Even now, as Brande made his way through the broad, unpaved streets of the city, he passed people dressed in demon costumes or sporting pumpkins for heads. The fayre was merry, but it would slowly degenerate into Nachmair's Night, a night when the city folk would get drunk amid merriment and debauchery.

He had waited one day at the insistence of the others. Eberhard pointed out the tactical advantage of entering during the festivities. As such, only Aldway had entered the city. He had been sent to buy food and clothes. He returned with such a bundle of garments that Brande was sure they had not all been acquired legitimately, even though Aldway protested they had. The food was very welcome and devoured without conversation. They hid out in New Forest, not far from the city, sleeping in the ruin of a long-abandoned watchtower. As they waited for the next day, they washed some of their bloodstained clothes in a stream that, for a while, ran red.

Brande absorbed the sounds and smells of the city. He had never liked densely populated areas, associating them with battlegrounds, not places to call home. Githa and the others were not far behind, so he made his way to the central market square where they had agreed to meet up. The law forbade him to carry a weapon. It usually also prevented the wearing of a mask, but that rule was relaxed during the fayre, so he had fashioned himself a crown of holly so as not to look out of place. He didn't expect anyone to recognise him, and certainly not in the smart new clothes Aldway had acquired for him.

The fayre was bustling with tradesmen hawking their wares and street performers juggling, sword swallowing and breathing fire. Brande had no doubt pickpockets and ladies of ill repute were also hard at work making their living amongst a crowd this size. He felt like the many years living in Bruton had caused him to forget so many people could exist in one place.

He noticed two men standing by a sword swallower. They were annoying him by asking him insulting questions he couldn't answer while the sword was lodged down his throat. He went over and stood a little way behind them. "Hello," he said. Eberhard and Aldway looked surprised to see him.

"We just got here," said Aldway.

"No problem getting in," said Eberhard.

"Picked the perfect day," said Brande, drolly. All the merriment hadn't distracted him from the urgent need to find Aithne and Fia.

They walked a little way together. "I don't think we

stand out," said Eberhard. "We just look like everyone else." He wore a hat with a feather in it.

"Oh yes, we look like everyone else," scoffed Aldway. "You're both a couple of heads higher than everyone. Eberhard has long blond hair like a Skullun, and Brande is built like a prize ox. You stand out a mile!" Aldway was dressed in typical peasant garb and wore a hood topped with a dangling tube that hung down his back. Brande wondered if he was hiding his face because he feared repercussions after procuring their outfits by illegitimate means.

Eberhard tilted his head. "Look, there's Githa." He'd spotted her across a crowded space burgeoning with craftsmen, entertainers and tradesmen. She was patiently trying to unburden herself of the attentions of a young knight who had taken an interest in her. "I guess she stands out too."

She saw them and excused herself abruptly. The knight looked flummoxed but walked off with his head held high. She worked her way towards them, ensuring their paths met.

"I don't believe it," said Aldway.

They all looked at him.

"In the pillory," he said. "Look!"

Children were throwing rotten vegetables at three men chained to pillories. One of the prisoners looked familiar.

"If you know him, don't be recognised!" hissed Githa.

They quietly drifted apart.

Brande and Alland found themselves by a vegetable stall full of plump, fresh produce.

"Who is he?" asked Alland, his deformed face squinting as he stared at the prisoner.

"From the skytes' cages," explained Brande. "Remember I told you of a crazy man we encountered going by the name Wylie."

"I recall. Didn't he sing something treasonous about the

king?"

"I guess this is where his singing got him."

"But didn't he pose some kind of threat?"

Brande nodded. "He seemed to know our purpose."

"Watch this," said Alland. He walked away from Brande and along a back street. He was out of sight for a short while then returned carrying a bucket. Brande didn't need to use his imagination to know what was in it.

Alland went over and stood before Wylie. Wylie looked back at him and then spat at him. "You are bad luck, hunchback. Stay away from me, ugly gargoyle!" A few people in the crowd laughed. Alland didn't answer, he just threw the bucket of waste over the man, who howled in indignation. A turd slid down his face, and he shook it off. The language that poured forth was as coarse as any Brande had ever heard. Parents of the children throwing vegetables dragged them away, covering their ears. Wylie invoked sexual organs, sadistic violence and Nachmair's own name as he cursed Alland, who was already walking away.

Alland didn't return to Brande, because he knew it would draw Wylie's attention to him. Instead, he found Githa, and they left together. A city guard didn't appreciate Wylie's vocal sentiments and was now shouting at him to be quiet. He threatened the thief with a strike from his metal gauntlet and the shouting died down.

Brande was irritated by Alland's prank. All he cared about was finding Aithne and Fia. He knew they were within the city walls somewhere. He drifted away from the market stalls and edged around a maypole that was surrounded by skipping children. A lutist played while walking on stilts. He ignored the shenanigans and ventured farther into the city. He came to tradesmen's quarters where many crafts were on display. He wandered through, keeping his eyes open for an indication of where the prisoners might be. He decided to head toward the garrison even though Githa said she thought the prisoners wouldn't be there.

Brande explored with his eyes, pretending to be enjoying the festivities. He paused very briefly to catch a theatrical performance depicting King Ignatius and his crusade against the Deft. Brande scoffed at the fallacy. Leofric had fought the Crusades, Ignatius merely happened upon the tail end of them. Ignatius had never truly been tested in a war with those of power dwelling in the east. Brande watched the actors tread the boards and grimaced at the heroics and winced at the melodrama. At the back of his mind, he kept going over the plan. Githa knew someone who would help them. She and her brother were in contact with someone who shared their revulsion at what was happening, and her connection was someone of local importance. They would meet with him, and he would help them.

When it happened, it happened quickly. Githa appeared and dragged Brande down a side alley and gave him a description of the address and pushed him in the right direction. He headed off in that direction, following her instructions and eventually finding an unassuming door to a modest building. As she had relayed, there was a sprig of holly on the door with two yellow berries. That was how he knew he had the right place. The man who had opened the door wore a stately green tunic and silk stockings.

"Quickly, you mustn't be seen entering here," he said gruffly, pulling Brande inside.

Once Brande was inside, the man relaxed, and his curt manner vanished. Wrinkles of kindness creased the corners of his eyes, and he shook Brande's hand, a limp handshake, but an earnest one. "I am Elderman Alewyn. Githa, your friend and mine, told me you would be arriving here first. I am so glad you have come to us."

Brande nodded, not willing to offer up any information. He was glad of the help, but why was this man glad he'd come? He wondered what Githa had told him.

"My name is Brande."

"Of course it is," said the man, eagerly, through a smile. "Brande. A common name, but a good one."

Brande nodded, unimpressed by the prattle. The Elderman seemed to notice his demeanour and changed tack. "Please, take a seat. You'll want something to drink." He scuttled off into another room and returned with a flagon. "This will warm your bones." He smiled.

Brande accepted it with gratitude.

A knock came at the door.

The Elderman opened it to find Githa and Alland waiting. He didn't need to say anything. They marched right in and took seats. Brande noted the lack of hesitation and knew they had been here before.

Another knock. Eberhard and Aldway.

"Ah, all at once," tutted the Elderman. "Too conspicuous."

"I did tell you to wait a while," said Alland to the two men as they entered.

"You also said there'd be food," agreed Aldway, looking about as if expecting to see a buffet table.

Alland rolled his eyes.

"Come, friends," said the Elderman. "There will be food enough later. It's the festival, after all." He looked to Alland. "Your assistance?"

"Why are we here?" asked Brande. He was growing impatient. He'd waited half the day because of the promise of help from inside, and now this old man wasn't even offering them food. He quaffed his drink and waited for a response.

"Is that mead?" asked Aldway, sniffing at Brande's cup. "Why don't I have mead?"

"Now you are all here," said the Elderman, ignoring him, "I want you to follow Alland. We have something to show you."

Brande didn't appreciate the showmanship. Alland helped the Elderman shift a cabinet that stood against the wall. It was stacked with ornaments, and the wood looked heavy, but when they moved it, it was apparently much lighter than the facade portrayed. The ornaments moved with it and didn't even rattle. Behind the cabinet was a wall. Alland pushed it, and a secret panel fell away. A gush of cold air swirled out of the darkness as a very narrow staircase was revealed. Alland went down first, holding a candle, and they all followed after.

"This better be where the food is," said Aldway. "I don't brave spiders for anything less."

"Child," scolded Eberhard.

"I loved secret passages as a child," Githa reminisced.

"I don't remember my childhood," grunted Brande.

"That doesn't surprise me," quipped Aldway.

They had to squeeze their way down the staircase which had evidently been made as narrow as possible to avoid detection within the architecture of the building.

"I was a beautiful youth," said Alland, sighing.

"Now only your mother could love that face." Aldway flashed him a grin to show he was joking.

Alland didn't look impressed. "Our mother died three years ago."

The staircase wasn't long. Brande turned his shoulders to squeeze down the last few steps.

"It's necessarily narrow," apologised the Elderman, at the foot of the stairs. "I didn't want the thickness of the wall becoming a telltale sign... ah, we're all down."

In the flickering candlelight, Brande could see metal glistening. Alland and the Elderman lit more candles from their own.

Elderman Alewyn waited until they were all gathered around. A row of weapons was stacked in a wooden rack against the wall. The low-ceilinged cellar also contained a table with a map of the city on it and small figurines positioned in various places. Brande and Eberhard made straight for the weapons.

Brande touched the silvery blade of a newly forged, double-headed axe which was attached to a thick oaken handle as long as his leg. He smiled and determined not to leave the building without it.

He looked up at Githa. "Love at first sight?" she asked, a twinkle in her eye.

Brande muttered something incoherent. He wasn't used to being wrong-footed and was glad the shadows hid the rise of blood in his cheeks. He smiled, realising his thoughts must have been open for all to see as clearly as if they'd been inked on his forehead.

The Elderman chuckled. "You can arm yourselves later. We need to talk tactics."

Instantly, Brande's mood changed. "This looks like a military campaign," said Brande. "I just need help releasing a woman and child, wherever they're held."

The Elderman shook his head. "And we must achieve that, Brande, but there is also a larger picture, there is more at stake than you know."

"I realise that you, Githa and Alland are involved in some campaign here, but that isn't my fight."

Githa put a gentle hand on his chest. "Wait, Brande. We are not the enemy. Hear us out."

Brande nodded perfunctorily, willing to back down and listen.

The Elderman shuffled over to the table. "I'm afraid your family won't be in the garrison any longer," he said. "That is not the King's way." Perhaps it was the candlelight or the subject matter, but the Elderman's face seemed to have taken on a grave visage.

"What do you mean?"

The Elderman looked at him. "What do you know of King Ignatius?"

"I fought for his brother, King Leofric. He was a strong

leader, a brave man, practical in all things. He used to say, 'eyes to the earth, not to the skies'. His hatred for the Deft is legendary. I remember when he died. People were sad to see him go. His younger brother was not a great warrior like he was, but he professed the same ideals. From what I have heard Ignatius is a fair ruler with a keen sense of justice, if a little paranoid at times."

"Yes, he executed four of his advisors not long ago," revealed Alland.

"That's true," acknowledged the Elderman. "And he was a true and fair king, until about a year ago. Something happened. Suddenly there were rumours of dark dealings and unnatural occurrences in the castle. A religious cult sprang up. It was said that one of the King's advisors was Deft."

"I heard a rumour that people from the east were making their way to live amongst us," snarled Alland, clearly upset at the idea.

"But most noticeable of all," continued Elderman Alewyn, "were the acolytes. Devotees of this new religion. He surrounds himself with them. They are like spectres, floating around the castle day and night, doing his bidding. It seems that the King has strayed somewhat from his brother's ideals."

"It is said they are followers of Nachmair," whispered Alland. "They have powers from the Rift."

"That has not been proven," interjected the Elderman.

"We fought one," related Githa. "We fought one in the garrison at Stonenife. He brought soldiers back from the dead. There can be no doubt now, Elderman. And we must act fast."

Brande frowned. "But this was a sudden change? A year ago?"

The Elderman nodded. Githa spoke, "We cannot know for sure."

Elderman Alewyn shrugged. "We cannot know because

very few have seen him these last few years."

"It is my belief that the King has been indoctrinated into this cult," said Alland.

The Elderman frowned. "At the very least, someone has the ear of the King. He has been led away from his brother's noble values."

Brande snorted. "What has this got to do with my family?"

"Your family, Brande, will have been taken into the keep. There are strange goings on in there. People have heard children crying in the chapel, but no one is allowed access. Recently, women and girls have been taken into the keep in droves, but none ever emerge. As far as I know, there haven't been any escape attempts. Meanwhile, these cloaked acolytes with their grey faces patrol inside and out."

"So Fia and Aithne are in the keep?"

"Yes, most likely. But so are a great many dangers and unknowns."

Brande snorted again. "I'm a pretty dangerous unknown, myself. When do we leave?"

"You must listen, Brande. There are dark forces at work here. Powerful individuals. I have heard tales of ghostly sightings, strange lights, terrible screams, and one morning a party of workmen passed the outside walls of the keep before dawn and saw they were bleeding. Of course, there was nothing there to see by sunrise."

"I don't like it," said Eberhard. He was sizing up a longsword in the rack. "But I agree with Brande. We shouldn't wait."

Githa moved some of the pieces on the tabletop map. "The tide is turning. People have had enough of closed doors and nameless acolytes attending to the King. They are ready for a change. Every day now, we hear of more people willing to take up arms. Just yesterday, a blacksmith was hauled away by guards who were taking orders from an acolyte. That isn't right!"

"You see these weapons?" The Elderman directed their attention to the wooden rack. "He was producing and supplying these to our comrades. Many support our cause and are ready to take action. Here..." He handed Brande a large black key that had been sat on the table. It was cast iron and the teeth on it were bent and curved, rather than standing straight. It didn't look functional.

"Big door?" asked Brande, sullenly.

"The Elder Key. It is a token, passed down for generations amongst my kind. Show it, and it will get you inside the keep. Don't lose it. Keep it safe. Don't discard it. Do you have a pocket? Good. Keep it in your pocket. One of the women of the court is on our side. She is called Lilly. She will meet you within the postern gate. Show her the Elder Key and-"

Brande sighed. "I am not one of your rebels."

"The time is ripe," urged Githa. "People are willing to move. Now is as good a time as any to storm the keep. This is why I wanted to bring you here, Brande. Your aim tallies with our own."

"It doesn't," said Brande. "I plan to get my family out and away, today. You want to overthrow a rightful king. Our goals differ."

"If you're to stand any chance, you need us with you. You need a massive assault to even stand a chance of making headway here. Think of all the soldiers camped here at the moment. Not just Lance Company who took Bruton and Bruke. There is an army here. Use us as a distraction, then get your family out."

"Brande," said Alland, imploringly. "Join us. You fought in the Crusades. You hate the Deft as much as I do. If they have a stranglehold on our King, they must be stopped. You've fought their type before and survived. You could help us. Lead us."

Brande shook his head. He would not be appealed to. He would not be flattered or offered some kind of position of leadership. "My family is the only thing that matters to me. I am here for them. If our paths have to separate at this late hour, so be it."

Githa and Alland looked meaningfully at each other.

"No need for that," said Githa. "Alland and I are beside you, regardless."

Alland nodded. Brande wasn't sure why Githa would feel any loyalty to him, but he nodded thankfully anyway.

The Elderman gasped. "Someone's coming!"

"How can you know?" asked Eberhard, usually the one to keep a lookout. "I heard nothing."

The Elderman looked like he was about to offer an explanation, but decided against it and ran up the stairs. "Stay here," he yelled down to them. They heard the cabinet closing over their exit, and then a knock on the front door of the building. Eberhard placed the sword he was inspecting back on the rack, so he wouldn't accidentally make a noise with it. "Sit," he told everyone. They all sat on the cold, damp floor and remained absolutely still.

The knock repeated, louder. They heard the Elderman open the door. They could hear everything as they sat quietly.

"Where are they?" demanded a voice, the moment the front door was open.

They heard the Elderman gasp and splutter, not providing any kind of a coherent response.

"They were seen entering here. Let me pass."

The sound of the Elderman's shuffling feet was followed by loud footsteps. It had to be a soldier by the tone of voice. He entered the main room, then more heavy footfalls as another soldier joined him.

"I don't know of what you speak," spluttered the Elderman convincingly. "I am alone here."

"You! Pull away this furniture."

Brande and the others looked at each other apprehensively. Aldway leapt to his feet and silently walked around the room, blowing out candles, then sat down again. Brande didn't like hiding. He would rather have grabbed the double-headed axe and stormed upstairs. Gentler steps seemed to enter the property. "Search everywhere," said a raspy voice. An acolyte.

They heard the cabinet being shifted.

"Really, there's no need. There's a trapdoor over here," said the Elderman.

Brande gritted his teeth.

They heard the trapdoor opening. It wasn't directly above them, but perhaps in the larder. He heard the men shuffling and searching. "Nothing here but wine and cheese," said the voice of a soldier. Clever, thought Brande, show them a real hiding place, but one with temptations instead of stowaways.

"Tear this place apart," shouted the acolyte. "I know they came in here."

"No, please…" The Elderman pleaded, but the sound of the place being smashed apart was unmistakable. There were more words they couldn't make out. Brande hated being idle. He hated waiting impotently while the Elderman quaked in his boots upstairs. He wondered if they'd find the secret entrance behind the cabinet. It was well hidden, but if they put a boot through the wall, then the stairwell would be revealed.

"You are a traitor. Take him."

"But!" The Elderman's voice was choked off. They heard him being dragged away.

"You, stand guard on the front door. You two, bring him."

There was silence for a short while, then they heard the soldier on guard come back inside and start poking around amongst the wine and cheese they'd found. Finally, the steps moved to the front door, went outside, and the door closed. Brande assumed the soldier had found the temptation to steal some of the goods too much and had headed off home with them, no doubt hoping to be back before anyone noticed.

There was quiet.

"We should have helped him," hissed Alland.

There was a striking noise. Aldway lit a solitary candle.

Githa had her hand on her brother's knee, placating him. "What could we have done? Only brought all the King's forces down on us. Their power is strongest here, near the keep."

Brande stood up. Stretched. Banged his head on the ceiling. He paused and looked chagrined. He moved to the rack and carefully removed the axe. He examined it, turning it in his hands a few times. It was a beautiful piece of work. He admired it for a long moment, then his eye caught something else. He leant down and picked up a saddle axe, which he identified as being the work of a different blacksmith, perhaps a foreign one. It had a long handle and a steel head decorated with symbols unknown to him. He grinned. "Time we got out of here."

"We need a plan," said Eberhard.

"I have a plan," said Brande. "I'm going into that keep, and I'm going to get my family out."

"And how do you intend to do that?" asked Alland, acerbically.

Githa shook her head. "It'd be suicide."

"We have this," said Brande, matter-of-factly. He held up the strange looking key the Elderman had given him. He studied it for a moment, as if recognising it from somewhere.

"If you go in with the Elder Key and don't cooperate you will be suspicious to Lilly."

"That's my plan," retorted Brande, flippantly, "to go in and not cooperate."

Githa rolled her eyes. Alland hissed annoyance. "Brande, you know the value of what we do."

"Then come with me," said Brande. "Or don't. It's your

choice. Eberhard? Aldway?"

He wasn't sure why those two rogues were on his side in this, but they had given him no reason not to trust them so far. Eberhard drew the longsword from the rack. "Fine work," he commented. Aldway took a longbow that was lying flat along the edge of the rack. He examined it closely then strung it. He took a leather quiver and attached it to his belt. A wooden tube full of arrows was built into the side of the rack. He measured some of them against his arm, and eventually had enough to fill his quiver. He drew them, testing them against his draw length on the bow. He nodded, satisfied. The whole thing had only taken him moments. He grabbed two short daggers and a throwing axe. There was a thin knife to be had, so he took that too. He tested the weight of a flail in his hand, then put it back with a shake of his head. "Too heavy," he muttered.

Eberhard was trying not to laugh. "Equipped?" he asked. Aldway grinned and nodded.

Brande turned to Githa and Alland. "Thank you for all you have done. There, I have said it. I won't repeat it. Now you have a decision to make. I have waited, I have heard what you have to say, but I am going to fight. Are you with me?"

"Yes," said Githa. "No," said Alland. They had spoken at the same time.

They looked at each other, consternation on their faces. They were twins and not used to disagreeing.

"I will go with you," confirmed Githa.

Alland looked at the floor.

CHAPTER FIFTEEN

"Who goes there?" shouted the guard as the front door burst open. He was drawing his sword as he exploded into the house, responding to the crashing sound of Brande shoulder-barging his way through the false wall in the Elderman's property. The guard saw Brande brushing the dust off himself and then saw the hole in the wall. His eyes widened in surprise, then narrowed as anger set in. "Halt, in the name of the King!"

Brande lifted his shiny new axe and smiled through gritted teeth. There was a twanging sound, and the guard grunted. A confused, disappointed look crossed his face, then he clutched at his neck and started to scream and gag at the same time.

A similar expression of disappointment was reflected on Brande's face. Brande glanced at Aldway, who had shot the arrow from where he stood in the secret doorway. "I wanted to try out my new axe," said Brande reproachfully.

Aldway laughed. "I wanted to try out my new bow."

The guard was on the floor now, howling and clutching at his neck. He was tugging at the arrow in some confused understanding of what good it might do. His large body thrashed against the wall. Blood gushed from his neck, leaving a circle of red around him as he twisted around on the spot. Brande rolled his eyes. This was meant to have been a quiet exit. He hefted his axe and halted. Alland had stepped past him, and a flanged mace of heavy steel came down on the man's helmet, crushing both it and the skull beneath. The sound of metal on metal rang out as loud as a church bell. It was a good hit at close quarters, and Brande nodded approvingly, although still looked put out that he hadn't had a chance to try out his new axe. There was a squelching sound as Alland retrieved the mace.

"We'll need to be quieter than that in the keep," said Aldway.

"Let's go," insisted Alland.

Brande turned to him. "Where will you go?"

Alland's lips twisted in an unreadable expression, although whether due to his deformity or because he was keeping his thoughts hidden was impossible to say. "Someone told the acolyte we were here. There's only one person that knew we were here and held a grudge against us, and I tipped a bucket of shit over his head."

"You're going after Wylie, instead of coming with us?" asked Githa in surprise.

"No, I'm going after Wylie, and then I'm going to rescue our elderman. There'll be an uprising here soon." He looked at Brande with a transparent look of contempt. "Some of us are going to be part of it. Without Elderman Alewyn, the rebellion will lose impetus."

"Will you go with him?" Brande asked, turning to Githa.

"No," she insisted. "It's also my cause, but I told you, I'm with you."

Brande looked at his companions. There was Githa, who said she was a cousin of Silas, a man he'd let die, and with a brother who had his own agenda that did not wholly coincide with Brande's. He glanced at Aldway and

Eberhard, men, lovers, whose motivation for sticking around was still unclear to him. So, three he was unsure of, and one who was leaving. It was not like the old days, not like the Crusades. Yet it mattered more. For him, the stakes were higher. Aithne and Fia flitted through his thoughts and his stomach twisted with anxiety.

In his mind, for a moment, Fia was eight again. Aithne was there and beautiful, flowers in her hair, her smoky eyes laughing at some mischief. They had been stood by a pixie well which was sat on a natural spring and surrounded by old stonework. They each tossed in a small pebble and made wishes. Brande wished for a peaceful life. Aithne had said she'd wished they would all be together forever. And Fia, she wished she could have a tame dragon for a pet. So far, it looked like none of their wishes were coming true. He saw Fia fleeing for her life, a yellow band of flickering light catching her, turning red, and tracing her as she ran. He saw Aithne peering at him from a cage. He saw the girls in the inn chained to beds. He gritted his teeth. If these three would help him, he'd take their help. It was better than storming the keep alone.

Alland slipped away. Only one guard had been placed on the building. Presumably, the acolyte didn't expect anyone to return with Elderman Alewyn gone. How confident they were in their security and superiority. Brande didn't like it.

"Plan?" asked Eberhard.

"I have this," said Brande, showing the key with the warped teeth. "I get to the postern door, and Lilly lets me in. I'll leave first."

"Carrying that axe?" asked Eberhard.

Brande tutted. "Good point. Here, you take all the weapons. You'll look like a blacksmith bringing goods to market."

"There are so many people. I don't see how we'll manage this," remarked Githa.

"Because there are so many people," said Brande. "We'll hide in the crowd."

Brande banged on the wooden door with his fist. He waited.

The woman who opened the door was short and had fiery red hair in a braid that hung down over one shoulder. She looked at him with large blue eyes, slightly alarmed. "You are not expected."

Brande inspected her. She wore silk and had youthful features and delicate hands. She was no warrior. The Elderman had said she was a lady of the court.

"You guard this door?" he asked.

She shook her head. "I was waiting for someone," she said. "What do you want?"

Brande pulled out the key. "Recognise this?"

She studied it for a moment. "How did you get that?"

"What is it to you?"

"It belongs to an Elderman."

"Belonged. He gave it to me, saying you'd grant me access."

"He would never give it away. You must have stolen it."

"He said you'd let me in with no questions asked," said Brande, a little flummoxed.

"Oh…" She looked confused. "I don't know."

Brande let out an exasperated sigh. "Look, either-"

"What's your purpose?"

Brande glared at her. "Is there anyone within earshot?"

She looked behind her for a moment. "No."

"Well, personally, I aim to cause havoc."

"Oh? For whom?"

He considered the question. "Everyone."

"Who sent you?"

"Alewyn. He said you were Lilly."

Her eyes widened. "Is this the start of the uprising?"

Brande looked at her, perplexed. She wasn't doing a very good job of whatever it was she was meant to be doing. "Not yet."

"Are you alone?"

"Not quite."

He lifted a hand and placed it on the keystone above the doorway for a moment. "A sign," he explained, hoping Aldway was observing carefully with his archer's eyes and would soon lead the others up here.

She ushered him in and closed the heavy door.

"I can get you in from here," she said.

"Where's the King?" he asked, a glint in his eye.

Aldway muttered under his breath. "Does no one know?" he asked.

The girl, who had told them her name was Lilly, looked upset, like she had betrayed them. "You don't understand," she said. "They protect those areas very well, and only acolytes and chosen soldiers are allowed to enter."

Aldway opened his mouth to retort, but Brande cut in. "How do they choose the soldiers?"

"I don't know about the selection criteria," she replied, "but you can tell the chosen soldiers because they wear a red rose entwined with a snake embroidered on the left arm of their uniforms."

"The king's emblem is the flame and three arrows. Why a snake and rose?"

She shrugged.

Brande stroked his beard, which had grown long over the days of travel. It was thick, woolly, and tangled, the way it had used to be, back during the Crusades, although now flecks of white wove through it like the first signs of winter. "From what you're saying, this whole keep is some kind of prison. When did the king last receive guests?"

She shrugged. "Not in recent times, that I know of,

although dark figures come and go all the time."

"Don't speak to me of dark figures," he growled, a little too aggressively.

Githa stepped forward. "Lilly, your help is much appreciated. There is much we would know, but I fear you don't have all the answers."

Lilly shook her head sadly. "There's not much I can tell you. Elderman Alewyn should have told you all you needed to know."

No one had yet told her that he'd been taken because no one quite knew her role in all this or her connection to him.

"There are a lot of unanswered questions," said Eberhard. He was by the door with an ear out for trouble.

"I think we need to make a move," said Githa. "The evening is close and the Nachmair's Night will be a distraction. Brande?"

He tugged on his beard. Options rose and fell before his eyes. In the end, all he saw was Aithne and Fia. He could imagine them being hurt and that made him deep down angry. He stoked the embers of the rage inside him. "It's time," he agreed.

"Did the Elderman tell you anything that might help us?" asked Eberhard.

"He thought the entrance to the chapel was a good place to enter. That is where the children are taken."

Brande paused. "And the women?"

"The girls and women are taken into the keep proper, but the chapel is where the children go."

Brande looked at the others. Aldway and Eberhard had their mouths turned down. Githa was frowning at the floor. In truth, none of them wanted to go there and see what was happening. They had all heard late night tales about what happened to children that were snatched away by cultists.

"None of them ever come out," said Lilly, as if reading their minds and confirming their fears.

"Did you have a child?" asked Githa.

"Once," she said.

No more was asked. Brande realised now that he had seen very few children in the market town as they approached the keep. Either they were gone, or they were hidden by parents not wanting them taken from them. The whole of Charstoke was sick to the core, but maybe he could do something about that.

"Lead the way," said Brande. "Time's wasting. I can hear the horn of Naril sounding to indicate the approach of Nachmair. The night's festivities begin."

They followed Lilly. She took them a circuitous route to the keep, winding through alleys and taking shortcuts through the homes of people who just nodded at her and ignored her presence. Brande began to get a sense of how many people were in on this uprising. They really had stumbled into the midst of a rebellion. He could see now why they needed the Elderman. If he was the ringleader, they needed him to lead the charge. It would be a disaster if all their preparations went to waste because people lost confidence due to his absence.

The cathedral adjoined the keep. It was an ugly building, designed to look grandiose. Gargoyles leered from the walls. Spires rose upward at irregular intervals. Stained glass windows depicting Hungrar, the world dragon, fighting Nachmair, the demon lord, rose in bright colours on either side of the front facade, which they entered through large double doors.

Inside, it was cold, despite candles left burning on a table in the chancel and the occasional torch burning in a wall sconce. Tapestries were draped along the stone walls that ran along far edges of the aisles. More gargoyles, their ugly faces reminding Brande of Alland's, hung from columns spaced along the length of the nave. The place was empty.

Brande didn't like all this creeping about. His was a world of open forests and, once, open battlefields. He had never liked sneaking around, not knowing where the enemy was.

"Through here," whispered Lilly, indicating to a door. "The children get taken this way. The acolytes come and go, but they don't talk to anyone."

"Thank you," said Githa, quietly, placing a reassuring hand on the young lady's shoulder. "You've been brave, but it's best you go now. What's up ahead will be no place for a lady."

Brande watched her hurry back through the chapel and leave. He hoped she could be trusted. Perhaps it didn't matter now.

She had left the four of them standing by a doorway, which he assumed led into the keep. He could tell from the rough work around the frame that it was not part of the original building. He looked at the others, who seemed impatient to get going, so he opened it carefully, trying not to make much noise. The door opened inwards. They found themselves looking at a piece of fabric which covered the entire portal.

Aldway spoke very quietly. "They've hung a tapestry over the hole so the door can't be seen from the other side." That made sense to Brande. The entrance was hidden from the keep's side.

They stood quietly and listened. For a moment all they could hear were each other's jostling, but experience taught Brande that being still might give them vital information.

"Screams," hissed Aldway. His hearing must be as sharp as his eyes, thought Brande, who could hear nothing.

"Children," whispered Githa. "I hear them now."

Brande stayed put. He thought he might be able to hear something, somewhere. Some shrill sound. "Anyone in the next room?"

They waited. After a moment, there was a sound, as if someone had stood up from a chair at a desk, pushed the chair backwards an inch, then held fast. A moment later, they heard quiet, deliberate steps approaching.

Brande looked to the others, who were wide-eyed, like him. Any moment now this person would pull back the tapestry. Brande indicated to Aldway, who pulled out his dagger. Githa rested her hand on her sword. Brande and Eberhard pulled back, their larger weapons less useful in this small space between rooms.

Someone stood on the other side of the tapestry. Any moment, they would all be discovered. Why hadn't they pulled back the tapestry? Perhaps the person on the other side was suspicious of some noise but had no knowledge of the secret entrance and was wary about moving the hanging fabric.

They waited. They could hear their own breathing and that of their companions. Brande could hear his own heartbeat. He imagined it might be an acolyte standing on the other side. That might prove highly disadvantageous to their mission. He didn't know if they could afford such a battle before they had a chance to explore.

The world seemed to stop. No one moved. No one breathed. Without a doubt, someone stood waiting on the other side of the thick fabric, just as they did on this side. He decided they had made too much noise and were already discovered.

"Attack!"

Aldway dug his dagger into the fabric and dragged it to the side, going with it, tearing it and pulling it away to reveal what lay behind. Githa charged forward and plunged her sword into the person standing there, then gasped. She hung in front of the crumpling body, watching it collapse to the floor with a grunt.

They poured out into the hall. Aldway stepped away from the thirty-foot tapestry which hadn't born the weight of him pressing into it well. It ripped away from the wall, and thundered to the stone floor, falling and collapsing before their eyes, landing on Githa and her victim. The sound of it falling echoed around the room, but there was no one else there. Brande and Eberhard dragged the fabric off Githa as quickly as they could. She stood straight, pushing the material away from her, and looked at them with horror in her eyes.

Lying on the ground, a large gash in his chest, was a tall child of no more than twelve years. He was dressed in nothing but a ragged shift of cotton. Even his feet were bare.

They stared at what she had done. Not one of them said anything. The boy lay on the ground, as still as the flagstones he lay on.

Aldway frowned and moved forward, he grabbed the boy by the shoulder and rolled him over. The back of the shift was soaked with blood from the wound left by the sword which had punched right through. Aldway's fingers traced a mark on the boy's neck, then he ripped away the shift, revealing bloody gashes on the boy's back. He'd been whipped, and the wounds still bled.

"I don't, I can't-" stammered Githa. "What have I done?"

"You weren't to know," reassured Eberhard. "You couldn't have known it was just a child."

Aldway spoke the obvious. "He's been whipped. Poor lad. His back's a mess."

There was no sign of life left in the child. Even as they looked on, his skin appeared to develop a tallow-like complexion. "We killed him," stated Aldway, sharing Githa's blame. Even in the shadows cast by the flickering torches, his eyes showed sorrow. He tugged at the tapestry, pulling part of it back over the boy to hide his body.

"Come," said Brande. "There will be more like him. We might have a chance to save them." He said this, but in his mind he still had but one purpose and that was to find and free his wife and daughter. However, if he had the chance to do good along the way, so be it. Aithne would demand it of him.

He wasn't sure what the room had been used for originally, but it was deserted now, except for a table and chair. The boy, it seemed, had been left alone to copy writing from scrolls. They examined the manuscripts for a moment, but the language was unknown to them. Brande showed no interest in the texts, his concern was to get moving before they were found and their mission became impossible.

The fallen tapestry was an obvious sign of intruders. If someone came looking for the boy, they would all be found out. He hated all this sneaking about. He hefted his axe to his shoulder. "Come on," he hissed. There were several possible exits.

"I can hear the screaming again," whispered Eberhard.

"It's not far," agreed Githa.

"It's time to do some real damage to these child-stealing bastards," he growled. He had spoken at full volume. Would anyone have heard? He didn't have to wait to find out.

"In here," urged a child's voice. A door flew open. A naked boy, younger than the one that lay dead, entered the room. They stared at him. His body was covered in dried blood. But for his untouched face, he was barely recognisable as human. He must have been whipped to within an inch of his life on more than one occasion. He pointed at them. "There!" He sounded triumphant. "Intruders!"

An acolyte swept into the room, his dark cloak billowing behind him. Another followed. Their bodies were skeletal despite being wound with thick black cloth. They looked like scarecrows not yet stuffed with straw. Their pale, grey faces were screwed up around dark eyes burning with hatred. The first raised a hand and began to incant.

"Quick," shouted Eberhard, running for a door.

The acolyte's gaze followed him. The distraction gave

Alastair Pack

Aldway time to shoot an arrow into the cultist's chest. The acolyte squirmed and staggered, but didn't drop to the ground. The sickly green light being woven on his palm faltered for a moment, then flickered, and grew in strength again as the incantation continued. He threw it at Eberhard, who threw himself to the ground and watched it rebuff against the wall above him, sending splinters of stone in all directions.

Two more arrows thudded home. The acolyte stumbled. Brande was on him, his battleaxe cleaving the monster in two and then smashing into the crumpling body over and over, hacking it to the ground. He turned on the other one.

The boy screamed and ran at Eberhard, with no apparent concern for his wellbeing. Eberhard paused, perhaps because the boy was so young. An arrow took him down. Githa looked at Aldway in horror, and he gave just the slightest of shrugs. Brande understood. The boy would raise the alarm. He had to be dealt with.

Brande moved toward the remaining acolyte, lifting his axe up high, ready to deal a devastating stroke.

The acolyte didn't move at first, just taking it all in, then he spoke and began to wave his hands around an imaginary ball in front of him. "You have killed two of my slaves and my apprentice, but you have not come prepared for me."

As he incanted, his lips moved, though no sound emerged. A black ball of ethereal fabric, like the one they had seen the acolyte in the prison cell conjure, formed between his crooked hands. It increased in size, pulsated, then blasted through the air at Aldway. The acolyte hissed, showing pointed teeth and a thin, pointed tongue that looked like a worm. That reminded Brande of something, but he had no time to think what. Aldway rolled away, leaving the black mass to strike a flagstone, melting it and leaving a glowing hole in the floor. Aldway was already nocking his next arrow.

Brande walked calmly toward the acolyte. "I once let

236

one of your kind escape. I won't make that mistake again."

The acolyte sneered and began incanting again. Brande charged. He swung his axe and brought it down on the acolyte, who screamed, unable to respond in time. The monstrous being collapsed in front of him. Githa was by his side, and she brought her sword down on its neck, decapitating it. Brande brought his axe down, again and again, hacking it into pieces. He'd already seen one corpse reattach its head and it wasn't a sight he was eager to see again.

"This one had none of the strength of the one in the dungeon," said Aldway, astutely.

"We've been lucky," agreed Githa. "These were not soldiers."

"We should move," grunted Brande.

The screams from the other room were unmistakable now. The thick door no longer blocked their sound.

"I don't want to…" said Githa, hesitating.

"Come," ordered Brande. "This is your rebellion."

Githa nodded and then steeled herself. She went first through the door. Brande was impressed by her bravery, but he knew they had all yet to be properly tested. This was nothing. The Crusades had taught him that.

Githa gasped as she entered the room.

"I've been waiting," said a voice. A figure on the far side of the room drew their attention. Another acolyte, it seemed, but in tattered black clothing, a cowl pulled over his head obscuring his face.

Brande entered. It was a massive room with no windows, lit entirely by candle and torch. What he saw confirmed all his concerns. Eberhard followed after him, with Aldway at the rear, arrow nocked and half-drawn.

"What is this?" demanded Eberhard, horrified.

"The children!" gasped Githa, breathlessly. Tears were already in her eyes.

Brande looked to Aldway and his companion. They

were all stupefied into non-action. Brande felt a pang of hurt in him, a realisation that they all had something still to lose in them that he had lost a long time ago. Some kind of innocence. For all their battle-hardened behaviours, for all that they had seen, none of them was ready for the horrors associated with the Rift.

This had once been a place for grand feasts and celebrations, but now it was something else. In the centre of the room, floorboards had been ripped up, stone removed, mud dug away, and before them now was a deep pit with smooth stone sides to prevent anyone escaping it.

Brande inched forward, looking down, trying not to take an eye off the person who had spoken.

The pit contained children, maybe thirty of them. All had deformities. Most of them had the deformities on their backs. All were covered in blood. Some were moaning, some were screaming. All were in pain. Some were fighting. Some were eating the ones that had fallen.

"What is this?" repeated Eberhard, shuddering.

"An experiment," answered the figure on the other side of the pit. He was alone. He moved toward them, around the edge of the pit. His ragged black cloak fluttered about him, tatty and grey in places. It woke a memory in Brande.

He had been standing by an altar. Empty chains hung from it where presumably a child had been held but was there no longer. Candles, seemingly placed at random, burned throughout the room. Some were on the altar, some on the floor, others on tables or balanced on pots or chairs. Bowls full of blood were also arranged across the floor, surrounded by etchings of strange symbols. In the background to it all, a silver statue of a man with a goat's legs and a woman's breasts, with the head of a giant snake and wings protruding from its back, stood tall, looking over the scene.

Brande sneered at the statue. "They worship Nachmair," he spat. "We thought as much."

"Oh, yes," rasped the figure. "We worship him. Revere him. We make sacrifices. But I am his High Priest. It falls on me to replicate him." He gestured to the children in the pit. Brande looked again and saw that the deformities some of the children had on their backs were stumps, but on others, they looked like tattered, fleshy wings. None of them looked like they could fly. Some of them had scales on their skin. A couple had snake-like tails. All were covered in each others' blood. "I will change them. Make them into little Nachmairs so our Lord can return. He will claim a body. But my experiments fail. I need more subjects. More children." The figure chuckled beneath its cowl. "Of course, the last test is seeing how badly they want to survive. I need ones that want to survive above all else."

"Monster!" cried Githa.

"They're monsters. I'm a monster. You killed a child, Githa… you're a monster. We're all monsters here."

She started at that. The acolyte's declaration was like a punch to her gut, not least because he somehow knew her name.

The acolyte in the tattered, feathery cloak pulled back his cowl and Brande saw what he expect to see. It revealed the bird-like features of the creature he'd met in Stonenife, the one that had tormented him in the garrison prison. Last time the creature had fled the sunlight and escaped. Brande tightened his grip on his axe, swearing to himself that this time only one of them would leave the room alive.

CHAPTER SIXTEEN

The creature continued its progress towards them. There was no hesitation or fear in it. It was alone but utterly confident that it was in no danger. Brande didn't like that one bit.

"Monster!" shouted Githa again, barely controlling her outrage. Brande knew she was struggling to deal with the horror in front of her. Her face was a pale mask of fright, her eyes hollowed out holes in her skull.

Eberhard was breathing deeply, almost panting. Aldway was looking at the children, and Brande knew what was going through his mind. He could never have explained how he knew it, but he could tell Aldway was counting the children, and comparing that figure with the number of arrows in his quiver. There were too few arrows.

Brande looked at the children, and all he could think was that Fia was too old to have been included in this. She would have been with the women and girls taken to the keep. For that, he was thankful. What he saw before him went against all that was natural and decent in the world.

"What will you do?" asked the High Priest of Nachmair.

It held open its talon-like hands in a symbol of hopelessness. It was mocking them, utterly confident in its control over the situation.

Brande stared at the priest's upturned hands and asked himself the same question. What would they do? It was him against the High Priest since his companions seemed lost in the horror of it all.

Brande had witnessed many unnatural things during the Crusades. The only thing that kept away the perpetual nightmares was the knowledge he had ended the lives of those who had committed the atrocities he'd witnessed. Some called them blood rites or scarlet sacraments, but they all had the same purpose: to draw power from the Rift.

As legend had it, the Rift was a place in time and space where Nachmair had entered the world and from which he still drew his obscene power. Some of this power he granted to his acolytes. They had found the High Priest performing blood rites here in Charstoke Keep, right under the King's nose. Brande looked at the children again, and something in him snapped. His blood began to boil. His teeth began to grind. He had fought against this for years under Leofric and hated it then and hated it now. The tiniest prospect that Fia or Aithne were caught up in this would have made him explode, but the certainty of it in his mind was too much.

The High Priest sensed his fury and laughed. "There's only one way you can beat me, and if you take that route, then Nachamair will have won. Isn't that right, Brande?"

Brande focused on his battle axe. He tried to keep his mind clear. Somewhere, locked deep within him, was a fury that no living being should possess. The excommunicated Sister of the Stone had locked it away for him, tied it off, dampened and sealed it in a terrible ritual performed atop the Strangled Mountains. Aithne had helped him keep it subdued all this time, all through Fia's younger years and as she grew into the young woman she was today. He had kept it at bay, but now, here, in this place, surrounded by blood and deformity, facing off against this creature of Nachmair's, all warped and shrivelled by powers drawn from the Rift, he felt something tug inside him, something loosen, something snap. It was free. After all these years, this is what it took to shake that darkly woven enchantment which held his own Deft power at bay.

Last time he had been in a situation like this, he hadn't spent any time thinking. He hadn't assessed the situation. He just brandished his axe, charged right in, and swung the blade with all his might. This time was no different.

A roar of defiance exploded from Brande's lungs. The children stopped their fighting and stared. The High Priest's hands dropped by his sides in surprise. His companions awoke from their stupor.

Brande ran, skirting the edge of the pit with the speed of an eagle dropping on its prey. The High Priest saw him coming and raised its hands. A black-purple mass swirled in its grasp, turning and warping and moving with a life of its own. The High Priest fired it at Brande, the strange churn of otherworldly colour streaking through the air toward the enraged warrior.

Brande swung his axe, its blade curving through the air. It hit the ball of blackness and knocked it down into the pit, where it exploded in a furious spluttering explosion which rocked the room. The pit was blasted to pieces, and gory remains blew into the air and splattered to the floor. Brande didn't miss a step, but span with the axe, the blade never stopping, curving round, rising up in an arc while he faced away from the priest, then down again with force as he turned to come face to face with the hellish creature.

His battle axe sliced through the High Priest's collarbone, down through its chest, its dry guts exploding like ancient papyrus. The creature's beak opened wide, and its worm-like tongue struck out amid a terrible cackling. It was laughing. The axe sliced down through its thigh bone and emerged just slightly bloody. Brande carried on round and forward, his axe swinging in a circle and striking down into the High Priest's face, cleaving it in two. He didn't stop. He spun. His eyes saw nothing. His heart pounded furiously. The fire in his belly raged like the eternal sun. His axe came down again and again. Finally, he bellowed a war cry and kicked the High Priest's messy remains into the pit, where a few remaining, living, child-like things descended on it and ripped it to pieces with their teeth, gnawing on its grisly flesh.

Githa looked on in horror. Aldway turned away. He still did not have enough arrows to end those little lives that remained after the explosion.

Brande tried to quell his anger, but it was lit. He pushed it down, but it sprang back up. Inside him, the fire was raging.

Eberhard looked not at the children, but at Brande. "You knocked it away," he said, reproachfully. "How can an axe do that?" Brande was always impressed by Eberhard's alertness to his surroundings, and this time Brande cursed the very trait that made Eberhard such a good travelling companion. He was not ready to explain, but it was true that the bolt from the High Priest should have smitten him to nothing more than a dusty shadow on the floor.

"Conviction," he growled, by way of an answer. He was in no mood to elaborate. Eberhard didn't press the point.

Brande looked into the pit. Some of the children were starting to climb up the rubble left from the blast. They were eyeing up the party and pointing towards them.

Outside a horn sounded. It was loud, a city-wide call to arms.

"They know we're here," said Aldway.

"No," Eberhard disagreed. "Something is happening out there."

"There's something happening in here," growled

Brande. He moved toward the children, waiting to see what they would do. Some crawled out of the pit, using the damaged floor and debris to escape, and fled the room. Others grouped together and moved toward them, like a pack of rats, hissing, some crawling, all getting closer.

"I can't," said Githa, moving away from them.

"I will," muttered Aldway, with a sour expression. He loosed some arrows. The children screamed and fled from the main chapel.

"Lilly said she thought there were more secret passageways, ones that lead deep into the keep," reminded Eberhard.

"Probably guarded," said Githa, pleased to think about anything but the children.

Brande was already halfway to the altar as if he already knew what he would find. He went behind the towering statue of Nachmair and tore down the tapestry there. Sure enough, there was another passageway. He grabbed a flaming torch from the wall. "Let's go," he said. "The whole damn keep will know we're here by now."

They descended stairs into the darkness. The way turned into a tunnel, little more than a mud floor with stone walls and wooden slats for the ceiling. Occasionally, there were sconces, but the torches were missing. It seemed the passage had been out of use for some time.

"This looks like it will lead under the lower bailey," said Brande.

"It might come back on itself," said Githa.

"Or fork in several directions," added Aldway, who had followed after with another torch.

"We need to get into the keep," said Brande. "We hold to account anyone we meet. We find the prisoners."

In his head, he was shouting to Fia and Aithne to let them know he was near. He loved them, he was coming for them, nothing would stop him, not deranged children, not Nachmair's High Priest, not Nachmair himself.

The tunnel went deep underground. At first, they sensed something was wrong, but as time passed, they realised they had travelled much farther than the boundary of the keep. "It's a maze down here," complained Aldway.

"A warren," suggested his partner.

It was not as simple as choosing one path or another. The tunnel twisted and turned and rooms and other tunnels shot off in all directions. "What purpose does this serve?" asked Githa. There seemed to be miles of tunnels down here, endless routes. "Who made this?"

Brande shook his head in the near-darkness. "I've no idea. It's too big to have been made recently. Look at this wood." He tapped the ceiling. Dirt and splinters of ancient wood crumbled away under the impact of his fingers.

Eberhard grunted agreement. "It could be the very reason this is the capital. Who knows what went on here in the past? These look like claw marks on the walls."

"Couldn't be worse than what was going on up there now," remarked Githa. Her voice trembled slightly at the memory of the children hurting each other.

After some time, Aldway's torch spluttered out. Brande still carried one. Occasionally, now less frequently, there were sconces on the walls holding unlit torches. Brande stopped to light one and gave it to Eberhard, who lit one and gave it to Githa.

The tunnel split into two, and each path split again. Brand let out a puff of resignation.

"Are we lost?" asked Aldway, cheerily. "I do so like to be lost below ground level with limited torchlight and demonic children running around upstairs. And what in the name of Hungrar was that thing calling itself the High Priest? There must have been a morning, a few days back, when I could have stayed in bed instead of getting up, and I'd have missed bumping into you lot, and this wouldn't be happen-"

"Stop gabbling," warned Eberhard.

"Yes, we're lost," confirmed Brande.

They halted. "Can we find our way back?" asked Aldway.

"I think so," said Githa. "We haven't really turned off a side shoot. We've always kept to the main path, the largest tunnels."

Brande nodded. "I think we came back on ourselves. I could be wrong, but I think we're near the perimeter of the keep. Look how much straighter the walls are here. And the tunnel is bigger. We've seen stone foundations in the walls and more wooden struts. Something heavy is above us. People worked down here securing the tunnels, some of the struts are of slightly newer wood. We've gone beyond the limits of the keep and have turned and are back at the walls, probably on the east side. I'm fairly sure of it."

"I hear something," said Githa. "That way." She pointed along the tunnel ahead of them.

"We should avoid that way, then," said Aldway. "Probably demonic moles, blindly making their way towards us with their giant claws. I hate small spaces. This is much worse than the skyte's cage."

"No," said Brande. "We should find who is making the noise and if possible question them. They may be able to bring us out somewhere useful."

"Probably acolytes," said Aldway. "Bird-faced priests and the like."

There was a moment of quiet as each of them made up their mind about what they thought was the best option, then Eberhard said, "Let's find them."

Aldway groaned. "Can't shoot arrows down here, you know. Who's going to keep you safe? Oh, come on then."

The decision was made, and Brande plunged forward into the darkness, holding his flickering torch before him.

They followed the noises, which didn't seem to remain

in one place. "They're on the move," remarked Aldway.

"Approaching us," said Brande, suddenly. The sound was increasing.

"We've been heard," whispered Githa.

"Good," said Brande. "I'm sick of these tunnels. Let them come to us. We'll get some answers out of them."

The earth around them seemed to reverberate with the footfalls of the approaching party.

"There could be a few of them," suggested Aldway.

"Back here," said Eberhard, who had dared wander off the main track on his own. They stumbled backwards and fell into a large chamber where Eberhard had been exploring. They lifted their torches and tried to identify the limits of the space. There was a slight ramp down into the room, and the ceiling must have been twelve foot high. It was a barren mud hole, an empty room no longer used for anything.

"Here is a good place to fight," said Githa.

"Yes," agreed Brande.

There was a hissing noise from the tunnel, like someone annoyed that they couldn't find their quarry.

"Oh dear," said Aldway.

"What?" asked Brande.

"It's not going to be human, is it?"

The rest of them drew breath. Even Brande hadn't considered the possibility, although he should have. It was quite likely the approaching thing was another of the High Priest's dark experiments. What could be worse than children with deformed wings and a taste for blood?

"Put the torches on the walls," said Brande, quickly. "We need free hands to fight."

The footfalls were heavy, but there was just one set. It was not a party approaching, just something big. There was an accompanying shuffling sound. And hissing.

The same image filled all their heads. Nachmair.

It was huge and filled the tunnel. The creature roared as

it stumbled down the ramp into the room with them. They had it surrounded, but that didn't count for much. Even now, it was unclear if it was at full height or stooping. Hard lumps on its lizard head scraped across the cavern ceiling. It had two muscular arms, two sturdy legs, and a tail with sizeable spikes on the end which switched behind it, making the shuffling sound. The traces of human were unmistakable. Its torso was flesh coloured. Its eyes were all too normal and looked wide and innocent in its serpentine head. Its legs and chest were hairy. Its left hand was a claw, but its right, though reptilian, was more like a man's, and in it, it held a mace. The object was two foot long, steel, a long handle leading into a thick, tapering cylinder with a spike not unlike those on the creature's tail jutting out from the side of it. It looked heavy, heavier than an average man might use, and with the creature's extended reach it would be utterly deadly if it made contact.

"Was this part of the plan?" asked Aldway. "I thought we were rescuing people. I don't remember this being part of the plan."

The creature snarled. Its wide eyes looked panicked, and it started towards Githa, who backed off slowly, raising her sword. "That's right," she taunted. "This way."

Brande moved around the creature, thinking to get behind it. Aldway loosed an arrow towards its face but missed as the beast lunged for Githa. It struck with its clawed hand. She was hit, knocked to the ground. It raised the mace.

Eberhard's longsword found its way across the creature's arm. He had probably hoped to sever it, but all that was left from the blow was a deep cut. The deformed monstrosity roared and turned to him. Githa didn't lie still, she grabbed her sword from where it had fallen and rammed it into the creature's foot. It screamed in pain and went to kick her, but an arrow struck it from behind.

She rolled away. It watched her movement, and Brande

didn't waste a moment. He brought his axe down into its back, hoping to sever its spine. The cut was shallow. The creatures hide was thick, and although it shrieked in torment, it shrugged the axe away and rounded on Brande.

Brande backed away, realising he was holding back the rage inside him. He owed that to Aithne. Didn't he? He had broken the Sister of the Stone's seal, now only he could hold it back. He thought he could feel it growing inside him. He had loosed it on the High Priest, and it was out now. This beast could not be allowed to live. He still had hold of his battle axe. He turned it around in his hands and ran at the creature. He planted the axe blade into its chest, then fell between its legs and scurried through them. He grabbed on to its tail and clung to it, as it swung him back and forth. The beast tugged at the axe, drawing it from its chest and tossing it away. Aldway loosed more arrows into it. Eberhard swung for its head, but it retaliated, knocking the sword away with its mace. It was quicker than it looked.

Brande held on to its tail but now with his legs wrapped around it. Aldway drew a dagger, aimed, and threw it directly into the tail, right next to Brande, with immense precision. Brande pulled the blade out of its flesh and started hacking. The mace swung past close to his head, a near miss.

His axe had been thrown to the side of the room by the creature. He hoped to slow it, maybe sever the tail, but it was a half-done job. He didn't want his skull turned to paste by the creature's mace. He let go and rolled away. At that moment, Githa jumped on the creature's back and drove her sword deep into the gap between its clavicle and its throat. The beast staggered. She thought she'd delivered the killing blow.

It threw Githa away, and she landed hard, grunting. The creature stumbled close to Aldway, and its left claw-hand pounded him into the wall. He slumped there, stunned.

The half-man, half-lizard was in agony and absolutely

manic. Brande used the moment to snatch back his axe. He and the others backed away as the creature thrashed back and forth trying to manage its pain. It reached to its shoulders and somehow pulled Githa's sword from its body. It threw it out the door. It had learned not to let them recover their weapons. It was at least that smart.

It crossed Brande's mind that this could just be another child that had undergone experimentation. Due to the partial success of the experiment, it may have been left to grow in the tunnels, to see how it fared. Or it could be anyone, turned into something nightmarish, a more advanced version of what had happened to Alland.

For all its injuries, the creature bled very little. It roared again and charged for Eberhard. He swung at it, slicing its chest. It was fast and struck him with the mace. He blocked with his sword, but the force of its strength sent him reeling. It was fast, too, and getting faster. There was some dark power assisting this beast. "It's not bleeding," noticed Eberhard, pointing to the wound that Githa had inflicted. "It's healing fast."

The creature bellowed, frustrated that its prey was proving so difficult. It followed Eberhard as he backed away. Githa retreated to the exit to get her sword from the tunnel where the creature had thrown it. Aldway was crouched on the floor, holding his head. Brande was relieved to see him get to his feet and start looking for his bow.

"Do you have any poisoned arrows?" asked Eberhard.

"Good idea," shouted Githa, from the door. She had her sword in her hand again.

Aldway staggered, finding his balance with difficulty. "I have one. I'll try it. But this thing hardly bleeds and poison works in the blood, so I don't know if it'll work."

"It might slow it," urged Eberhard.

To distract it, Aldway released a regular arrow, aiming low because of the close confines. It struck the creature on the side of its head, next to the hole that must have been its ear. It bellowed again and pulled the shaft from its head, snapping off the arrowhead in doing so. It threw the remains of the arrow to the ground.

Aldway started nocking a new arrow to his bow. It had a red cock feather, telling him it was different from the others. He didn't shoot it immediately, waiting for just the right moment.

The creature turned and started toward the exit. It had had enough. It bellowed in pain, clutching its ear where the arrowhead was still under the flesh. It found Brande and Githa blocking the exit. It staggered, off-balance because of the pain and its maimed tail, which hung, unmoving behind it, dragging and slowing the creature. Brande realised he must have done a better job than he'd realised with Aldway's dagger, severing nerves and muscle.

Brande edged forward with his axe. This time, he was going to go for the head. There weren't many things that could survive having their skull split down the middle.

The creature, seeing it was surrounded, and roaring in frustration, moved to the wall and knocked a torch from its bracket. The flame hit the ground, and the creature stamped on it, making it splutter out.

There was a twang as Aldway shot his poisoned arrow. The beast roared defiantly as it hit home, straight in its neck. The lizard-man screamed and charged at Aldway, but he was ready this time and dived out the way. The beast roared and struck another torch from the wall, grinding its clawed foot into the flame.

"It's deliberately going for the lights," warned Githa.

"This isn't going our way," growled Brande.

Eberhard nodded. "Brande, you go with the others. I'll stall it."

"You're doing nothing without me," promised Aldway.

"You'll be fighting blind," she said. "It probably sees in the dark."

251

There was no wind down here, but Brande's torch, the one he had left in the tunnel outside, guttered. "We don't have long."

"Go!" said Aldway. "Githa, Brande. Go. We'll hold it. Then we'll run for it."

The creature didn't seem to like Aldway's shouting. It sprung at him. He dodged, and it collided with the wall. Roaring in anger, it charged Eberhard, who managed to land a good blow across its arm as he moved away. The creature's left arm hung limp for a moment, but then it seemed to regain strength and moved. "Its tail," said Brande. "It's moving again. There's some unusual power here. Try to behead it, or burn it, but otherwise, just get away."

"You're not going!" yelped Githa.

"I am," said Brande. "I need to find my wife and child."

Githa frowned but nodded. Her look suggested she doubted his family was still alive, but she again made up her mind quickly. "I'm coming too."

Together, they took one last glance back. Aldway had the one remaining torch in the room. He was determined to keep it alive. Seeing that no side was obviously going to win, Githa and Brande hurried away into the darkness with the guttering torch.

They heard Eberhard cry out as they raced down the tunnel and looked at each other, just shadows now. Moments later, the torch died and there was pitch blackness.

They ran for a time, running their hands along the walls to keep a sense of where they were. They listened for each other's breathing. They seemed attuned to each other and occasionally would reach out and just touch the other's shoulder or arm for reassurance they were there. They didn't need to explain what they were doing, both just seemed to know. In the darkness, there was an understanding between them.

Suddenly they were separated. "Stop," yelled Githa.

They both retraced their steps, four or five large paces. Githa held Brande's shoulder. "There's a divider. The tunnel splits. I went this way, you went that. Which way?" They couldn't see each other, but they could tell from their ragged breathing that they were both getting tired of this underground maze and its absolute darkness.

Brande closed his eyes. The darkness didn't change, but he thought he could hear things above him. There was a commotion, stamping. It penetrated the ground above them. "This way," he said, taking her down his route.

They ran in the darkness. At some point, they had stopped being able to hear the battle between Eberhard, Aldway and the lizard-man. It felt like they had travelled a great distance, but the keep was not that big, and Brande insisted it was still above and around them. "The length of these tunnels is deceptive. They curve and twist and fold back on themselves. It's clever. Whoever designed this labyrinth knew what they were doing."

"Who? Who made these tunnels?"

"I don't know. They're probably older than the keep. Older than the city, perhaps."

"Then who?"

Brande let out a cry of pain.

"What?"

"Knee. Hit something."

He knelt and clutched his knee for a second, letting the pain subside. He put his hand out in front of him, hitting something wooden. He patted it. He patted the thing above it. And the thing above that. Githa reached out too.

"Steps," she said.

They looked up and realised there was a shimmer of greyness in the darkness.

"We need to leave something," she said, "so Eberhard and Aldway know we went this way."

Brande took Aldway's dagger, the one he'd used on the

creature's tail, which he had in his belt, and swung it into the wooden step. It stuck.

"Good. They'll know we went this way."

"I was just getting my own back on the stair," grunted Brande. He couldn't see if she smiled. "Come on," he said, clambering forward, slightly unsteady on the knee he'd just knocked. "This goes to the tower."

"How do you know?"

"Look how high up that light is. We're not that far below the surface."

She nodded in the darkness, accepting his logic.

They bounded up the stairs. It was a long climb. The steps were old but stable. Both of them were trying to be quiet, but the old wood creaked as they pounded up it. The steps stopped, and they found a ladder attached to the wall in front of them. It seemed solid, though they could hardly see it. They started climbing. Brande went first. Climbing sapped the last of their energy after the fight, the long run through the tunnel and ascending the stairs.

Finally, Brande clambered on to a solid deck. He helped Githa on to it. She gasped, feeling his strong hands pulling her up on to it. She didn't begrudge his assistance, her legs and arms were like lead.

More stairs spiralled upwards, but there was some visibility now. The walls had turned from mud, to stone, to wood, as they had climbed. The quality of the wood had improved. This was newer. The tower was newer. Light broke through a slight crack in the wooden wall, and they could see again. They could hear shouting and metal on metal outside the tower. The noise had been going on for some time, but it was loud now. Brande's senses had been right and had led them towards it, towards the fight. They climbed and came to a door. Brande opened it. It wasn't even locked.

Light. It poured in around them, and they both sighed in relief, blinking as they grew accustomed to it. It felt like a weight being lifted from them and seemed to renew their energies. "We're in some secret passage in the tower," stated Brande. "Such noise outside. It's Nachmair's Night, but I'd recognise the sound of battle anywhere."

"Up the stairs," she said. There was an arrow loop in the external wall of the stairwell. They looked out of the thin slit at the setting sun. There was fighting outside in the inner ward of the castle. Acolytes stood motionless behind soldiers who were defending the keep. The townsfolk had risen up. A blast of noise filled the air. They looked for the source, and there was Alland. He had a large horn, made from a curved tusk as long as a man's arm, pushed to his lips.

"There!" said Githa, trying to point through the narrow window.

Brande looked and saw Elderman Alewyn in his green robes. Somehow he was free. He was on horseback. Along with other men, he rode into the fight.

"I told you," she said. "The people were ready. We should have waited. It would have been easier."

Brande snorted. He would use it to his advantage. He carried on up the stairs, leaving Githa behind him, looking out. He glanced back. She was smiling and looking out at her brother.

He moved on.

After a moment, she chased after him. He heard her mutter to herself in wonder. "Alland brought an army!"

CHAPTER SEVENTEEN

From the top of the tower, despite the dwindling daylight, they could see carnage unfolding all around the keep. Alland seemed to be in charge of a large group of commoners armed with swords, pitchforks, and seemingly anything they could get their hands on that was sharp or heavy and blunt.

The Elderman sat astride a large, bay stallion. Other riders were positioned alongside and in file behind him. Many of their fighters were still dressed for Nachmair's Night, wearing garish colours, horns or vegetables. That explained how they had amassed so quickly and got past the guards, thought Brande, looking down from atop the tower. Nachmair's Night. A night when chaos was already present. A night when these worshippers of Nachmair would feel most confident and so, being unwary, actually be at their weakest.

The King's soldiers fought against the commoners. But not all of them. Brande saw soldiers shifting allegiance before his eyes. He was sure most of them would want to fight beside their own people, not against them. Why side with the acolytes who were clearly monsters? No wonder the Elderman and Alland had felt such confidence. "You knew this? This evening?" he asked Githa.

She shook her head. "Not when or exactly how. Elderman Alewyn never revealed those details."

Brande nodded acknowledgement. "The secret passageway brought us to the top here," said Brande. He knew it had wasted time and sapped their strength. "But we can go down through the tower now. We're in the keep."

"Seeing all this fighting is making me edgy," she replied. "I want to be a part of it."

"I don't suppose you'll have long to wait."

They were just about to head for the stairs when one of the motionless acolytes below decided to join the battle. Instantly, the nature of the fight changed. Colourful strands of woven energy sucked from the Rift and manifested in the air sparked across the battlefield. There was blood. The commoners were pushed backwards, many engulfed in purple and yellow flames. Just one acolyte had turned the flow of the battle. Alland was crying to his men to reform, to hold fast, to attack, anything but run in fear. To their credit, they surged forward and swamped the acolyte. "Watch this," ordered Brande. "If they can kill one acolyte, they can kill more."

Githa watched.

The acolyte used everything at his disposal. He shapeshifted and grew, claws extended from his hands. Black sparks flew from his eyes and a weave of power started to form above him. His face grew jaws which bit at his attackers as they swarmed over him. Black shadows, like solid silhouettes, rose around him, as if summoned from the earth, and started grabbing at the rebelling townsfolk, dragging them to the ground. "It looks bad," said Githa. She glanced around to make sure Alland was still alive. She caught sight of his deformed face. He looked up, somehow sensing her, and locked eyes with her. His face was set with determination.

The Elderman shouted to the men of the city, as the acolyte and surrounding soldiers drove them back. The peasants rallied and rebuffed their efforts, driving forwards again. There was a cry of surprise as the acolyte fell under the attack and was trampled and hacked to death. The shadows and the supernatural powers disappeared with a crackle of energy. The tide turned, and the acolyte was carried away over people's heads, a victory trophy. Like a swarm of ants, Alland's men crossed the courtyard, cutting through the line of soldiers. The body of the fallen acolyte was dumped unceremoniously and left in their wake.

"There's hope," she said.

"Come. Let's get into the keep," said Brande, heading for the stairs.

They stopped in surprise. Two archers were climbing the stairs, bows in hand, hoping to reach the top of the tower and use the vantage point to pick off important targets. Githa was just ahead of Brande, and he later remembered the word that left her mouth was, "Finally." She felled the first soldier before he knew what was happening, and the second before he could draw his sword. She kicked them to the side and pressed on down the stairwell as if nothing had happened. Brande laughed, impressed, and followed after.

"This won't take long," he thought aloud.

Behind them, the sun touched the horizon and spread out like it was melting in the sky.

"Defend the King!" yelled a guard, as Githa and Brande turned into the antechamber outside the main hall. The commotion outside meant the room was well guarded. If that guard had meant what he said, then the king was waiting for them behind the massive oak doors in front of them. Eight soldiers stood outside the door, four either side of it. Brande noticed that they wore the same black kerchiefs as the ones in the prison under the garrison at Bruke. They were working with the acolytes. Fortunately, none of those servants of Nachmair was about.

"I've got this," said Brande and Githa at the same time. They both smirked and charged into battle. Githa took the four on the right. With incredible precision, she blocked and parried the thrusts of the first two that responded to her. She seemed to swirl and strike in one simple motion, almost too fast for the eye to see, and as she took on the second two guards, the first two fell to the ground with a clash of metal against stone. She despatched them all in almost no time at all. She turned, and Brande was standing holding a dripping axe. Four men lay at his feet on the other side of the door.

"I'll get the door," he growled. He barged it with his shoulder, and Githa gasped as the door didn't just give way, but shattered and exploded into the great hall beyond. She had no way to know he was tapping his Deft abilities, harnessing the rage within him.

Just within the door were more guards. Closer to the King were men loyal to him, some knights, with their weapons already drawn. The King sat on his throne looking alarmed and angry.

A woman was draped against the side of his throne. Brande blinked in disbelief. It was Aithne. She was perched by the King, curled at his side like a fawning cat. Brande had no time to make sense of it.

A swinging flail narrowly missed his face by an inch. Brande was confused by what he'd seen and had paused just a second too long. The flail caught his axe blade and almost tore it from his hands. He quickly regained his senses and kicked the man on the side of his knee, destroying the leg joint. The man cried out and began to collapse. Brande drove the spike atop his axe up under the man's chin, just above his gorget. Blood bubbled out of the soldier's screaming mouth.

Others came at him, brandishing swords, but Githa parried one blow in passing, and Brande blocked the other with the haft of his axe. He needn't have worried about his moment's hesitation. Githa, her blonde hair tied back in a warrior's plait, swung like the wind carried her, decapitating one enemy and severing the throat of another. Brande brought his axe down on the nearest man's arm, smashing his sword out of the way. The man fell to the floor screaming, and Githa stepped in to finish him. They stood there, soaked in blood, staring at the King.

The amassed warriors and knights, no less than seven of them, approached cautiously. They were all shapes and sizes, a motley crew of loyal but deadly men. The King was not a fighter. He surrounded himself with these men to make himself feel secure. Seeing Brande and Githa standing blood-soaked before him, he looked nervous but, for some reason, not afraid.

A small man with a long black beard hefted an axe. A broad, fat ox of a man carried a morning star and a small round buckler. Another taller, thinner man held a double-bladed punching knife. Brande could see from their eyes they weren't the usual quality of soldier. These were warriors.

Brande looked up and saw Aithne rise and stand close by the King, resting a reassuring hand on his shoulder. "Aithne!" he called to her. Just a flicker of recognition in her eyes would be enough to set him alight, make his heart rise up, and he would tear toward her, but her eyes were dull, and she looked at him with little interest, even slight menace. "Aithne!" he called again. She did not respond.

"I don't understand," he growled, grinding his teeth.

Githa looked from him to the woman. She was a beautiful woman with long auburn hair, wearing finery fit for a princess, including a necklace of tiny sapphires. She did not look like a prisoner. "That's your wife?" she asked, incredulous.

Brande nodded. Something was very wrong. He needed to speak to Aithne and find out what. Not for a second did he imagine she would ever betray him.

The men attacked, but not as one. They had seen the quick demise of the soldiers. The bravest came first. The man with the punching knives went for Githa, but despite his skill, she seemed to curve and slide in the air, like she knew the dance to music no one else could hear. Brande caught this from the corner of his eye and was again impressed. No one around here fought with such grace. Her blade sliced up between the punching daggers and across the man's jaw, ensuring he'd never speak again. She whirled and spun, cutting him down with deadly finality. The longsword bearer decided it was time to jump in, but she wasn't taken by surprise, and she dealt with him just as surely. The axeman attacked, and she took her time, but he was no match for her. It was the little man with the sabres, one in each hand, that caught her unaware. One of his blades sliced her shoulder, and she cried out in pain. Brande had been fighting too, tapping into the anger within him to make quick work of the warriors who pressed into him. He saw Githa stagger under the blow, but already his arm and battle axe were at full extension, momentum carrying them around with terrific speed. The sabre user's neck caught the attack full on. His head tumbled away as his neck gushed like a fountain.

"Grateful," said Githa, holding the cut on her shoulder which was dribbling thick blood.

Three women had slid into the room through a door behind the throne. They were all tall, slender, and wore black kerchiefs about their necks. Each held a weapon Brande hadn't seen before. They were long staves with wildly jagged blades on each end, like lightning forks spreading out at all angles. Brande figured the blades were designed to snare an opponent rather than kill it outright.

They circled the throne and began swirling their staves around at astonishing speed. Brande was almost impressed. He threw his axe and rather than deflect it, the woman closest to him staggered away with it in her chest. She dropped to the ground, dead before she hit the flagstones. "The other two are yours."

"Pleasure," grunted Githa. She moved forward, but they both knew it would be a difficult fight with one arm injured. Brande left her to it. He had Aithne in his sights.

He walked toward the throne. The King was on his feet. "Halt!" he ordered as if Brande would accept his authority. There were some courtiers in the room, but they had all shrunk away from their king, frightened of this intruder who had cut through the guard like it was nothing.

Aithne grabbed the King's wrist in fear. The King, to Brande's mind, did not look worried enough. Brande felt in his gut that something was wrong and he snatched his axe from the woman's body where it had lodged.

"Aithne," he appealed. "Come down from there."

She laughed nervously. "Why would I do that?"

Brande felt like someone had punched him in the gut, forcing the wind from him.

A cry of pain was silenced behind him, and Githa was suddenly by his side. She had defeated the last of the women.

"Are you Aithne, wife of Brande?" asked Githa.

"I was," said Aithne, looking at Githa with surprise. "And who might you be?"

Githa didn't answer. "What now?" she asked Brande.

Brande could barely speak. "Aithne, what is this?"

There was laughter, but it came from none of them. Above, there was a balcony, such as where a band might play while people feasted in the Great Hall. For the first time, they noticed a man in the shadows. Perhaps he had been standing there the whole time. He wore a black cloak, like the acolytes, but this one was threaded through with gold, and he wore a golden serpent emblem about his neck, hanging from a leather cord. His face was sallow and quite plain, save for a black goatee and thick eyebrows. He was younger than Brande, but older than Githa. He chuckled quietly now, watching them with interest.

"Aithne," whispered Brande, imploring her to respond the way he expected.

"How dare you stand before your ruler and not address him," barked King Ignatius. He sat rigid-backed on his throne with an undeniable sense of authority. His body was wiry and lean, and he had a long, thin face with many lines and wild hair unbecoming of a king. His lips, set in a snarl, were thin and bloodless. "You will not address my concubine unless I command it." The man on the balcony laughed at that, as well.

Brande took a deep breath. The anger in him was bubbling like a pot ready to overspill, but he held it in check. The sight of Aithne somehow helped him with that, even though her strange behaviour twisted a tight knot in his stomach. It was all he could do to grip the handle of his axe more tightly and say nothing. He ground his teeth together, and there was no doubt everyone in the room could hear him do it.

Githa stepped forward and bowed. "My liege," she said. "We come for the lady by your side. She is this man's lawful wife."

The King snorted. He turned to Aithne. "It is your choice, my dear."

Brande stood motionless, and Aithne turned to him with a sneer. "Why would I want this ugly, penniless brute?"

Brande's world rocked under him. He could not tell if it was in his mind or if his legs actually buckled. He shook his head. "Aithne, have I wronged you?"

"I have chosen Ignatius. He's twice the man you are," she mocked, grasping her own crotch as if the point wasn't clear enough.

The man on the balcony tried to suppress his guffaw. Brande looked up, but the man slipped away through a door and into the shadows. The King was laughing too.

Githa grabbed Brande's shoulder, responding to the confusion and hurt in his eyes. "Look in her eyes, Brande. There's madness there. The King's too. They're bewitched, this is something else from the Rift." There was a gasp from some of the courtiers, whether because it smacked of treason or because it rang with truth was hard to say. "Come with me, Brande."

Brande blinked in surprise. He saw the truth of it as if he too had been bewitched and was now released from the spell. "Yes," he mumbled.

"We can still rescue her," promised Githa. "She's not harmed. Let's go and find Fia. She may be in more danger."

"Fia…" said Aithne, she seemed struck with confusion for just a moment, then her face darkened again. "You cannot rescue me from a choice I have made! Guards! Guards!"

"Guards!" yelled the King.

"Don't you have your own quarrel with the King?" asked Brande.

Githa paused, not expecting the question. "I've seen enough. He isn't the enemy."

They ran. Brande cast a glance back at Aithne, but just saw a stranger. He and Githa slipped through a door at the side of the hall as the King continued to yell for his guards.

Githa spoke first, "She's not herself. We must kill whoever enchanted her to break the curse."

"The man on the balcony," realised Brande. He understood it all too clearly now. He had been unprepared for such emotional hurt, but now he was away from Aithne he saw what this was. "He has enchanted the King and Aithne. I am sure of it."

"Another High Priest?" asked Githa.

He cast his mind back to a distant memory, an order of

damnable cultists he had fought during the Crusades. "No. He wore a gilded serpent. That symbol once denoted that a person was a warlock."

"A warlock? I thought them myth."

"King Leofric spread that misinformation after the final Crusade. People here feared warlocks. He neutralised their fear."

Githa shook her head in frustration. "I think he went that way. What lies that way? Isn't that the dungeons?"

Brande stopped running. He closed his eyes and placed a hand on the wall. Suddenly, he felt sick. "He had Aithne," he stammered. Something felt terribly wrong to him. "Why Aithne?" he managed.

Githa shrugged. "He knew you were coming, so they chose your wife to punish you… wait! You think he has Fia too?"

"The dungeons!" gasped Brande. "Come!"

They charged along a hallway, and two guards in plate armour emerged in front of them. Brande growled. Githa raised her sword and adopted a stance Brande was unfamiliar with. The guards were heavily armoured, and both wore swords but carried flails. The soldiers looked at each other and then at Brande and Githa. They attacked, but not for long.

Brande and Githa made their way down a flight of stairs. Several more castle guards tried to stop them, but Brande's anger and Githa's aptitude made them formidable. Some servants had also tried to stop them, out of some misplaced sense of duty. The pair shoved them aside roughly, not meaning to harm those who were merely foolish. They were lucky that the resistance they met was minimal, a fortunate side effect of the battle still raging outside the keep's walls that demanded the presence of soldiers and acolytes alike.

"This door is bolted. I think this is the way to the dungeons, though," said Githa.

"Step aside," ordered Brande. He brought his axe down

on the door and cut through iron and wood like it was meat on a plate. He kicked the door, and it opened.

They entered an empty room, barely twenty paces across. The floor and walls were stone, and only a small archer's loop provided light, although that was limited as night was now descending. A colossal trapdoor dominated the centre of the floor.

"Are these the dungeons?" he wondered. It seemed unusual to have a trapdoor as access.

"Nothing about any of this feels right," said Githa.

Brande nodded grimly, then went forward and grabbed the metal ring atop the trapdoor and pulled. It was heavy, but inch by inch it came. He shoved and grunted with the effort of lifting it. Githa ran forward and added her strength. It passed the vertical, flipped over on its hinges, and slammed backwards on to the floor, leaving a gaping hole and revealing a stairwell going down into the darkness. As soon as the trapdoor had crashed down, they heard the sound of wailing rising from below. The thin voices of girls and women who had lost all hope cried out to them in despair. The sound was outrageous and unbearable.

Githa whitened. "You first," she said, unashamedly.

There was a movement to the side of them. They'd been found. "Halt! How dare you enter here?!" Three men in leather tunics entered the room, holding swords with rough edges that were badly in need of repair. Brande took them for servants that were attempting heroics on behalf of their king.

"I'll deal with them," Githa said. He saw her rotate her injured shoulder and there was good movement in it. He felt assured that she could handle their new assailants.

Brande nodded his appreciation and descended the stairs. He headed down into the darkness, toward the sound of crying and screaming. He quickly glanced back at Githa. She was like a cat. One leg bent, one outstretched, her pose gave her the strength to reflect heavy blows, yet provided a springboard for attack. She swung her sword in patterns that struck nothing but dismayed her attackers, never giving them warning about where the next blow might originate.

Brande ducked down, and she was lost from sight. There was a dark room at the bottom of the stairs, barely lit at all by the light from the room above despite the trapdoor being open. Something was swarming on the floor. His first thought was rats, but as he approached he could tell from the noise it was children. They were huddled on the floor, maybe fifty of them. Some were naked, some still wore woollen rags. Older girls stood around the edges, forlorn hopelessness on their faces. The smell of fear and faeces was acrid and overwhelming. Brande looked for Fia's face amongst them, but it was too dim to see. "Fia?" he tried, but they all wailed and shied away from him.

Brande had seen many terrible things, but this sickened him to his core. "Out!" he bellowed at them. Suddenly he was annoyed that they were cowering instead of fleeing, but realised they had no way to know if he was friend or foe. "Out!" he ordered again, running up the stairs, pointing the way for them. "Out!"

Unexpectedly, a small boy rose out of the shadows and put a foot on the bottom stair. "Good lad," encouraged Brande, motioning him forward. "Everyone, up the stairs!"

He climbed out of the way. Above, he found Githa's opponents had been joined by several men in chain mail. She had despatched two of the servants but was under strain holding back the newcomers. Brande joined her, his great axe carving through them. As the children poured from the hatch into the light above, Brande felt he was clearing a path for them and was swift and merciless.

Githa gasped in shock, seeing the prisoners for the first time. The children were covered in dirt, blood, faeces and very few were clothed. "People must have known about this," she said bitterly, still panting from the effort of fighting. "How could this be allowed to happen?"

Brande offered no explanation, for he knew none.

Some of the prisoners were injured. Brande and Githa pulled them up out of the hatch. "Don't go outside," Githa warned the older ones. "There is a battle. Find a quiet place. Hide. Stay together."

"Thank you," said one older girl, standing in rags before them. Githa managed a smile.

Brande ducked back down the hatch to check for others. He helped the last few girls make their way up the stairs. They were uninjured but too frightened to move. The sight of dead bodies strewn across the floor did little to encourage them. One had a broken arm, she said she'd been thrown down into the hole by soldiers. He didn't want to further upset them with questions.

"We should help them," said Githa.

Brande took a moment to compose his words, then said, "Fia was not amongst them." It was a refusal.

Githa pursed her lips for a moment, then said, "To the dungeons."

He nodded. "Are you with me?"

"All the way," she replied. It looked like she was going to add something else, but whatever it was died on her lips.

Something had broken inside Brande. He had broken the seal cast by the Sister of the Stone. All the gentle words Aithne had whispered into his ears were fading away to nothingness. She always reminded him that the Crusades were over and that he was a different person now. Together, they would create a new life for him, a new world. They would live with their daughter, and they would be happy. But it all died away in an instant.

This was the Crusades all over again.

These men would learn to fear his name like others once had. He felt the fire in him burning again, an inferno of rage, his anger stoked until the flames in his gut writhed and churned, driving him into a mad fury. Once again, he was Brande the Butcher and all who came before him would tremble and die.

"It's time to finish this," he growled.

They found the entrance to the dungeon. Strangely, it was unguarded. The sound of fighting outside the keep was still audible so they knew this was the best chance they would ever have to infiltrate the dungeons and find out what horrors lay within.

"If we do find Fia…" she began, trying to warn him that he might not like what he found, trying to soften the impact of what they might encounter.

"Come on," urged Brande. Somehow, he knew Fia was down there and that the warlock he had seen was hurting her. The anger in his gut was unbridled now, the fire inside raging, tearing at his insides. He ground his teeth and plunged forward into the dungeons.

They quickly picked their way down a spiral stone staircase. Reaching the bottom, the ground was damp, and it was pitch black. They stumbled along blindly for a time, then sensed they were reaching the end of this stone tunnel when the darkness turned to grey, and evidence of flickering torchlight made the walls visible. They emerged from the darkness at the entrance to a corridor lined with prison cells. A lit torch flickered dimly on the wall. A stool and a small table were unoccupied, a place where a guard might typically sit. A rat scurried past them. Githa watched it for a moment. It didn't seem anyone was down here. They checked a few of the cells, but they were empty. "This way," said Brande, in hushed tones, taking them forward toward a closed door at the end of the walkway.

Before they got there, the door opened, and an acolyte stepped through. They hesitated, cursing their ill fortune. The acolyte paused only momentarily, then pushed back its hood to reveal the face of an old, shrivelled man smiling at them. He did not seem as monstrous as some they had seen.

Githa picked up the stool and charged the acolyte. The figure in black waved his hand. A flash of blue light knocked her to the side of the corridor, wrenching the stool from her grip. It seemed as if she had planned for this, for instantly she rebounded from the fall with her sword drawn, suddenly more deadly than before the acolyte had disarmed her of the stool. The acolyte was forced to step back. He wove another gesture in the air and Githa was thrown aside before she could reach him.

The distraction was all Brande needed. He barrelled forward and drove his axe's spike into the acolyte's gut. Room for movement was limited in the narrow space and swinging a weapon as large as his battle axe was awkward, but driving it like a spear into the demonic figure was just as effective. The acolyte absorbed the attack and barely budged. His face showed no sign of pain. He grabbed the axe's handle and immediately Brande felt stabbing pain shooting through his hands and arms. He dropped the weapon.

The pain stopped.

He had been surprised, but he had fought worse than this in his youth. He laughed, the look on his face more demonic than that of the acolyte's. "You ever hear of Brande the Butcher?" he asked. The acolyte's eyes widened with interest, but there was no sign of shock there.

Brande launched at him. His fists pummelled the figure's face and then grabbed his throat. A withered, purple tongue protruded in a panicked spasm. He was trying to speak, but couldn't. Brande saw the man's fingertips glow, but before anything happened, he crashed the acolyte's skull against the wall and pinned him there.

Githa had her sword through the man's heart before he could make a move. He burbled and then swung an arm. Brande was lifted up through the air and smashed against the ceiling. He collapsed to the ground with a dull thud.

Githa drove the sword higher and higher into the being until the tip came out the back of his neck. His sad, old face looked at her with strange dark eyes, then he hissed violently, but the eyes faltered and then stared past her. The acolyte's body slid down the wall, landing like nothing more than rags on the ground. She extracted her sword with a swift yank, watching the whole length of it slide from his insides. There was barely any blood on it.

Brande was already on his feet. He reclaimed his weapon. "You did well," he said.

Githa's looked like she might smile, but it never came. She nodded grimly. "Through here," she said, leading the way through the door. "No point keeping quiet after that."

"I can hear people running," said Brande. "Approaching from behind us."

The next corridor had no prison cells, just stone walls. "Where does it all go?" asked Githa. There was noise from behind a door hanging ajar at the end of the corridor from which light poured in.

They approached it cautiously, and Brande threw the door open and found two acolytes gliding up a lengthy set of stone stairs towards them from some massive room. A shout came from behind them. Brande looked back and saw several soldiers bolting their way toward them.

Brande hesitated. Githa stared with wide eyes around her. This was no dungeon they'd entered. They found themselves at the top of a stone staircase, leading down into a large hall, surrounded by a viewing balcony that ran right around the room. The room was busy with more acolytes than they had ever imagined existed. Brande estimated fifty of them, but it could have been twice that. Other, smaller, figures hurried about too. There were children in grey robes, with a bloody red serpent carved into their foreheads.

It was a sacrificial chamber. Hundreds of candles lit the room, they burned on every wall and in every corner. In the centre, surrounded by acolytes, was a stone altar. Standing at the head of the plinth was the warlock, a long, curved dagger in his pale hands. He looked up and saw them. A wide grin broke across his face. He said something which was lost amid the noise and bustle, but Brande found he could read his lips: "At last!"

Brande didn't even need to look. He knew who would be lying on the altar.

CHAPTER EIGHTEEN

"Fia," he whimpered. His heart was broken from seeing her there, lying on the stone plinth, motionless and naked. He stood transfixed at the horror of the scene. His eyes flicked up and caught those of the warlock, and for a moment their gazes locked. The warlock smirked.

"Brande!" warned Githa, jostling him. "Acolytes. So many." Her immediate concerns differed to his. The sacrificial chamber held a great many acolytes. The warlock was an undefined entity, possibly more powerful and more dangerous than any of them. Other followers in grey moved between them, but there were also soldiers guarding a balcony and a couple of other exits. Behind them, the pursuing soldiers were shouting at them to halt.

The narrow staircase hugging the wall of the room was a long one, but the two acolytes were almost at the top. They were chanting under their breaths and twisting their warped hands, coaxing the air to bring forth substance.

"Brande?" she asked, backing towards the door they came through. "Brande? Run!"

Brande looked at his baby girl, lying there; the cold, hard

altar like a symbol of death. She lay unmoving, not seeming to breathe. Her midriff and hips were awash with blood from some ritual. Her face was placid, her eyes closed. One arm lay by her side, the other hung over the edge of the plinth. Her dainty fingers seemed to point, but at nothing in particular. Brande felt a madness descend on him. He felt the fire in his gut engulf his sense of self. The flames of it licked at his heart, burned up his throat, entered his mind and seared any self-control that was there. The inferno consumed him. There was a noise in the room, a noise filling the grand chamber, and he realised it was him, him screaming, screaming with rage.

He was no longer himself. He had regressed. He was a previous version of himself, a younger one. A terrifying one. Brande the Butcher, they called him. Brande the Slayer. Brande the Brutal. And something else, eventually. Something worse.

A vision swam in his mind. It was the first time he had ever fought alongside King Leofric on the battlefield. It had been an honour. At first, Brande fought like the other men. They stood together, their shields linked in a wall, progressing toward an enemy that potentially wielded Deft power. Their mission was to destroy that power by killing those who possessed it. The land was barren, seared rock and dry mud. The Scorched Lands. It was a good place to fight. An even field. The soldiers of Leofric's army versus the Deft. He had been a part of something, back then. They had marched together, eaten together, and now they would fight and die together. It had made him proud. He marched alongside them, his head held high. They had stood before a terrifying enemy that poets would later name the Blackened Foe. They were the black-clad monks of an order whose name it was now illegal to utter. Leofric's men used steel, wood and fire, like any army. The enemy used their Deft touch and, worse, power drawn from the Rift. The monks worked in small teams, chanting, dancing, creating terrible images and figures out of the blackening air. Things tore from the ether and fled toward Leofric's men, and they fought them, as best they could. Their strength lay in sheer numbers. Leofric's men outnumbered the opposition fifty to one. The odds were probably even. The Blackened Foe sent forth their demonic creatures to tear through the ranks of men. Brande had fought, and somehow survived, but he had felt something then. He had felt an inexplicable anger building inside him. It was a tangible thing in his gut. He could sense it there, like a ball of molten lava. He could play with it, inspect it, turn it with his mind. Finally, though, he quashed it and forced himself to forget about it. Until the next battle.

As Leofric's men came upon the Tower of Insegmi, in the outer reaches of the Silvered Isle, where ice covered most of the land, they fought another terrible enemy. By now, their numbers were much depleted. They faced creatures that had once been men. The Fnagir were hideous, all fur, tooth and claw. Brande fought and was injured. A poisoned tusk pierced his chest and the pain flared in him like a god's wrath. His ball of molten anger, the one he'd been suppressing for months, suddenly burst and flooded him. He rose from the ground, took up his sword and attacked the creature with a viciousness he did not know he possessed. He severed its limbs and finally ripped its head from its body with his bare hands. He plunged forward, barging past his own men, now taking the lead, now out in front. He forced a path through the creatures, hacking, cleaving, biting, punching, kicking, and, after mowing down twenty or thirty of the vile beasts, he caught hold of himself. He cast a glance backwards. The other soldiers looked on, slack-jawed. They had just witnessed the turn of the fight. They went home early that night, with warm, freshly acquired pelts, cut from their enemies.

Brande knew then. He knew that inside he was a traitor.

He was fighting to rid the world of the Deft and those who drew from the Rift. Yet, he had something in him, some power he could draw on, and it was more than just anger, more than just rage, more than the fire found in any seasoned warrior's belly. He tried to hide it, but it was growing. With every battle, with every slaughter, it was growing.

They stood before the walls of Contrapolli. The great city rose before them. He rode by Leofric's side now, a Major General. This would be one of their most important battles. They did not fight Deft this time, but a political enemy of the King. Two thousand men remained loyal to them and were at their back. Archers. Infantry. Cavalry. But when the high gates to the city were finally smashed opened, after two weeks of fighting, it was Brande that they unleashed. He stormed the citadel by himself. Brande the Butcher was born. The poets called him Brande of the Five Thousand, for that was the number of men, women and children he was reported to have killed that day. When he finally regained control of himself, he fled. He could not live with others, and he certainly could not live with himself. He had taken himself off, into the mountains. He had gone to ground, and none of Leofric's search parties ever found him. If the enemy had ever come looking, they did not leave the mountain to tell the tale. And as years passed, he became improbable. The stories grew absurd, and he became a figure of myth. Brande of the Fifty Thousand. A fiction. Slowly, the stories got told less often.

Brande had found a small town he liked, called Bruton, near the vast forest of Skirtwood. He made a home there, buying a thatched hut and taking work as a carpenter and woodsman. It was good work. Clean. Honest. He had hoped to live out his days there, and to die there. Always he had kept to himself. Always he had controlled the power inside him, reining in the terrible burning rage. Until one day, he met Aithne, and everything changed. She whispered in his ear, and he knew he could be a new person, a better one. The fire in him subsided, and slowly, surely, Brande stopped being Brande the Butcher and became Brande the Woodsman. They visited a Sister of the Stone in the Strangled Mountains, and through some terrible ritual she had tied off and dampened the power within him, warning him that it could come back under duress if he gave in to his rage. Aithne kept him calm. And they had a daughter.

His daughter lay on a sacrificial altar at the centre of the chamber. A goat, its throat slit, dangled from a chain above her. She was awash with blood and the thing span in the air, dripping on her. Her body was still, frozen, calm. But Brande was not. Inside, he was volcanic.

"Brande!" shrieked Githa. "We must run!"

Brande leapt from the top of the stairs into clear air. He felt the fire in his belly spread. His muscles burned as they caught fire. His skin exploded into flame. This is what he remembered. This was a much different Brande from the one Aithne married.

Flames tore from his hair, from his skin, from under his nails. His clothes were alight. As he fell through the air at the acolytes, who even now spun black weaves in the air and tried to strike him, he became more demon than man. He was a figure of fire, a burning effigy of the thing that had once been Brande the husband, the father, the man. In his hands, the war axe gifted to him by Elderman Alewyn also exploded into flame, burning like Nachmair's own trident. It swept in a burning arc, cleaving both approaching acolytes in half as he landed. He leapt again.

The axe was behind him, batting away a black web of Rift power coursing through the air at him. It was nothing to him now. They were but novices compared to the seasoned warmonger suddenly resurrected.

Soldiers approached. He descended on them, grabbing one and throwing him so forcibly at the other that they were swept away like skittles made of delicate flesh and became ripped and tangled in each other, never to rise again.

Now the warlock was shouting. The smirk had gone from his face.

Everyone in the room turned on Brande. He revelled in it. Nachmair forbid, as more soldiers and acolytes entered the room, he laughed.

His axe was like a slice of the sun, moving so fast it seemed like a firefly, darting, changing direction, flitting from place to place. His body burned like a raging funeral pyre. His rage was everything. The acolytes moved as one, facing him, chanting. A green mist swirled at his feet. A red glow surrounded him. Their power had no effect. Black web fell on him. Brande shrugged, burning it off, and charged. He slaughtered them, one, two, three at a time.

In the centre of this hurricane of fire was a place of solitude, an eye of the storm, a plinth, where a girl lay. In the midst of his fury, fire consuming his vision, he remembered a night long ago.

It was a cold night in Bruton. A thick frost lay outside, and the fire in their small hearth was struggling to survive. Brande had kept awake as long as he could manage, shivering under a rug, poking the fire, feeding it. Fia slept in her bed. Aithne in theirs. Finally, he crawled in and joined her. Aithne had grumbled at being disturbed, and he tried to wake her, hoping to make heat between them, using their bodies to warm each other, to create pleasure where there was only cold. She shuffled away from him, muttering that it was the middle of the night, that she was cold, that she was tired. He gave up after a moment and put the hearth rug over their bedcover, then, changing his mind, he took it over to Fia and placed it over her covers instead. He climbed back in with Aithne, and he fell asleep.

Fia was sobbing her heart out. She was seven or eight years old at this time. Aithne was out of bed before Brande could make sense of what was happening. She put an arm around Fia, who was sat up in bed, crying. Her shoulders shook. Aithne brought the girl over to their bed and sat her between them. "There, there," she said. Her dark eyes looked troubled. It was not like Fia to be disturbed in her sleep. "What's the matter, my love?"

"The man. The man at the window," she said. "I dreamt of a man at the window. He was-" She broke down in tears again. Aithne hugged her close, clinging to her, letting the sobs subside.

Brande attempted to help, and he said, "Fia, my love. They say that Nachmair sometimes comes into our sleep and invades our dreams, but he is locked in those dreams, mistaking them for reality. Once you awake, you leave him trapped there for a time, and no harm can befall you."

Fia didn't stop crying, and Aithne gave him a look colder than the last dying ember of the fire. Brande realised a soldier's tale was not the way to comfort his daughter. He whispered that he was sorry.

He was still learning to settle into this new life, with Aithne's help. For all the years they had known each other, most nights he would awake from terrible dreams, and she would be there, with her smoky eyes, gentle touch, tangled hair and wicked laugh, to tease him, comfort him, and make love to him. She had taught him to be a man, not the monster he knew he was inside.

"Sorry," he said, to his little daughter. "I guess that didn't help. Look, if any man comes to the window, don't worry. My axe is by the door. I'll go out there and-"

Aithne slapped his wrist. "Quiet."

She held Fia against her. "It was just a bad dream," she told the girl. "There's no one at the window. No one. We're here. Come, lie down in the bed between us." She gave Brande a look, telling him not to complain. "Lie here, sweetheart, and fall asleep. We'll be either side of you." The girl gratefully accepted and fell asleep between them, taking up far more of the bed than Brande felt she had any right to. He lay awake for a while, thinking about how inadequate he was. A great warrior. A poor father. But he was so lucky, and he had come so far, and he would make a new man of himself, for Fia's sake, for Aithne's, no matter how long it took. He had been poor comfort to his daughter that night, being too hard, too rough to think of kind words. He would somehow make it up to her in the morning. She slept well, lying there, between them.

Now she lay here, in the eye of the storm. Cold as a corpse.

Brande crashed the skull of a soldier against the floor. Three acolytes were almost on him. In one swift motion, he leapt up and took hold of an acolyte's shoulders. Being short of time and options, as the two others reached for him, he bit into the thing's face, ripping away more than just soft flesh. He headbutted what was left and watched it fall away from him. He turned to the next and screwed its head off under one arm. They were slight creatures, he realised, but they were strong. The final acolyte of the three punched him in the gut. It winded him, but his rage and the power emerging within him meant his recovery time was next to zero. He flung himself on the creature and clung there until it was ablaze, then he picked up the cloaked, skeletal being and threw its burning, still-living, body at the warlock.

A wave of the warlock's hand changed the direction of the corpse's flight, and it spun away harmlessly. "We meet again," said the warlock, and laughed.

Brande charged into the warlock and was rebuffed by some invisible shield. Brande found himself standing ten foot away, his rage increasing. The warlock smiled. Brande snarled and moved away, vowing to return any moment. He turned on a group of soldiers. They had seen what he did to the acolytes, and they knew they stood no chance against him. They turned to run but were not fast enough. Brande's axe cut through their backs and hamstrings. There was no escape for them. They had aided the capture of his daughter, and their lives were forfeit.

The acolytes, with their awful twisted faces and skeletal frames, drew toward him at their master's bidding. Brande felt his axe tugged from his hands by some unseen force. He tried to hold on, but it was ripped from him. The flames surrounding it died, and it clattered to the ground. Brande growled.

He ran forward and took hold of the first acolyte he could. Their deadly weaves landed on him but were consumed by the fire that raged around him. He was a ball of raging fire. To stand next to him would be to immolate. The acolyte he grabbed began to burn but might as well have been made of ancient papyrus when Brande tore him apart, skin, flesh, bone, as if it were nothing. Blood sprayed across Brande's face and was burnt away before it touched his flesh. He plunged his fist through the next acolyte and hauled him into the air, his clenched hand in the man's entrails. He threw him towards the warlock who was descending on Fia with the dagger. The long, silver blade flashed orange, reflecting Brande's power.

Brande snatched his axe from the floor. The room was emptying. Soldiers ran. Acolytes slipped away through secret passages and side doors. Brande assessed the scene and laughed without mirth. He saw Githa beginning to make her way down the stairs having dealt with the pursuing soldiers.

Other soldiers were trying to escape by running up the stairs towards her. She was game and readied her sword. He looked around for archers on the balconies, but there were none. She was safe to face the new threat head on. Brande looked away, already knowing the outcome.

He turned now to see the warlock, and he did not like what he saw. He held the dagger above Fia, ready to strike. Thin trails of black smoke slipped from between his lips as he incanted some terrible rite that would make a sacrifice of her.

Brande went for him, axe swinging. In memory, he would later believe he had not run but flown. Whatever shield had been in place, toppled under the intensity of Brande's Deft power, his conviction and the erupting volcano of his rage.

The pair tangled, and came apart. The axe clattered to the ground, and the dagger skittered after it. Brande punched with flaming fists, and the warlock defended himself with swirling shadows that absorbed the attacks. Brande had never met his match in a single individual before. He tried to grab the warlock, hoping to smash him into the stone plinth, but the warlock was like a black mist, and his hands couldn't find purchase on the man's cloak or shoulders.

Fia sighed. Brande looked at her, distracted, but suddenly aware that she was alive. He saw her breathe, the slightest rise and fall of her chest. He turned back to the warlock, dismayed at his own hesitation. He growled, and the flames surrounding him grew higher. The warlock's eyes widened, and suddenly there was an otherworldly flapping, screeching, a wave of black, a swirling mist, and the man was gone, leaving just space and the charnel stench of foul smoke where he had stood. Brande cried out in anger, frustrated that his foe had fled and escaped. Where might he have gone? Brande thought he knew.

A scream of defiance drew his focus, and five remaining acolytes started weaving their black arts. Brande instantly saw the subject of their attention was not him, but Fia. He grabbed the nearest weapon, the dagger the warlock had dropped, and threw it. It was still flaming when it hit the first bird-like acolyte and ripped through its chest. Brande was on his axe a moment later, and the acolytes turned their attention back to him. That was what he wanted. They were his now. He slaughtered them like farm animals, scattering parts of them all around him.

Brande finally caught at his own anger. It began to subside. Githa had descended the stairs to join him and was suddenly by his side. He cast his eye over the carnage all around him. Bodies and body parts littered the chamber. Blood ran freely along the floor, forming pools. Much of the room was alight and many of the corpses were burning, some had blackened holes punched into them that still smoked. The air smelt of burning flesh. The tapestries around the walls were disintegrating as fire spread across them. One tore away from the wall and fell in a mound of smouldering fabric across the floor.

Brande walked solemnly and slowly towards Fia. The flames he generated died down and puffed out in wisps of white-grey smoke. The burning in him began to subside. He reached her and placed a hand on her chest. He felt her heart beating. He leaned in close to her face and felt her breath on his cheek. He kissed her on the forehead.

"She's alive," he gasped. He crumpled forward, one large hand clenching the stone altar for support. His chest heaved. Great breaths were sucked in and released as tears squeezed from his eyes. He looked to Githa, a smile almost breaking through his trembling face. "My daughter is alive." He allowed himself, finally, to acknowledge the deep fear he had held inside himself, the fear that she was gone forever. She was alive!

"She must not see this place," he said. He picked her up in his arms. She felt weightless to him. His heart felt like it might burst. Great sobs rose up in him, and Githa looked away as he held Fia tightly and tried to control the release of pent-up emotion escaping him.

His breath steadied. "We need to go."

"Where?" Githa was resting against the plinth, cleaning her sword on her thigh before sheathing it.

"You said the warlock enchanted Aithne. I need to find him. Kill him."

"He'll be with the King," she said, with some certainty.

"Yes. The Great Hall is above us. Let's go."

She eyed him warily and opened her mouth to say something, no doubt dismayed by the existence and extent of his Deft power, but no words came out.

"This is no time for explanations," he growled. "Are you still with me?"

"Of course," she smiled. Not for the first time, Brande wondered why. He wondered where her unfaltering loyalty stemmed from.

"You fought well," he said.

She beamed.

"But I need you to take Fia to a safe place. I cannot protect her while I fight him."

She grimaced. "I understand. I'll look after her. You can trust me."

Brande felt that he could. He carried her past the burning bodies, some of which burned like candles. He paused only to retrieve his axe.

"It's a fine axe," commented Githa. "Perhaps you should name it."

"I want to kill with it, not make love to it."

She laughed and walked past him, picking her way over bodies, and made her way up the stairs before him. Brande carried Fia up the stairs and out of the room, blinking away the black smoke swirling up towards them. They passed through the corridors, up the spiralling steps and back into the main body of the keep. Brande bore Fia carefully all the way, barely able to contain the tremendous relief within him.

"The battle is still raging outside," commented Githa, hearing the sound of it. It seemed so close.

"Through here," instructed Brande. The place was deserted. They found an empty room containing some tables and some old books. Its purpose was not immediately obvious. He placed Fia down on a table. "If you find somewhere better, move her. Protect her."

"I will," said Githa.

Brande grunted his thanks and was gone. His wife was still in danger, immense danger.

Brande could see the entrance to the Great Hall from where he stood, next to a pillar. Once again, the Great Hall was protected by a group of soldiers. There were a dozen of them and they had not yet seen him. The door they protected still hung in disarray from bent hinges following Brande's earlier assault on it.

The soldiers were there to protect the King from the rebellion, from Alland and Elderman Alewyn and the rabble, not from the likes of Brande the Butcher. Briefly, he considered that with so many of the acolytes disposed of, he had made Alland's job much easier. That was assuming Alland and the Elderman were still alive.

The King would have assumed the warlock would deal with Brande, but by now he would know better. Brande wondered what they were discussing. Perhaps the warlock's hold on the King was so potent he wouldn't even be questioned. Either way, Brande was coming for them, but they still had one advantage over him.

Aithne was in there. She wasn't herself, not in her mind. But it was still her body. If they threatened to harm her, he wasn't quite sure what he would do. He kept his plan simple. He would rescue her. She would recover and remember who she was. If she didn't heal quickly and naturally, he would take her to the best medicine men and the strongest Deft healers he could find. He didn't think it would be necessary. Past experience told him that if you cut the head off the snake, the body dies too. He would kill the warlock, and the power he had over her would be undone.

He still hadn't decided what to do about the King. He might just leave him to the rabble.

He walked out in front of the soldiers. The burnt rags he

wore barely covered him, but he did not care.

"Halt! Stop in the name of the King!"

Brande felt the rage in him. He stoked the fire. It felt good. It churned inside him. He approached the guards, his axe over his shoulder. "I seek an audience with the King and his warlock," he shouted, loud enough that all would hear him. They didn't get a chance to refuse. He only swung the axe once. What happened next, happened quickly, and he still had hold of three of them as he burst into the Great Hall. He scattered their bodies like seeds before him, throwing them down for all to see.

Aithne was still there, positioned next to the King. She looked unperturbed. She may have been stood in the room, but her mind was elsewhere. She was being controlled like a puppet on a string.

The warlock was by her side, cloaked in black, his serpent pendant at his neck. He was also cloaked in an eldritch swirling smoke of black fibres, something deadly and otherworldly. Knights and soldiers had amassed in the room, ready to protect the King from the invasion outside. Brande spat on the ground. Ignatius' brother, Leofric, would never have proved so weak and malleable. He knew it was an unfair judgment, this king was enchanted and not to be judged on ordinary principles, but still, he felt disgusted.

"Brande," said Aithne. "Turn around and leave. You're embarrassing yourself. I don't want you. You betrayed me. You broke the seal we constructed with the Sister of the Stone. You have let me down."

Her words were like knives plunging into his chest, but he knew it wasn't really her speaking. He ignored the hurtful words. He knew they should mean nothing to him, but it knocked him off his stride.

The King raised a hand. "Guards, this is no man, this is a monster before you. Attack!" Brande realised how like a monster he must look, stood there in scorched rags, covered in blood and carrying a weighty battle axe. He was a big man with thick-set features. He must look like a troll.

Brande grinned. This unnerved the men. They had just seen him throw their comrades to the floor like rag dolls.

"Attack him!" demanded the King.

They did. Brande blazed through them, all the while watching the warlock and the King to make sure they didn't lay a hand on Aithne. The soldiers died. As he removed his arm from the chest of the last man and shook his corpse free from his bloody fist, he noticed he had been joined by others who now poured into the room. The battle was all but won. Githa, Alland and the Elderman stood behind him, and many of their fellow citizens who had taken up arms.

Brande stood before the King. "My wife loves me," he proclaimed.

"Don't fool yourself," she spat. "I never loved an oaf like you."

"Enough," commanded the warlock.

He raised a hand. Aithne and the King fell silent, unable to speak. He raised another hand and Alland and the Elderman were knocked back against the wall, as were their men. They were pinned to the side of the room, mere spectators.

The warlock stood before Brande. Brande nurtured his anger, it was still white hot.

The swirling cloak around the warlock spread out and filled the room.

The room went dark.

The whole world consisted of just Brande and this man, this warlock, this conjurer of demons and Rift power. The others in the room seemed to have faded into shadows or ghosts that flickered like flames on the edge of what was visible in the spreading gloom. The ceiling looked low, just over his head, like a dark cloud. An unexpected wind whipped at his clothes, blowing at him from all directions.

"I need you, Brande," smiled the warlock. He laughed darkly.

Brande tightened his grip on his axe, looking about him, trying to work out what to do next.

The warlock floated down off the dais and landed in front of Brande, just out of reach. "I am obsessed with you," he cooed.

Brande snarled. He wasn't interested in the warlock's words of distraction.

"I have had a burning passion for you my whole life, every single day of it since I first saw you."

"You took my wife, bastard," growled Brande. "You took my child." They were statements, but they were also threats.

"I have yearned for you, Brande. Yearned for this meeting."

"Well, here I am. The last thing you'll ever yearn for."

Brande decided the strange surroundings weren't a threat to him, just an illusion designed to keep them focused on each other. The warlock himself was another matter. This man had used the King like a puppet for over a year. Brande was an unstoppable force in battle, but how would he fare pitted against a single foe with powers like that? He gripped his axe and started to raise it.

"No need for that," smiled the warlock, who was wrapped in blackness now, his face darkening, smoke swirling around his feet. He waved a hand and Brande felt the axe torn from his grip. He tried to hold on, but the force that struggled it away from him was far greater, more like a hurricane uprooting a tree than a man grappling possession of a weapon.

Brande turned his focus inward. He felt that molten core inside himself. He stoked it. He fanned the flames of his hatred. This man was responsible. He was responsible for Bruton being sacked. For Bruke. For the skyte's nest. For Silas's death. For his daughter and wife being kidnapped.

For the fear they felt. For the terror. For all that he had been through since that first day in Bruton when they were attacked by two soldiers on horseback.

Brande looked the warlock in the eye and said, "I don't need a weapon. I am a weapon. I'm the weapon that won the Crusades." He felt blistering around his fingers as flames licked between them. He could feel his insides burning away like a furnace, a furnace of rage and spite. He had never felt such anger in him before, it was something new, something that made even him feel afraid.

The figure before him changed shape. It grew. Dark wings spread from its back. Its face elongated and horns sprouted from its head, which it threw back as it laughed. "How appropriate you should try to end me," spoke the demon-like visage before him, its deep voice reverberating around the dark shadow-chamber they were encased in, "for it was you, Brande, who made me."

CHAPTER NINETEEN

Brande's eyes narrowed. This was not his first encounter with a warlock. They were powerful, but they weren't demons. A demon was a creature from the Rift, whereas a warlock was merely a person who harnessed the power of the Rift through worshipping Nachmair. This had to be an illusion. It only served to make him angrier.

"You made me," said the thing, extending claws as long as swords. Brande tried to move toward it, but his feet were clamped to the ground. "No," it ordered. "You will hear me out. Your Deft touch is strong, the strongest anyone has seen in a long time, but I have conquered the mysteries of the Rift."

"You suckled Nachmair's tit and learnt some new tricks," growled Brande. He attempted to move but was held in place by the wind whipping around him. It battered against each limb as he tried to push forward, thwarting his ability to approach his enemy. He inched forward, but the wind beat against his chest driving him back. The flames of his rage poured forth from him but flickered away in the air.

The creature stretched its wings and flapped them. It

rose into the air, hovering before Brande. Its muscles grew, its back arched as its flesh blackened and thickened, adopting a rough, spiky texture.

"Brande the Brutal, Brande the Butcher," laughed the demon. "I was just a boy. A boy who lived in fear of the Crusaders. A poor boy, with parents who loved him. My father, a soldier. My mother, a seamstress. A simple life. It was ours. We had nothing, Brande. And in having nothing, we had had everything, for we had each other. My father was going to give up fighting and become a woodsman. Sound familiar?"

Brande growled. The wind was tugging at his face, drying his eyes. He closed them and concentrated on that furnace within himself, the one he knew he could now unleash. Aithne rose in his mind, quelling it, quashing it. He pushed her aside. The survival of his family and his kingdom depended on it. For a moment, he saw King Leofric's face before him, telling him, "All Deft must die!" He felt that old hatred. He didn't want to become like the demon before him, a thing of ethereal power and destruction, but he knew he could rival it, equal it, maybe surpass it if he could tap into that old rage, that deep-seated dedication to Leofric's cause.

Could he raise that spectre? Through the noise of the wind whipping around the darkened room, Brande could hear the demon taunting him, talking to him, and he could barely hear himself shouting in response, "I. Will. Destroy. You."

"I feared the stories of Brande the Butcher. They gave me nightmares, but never more so than in the days and weeks after you came to our great city and killed our people. Five thousand of our people. You slaughtered my parents, and you didn't even slow down as you moved on through the street. We weren't at war with you. You just came at the head of an army and slaughtered us all."

Brande felt a knife in his heart. He could imagine

Aithne's eyes on him, seeing him for the barbarian he was, the murderer of children and children's parents. How could a person ever escape such a past? He owed it to Aithne not to be that person! Not to be Brande the Butcher. But this is who he was. He could not hide this person away.

"You didn't kill me, Brande. I don't know why. You killed other children. Hundreds of them. But you spared me. And I hated you with every fibre of my body for it. But I loved you too. You were like a god. I had to know where you came from and if I could ever be like you. Imagine when I learnt you were trying to destroy the Deft. The hypocrisy of it. It kills me, Brande. It kills me to think of it." The demon looked like it would weep from its red eyes. "I loved you, Brande. I devoted myself to you. But I knew that love was not reciprocated. I meant nothing to you. You didn't even know I existed."

The wind battered into Brande, somehow strengthened by the beating of the creature's wings. It forced Brande down on his knees. The flapping wings beat faster and faster, and the wind grew fiercer and fiercer. Its voice rose to combat the howling winds of darkness that stole light from around them, making Brande's world a dark maelstrom of pummelling void.

"I found Nachmair, and I became powerful."

"You. Will. Die!" screamed Brande into the night around him. He had to destroy this thing, but its words caused conflict within him. It spoke of who he had been. He could not summon the totality of this Deft power while this creature reminded him of his promise to Aithne.

"I couldn't find you, of course. You were hiding. So I decided to smoke you out. Rumours came to me. You had a family. You took my family, Brande, then went and made your own. Is that fair? A woodsman with a wife and child. I laughed when I heard that. It reminded me of my childhood, of what you took from me. I knew I would have to strip that from you before I killed you."

"You. Have. Failed!" screamed Brande, "And. You. Will. Die!" Brande ground his teeth. He could no longer see the demon. He was on all fours, being shunted backwards along the ground by the indefatigable wind buffeting and battering him. Flames burst into existence all around him but were whipped away on the air just as quickly. A trail of flame poured out behind him, disappearing into nothingness.

"You killed so many people. I decided no number of deaths could be too many in my hunt for you. Eventually, I had the ear of the King. He became my puppet. And I took away all the wives and children, knowing eventually I would find yours."

"No," growled Brande. It was another knife to the heart. Bruton. Bruke. It was all his fault. All that death, all those kidnappings. They were his doing. He felt the fire in him flicker and fade. He tumbled and found he was on his back, spinning. His past had caught up with him. After all these years, people were still dying, towns were still being sacked, just so someone could root him out and make him suffer. He was still causing death. He couldn't even say he fought the evil Deft for King Leofric because he was one of them.

In the blackness, in the fear and confusion, he wondered if the world might be better off without him. His rage weakened, and, in a moment of self-realisation, the fire inside him spluttered and died.

He was just a man at the mercy of a demon.

"Now you see," laughed the warlock. Brande could hear, but could not see. "You are responsible for all of it. I have found you. I have won. Your wife is enslaved. Your daughter sacrificed to Nachmair. And you will be tortured until I know everything about you, everything about the man who made me what I am. I need to know, Brande. I need to know everything! That's the only way my need for you can end, when I am satisfied about my parents' killer." He paused, his wings slowing, his feet settling on the ground. His voice was a whisper. "And then I will make you beg me to kill you." There was no hint of laughter now. This was the warlock's ambition laid bare. He had spent a lifetime working to accomplish this.

Brande wallowed in self-loathing. He was no better than this being. No, he was worse. He had created him. His actions had killed Eadlyn and Silas, had caused Fia and Aithne to suffer. He was not Brande the Butcher, he was Brande the Destroyer of All. He deserved to die.

In the darkness, devoid of power, devoid of hope, Brande closed his eyes. He gave in.

For some reason, in what he knew would be his last moments, his mind took him home to Bruton. He remembered the woods. His little home. The fireplace. The wooden dragon he had carved and given to Fia. He recalled Fia laugh with delight when she saw it, pleasure twinkling in her eyes. Her eyes were so like Aithne's. The eyes that had taught him peace and showed him love.

And he opened his eyes. And he stood up on his two feet. And he was just a man.

The demon shrieked in anger, "What is this?" It rose before him, beating its mighty black wings. The winds howled but no longer pushed Brande to the ground.

Brande took a step forward. Of course, he had been right. The demon was an illusion. The black maelstrom surrounding him was an illusion. The warlock was using his own power against him, encouraging it so as to defeat him with it, not unlike the bird-like acolyte in the garrison prison at Bruke attempted to do. A gentle smile played across Brande's face, crossed with sadness. "You and I share something. Our power is fuelled by the darkness inside us. But that is not who I am anymore. And you cannot oppose my power if I don't use it. I learned this during the Crusades: darkness fuels darkness. It never destroys it. The more I killed, the more I became the very thing I had been taught to hate."

"And you shall suffer for it!" bellowed the demon, stretching out an arm and striking him across the chest with its claws. It crushed him. He heard a rib pop, and he was thrown to the ground. "Maybe I should finish you now," it deliberated, moving closer. It seemed unsure.

Brande coughed. Blood specks flew from his mouth. He stood again, ignoring the pain. The demon grabbed him by the head, between two large claws, and started to squeeze. He knew if this continued he would die in a moment. His hands dropped to his sides. He grimaced, his teeth red with blood.

He felt for a metal object by his leg. There it was. A large, black key with curving, twisting teeth jutting out at odd angles. The Elder Key. He slipped it from his pocket and lodged it firmly in his palm, arranging it, so that it stuck out between two fingers of his clenched fist. He punched, stabbing the demon in the side. He drove the key right in, twisting it until the head of it pressed against the creature's flesh and prevented it from going further.

The demon howled and fell back. Its facial expression was one of confusion, then comprehension, and finally fury.

Brande spoke calmly. "During the Crusades, I encountered artefacts of Deft power. I felt the power in this one the moment I touched it."

The wind lessened. The demon sank to the floor, holding the wound in its side. It seemed smaller than before, more like the size of a man, more like the size of the warlock. The darkness began to lift, and Brande saw that he was still in the Great Hall and people surrounded him, still pinned to the walls, unable to advance.

Brande turned to the demon. "The other thing the Crusades taught me," he added, "is that no matter the circumstances, no matter how powerful the enemy, no matter the odds, I always, always win."

The demon tried to reply, but only a howl of pain emerged from its lizard-like lips. It began to thrash on the ground, wriggling and clutching at its side. The head of the key started to glow green, and yellow flames flickered out of the demon's wound. The wings on its back turned to ash and fell away. It began to look more human, the warlock's face returning, his skin returning to its standard colour. He screamed and gnashed his teeth, wracked by pain, unable to do more than claw at the key which was too hot to touch.

The key's teeth spread like tendrils throughout him, squirming their way through his demonic body, tunnelling through it, then breaking out through the skin and wrapping themselves around him. The warlock, once again a man in a black cloak threaded with gold, wearing a serpent pendant, writhed on the floor, shrieking in agony, all vestiges of the demon gone.

He began chanting, spell-casting. He was battling it. But the key had done its job. It no longer glowed. He was human again. The tendrils retracted. Now, it was just a metal object implanted in the side of a man.

Brande staggered over to his axe and snatched it up.

The warlock grabbed at the key's head and yanked it clear of himself. The key came loose amid a spurt of blood. He held it up in front of him. "The Elder Key!" he gasped. "How did you come by this?" He turned on to his knees and staggered to his feet, blood leaking from the wounds left by the key's tendrils. The warlock managed a smile. "I have looked for this artefact." His voice was broken with the pain he was enduring, but he bore it and continued. "Thank you, Brande."

It triggered him. Brande burst into flames, his anger returning all in a moment and hitting a new peak. He growled like an earthquake and swung his battle axe overhead, bringing it down toward the warlock. The blade burned white as flame leapt from it. It sliced through the air leaving a trail of vapour behind it, hitting nothing. It smashed off the flagstones, and he caught it before it rebounded into him.

The warlock was gone, just a tendril of smoke remaining where he had been. The key was gone too.

For a moment, Brande considered his options, considered giving chase in some way. But he stopped himself. He looked over to Aithne. She was passed out by the throne. He looked to Githa. She stared at him in wonder, and he hoped she had left Fia somewhere safe.

Brande breathed out.

Githa ran out of the room, suddenly free of whatever enchantment had held her against the wall. The many spectators were no longer pushed up against the wall either. They staggered forward, exclaiming aloud to each other about what had happened. Brande wondered if they had seen the whole event or just the demon-summoned darkness he had endured. Ignoring their clamour, Brande ran forward to Aithne. This is all he wanted now. He dropped to his knees by her side, brushed the hair from her face. "Aithne, my love," he said, frantically. "Can you hear me?"

Her eyelids fluttered.

"I have come a long way and betrayed everything we worked to achieve, but I have you now, and we are free to go. That is all that matters."

"Fia…" she said, her eyes drifting open.

"She is safe."

"Brande," she whispered, and smiled, "my love."

His heart exploded in his chest, and he knew he had her back. The warlock's control over her was gone.

He spoke gently to her for a moment.

King Ignatius sat in stunned silence, watching them both, and looking around the room as if he could not comprehend where he was or what was happening. Words kept trying to form on his lips, but it was as if he couldn't bring himself to say them.

Brande helped Aithne to her feet. She put an arm around him. He kissed her on the cheek and hugged her tightly. He looked around for Githa, but she was nowhere to be seen. He frowned. He thought he could trust her, but what was her reason for supporting him? He still didn't know. Suddenly he felt a chill in his heart. Where was Fia? Where had Githa gone?

Aithne was supporting herself now. "I am alright, Brande," she said. "Where is Fia?"

"Safe, I think. Can you walk?"

"Yes, I'm fine. Let's find Fia."

Brande hesitated for just a moment, then nodded and made for the exit. Alland jumped forward, blocking his way. He held his flanged mace at his side. His deformed face was twisted into a snarl. "You!" he sneered. He stood before Brande, hunched, pointing a gnarled finger at him. "Don't think we didn't hear all of that. You are responsible for this. You are responsible for that demon. You are Deft!"

"Alland," growled Brande, "you don't know the half of it."

"I know enough! You have betrayed all of us, from Leofric to Ignatius, to me, to Githa, all of us! You are one of them! We shall not permit a Deft to live."

"Now, stop there!" demanded the King, rising from his throne, suddenly finding his voice. "This is Brande. I recognise him, although it has been many years. This is Brande, my brother's champion, a war hero. And he has saved me and rescued this kingdom once again. It is Brande, isn't it? I remember you. You were Leofric's man, am I right?"

"No, my liege, please understand!" cried Alland. "He is one of them. He must die. He is just as bad as them!" Alland's hatred of the acolytes and all things Deft now extended to Brande. Why Alland should feel so strongly about the matter, especially after all they had been through together, Brande couldn't fathom.

"Alland," growled Brande, lifting his axe, "get out of my way." He had to find Fia.

"If you only knew what I know," said Alland, the disgust showing on his unpleasant features. He spat on the ground. "I looked up to you. Githa looked up to you. But now you disgust me. I will not let you pass. I am going to end you. You see, I am your judge, I am your-" Alland dropped to the ground like a sack dumped from a farmer's shoulder. His head bounced as it hit the ground. The butt of Brande's wooden handle left a mark on his temple. Alland's strangely hunched form lay unconscious on the ground.

Brande stepped over the still form of the hunchback and towards the exit. The King called to him to stay, but Brande turned and shouted, "I must find my daughter."

Ignatius was determined to speak to him. "You saved my kingdom. I am in your debt."

Brande realised there was still a problem here. Elderman Alewyn had stepped forward. There had been another battle fought this day, and now that the acolytes were beaten, Brande wondered if the Elderman and his allies would forgive the King his role in it since he had been in thrall to the warlock.

Brande asked the Elderman. "Do you understand what happened here? Are you content?"

"I saw, Brande. I understand now. And I am content," said the Elderman. "The King is not to blame for what has happened. I will call off my men, but Brande... you should not have let him take the Elder Key."

Brande nodded his understanding. The warlock was gone, but not finished.

"I must find my daughter." He had seen Githa, but she had rushed off. He had to find out why.

"Go, with my blessing," urged the King. Brande was already halfway out the door. Aithne was by his side. He took her hand.

He knew the King would want to speak to him later, but he had already made up his mind about what to do. As soon as they found Fia, they would get away, far away. They would travel beyond the reach of the King, beyond the scope of the warlock. They would vanish together.

He and Aithne searched along the corridor. "She's this way..."

They found Githa in the room with the tables and books where they had left Fia. It was deserted, but for the two women. Githa stood by Fia, whose slender form still lay on the table where they had set her down. She remained covered in goat's blood. For a fleeting moment, Brande thought Githa had completed the sacrifice. A second glance told him that she was protecting the still body of his daughter, as he had entrusted her to do.

Aithne screamed and ran to her daughter. She fell on her, hugging her, grasping her with everything she had. "Fia, my little flame!" she cried. Brande had given his daughter that nickname. Githa looked over at him. He smiled at her, and she took that for thanks, as it was intended. Brande moved to stand by Aithne and rested a hand on her shoulder.

Fia stirred a little but did not wake.

A cry came from down the corridor. Brande's ears picked up, and he listened to hear the nature of the commotion. The second time, the words were clearer. "Fire below!"

Brande thought he understood. His Deft power had set the sacrificial chamber alight, and between the fabric of the tapestries and the burning bodies, there must have been enough fuel to keep the fire burning long enough to catch the timbers alight. From there, the fire would have spread upwards. He scooped up his daughter in his great arms as gently and quickly as he could. To Githa he said, "Lead us out of here."

Githa smiled, relieved to be leaving.

"I can smell smoke," said Aithne. She put her hand on the floorboards. "Hot," she said. "This floor will give."

They rushed out of the room. From a window, they could see black smoke billowing up into the sky. "Hurry!" urged Githa, moving along the corridor ahead of Brande and Aithne who were close behind. Brande found Fia as light as air. He invoked his Deft powers to give him strength and energy and to reduce the pain of his broken rib. Occasionally, she stirred or moaned as he turned her to pass through a doorway, or move downstairs.

They sighed with relief as they came out into the fresh night air, leaving the keep behind them. But the day had been one of war, and a hostile guard was present as they emerged.

"Halt." A soldier wearing a black kerchief around his neck stood before them, pointing a spear at them. "Not another step!" he ordered. Aithne halted. Brande was carrying Fia and hesitated, not sure whether to put her down or not.

Githa's sword flicked out like a frog's tongue, licking the knight under his chin. He fell to the ground, choking on his own blood.

"You're useful to know," said Aithne, not looking happy at what she'd seen.

Githa looked at Aithne strangely. Brande saw it, found it impossible to interpret. Aithne chose to ignore it and stepped past the fallen knight.

"Githa," said Brande, "you should go back for Alland. He was in the hall." He said nothing about Alland's challenge to him.

Githa looked undecided. She looked at the three of them, then at the doorway.

"He was unconscious," said Aithne.

"Thank you," said Githa. She bit her lip, still undecided. "Will you be heading to Bruton?"

"No," said Brande, a little too abruptly. He offered nothing else.

Githa looked pensive, realising they would be gone

when she re-emerged from the building. "Goodbye," she said. Not waiting for a reply, she ducked back into the keep and out of sight.

Outside, there was still evidence of the festivities and Nachmair's Night. The town was full of empty stalls, and the deserted marketplace was smashed to pieces by the fighting. A few groups stood looking toward the castle, speculating on what was happening. Mostly these would be traders from afar, who did not count this as their battle. The elderly and apathetic also clustered for protection, chatting away to convince themselves they were right not to get involved. Soldiers traipsed past clutching their wounds. The sound of fighting could still be heard from some quarters, but the word was spreading that the battle was over. For the briefest of moments, Brande thought someone was standing watching them. He turned to look, but the shadow slipped away behind a building. He felt vulnerable with Fia in his arms, and it was making him paranoid. "Come on," he urged. "Let's go."

Brande carried Fia and, with Aithne at his side, they made straight for the way out. Brande glanced back to see the keep being torn apart by the blaze within. He felt no sorrow for having caused it.

They were not challenged again and soon put some distance between themselves and Charstoke Castle.

Brande paused while Aithne touched Fia gently on the chest, checking her heart still beat and she was still breathing. Fia shuffled in Brande's arms, where she lay in a dream.

"I'm glad," said Aithne. She leant forward, looking deep into his eyes. "I'm glad you came for us. Even if it meant you sacrificed everything we worked at."

She placed a kiss on his lips.

CHAPTER TWENTY

"Down," said a little voice. Brande halted and slowly let Fia down on to the ground where she unsteadily found her feet. "I'm weak," she said and slung an arm around his shoulders for support. He leaned down, being too tall to help otherwise.

Aithne came about and grabbed her other arm to help keep her steady. "You're safe now, Fia," she said. "Your father is here. We're going home."

Fia smiled weakly. Aithne removed the cloak she wore and hung it around Fia's starving, naked frame. It was a crisp autumn night, and Fia looked cold, though her shaking was from exhaustion and maltreatment.

They stumbled on by the light of the moon and the stars, also aided by the glow from the castle burning behind them.

"Are you harmed?" he asked her. It was a loaded question. Anger still smouldered inside him, and it wouldn't take much to rekindle the fire. This should never have happened to his baby girl. Yet, in some way, it was his fault. His legacy was to blame for this.

"No," she mumbled. "The warlock wanted me to be pure... for the sacrifice."

Aithne gave Brande a relieved glance.

Fia continued, "He seemed to know who I was. He singled me out."

"He didn't want you at all," said Brande, trying to comfort her. "He just wanted revenge on me."

"You know him!?" She seemed aghast.

"No, no," he said gently, "but he thought he knew me." He left it at that for now.

He knew Fia would not give up until she got a full explanation, but it could wait until her strength returned. He kissed her on the forehead, and she smiled.

"Where are we going?" she asked.

"Far away," replied Brande. "But we'll stop and rest soon, I promise."

They pressed on and made it to a small river that stank of effluence, a familiar smell in any town. They crossed a small but sturdy stone bridge and made their way out into the open fields. A dog was roaming, looking for rabbits.

"There they are!" yelled a voice behind them.

Brande shifted Fia's weight on to Aithne and spun around, readying his axe. Racing up behind them were two men in chainmail, and another, in the torn clothes of a beggar. "Halt!" yelled one of the soldiers.

Brande stepped forward, putting Aithne and Fia behind him. He wrung the haft of his axe like a towel, waiting for the fight to come to him. These men wouldn't be a problem for him.

The three men slowed their pace as they approached, although one drew his short sword. "This is them," said Wylie, the thief that Brande had last seen in the pillory in the castle, covered in the waste that Alland had thrown over him.

Brande growled, deep in his throat.

Wylie hissed at him. "You are traitors to the crown. I

was sent to identify you by the captain of Lance Company. These men will bring you in."

"You're a bit late for that," Brande informed him. "Whoever gave you those orders is most likely dead by my hand. The King has thanked me for saving his kingdom."

One of the soldiers pushed forward past Wylie. "We'll deal with him!"

"You won't pull the wool over our eyes," promised Wylie.

"Go back to the castle. The warlock is gone. The acolytes are dead. The king is himself again." He was talking to the guards. "I have rescued my family. If you think you can stop me from leaving this place, you are mistaken."

"Just take him!" shrieked Wylie. He pulled one of the soldier's arms in Brande's direction as if that would make him attack. The soldier shook him off. Anything could be the case after the day they had experienced, with the peasants attacking the keep and the sight of acolytes casting dark powers. The keep was ablaze and who was to say what was true and what was not.

"I recognise you," said one of the soldiers. He peered at Aithne over his hooked nose and bushy moustache. "I've seen you with the King. Are you this man's wife?"

"I am," she confirmed. "He has rescued me from the injustices of the King and his warlock."

"I've seen that girl," said the other, lowering his short sword and using it to indicate in Fia's direction. "She was up at the castle. He must have rescued her, or she wouldn't be here."

"Stop discussing it!" yelled Wylie, infuriated. "You heard the acolyte. He is to be captured and brought before the King. Your own captain ordered this!" He was close to stamping his feet. Alland had tipped a bucket of shit over his head, and he wanted revenge. Brande realised Wylie must have seen him talking to Alland beforehand and the cunning thief had put two and two together. No doubt he reported them, leading to the Elderman being taken from his home after their clandestine meeting.

Brande snorted. "They can't stop me, Wylie. I could kill all three of you, but I don't think I need to."

"Don't listen to him! Attack him now!"

The soldiers looked at Wylie going red in the face and took a step away from him. "I think he speaks the truth," said the one with the short sword. He knew bad luck when he saw it and fighting this large, bloody, half-naked man brandishing an axe to defend his family looked like more trouble than it was worth.

"Give me that sword," said Wylie, wrestling it off the guard. Taken by surprise, the soldier released it. Wylie turned to face Brande. Physically, he was much smaller, but there was a handiness about Wylie that made him menacing. His wiry body told a tale of survival through violence and desperation. He leapt forward, trying to get past Brande to strike at Fia. "I'll make you pay!" he shouted. Fia screamed.

He didn't get far. The other guard with the thick moustache grabbed Wylie from behind, wrapping his arm around his neck. Between them, the guards pinned Wylie's arms and lowered him to the ground. The short sword was wrestled from him and pressed against his neck. "Get along with your family," barked the soldier with the moustache. "We'll deal with this miscreant." Brande guessed that perhaps the soldier had a family of his own and harboured rebellious sentiments towards the King. It wouldn't be a surprise, most of the city seemed to.

Wylie screamed oaths of murderous intent as the soldiers dragged him away, kicking, screaming and biting.

Brande watched them leave, saying nothing. He preferred to kill his enemies, but he didn't suppose Wylie would ever prove a threat. The soldiers wouldn't want him blabbing about them disobeying an order and allowing a wanted man to escape. They would toss him in a cell to rot until his mind was gone.

Brande turned to embrace his family. Fia was sobbing from the shock of Wylie's attempted attack. He let her calm down before they moved on. Slowly, they made their way, side by side, away from the city. Fiery smoke billowed up over the castle and was more than enough distraction to let them get away without being conspicuous.

Brande thought that some colour was returning to Fia's face.

"You came for us," she said, suddenly, smiling and falling into Brande to hug him.

"Of course I did," he laughed, tears pricking his eyes.

He walked holding Aithne's hand, with one arm around Fia's back, slipped under her arm to help her walk. She had been travelling in cages, then drugged into unconsciousness, so was still struggling to find her strength.

"How did you find us?"

"I followed you from Bruton."

Aithne looked troubled. "Brande, those things I said-"

Brande shook his head. "Don't mention them. They were the warlock's trickery, nothing more."

"But there something you should know."

"I don't need to know. My wife left with soldiers, she came back with me. The woman in between was someone else."

"I'm not a soldier, Brande. You can't just dismiss things, saying they happened at war."

Brande looked apologetic and nodded, suddenly understanding her need to talk. "We're a family. You tell me anything you need to," he said. "Whatever you have to say, I will-" He stopped abruptly. Fia stopped with him. Aithne turned to look at him, alarmed.

Hoof-beats pounded toward them. Aithne pointed. Two horsemen appeared over the rise, galloping toward them. Brande had no doubt about their intention to intersect with his family. They moved like the wind, bearing straight down on them.

"It's too dark to see," cursed Brande. Only dark silhouettes against the sky were visible, making it hard to assess the threat. Even so, two armed soldiers on horseback posed a threat. He would have to go after one before the other. What damage could the second do while he concentrated on the first? He didn't like it. It brought back memories of the attack on them in Bruton, but his power had been sealed away then. He let the fire inside him simmer in preparation for what was to come.

"Stay close to me," he said. "They will have weapons. If you separate from me, they'll ride you down. Stay by my back, turn with me. I'll take the first one out, and then the other will have to come through me."

"Get close," said Aithne, pushing Fia in behind Brande and holding on to her. She looked grim, determined to follow his orders without showing fear.

"Not again," wailed Fia. "Don't let them take me again."

"We won't," soothed Aithne. "We won't. There, there. We won't."

Brande peered into the night. The riders still seemed shadows against the night sky. Being out amongst the fields and the farmland made them an easy target. There was no shelter to run to. He readied his axe. It was stained thick with congealed blood. He smiled, and slowly the fire rekindled.

The horsemen drew close. As they approached, they slowed to a trot. It was not a hostile gesture. Brande could now make out the shape of the two figures. He laughed and dropped his axe to waist height.

"Who is it?" asked Aithne.

"Two good men," said Brande. "Well, not that good. But good to me." He managed a welcoming smile, although it was mostly relief, as Eberhard and Aldway approached.

"Hail!" he called out, making sure he got a friendly response. He was not so trusting that he didn't need reassurance.

"Well met, friend!" called Aldway. Brande relaxed. "What brings you out this far, Brande? The sheep? I hear you folk from Bruton like sheep."

Eberhard scowled. "The women," he hissed, reprimanding Aldway.

Aldway looked unabashed. He had a dazzling grin, and he flashed it at Fia. He drew his bay gelding around in a tight circle and then brought it to a halt. "What do you think?"

"Where did you get them?" asked Brande.

"We borrowed them from two men who, after parting with them, chose to lie on the ground until we left. Probably longer. Probably still there."

"Because you unnecessarily put arrows into them," grumbled Eberhard disapprovingly. He dismounted from his own gelding. "But here, you'll need one of these, Brande."

Eberhard passed the reins to Brande, who took control of the horse and stroked its nose. The horse seemed to like him.

Eberhard walked over to Aithne and Fia. They both recoiled from the huge, blond-haired, muscular figure.

"Now who's upsetting the women?" jeered Aldway, meanly.

"I'm so glad you're safe," said Eberhard to them, but he kept his distance. Fia smiled weakly.

"Thank you," managed Aithne.

Brande saw that Fia was looking shaky, so he helped her up on to the horse. Aithne followed. Brande held the reins.

Aithne leaned down to the two men. "Thank you," she said. "This will be a great help to us."

"Not a problem," replied Aldway, from atop the other horse. "Now, we better get going. See this?" He banged the saddlebags by his legs. The satchels chinked loudly. "We need to get this stuff somewhere safe."

Brande snorted. "I knew you two had an ulterior motive."

"It's a hard life," said Aldway, "but when you know there's going to be spoils, you've got to follow your nose."

Brande suspected they were mercenaries, or thieves, or something of that sort. He had feared they might betray him, but betrayal was not one of their failings. He imagined there were many others. He believed them to be a pair of travelling rogues, lovers and fighters with nothing to stop them roaming or taking loot where they found it.

"How goes things at the castle?" enquired Brande.

Aldway laughed. "They won't forget you for a while."

"The soldiers and city folk were assembling to listen to an address from the King when we left."

"You didn't stay for the address?"

Aldway shook his head. "Having helped ourselves to gold from the cathedral, the treasury, the stately rooms and the King's bedchamber-"

"I think he gets the picture," cut in Eberhard. "What about you, Brande? Where are you headed?"

"Away. Home won't be safe. We'll find a new place."

Eberhard grunted, realising their woes were not over. "You have a friend in us, Brande. I hope our paths cross again, one day."

"Yes," agreed Aldway, sombrely. "I like the way you wield that axe."

Brande shrugged. "Back to chopping trees for me."

"Come on," said Eberhard. "Time we hid this stuff." He patted the saddlebags, making them chink again.

"Goodbye," said Aldway. They all exchanged parting words.

Eberhard climbed up behind Aldway on the horse. They turned to ride off, but as they did, Aldway turned back and said, "Oh! One more thing. For you!" He unlatched a satchel. It fell to the ground with a thud.

"Thank you," said Brande, grateful for a share of the

spoils.

"Don't thank him too much," laughed Eberhard. He kicked the horse into a trot. Neither gave a backwards glance as they rode off into the night.

Brande picked up the satchel. It didn't feel heavy. "Strange," he said, unlatching the buckles.

"Have they left us gold?" asked Fia, excited at the prospect.

Brande lifted the flap and looked inside. Confusion crossed his face. He turned the bag upside down. A green ball-shaped object tumbled out. Fia gave a little exclamation. Aithne peered down from their horse at the strange item. "What is it?"

Brande nudged it with his foot, rolling it until two lizard eyes stared up blindly at the sky. It was the head of the creature they had fought in the labyrinth under the keep. He had forgotten to ask them how they had faired, so much had happened since then. They had done well to defeat it.

Aithne asked again, "What is it?"

"The head of a monster. There is much I need to tell you."

Aithne and Fia asked about the two strangers, and Brande, no storyteller, did his best to explain who they were as he led their horse away across the fields. He left the head where it lay.

The castle grew smaller and smaller on the horizon. They had encountered no confrontation and, having passed farmsteads and remote huts, they finally came to the edge of the forest and followed it northward.

"We will need to travel all night," he explained. "You saw how quickly those two caught up with us. If we're followed, we'll have to fight, but it may be we're spared that now Ignatius is his own man again and most of the acolytes are gone. Fia, you might be able to sleep while you ride, if you try."

"Do you think the warlock will return?" asked Aithne.

Brande didn't answer straight away. He considered the likelihood of the warlock returning to Charstoke and thought it slim. The warlock's personal vendetta against him would never end, but it might be some time before he had the wherewithal to attack again. "I don't know," he admitted.

Aithne leant down from the front of the horse and ruffled his hair.

"You saw me fight," he said, miserably, "and lose control."

"I saw you fight for your family."

He looked up, grateful. His wife smiled down at him. "We're together again, Brande. That's what matters. And we'll make a life for ourselves somewhere. And we'll be happy. Away from all this."

Fia looked up, perhaps from a dream, and asked, "Are we safe now?"

It wasn't in Brande to lie, nor to offer platitudes, but he reached up, gave her leg a reassuring squeeze, and said, "Yes, we're safe."

Together, they rode on, through the night, heading towards their new lives. Brande let out a long, slow sigh of relief, glad beyond all measure to be reunited with his family. He would put Charstoke and all the fighting behind him, relegate it to the back of his mind, forget it and forgive himself for it.

But his legacy remained. And within him still burned the fire of the Deft.

The End

Acknowledgements

Writing a book is a long and lonely process[1], but the end is always fun when others get involved. I'd like to thank my beta readers, Pab Roberts, Morven Pack and Mark Wilson, for their pernickety perusal. My greatest thanks go to my wife Emma, whose love and support seems to know no bounds. Her horse knowledge comes in handy too, though any mistakes are mine.

I hope people will judge this book by its cover. Christian's wonderful design deserves it.

[1] It's not, I love it.

Printed in Great Britain
by Amazon

28024319R00182